Other Books by Kristine Smith

CODE OF CONDUCT
RULES OF CONFLICT

KRISTINE SMITH

LAW OF SURVIVAL

An Imprint of HarperCollinsPublishers

This is a work of fiction. Names, characters, places, and incidents are products of the author's imagination or are used fictitiously and are not to be construed as real. Any resemblance to actual events, locales, organizations, or persons, living or dead, is entirely coincidental.

EOS
An Imprint of HarperCollins*Publishers*
10 East 53rd Street
New York, New York 10022-5299

Copyright © 2001 by Kristine Smith
Excerpt from *The Gambler's Fortune* copyright © 2000 by Juliet E. McKenna
Excerpt from *Sky of Swords* copyright © 2000 by Dave Duncan
Excerpt from *Ascending* copyright © 2001 by James Alan Gardner
Excerpt from *Wheel of the Infinite* copyright © 2000 by Martha Wells
ISBN: 0-380-80785-8
www.eosbooks.com

First Eos paperback printing: October 2001

Eos Trademark Reg. U.S. Pat. Off. and in Other Countries, Marca Registrada, Hecho en U.S.A.
HarperCollins® is a trademark of HarperCollins Publishers Inc.

Printed in the U.S.A.

10 9 8 7 6 5 4 3 2 1

Acknowledgments

To my newsgroup regulars, for keeping me motivated and making me laugh when I needed it.

To Julia Blackshear Kosatka, Dave Klecha, and Secret Dave, for First Readership above and beyond the call.

As always, to my parents, for their understanding and support.

And finally, a postscript . . .

I've been asked how to pronounce my idomeni names and places often enough that I felt I needed to do something about it. I've therefore added a Pronunciation Gazetteer to my webpage, which is located at *www.sff.net/people/ksmith*. There, you'll find some how-to's, along with a few whys and wherefores.

CHAPTER 1

"Come look at these."

Jani Kilian maneuvered through the morning workday crowd and joined Lucien Pascal at the shop window. The display proved typical for an establishment bordering Cabinet Row, quiet and opulent at the same time. The store specialized in fine tableware—the cutlery and metal plate that filled the velvet-draped display niches seemed to glow in the Chicago morning sun.

"This is a very good thank-you gift for your better clients." Lucien pointed to a small silver bowl that had been shaped into a half-shell, then satin-polished until it appeared lit from within. "Not too expensive, but not cheap either. It implies that the document business is good, but you're too astute to throw money about without good reason. It just so happens that you consider the recipient to be a good reason." He bent closer to the window to get a better look, his white-blond hair capturing the light like the silver. "Hand out a few of those, then sit back and watch the commissions pour in."

Jani examined the bowl. Lucien had acquired his eye under the tutelage of Exterior Minister Anais Ulanova—his taste, as always, proved sound but expensive. "I already have more commissions than I can handle." She turned away from the window and continued down the walkway. "I should be home working on a few of them now instead of walking you to the train." She slipped her hand inside her trouser pocket, working her fingers through the assorted vend tokens and keycards until they closed around a slip of paper. The crisp, Cabinet-grade parchment crackled—she jerked out her hand, then folded her arms and turned back to Lucien.

He stood in front of the window, watching her. He looked like a fairy tale soldier in his dress blue-greys, the steel-blue tunic cut on the diagonal with a black leather crossover belt, the grey trousers slashed along the sides with mainline red stripes. He'd set his brimmed lid with geometric precision. Even his red lieutenant's bars and expert marksman badges glittered like costume decoration.

Only the fully packed holster on his waistbelt belied the romantic image. That, and the light in his brown eyes, as cold as the metal on the other side of the glass. "Why are you so edgy?"

Jani forced a smile. "What makes you think I'm edgy?"

"Because you're answering my question with a question, for one thing."

"I do that all the time. You're not the only one who complains about it."

"But I'm the only one who knows what it means in this particular instance." Lucien strolled to her side. "At oh-six, you get a call from the lobby. It's your building manager, with an early morning documents delivery from Cabinet Archives. Nothing unusual in that—you've gotten those before. You tumble out of bed, throw on some clothes, and go downstairs to retrieve them." He leaned close to her, bringing with him scents of soap and freshly washed hair. "Except you don't return right away, and when you finally do show up, you're snappish and distracted. You refuse to eat breakfast, and you hustle me out the door before I've even swallowed a cup of coffee." He drew even nearer, until he brushed against her arm. "John would be upset if he knew you didn't eat. You know that you can't afford to mistreat yourself, considering your condition."

Jani backed off a step so that she could look Lucien in the face. And what a face, the full mouth and strong bones still softened enough by youth to imply innocence. An angel, perched on the brink of damnation. *Stay focused.* She knew he could distract her, then trap her with a question or an off-hand comment. "I'm fine. It just hit me how much work I have to do. I've got that meeting at the idomeni embassy today, and if form holds true, it will run longer than expected. I've got three Treasury summaries due next week, and I haven't even looked at the data."

"So as you said, why waste the time playing escort now?" Lucien stood easily, arms at his sides, head cocked in artless curiosity. "Where are you going after you leave me at Union?"

"The only place I'm going after I leave you at Union is home." Jani turned her back on him and started to walk. Her weak right knee sagged with every step, the persistent reminder of an eventful summer. "I've found that the occasional break clears my head. Maybe I'll take another one later today, come back here and buy something for my best clients." She took a deep, steadying breath. The crisp fall air held a city melange of restaurant aromas, overheated skimmer batteries, and a whiff of pungent cologne from a passing pedestrian. "What time's your train?"

"Oh-seven and a half. Same as when you asked five minutes ago." Lucien moved up beside her, matching her stride for stride. "What's wrong?"

"Nothing."

"How can I help you if you never tell me anything?"

"I don't need your help."

"Who are you meeting?"

"I'm not meeting anybody."

As they continued up the walkway, Jani noted that people stepped aside for them. They glanced first at Lucien, then at her, their eyes questioning. *Who are you, lady?* A Family member on an early morning shopping spree with her officer boyfriend? A colonial diplomat out for a stroll with her bodyguard? She knew she cut an imposing figure in her black trousers and crimson shirt-jacket. She matched Lucien in ranginess and almost matched him in height, her short black hair and brown skin serving as dark contrast to his brilliant blondness and paling summer tan. *That's who I am—the soldier's shadow. Not the real thing—please don't make that mistake.* It was an error she'd made herself once, thinking herself a soldier. As was usual with those sorts of lapses, others had paid a steeper price for it than she.

They turned the corner, and Union Station loomed into

view. Commuters streamed out, on the way to posts in the Cabinet Ministries, NUVA-SCAN, or Neoclona, and in, travelling to Fort Sheridan or other more distant points in the Michigan province. They entered the station, a train cathedral of stained glass and vaulted ceilings; the pound of footsteps and the keen of voices ricocheted off the walls and seemed to increase in volume with each successive bounce. Jani's pulse quickened as she elbowed through the crowd. She had hurried through many train stations over the years.

They reached the embarkation platform and scanned the Outbound display, then hurried along the line of trains and down the track just as the first call for the Sheridan Express sounded. Lucien stopped before an open car, then turned. "I'll see you at the embassy?"

Jani hesitated, then nodded. "You're going to be there?"

"I'd never miss a chance to watch you and Nema cause trouble." He pulled her close and kissed her, his lips warm and bruising. "Enjoy your *break*," he whispered as he pulled away. He boarded the train, remaining in the entry as the door slid closed and the sleek bullet pulled away. They didn't wave good-bye, just as they never held hands, or hugged—it wasn't their style. They just stared at one another until the angle grew too sharp and Lucien disappeared from view.

Jani stood on the platform until the train vanished around the bend, then reached into her pocket once more. This time, she removed the piece of paper, her actions of earlier that morning replaying in her mind.

I met Hodge at the front desk. No one else was in the lobby. The only person outside was the doorman. I opened the documents case in Hodge's presence, like I always do. If the seals appeared tampered-with, or if anything looked strange, better to uncover it before a reliable witness. I found nothing amiss. Seals appeared intact. The papers had been filed in an orderly manner.

Then she had caught sight of the slip of pale green parchment sticking out of the corner of one of the slipcases like a marker tag. She had gone ahead and closed the case, waiting until she boarded the lift before opening it again and removing the scrap with a hesitant hand.

You possess hidden talents, Niall—it takes skill to crack a Cabinet-grade seal. She unfolded the note and studied it as she had earlier. A short sentence, written in the neat script she'd grown accustomed to over the past months.

Meet me at oh-eight. You'll know where.

"I will?" Jani turned over the scrap and examined the back for any clues she had missed during previous examinations. "Why the mystery, Colonel? And why the rush? We're meeting for lunch tomorrow—can't this wait?" She folded down one of the corners, then unfolded it—the weighty paper still rustled like new. "Pale green—that's the color Commerce is using for their official documents this year—" She stilled. "The Commerce Ministry."

Now she knew where she had to go. All that remained was to find out why.

Jani crossed the pedestrian overpass that spanned the twelve-lane Boul Mich, Chicago's main thoroughfare, and entered the lakeside sprawl of government buildings, parkland, and open land known as Cabinet Row. She reached a vehicle dispatch platform, and boarded a Commerce Ministry people-mover amid a group of green-clad employees. After everyone sat, the lumbering conveyance began its slow float down the wide walkway toward the kilometer-long Ministry main building. As it approached a subsidiary gate that led to a small employee park, Jani stood. The vehicle stopped, and she disembarked.

Jani watched the roofless vehicle resume its glide toward the Ministry proper. Then she pressed her hand to the gatekeeper square; the device scanned her palm, and the gate swung open.

Colonel Niall Pierce stood near the entry, talking to a younger man in lieutenant's gear as he pointed to a late-blooming hybrid rose. Like Lucien, he wore mainline dress blue-greys, but no fairy tale Jani could think of would have claimed him as its hero. In contrast to the prince's clean, broad brow and high cheekbones, this weathered pretender possessed a narrow visage, sun-battered and lined, the appearance of length accentuated by the scar that cut the left side of his face from the edge of his nose to the corner of his mouth. Young blond was replaced by old bronze; springy fitness gave way to wary tension.

Only his eyes spoke to the humor in the man. The warm gold-brown of the richest honey, they hinted at depths of emotion that Lucien had never experienced.

Niall straightened when he heard the gate slam shut. "Captain." He touched his fingers to his forehead in a modest salute. "That'll be all, Pull," he said to the lieutenant. "Meet you back at the skimmer."

"Sir." Pull snapped a salute, then turned to Jani. "Ma'am." Jani nodded. "You're new."

"Lieutenant Randal Pullman, ma'am." The young man blushed. Since he was a pink-skinned redhead, the rouging made it appear as though he'd just popped out of a boiler. "Good morning." He backed away, his smile wide and fixed, then turned and clipped down the walkway that led into the Ministry.

"I've been telling him about you." Niall's voice twanged, middle-pitch and sharp, lower-class Victorian blunted by years spent on other worlds. "Suffice it to say that you have a new admirer." He moved from the rose to an autumn hydrangea, lifting one of the bloom-heavy branches to his nose.

"I wish you wouldn't do that." Jani wandered a wide semicircle until she stood beside him. He pushed the branch toward her and she bent to sniff the blooms, which were brilliant purple with a heavy, spicy-sweet scent. As she did, Niall released the branch and stepped away. Jani had flinched once when he accidentally touched her. Since then, he took care not to remain close to her for too long.

"Why not?" He drew up straight and locked his hands behind his back. "The work you did at Rauta Shèràa Base was admirable; even twenty years later, it manages to impress. And that flaw you found in Transport Ministry docking protocols was a marvel of critical analysis."

"Niall, I was forging manifests for a smuggling operation when I uncovered that flaw." Jani paused, then looked up from the flower. "I don't think I ever told you about that, did I?"

Niall hesitated. Then he jerked his chin toward the garden entry, and sniffed. "Pretty Boy waiting for you?"

"No, he's on his way back to Sheridan." Jani picked a shriveled petal from one of the blooms. "I didn't tell him I was meeting you, but he knows something's up. Don't be surprised if you get back to Sheridan to find someone had checked into your whereabouts this morning."

"Isn't he the crafty one?" Niall sneered, his damaged lip accentuating his disgust. "Is he still . . . *dating* that father of four who runs the Justice Ministry Appeals Division?"

"Yes, and a few others as well. I've explained to you before—I don't mind. That way, he doesn't get bored, and I get a few nights a week to myself."

"You call that love?"

"You know I don't. I never did. Between Lucien's essential nature and prototype augmentation, he can't love anyone. My . . . experiences have taught me the value of his sort of outlook. He doesn't know how to ask for what I'm no longer prepared to give. We have just the relationship we want."

"I think you're doing yourself a disservice."

"Can we please cut to the chase?" Jani backed away from the shrubbery until she stood in Niall's path. "What's going on? You didn't go through the trouble to break into a sealed Treasury Ministry documents case in order to lecture me about my personal life, did you?"

Niall reached beneath his brimmed lid to scratch the top of his head. Then he readjusted the braid-trimmed hat to its former dead-on level, and brushed a speck of nonexistent dirt from the front of his tunic. "Ever been to Tsing Tao Station?" He tugged at his own expert marksman's badge. "Biggest shuttle transfer station in the Pearl Way, last stop before you hit the GateWay and enter La Manche, the Channel Worlds—"

"I know what it is." Jani watched him take great care to look everywhere but at her. "A few years ago."

"Four and a half?"

"Yes. Four and a half."

"Just passing through, or did you work there for a time?"

"I did a few odd jobs to earn billet money. Same as I did at every other station I ever passed through. I think I stopped over there for a total of six months."

"Five." Niall yanked a brown leaf from the branch of a late-blooming rose. "Kill anybody while you were there?"

Jani studied him for any sign he joked. She'd learned to spot the hints over the months of their acquaintance—the narrowing of his eyes, the working of his jaw as he bit the inside of his cheek to keep from laughing. But she couldn't find them this time. Unfortunately. "No, I didn't."

CHAPTER 2

"Let's walk out to the lake, where we can talk in private."
Niall led Jani through the garden, past a triplet of clerks who
had intruded in a flurry of giggles and whispers. They exited
through the rear gate, which opened out onto the beach.

Jani shivered as the lake breeze brushed her. It was because of what Lucien referred to as her *condition,* she told
herself. It had advanced to the point that she only felt comfortable in heat most people found oppressive. Her discomfort had nothing to do with Niall's questions. Nothing.

She trudged after him across the combed sand to a bench
set at the edge of the breakwater. As always, he waited for
her to sit first before lowering beside her, an unthreatening
arm's length away.

They sat in silence. Overhead, seagulls swooped and
screamed. On the water, Commerce lakeskimmers glided in
silent patrol. Niall reached into the inner pocket of his tunic
and pulled out a flat silver metal case. He shook out a nicstick through the slotted opening and bit the bulbed end—
the ignition tip flared orange as it contacted the air.

Jani watched him smoke. He didn't do it often, she had
noted, but he did it at very specific times. When he felt particularly agitated or troubled, or as he tried to screw up the
courage to talk about what he called their "shared experiences."

"When to the sessions of sweet, silent thought I summon
up remembrance of things past." Niall leaned forward, elbows on knees, and studied the 'stick's glowing tip. "Shakespeare's Sonnet 30." He looked out over the water, his voice

so soft that the gulls threatened to drown him out. "I keep meaning to lend you the sonnets."

Jani folded her arms and tucked her hands up her sleeves. Her fingers felt like ice chips. "Tsing Tao Station, four and a half years ago. After a run of janitorial gigs, I managed to scrounge a non-Registry clerk's job for one of those seat-of-the-pants shipping companies. I don't even remember the name."

Niall exhaled smoke. "Mercury Shipping."

Jani watched the side of his face and waited for him to explain how he knew that. When he remained silent, she continued. "A brother-sister outfit. One rebuilt shuttle and a time-share lease on a thirty-year-old transport. Constant repair bills, high turnover, and the low-pay, bottom-feeder jobs that the bigger firms never touch."

"Sounds like the sort of outfit that might turn to a bit of smuggling to meet the payroll." Niall had wandered the wild side of the Commonwealth before deciding on the Service straight-and-narrow; his voice held the quiet sureness of someone with experience in the subject.

"Most of the time, smuggling was the payroll." Jani flinched when a gull screamed. "One thing led to another, and we got on the wrong side of a Treasury Customs agent. Not an official investigation—he'd just turn up unexpectedly and ask to see our records. Did that a few times. I figured he was trolling for a payoff, but he never got around to asking."

"He never got the chance. About the time he started digging into the inner workings of Mercury Shipping, he noted in his personal log that he began receiving threatening messages. He saved the paper ones." Niall took a deep pull on his 'stick—the dose ring moved halfway up the shaft. "Two station-days after the date on the last message, his body was found in his flat. Throat had been cut. One station-day after that, you upped and disappeared."

"I had my reasons, in case you've forgotten." Jani shivered as a bout of chills took hold. "Niall, what's going on?"

Niall again reached into his tunic, but instead of his silver box, he removed a folded-over documents slipcase. "I found this waiting for me in my mailbox this morning. After I read it, I figured I'd better pass it along." He handed her the slipcase, then reached into his tunic and once more pulled out his 'sticks.

Jani slid aside the closure and removed several pages of weighty, brilliant white Cabinet-grade parchment. "A joint ministry effort," she said as she searched the gold-bordered documents for a ministry ID code and didn't find it. She flipped back to the face page and read the summary header. "Commonwealth White Paper. Security Risk Evaluation— Jani Moragh Kil—" She fell silent as she found herself looking at a list of dates and page numbers arranged like a table of contents. Next to each date was the name of a city, or a settlement, or a station. The first page contained years one through five of her eighteen years on the run; the second page, years six through twelve; the third, years thirteen to the present.

"There's a data wafer tucked into a pocket inside the slipcase," Niall said. "It contains the full report. Names of companies you worked for, in what capacity, what sorts of . . . business you engaged in. Interviews with coworkers, acquaintances. Ex-lovers."

"I—" Jani swallowed a curse as her stomach cramped. She'd been doing so well on her new enzyme therapy—it hadn't ached for weeks. "I guess I should have expected this. I just didn't think it would turn up so soon." She tucked the papers back in the slipcase. "When do you need it back?"

Niall shook his head. "Keep it. There's plenty more where that came from."

Jani tucked the slipcase in the pocket of her jacket. "It's in general circulation?"

"In the various upper reaches, from what I could gather. PM got a copy. All the Ministers and their deputies. Security chiefs. It's been out for a week or so. Took a while to filter down to me, seeing as I'm on the second team."

"So the Admiral-General's office got one?"

"Oh, yeah."

"Mako have anything to say?"

"About what you'd expect."

Jani watched the dapple of sun on water. It calmed her enough to make her feel that things weren't as bad as they seemed. Almost. "I ran because I couldn't afford to be interviewed, not by trained criminal investigators. You know the drill. First would have come the encephaloscan, which would have revealed my Service augmentation. That would have given them just cause to call in a physician to perform a phys exam. After they'd found my animandroid arm and leg and all my other unique identifiers, they'd have assumed 'deserter' and moved on from there. Before I could whistle the first verse of The Commonwealth Anthem, they would have uncovered the Service warrant for my arrest."

"You could have stalled them."

"You think so? I don't know if you recall the last time we both met with Mako, but I don't interview particularly well."

"Really?" Despite the mood, Niall grinned. "Bit of a smart aleck, are you?" The expression wavered when Jani didn't respond. "Well, like you said, you expected it. How do you plan to counter?"

"Depends how bad it gets, and it could get pretty bad. I falsified shipping and receiving records. Stole scanpack parts. Reset credit chits. An entire host of Level A Registry offenses, any one of which could get me deregistered. Then there's my bioemotional restriction. If some psychotherapeutician decides my past behavior is an indication of future problems, they'll try to stick me in some type of permanent wardship. At the very least, they'll maintain the operational restriction—I won't be able to carry a shooter or drive a skimmer for the rest of my life." Jani stood and stepped to the edge of the breakwater. It was a short drop into the cold churn, only a couple of meters. The drops were always shorter than you thought.

"Maybe it's not as gruesome as you think." Niall's voice sounded rough comfort. "Read it first, then figure out what you need to do." Service tietops scraped on scancrete as he joined her at the edge. "I'll help in any way I can."

"Yeah." Jani gasped as her right calf cramped—her muscles tightened when she sat for too long. "I need to walk."

They strode along the breakwater until it ended, then followed the slope of sand down to the manicured shore. Gulls scuttered ahead of them, waiting until the last moment before taking to the air. In the distance, Commerce employees on break played a game of three-cornered catch.

Jani relaxed. She always felt better when she moved. Her limbs, both the real right and the animandroid left, adjusted readily to the shift and slide of the sand. "I wonder who drove it. The investigation."

"I hate to say it, but I'm betting it was someone on my team." Niall passed her and walked a little farther up the beach. "They probably started out gathering the evidence for your court-martial. When we medical'd you out instead, they wrote the report anyway. One thing Intelligence spooks hate is to let good garbage go unused." He kicked at a pile of pebbles, then picked one up and flung it into the water. "You've got your enemies at Sheridan, you know. They thought you should have been tried for Neumann's death, no matter what led up to it."

"I did shoot him, Niall."

"You had your reasons."

They headed back up the beach toward the Ministry. Jani slowed to give Niall a chance to catch her up. "Mako giving you a hard time about being seen with me?"

"A couple of closed-door talks. Reminders of 'the current conservative climate.' " Niall shrugged. "I remind him that you've got more experience dealing with the idomeni than anyone in Diplo, and that some of your recommendations over the past few months have saved us from some godawful blunders. He understands." His voice held quiet conviction, but he had followed where Admiral-General Hiroshi Mako led for over twenty years, and felt that the sun rose and set by order of the great man.

Jani didn't. "Niall, I'd bet my scanpack that Mako helped set this up."

"*No, he didn't.*" Niall's voice lowered to a warning growl. "It's the Base Command desk jockeys that are causing the trouble. The same ones that want to nail you for Neumann."

"Have they been reminding you of the current conservative climate, too?"

"Yeah. I hand them a little Milton, a little Shakespeare, tell them in my Master of Literature way to butt out. I don't interview particularly well, either."

Jani slowed more as Niall labored to keep his footing on the loose sand. "Don't screw yourself over on my account."

"You'd do the same for me if I got into trouble. I've seen you in action, remember?" He pulled up, removed one of his shoes, and tapped out sand that had leaked in. "I'm going to dig into this when I get back to Sheridan. See if I can find out who signed off on the expense reports." He brushed an invisible smudge from the black tietop's glassy finish, then slipped it back on. "You've got enough going on right now without dealing with this."

They walked in silence. Jani grew conscious of Niall's examination—he tried to hide it, but he never succeeded for long. "If you want to say something, I wish you'd go ahead and say it."

Niall drew closer until they walked shoulder to shoulder. "Earlier this summer, I was a shade taller than you. You're taller than me now. When are you going to stop?"

"No one knows. The average Vynshàrau grows one-nine to two-oh. I'm one-eight-two." Jani held her hand a handspan above her head to indicate how much she could still grow. "John says I might not get as tall as that, being a mixed breed. But even he's ready to give up on the predictions." She heard her voice grow tight. The anger built on its own now, no matter how she tried to suppress it.

"Your eyes look different." Niall leaned in for a closer look. "You've filmed them green! They were always so dark before."

"Neoclona's developed a new color-dispersive film just for me. What's underneath has darkened to green marble. I have nightmares about a film fissuring when I'm out in public."

"They look nice now, though. Stuff seems to work." Niall hurried ahead of Jani as they mounted the breakwater and cut through the rear yard of the Ministry. "I thought they were looking into the possibility of making you all-human again?" He held open the back gate leading into the garden and waved Jani through ahead of him.

"John did call in Eamon DeVries last month." Jani fielded Niall's look of confusion. "Eamon's the third member of the Neoclona Big Three. He's distanced himself from the company in recent years. You don't hear much about him."

Niall's brow arched—he'd detected the sharpness in her voice. "You don't seem sorry."

Jani shrugged. "I despise him. He despises me. He did his best to persuade John to declare me dead at the site of the transport crash. He'd heard that the Service had begun investigating Neumann's murder, and he knew they'd be looking for me. Because of the hybridization research he and John and Val had gotten up to in the basement of the Rauta Shèràa enclave clinic, he knew they couldn't afford to attract attention." And she had attracted attention. Many were the hours she had spent huddled in utilities chases while Val persuaded the Service investigators that Jani Kilian no longer existed. "Almost twenty years had passed since Eamon had seen me." Jani paced a circuit of the small garden. "First thing he says as he walks into the examining room is, 'Why aren't you dead yet?' "

Niall braced against a tree, removed his shoes one at a time, and tapped out more sand. "Bet he didn't say it in front of Shroud—ol' John would've killed him."

Jani smiled. "I never figured you for a John Shroud fan."

"I'm not." Niall brushed off his socks and slipped on his shoes. "Val Parini's all right. The doctor you see most of the time—Montoya—he seems sound. I know Roger Pimentel likes him."

"How is Roger?"

"Fine. Still Chief of Neuro, but the workload is wearing him down. He made vague noises about retirement when I saw him last week. Asked how you were." Niall shook his head. "We could spend all day talking about our doctors, couldn't we?" He watched Jani walk with the sharp eye of the experienced medical amateur. "So?"

"So, after Eamon examined me, he hunkered down with John and Val. They concluded that any attempt at retooling would most likely kill me." Jani stopped in front of a bird feeder and unplugged a stopped dispenser with her finger, sending a thin stream of birdseed spilling to the ground. "Sometimes that doesn't sound like such a bad risk."

"You can say things like that to me—I understand. But remarks like that tend to make psychotherapeuticians nervous." Niall gathered up a handful of the spilled seed and tossed it to some squirrels that foraged in the grass. "Trust me—I know what I'm talking about."

Jani gripped the feeder post and swung around to face him. "How did your last check-up go?"

"About as you'd expect." Niall flung more seed with such force that the squirrels scattered. "Get your augmentation removed—the risks of depression and psychosis outweigh the benefits. Yes, we know it could save your life in case of severe injury, but if the injury resulted from the fact that you just slashed your wrists, define the benefit please, Colonel. Cut back on the workload, take a vacation, transfer to another area. At least no one suggested retirement this time." He brushed off his hands and cut across the garden to the front gate. "Need a ride home?"

Jani tagged after him. "No, I'll take public. I've got to go to the embassy later. Sitting in a people-mover and watching the city float by helps me think."

"More fun with diplomacy?"

"Yeah."

"If I don't hear from you in a week, I'll send in an assault team." Niall once more cut ahead of her as they came to the gate so he could hold it open for her. "The Cup semifinals are set for next week. Acadia Central United's playing Gruppo in the first match."

"United got Desjarlais back just in time." Jani shivered as her body once more decided it was cold, and closed her jacket fasteners up to her neck. "The government will go nuts if a colonial team wins the Cup. They're afraid that's all it would take for some of the more rebellious colonies to attempt to secede from the Commonwealth."

"That's ridiculous."

"You're a colony boy, Niall. You know better than that. It's all about politics, even when it's not."

Niall sensed that she didn't feel like talking football. "Heard from your folks?"

"Yeah." The 'mover that would take Jani back to the walkway drifted up to the stand. "They've gone to stay with Oncle Shamus at his lodge near Faeroe Outpost. I guess he needs help with his systems again."

"You guess?"

"They're not being real forthcoming. I'm wondering if times are bad in Ville Acadie, and they needed to sell the business."

"Times are never bad for systems installers."

"Well, something's wrong." Jani stepped aboard the open-topped 'mover and took a seat near the rear. "I don't think they're comfortable talking to me. Maybe they don't think it's any of my business."

Niall shot her a "let's have none of that" look. "Or maybe Shamus did need help. Sometimes the answers really are as simple as they seem." He stepped back as the 'mover pulled away. "I'll look into that report."

"Thanks."

"Take it easy." Niall smiled his crooked smile and again touched his forehead. "Captain."

"Colonel." As Jani returned the salute, she felt the slip-case jostle in her jacket pocket, and tried to forget it was there.

Jani changed people-movers three times on her way home. As she had told Niall, sitting and watching Chicago drift past her window helped her think. Unfortunately, she couldn't control what she thought about.

They got me. She felt the slipcase every time she moved, saw the gleam of the white parchment sheets, heard their crackle as she had unfolded them under Niall's concerned eye. *I wonder how long it took them to uncover it all? When did they start? Last winter, when they realized that I lived? Or did they wait until the summer, when they had me in hand?*

The six-lane tumult of the Boul Mich Sidebar gradually veered lakeward, narrowing and quieting into the tree-lined elegance of Chestnut Street. Jani looked through the branches to the establishments beyond . . . the glass-walled terrace of the restaurant where she and Lucien had dined the night before . . . the shops in which they'd debated other presents for her clients. Jani hadn't realized that she needed to worry about presents for her clients until Lucien had broached the subject. Her comment that considering the way they ran her ragged, the presents should all flow in *her* direction had fallen on unsympathetic ears. *You're in the big city now,* Lucien had said. *We do things differently here.*

"Do you?" Jani stood as the 'mover slowed to a stop. "Could've fooled me." The only difference she had been able to discern thus far between the wilder colonies and the Commonwealth capital was that life in Chicago required more paperwork. And, at times, even more caution.

She disembarked and headed north, crossing Chestnut and turning onto the even more rarified gentility of Armour Place. Her goal rested in matronly repose in the middle of the block, a twelve-story sanctum of safety and security. Eighty-seven fifty-six—a sedate, marble-faced building with a live doorman and, according to Lucien, a century's worth of Family secrets buried within the walls.

Secrets . . .

I have secrets. Jani's step slowed. *The funny thing is, some of them are common knowledge. But still they're ignored, denied, not talked about, in the hope that they'll disappear. A peculiarly humanish habit, one the idomeni mock.*

My name is Jani Moragh Kilian, late of the Commonwealth Service. One of the conditions of my discharge disallows me from using the title Captain, Retired, but that's what I am.

Just as John Shroud resurrected me and rebuilt me as he saw fit, so my past has been gutted and reconstructed for the benefit of the few. What remains speaks to the facts, but the truth lies elsewhere. I tried to speak the truth, and they called me crazy. Now I stick to the facts, and bide my time.

Jani shook herself out of her grim reverie as she approached her apartment house, eyeing the entries of the buildings directly across the street. She did so mostly out of habit, but partly from unease. The small multilevel chargelot seemed quiet as usual. The commotion echoing from the building next door to it, however, scuttled the gracious ambience the avenue usually projected. Bangs and clangs, interspersed with the occasional muffled boom of a pinpoint charge and the whine of heavy-duty construction machinery.

The gutted former residence would soon twin its neighbor across the way—twelve stories of marble enclosing thirty of the finest flats money could rent. In the meantime, the carefully preserved white façades sheltered scaffolding, equipment, workers, and building materials sufficient to convert the shell into a hive.

Jani ducked beneath the low-hanging awning that sheltered her building entry and nodded to the morning doorman, who keyed open the triple-width door. The thick, ram-resistant scanglass swept aside and she stepped into the lobby, a low-ceilinged space filled with expensive furnishings, paintings, and sculpture. The sudden hush as the door shut behind her made her feel, as always, as though she'd been locked inside a vault.

She walked to the front desk, her shoes sinking to the ankle in the sound-deadening carpet; fellow residents passed her, their greetings muted, as though they spoke in church.

"You're back, Mistress Kilian." Hodge the manager smiled a subdued greeting. "Confound the racket across the way."

Jani sighed as she accepted the pile of paper mail he produced from beneath the desk. "Confound it, indeed."

"Not much longer." Hodge's voice held a hope-filled lilt—he'd mistaken her dismay at the amount of mail for weariness with the noise. "The rededication is scheduled for Thanksgiving weekend." He grew subdued. "Armour Eight Seven Five Five. Seems a rather dull name." He was a slight, older man with a schoolmaster's air. He'd worked in the neighborhood all his life and felt the changes like a father watching his children grow.

"Well, at least they're preserving the façade." Jani tucked the mail under her arm and looked out at the bustle across the street. "But for the noise, they're remarkably self-contained. You never see the workers."

"There are restrictions regarding these matters, to minimize the impact on the neighborhood." Hodge frowned. "But I have seen things. The workers are supposed to use a contractor lot three blocks west, near the University Annex.

But I believe they sneak vehicles into our garage to avoid the walk."

"Imagine that." Jani bit back the comment that if she'd been in their place, she'd do the same thing. But that was a colonial sentiment, and she lived in the Commonwealth capital now. As Lucien said, they did things differently here.

CHAPTER 3

The lift deposited Jani on the sixth floor. She walked to the last door at the end of the carpeted hall and keyed into her flat. The door slid open to reveal the large sitting room, an expanse of bare bleached wood flooring, unadorned off-white walls, and uncurtained windows.

Jani walked to her desk, the sole piece of furniture in the space, and pushed aside a stack of files so she could deposit her mail. Compared to the rest of the room, the desktop looked as though it belonged to another person. Masses of documents in multicolored folders and slipcases covered the surface from end to end, abutting her workstation on three sides and all but burying her comport. *I've got too much work.* But the commissions kept coming. The requests. The contracts. Niall had spoken the truth. Jani Kilian had more experience with the idomeni than anyone in Chicago, and Chicago seemed determined to take advantage in every way possible.

"Who has time to buy furniture?" Jani muttered as she cleared a space around her comport. *Give me a credit line,* Lucien asked repeatedly, *I'll get you whatever you need.* But she had turned him down because she didn't want him to become too well acquainted with her finances.

There are companies that handle this, Niall had commented, his assumption being that after years of living in the Commonwealth's outer reaches, she didn't trust her taste.

But it was her friend Frances Hals who had nailed the perplexity as well as anyone could have. *The two sides of Jani Kilian—paper and nothing,* she had said when she visited earlier that week to find the floors still bare. *When are you*

21

going to start filling in, and with what? She had served as
Jani's CO for only a few weeks that summer, but years spent
managing recalcitrant documents examiners had further
honed an already keen insight. She didn't want to hear that
Jani had no interest in life outside the documents realm, that
the workload was too heavy, the responsibilities too great.
*You're still running. You need to decide whether it's force of
habit or fear of what you'll find if you stand still.*

"Always a pleasure, Frances." The comport's incoming message light fluttered in mad blue abandon—Jani flicked the acti-
vator pad and watched a harried male face form on the display.

"Hey, Jan." Kern Standish, the Deputy Treasury Minister,
stifled a yawn. He'd already loosened his neckpiece, and sat
with both hands wrapped around a cup of coffee. "We're
having a meeting about you this morning, which will be a
continuation of the meeting we had about you last night. I'm
guessing that you know what I'm talking about."

Jani patted her pocket, and felt the outline of the documents slipcase. "Yes, Kern," she said to the recorded image.
"I know."

"Anyway . . ." Standish tilted his wrist to glance at his
timepiece, and sighed. "Gotta go. Just wanted to give you a
heads-up. I'd appreciate if you'd erase this after you listen to
it." His brown skin looked greyed in the harsh office lighting. "Most folks here think it's water under the bridge, but
you know Jorge. He's worried about Anais, and how miser-
able she can make his political life if she finds out he's on
your side." He smiled weakly. "I'll let you know what happens." The screen blanked. Jani duly erased the message,
then tapped the pad to open the next one.

"Ja-ni." The man offered a mouth-only smile. Devinham
from NUVA-SCAN Colonial Projects Division—one of her
errors in professional judgment. He kept moving the targets
and still expected her to hit every one with a single shot.
"The presentation I'm giving has been moved up to next
Monday, and I need the Phillipan dock data a little earlier
than I'd anticipated—"

"That's news, Frank." She tapped the pad again.

"—please help—"

Again.

"—if you have the time—"

Jani checked the counter. *Twenty-one messages*. Judging from the number of pleas she'd heard so far, the white paper hadn't yet scared off any clients. *Too bad—I could use the break*. She settled for taking refuge in her bedroom.

Unlike the rest of the flat, Jani had furnished her bedroom. Lucien had insisted. After all, he needed an armoire to store his clothes, a nightstand so he could reach a comport immediately in case of an emergency call from Sheridan, and lamps so he didn't kill himself when he arrived late at night to find her already asleep.

But most especially, Jani felt, he wanted a place to display his gifts to her. Last winter's tin soldier stood sentry atop the armoire. This summer's fatigue-clad teddy bear guarded the bed. They had since been joined by a set of nested matryoshka dolls and a watercolor of a costumed couple eyeing one another across a crowded room. The painting, which hung alongside the dresser, was exquisitely detailed and framed in tasteful gilt. The doll set, which had joined the soldier atop the armoire, had been hand-carved from wood and painted bright red and blue. Both objects contained flaws of use—the picture frame had been nicked in several places, and the fact that the tiniest doll in the matryoshka set could be opened implied that the littlest one had gone missing. In Jani's experience, only one type of person treated works of art like everyday objects, to be used as intended regardless of their value.

"Which of his Family lovers did Lucien steal you from?" she asked the largest matryoshka doll as she took her down from her resting place. "And why?" They certainly weren't the sort of gifts one usually bestowed on the object of one's rapture. Lucien took particular delight in showing Jani the clothes and jewelry that he received for services rendered— he ranked every present by its monetary value, and negligent admirers weathered the brunt of his indifference until they dug into their pockets and rectified the situation.

Jani returned the doll to its place. "Frances thinks that at heart, all men are children and that they show their truest feelings with childlike gifts." But then, Frances liked Lucien, and thought he had feelings to show. Jani liked him too, even though she knew that he didn't.

She walked to the window and deactivated the privacy shield. The milky scanglass lightened to transparency, revealing clear views of both the garden alley that ran along the rear of the building and Oak Street, a shopping lane that paralleled Chestnut and also merged with the Boul Sidebar. An escape route, one of many she'd worked out over the months. Not that she'd ever need them. She was yesterday's news, useful only as a subject of gossip and the occasional damning security evaluation.

Jani sat down on the bed, and girded herself for another go-round with her comport. And so they went in spite of the white paper. Requests for research updates. Meeting reschedules. Hat-in-hand queries into her availability. Jani demurred, assented, and rejected—if she applied herself, she could meet the most pressing of her deadlines and accommodate a few of the more challenging, and therefore more expensive, requests.

In theory. She'd been pushing herself the past few months, and only yesterday had caught several slips that would have proved embarrassing if they'd gotten into a final report. Niall had taken to calling her "the Red Queen"—her request for an explanation won her a lecture about the storied Alice.

Running faster and faster to stay in one place. She knew she spent too much time performing routine research. But she didn't trust the contractor firms, and her searches for help had left her muttering dark damnations about the current state of the documents profession.

When she had whittled the queue to the final message, she took a breather, sitting forward and letting her head drop between her knees to stretch her tightening back. Her stomach ached again. Hungry or not, she'd have to choke down breakfast. Her life had come to revolve around the care and feeding of her mutating body and her physician, Calvin Montoya, possessed a sorcerous knack for diagnosing patient noncompliance with a single look.

She hit the message pad, and stared open-mouthed at the face that formed.

"Hullo, Jan." Steven Forell grinned and pushed a shaggy

auburn lock out of his eyes. "Bet yer surprised to see me."
His lapsed altar boy face looked despairingly youthful.

"You might say that, yes," Jani said with a laugh. She'd
last seen him that past winter, when she left him hiding in
her Interior Ministry suite while she hunted down whoever
had framed him for murder. She had uncovered the true cul-
prit and much more besides, and almost died during the subsequent shakeout that wound up costing Evan van Reuter his
Ministry.

"We're back—Ange and me—froom Helier." Steve's
Channel-Guernsey accent ground his words together into a
single lumpy mass. "Bit of a bang job. In and out—word
from the nobbies—here we are and back again."

*You and Angevin received a short-term special assign-
ment from some higher-ups in Interior Colonial Affairs . . .
got it.*

"We'd heard about yer to-do, o'course . . ." Steve's brow
drew down as his look sombered. "Rum go you had, gel.
Ange thinks it were all a setup from on-high. She tried to tap
some of her late dad's friends fer info. You'd think she'd
asked them to give a few years off their lives." His words
stalled as he searched his pockets. He uncovered a nicstick,
ignited it, and was soon enveloped by the cloud of smoke
Jani recalled so well. "So we're here. Still a few days till our
return to the grind—Ange thought you might like a dinner.
Tomorrow night? Gaetan's? Our treat, since we never got to
thank you proper." He coughed and looked away. The seconds ticked. "Sevenish, then? Meet ya there." He turned
back to the display. His grin froze and faded as the message
ended.

Jani stared at the blank screen. *Ya see, there's this bang
job,* she thought in Steve-speak. *I don't have the time,* she
continued in her own. She reached out, her finger hovering
above the reply pad. *I don't have the time.* A very simple
sentence. By now, she could say it in her sleep.

Instead, she undressed. Showered. Chose a suit in dark
green from the conservative array in her closet and dressed
with absent care, her mind carefully focused on nothing.
Styled her hair. Applied makeup. Avoided the mirror.

Finally, boots in hand, she removed Niall's slipcase from the pocket of her discarded jacket, padded out to the sitting room, and inserted the data wafer in her workstation's reader slot. She sat down and pulled on her boots, concentrating on adjusting the fasteners to the proper tension before looking at the display.

It scrolled before her, cross-referenced and footnoted. The officially researched life of Jani Moragh Kilian, written in bland government style. The anonymous authors didn't spend much time on her first seventeen years—a single paragraph defined her parents and her early schooling in the Acadian capital of Ville Acadie. Only when they discussed her performance on a formidable array of Commonwealth-wide qualifying exams and her subsequent acceptance into the idomeni Academy in Rauta Shèràa did they become more verbose.

" 'After her arrival in Rauta Shèràa, Kilian's lack of Family connections and singular personality caused her to seek support and companionship in unlikely quarters. Kilian's ready adoption of idomeni languages and customs alienated her from peers even as it increased her value in the diplomatic sphere. While her singling-out as a favorite by the Chief Propitiator of the Vynshà, Avrèl nìRau Nema, alarmed Consulate officials, the general feeling was that even this could be worked to Commonwealth advantage. Her subsequent commissioning into the Commonwealth Service, while a sound decision on the face of it, only served to highlight her flagrant disrespect for traditional seats of human authority and intensify her estrangement from those who could have assisted her in her reassimilation.' "

Jani smacked the side of the workstation display with the flat of her hand. "This is a reference to Evan, is it? The only reassimilating he wanted from me was the illegal transfer of idomeni brain research data into his late father's hands!" She didn't find that out until years later, however. *Just last winter, in fact. The uncovering of that information led to Evan's downfall.* She stood and paced a circuit of her barren sitting room before returning to her desk.

Knevçet Shèràa, the authors touched on only briefly. The deaths of humans as the result of mind control experimentation performed on them by Laumrau physician-priests, well, they had to discuss that since it was a matter of record to which the idomeni admitted freely. The role that Colonel Rikart Neumann played in planning and gathering the research was glossed over as unsubstantiated rumor; his murder was blamed on his sergeant, Emil Burgoyne, who supposedly sought revenge for a recent demotion. "Except Borgie didn't do it. Mako made him the scapegoat so that Prime Minister Cao would accept the idea of my medical discharge." Jani felt her throat tighten. "Mako couldn't afford to let me face court-martial. He has his own bodies to keep buried." She blinked until her eyes cleared, then continued to read.

" 'As the Vynshà worked to weaken Laumrau defenses around the dominant city of Rauta Shèràa, the Laumrau sought to maintain strategic positions in the mountainous desert regions that surrounded the city. Knevçet Shèràa, which they considered a holy place, was one of those positions. The presence of human beings in the area was, they felt, a mistake that they needed to rectify in order to regain the favor of Shiou, their goddess of order. For that reason, as was admitted later in a closed-door session cited below footnote addendum et cetera et cetera, they planned to retake the hospital-shrine from the remaining members of the Twelfth Rover Corps. The battle would follow a night of prayer and sacramental meal-taking that they referred to as a Night of Convergence.' "

Jani's voice slowed as her sense memory of that night returned. The sear of pain as she hacked her left arm with a mess knife. The warm flow of her blood, captured with strips torn from a red machinist's rag, the closest facsimile she could find to a Vynshà soul cloth. The growing numbness in her slashed arm, the rough dampness of the rag between her fingers as she braided the strips into a skein that would house her soul, and shelter it from the actions of her body. The slip of the sand under her boots as she walked down the hill toward the Laumrau encampment. " 'As the twenty-six Laumrau based at the encampment took sacrament in their tents, Kilian crept in under cover of night and shot them one by one.' " That much, the fact-finders nailed perfectly. But then, they'd found it out from the idomeni. Unlike humans, the idomeni always admitted truth freely, no matter how damning the result.

After that, details muddied quickly. While unofficially, everyone knew that Evan van Reuter had arranged that a bomb be planted on the transport that had been sent to return Jani and the rest of the Twelfth Rovers to Rauta Shèràa, he had never been officially charged with murder. Even though everyone knew that John Shroud had salvaged Jani's shattered body from the wreckage and rebuilt her with illegally acquired idomeni genetic material, no one wanted to put the details to paper. John could have faced charges of kidnapping and illegal utilization of technology, and John was a powerful man. Evan, meanwhile, though no longer a powerful man, still had his memory and his mouth.

"You'd spill it all if they tried you for murder, wouldn't you, Ev? You'd drag all the Family members who conspired with Neumann and your father into the hellhole with you." Which explained why Evan remained free to nibble on the edges of the idomeni diplomatic pie, a peripheral presence at some of the meetings Jani attended. They took assiduous pains to avoid one another, much to the disappointment of those who hoped for an altercation. "As if it would make a difference." Maybe someday they would be forced to face their shared past. With any luck, *someday* would never come.

Jani broke off her meditation to look once more at the workstation display, and read of her escape from Rauta Shèràa during that final Night of the Blade, when the Vynshàrau asserted their claim to the city. Then came the details of her life on the run. The names she had used. Men she had known. Dirt she had done.

So they found out about the faked bank transfers in Ville Louis-Phillipe. The altered manifests and receiving documents she had constructed on a score of worlds. And the shipping clerk in New St. Lô must not have been at happy with her cut of the proceeds as she had seemed at the time—she had revealed everything about the scanpack parts skimming operation in which Jani had been involved. *No, not involved—it was mine from start to finish.* But her scanpack had needed refurbishing, and she had been desperate. *I just took a part here, a part there. I never got greedy.* Unfortunately, that qualifier hadn't made it into the report.

She paged to the top and read through once more. She searched for conclusions. A recommendation for censure or expulsion from Registry. A proposal to convene a grand jury to explore possible criminal charges. She didn't find them, though, just as she didn't find mention of certain other salient events. A small gap. One missed stop in her round-the-Commonwealth journey, but it dwarfed the other matters delineated in the security report.

They're probably saving that for the next white paper. She pushed the idea to the back of her mind and waited for her nerves to settle enough that she could consider eating.

Jani adjourned to the kitchen. She dug through the cupboards for a Neoclona prepack meal and tossed it label-unread into the oven, then poured herself coffee from the morning's dregs. By the time she flushed out the brewer, her breakfast was ready. She popped the lid on the container and stared at reactor-kettle meatloaf and a shredded purple vegetable that the container claimed was beets but that smelled like no vegetable she'd ever encountered. She excavated a fork from her muddled utensil drawer and boosted herself up on the counter. She ate and mulled until the buzz of her comport called her out to the sitting room.

"Jani." Colonel Eugene Derringer, adjutant to General Callum Burkett, the head of Service Diplomatic, regarded her with his usual air of impatience. He looked a study in tan—skin, hair, desertweight uniform. Burkett the Younger, with his clipped demeanor and horse face; it was a running argument among the rest of Diplo whether the similarities were happenstance or if Derringer worked at them. "I'm calling from my skimmer. I've just left the base. Why don't I zip by your building and give you a lift to the embassy?"

"It's a little out of your way, Eugene. And it's almost two hours early."

"We can use the extra time. There's something you and I need to discuss."

"What?"

Derringer smiled coolly. "See you in a few." His face fractured and faded.

Jani poked her fork into the remains of her meal. She suspected a bout of on-the-road reeducation in the offing. Derringer felt her behavior toward the idomeni too familiar, her relationship to the ambassador too close—

The comport buzzed again. She hit the receive pad harder than she should have, and the unit screeched.

"I heard that." Niall sat at his desk in his Base Command office. He paused to partake of his soldier's breakfast—a swig of coffee, a pull on a nicstick. "Things not going well?" He made no reference to which things he talked about. Neither of them trusted comports, even ones like his and Jani's that were supposed to be secured.

"Eugene just called." Jani rolled her eyes. "He's picking me up in person to take me to the embassy."

"Well, well. Fixing to pop the question, is he?"

Jani forced a laugh. "Yeah, I think he has the ring and the date all picked out. Right after I say yes, he's going to ask Nema to be best man."

Smoke puffed from Niall's nose and mouth as he laughed. "Has the esteemed representative of the Shèrá worldskein pulled anything since the Pokegrass Episode? Any more vegetation-stuffed chair cushions for our dear Eugene to sit on?"

"No." Jani smiled more easily, the memory of Derringer twitching about in his booby-trapped seat over the course of one memorable four-hour conclave replaying in her mind. "Nema's moved on to other torments. I keep telling him, 'You're humiliating a Service diplomat—stop it.' But he won't listen."

"He's idomeni. He knows Derringer doesn't like him, and he enjoys tweaking him." Niall sat back, nicstick clenched between his teeth at a jaunty angle. "So what's happened lately?"

Jani pressed a hand to her forehead. "They met in Nema's rooms last week—I forget what about. Somehow, Nema arranged to have an audio track of the Commonwealth anthem piped in, at a very, very low volume. So they're talking, and Eugene's just barely hearing this music—"

"And wondering if he should stand at attention or check into the Neuro ward."

"Nema said the look on his face was 'a sight to behold, and truly.' I keep waiting for Eugene to retaliate. Somehow, I don't think that will prove nearly as humorous." Jani sighed heavily and sat up. "That being so, I shouldn't aggravate him by making him wait. I better get ready."

Niall's eyes narrowed. "You OK?"

"Yeah." She nodded once, then again.

"You don't seem too sure."

"Just a feeling. Just—" She braced her hands on her chair arms and boosted to her feet. "We'll talk later."

"All right." Niall frowned. "Later."

Jani waited for the display to blank. Then she carted the remains of her meal to the kitchen for disposal. Washed her fork and coffee cup and stored them away. Wiped down the counter. Thought.

Here's my feeling, Niall—the white paper contains one important gap. Two serial events in the same botched scenario, the discovery of either one of which could result in her imprisonment for life.

Jani returned to her desk and stuffed her scanpack and a few pertinent files into her battered Service surplus duffel. *How could they uncover my one-week stint as a deckhand on a Phillipan cruise shuttle, and miss those two things?* She put the duffel aside and sat down, burying her face in her hands as the past returned, an unwelcome shadow in the doorway that said, *Hello, remember me?*

Document forgery as a whole was a crime, of course, but under the general heading came three classifications with steadily increasing penalty in proportion to the adjudged severity. Simple forgery, the construction of a unique document that had no legal right to exist, was the least grave— such objects were bastard children, embarrassing to the putative relatives but easily dealt with. Wipe them out, lock them up, take steps to make sure that particular avenue of deceit was closed and remained so. Second came alteration of existing paper. That misdeed carried heftier fines and sentences because something once pure had been sullied, something once reliable had been rendered untrustworthy.

But copying a document, divesting it of its unique identity by sending a twin out into the world as if it were the original, was considered the worst of the three. Simple forgeries were more sporting—a contest between the forger's skill and the investigator's ability to detect. But executing a copy of an existing document, down to the weave of the paper and the position of the insets, took that competition and warped it. Worse than a bastard, such an object was a changeling that subverted the rightful document's place in the paper world, and robbed it of its inheritance. It shook the stability of the paper system, a construct in which every document played a role, had a history, promoted order.

Jani lifted her head and rested her chin on her arm.

"I made a copy once." Five years before, in Hamish City, a dreary town as off the beaten path as a colonial capital could be. *The capital of Jersey, the hind end of the Channel Worlds.* She tried not to think of Jersey too much.

Jani could see out her sitting room windows to the bright sunny morning on the other side. Bright sun didn't evoke memories of Hamish City. For those one needed grey skies, grimy streets, the stinging odor of battery hyperacid mixing with the rank of desperation.

"Sasha needed my help." But then, Sasha had always needed somebody's help. Short and spindly, a shaggy brune with bitten fingernails and a nervous smile, he was a member of the loose-knit group of techs and clerks to which Jani belonged during her Jersey stay. Another member of the group had labeled Sasha clumsy, which was a shorthand way of saying that he missed warning signs and never listened.

"He decided one day that he wanted to pull out of Hamish." Jani rose, twisted back and forth to stretch her back, then walked to the window. "But he needed money." And someone offered him some, Sasha had told Jani, the excitement pitching his voice high like a young boy's. All he had to do was figure out a way to obstruct an investigation into the true ownership of a parcel of land on which someone wanted to build a fuel depot. "I should have known as soon as he told me about it that a Family was involved. The Families had a vise grip on fuel services in the Channel." But she was working as an inventory hack and going mad from the boredom, and the idea of throwing a wrench in somebody else's works appealed.

So when Sasha brought Jani the original deed of ownership and asked what she could do, she pulled out her scanpack and the best documents training extant and went to work. It had taken her a week to diagram the original, then two more to steal the necessary components and assemble the backdated copy. It was a sound piece of work, she knew, the best that could be done without a Registry copying device. It even got past her scanpack analysis, if she ignored some of the dodgier variances.

"But I warned Sasha that it wouldn't get past a Family examiner." Jani watched the well-dressed midmorning bustle on the sunny street below and envisioned a gloomier scene: the pedestrians bundled in weatheralls and field coats, late fall wind driving the cold mist like smoke. "I told him to arrange for a fifty-fifty drop." The buyer would leave half the money at a prearranged site; Sasha would take the money and leave the copied deed. "The next step would be for the buyer to pick up the copy and leave the rest of the money. A sucker bet, yes, but it didn't matter because I had told Sasha not to wait. The half payment was enough to get him off Jersey. I told him to take it and go. He took too great a risk if he hung around."

She still didn't know why she followed him the day he made the drop. Guilt, maybe, that she'd helped him get in well over his head. Shooter in hand, she tailed him to an alley behind some warehouses, watched him pluck the documents slipcase containing the first half of the payment from a space behind some empty crates, then insert the copy into the same niche. "I rousted him then, made him come with me, told him to get offworld *now*." She should have escorted him to the shuttleport herself and seen him aboard the next merchant vessel out, but he had promised her he'd leave, and she'd believed him for the ten minutes it took him to disappear from her sight.

By then, the realization hit. That Jani had asked Sasha to

leave a great deal of money behind, and that Sasha never listened. By the time she reached the drop site, she found him felled like a tree. A man stood over him, shooter in hand. A man like Niall. A coiled spring. A professional. But even professionals could be surprised—he spotted her an instant after she saw him. An instant too late. She had earned an Expert marksmanship badge in the Service and never lost the eye.

Jani knew she'd killed him—she could tell by the way he lay, like a rag crumpled and tossed to the ground. She left him and saw to Sasha, dragging him into the open as carefully as she could, then watching from a safe distance as the first passerby found him and called for help. Then she fled, the need to reach the shuttleport and nab a billet on the next ship out overwhelming the desire to remain behind and discover whether Sasha survived. Clumsy Sasha, who had needed a mentor but had been given a changeling instead.

"Copying. Murder." Of a Family agent, most likely. "How did they miss it?" Jani stood at the window, watching but not seeing. Then thoughts of Derringer intruded, and she trudged to her bathroom to brush her teeth. She did so twice, in deference to Vynshàrau sensibilities. All idomeni considered the act of eating a private communion between the worshipper and their gods, food and drink the links that forged that sacred bond, but the Vynshàrau were the most rigid in their beliefs. Even Nema, as audacious as he was, adhered to his sect's dietary laws, and Jani didn't want a whiff of coffee breath to further aggravate already tense relations.

By the time Hodge called her from the lobby to tell her that the colonel's skimmer had arrived, she felt prepared to face whatever Derringer had to throw at her. Before she left her flat, she removed Niall's wafer from the workstation reader, returned it to the slipcase, and tucked it into the safety of her inner tunic pocket.

CHAPTER 4

Derringer's steel-blue double-length hugged the curb in front of the apartment house. As soon as Jani hit the sidewalk, the doorman and Derringer's driver engaged in a footrace to see who would play the gentleman. The point was declared moot when Derringer popped the door open himself and stepped out of the vehicle.

"Jani." Even though the red stripe had been removed from his desertweight trousers in deference to the Vynshàrau's color protocols, no one would ever mistake him for anything but highly polished mainline brass.

"Eugene." Jani brushed past him and bent low to climb into the jump seat across from him. "What did you need to see me—" She fell silent when she saw a young man already sitting where she wanted to sit. "Who are you?" She could hear the sharpness in her voice, but she didn't savor being forced to sit next to Derringer. She scooted down the bench seat, as far away from the colonel as possible.

Derringer doffed his garrison cap and eased in beside her. "This is Peter Lescaux." He nodded to the intruder, who smoothed the neckpiece of his somber brown daysuit. "Exterior Minister Ulanova's new Chief of Staff."

"The storied Jani Kilian." Lescaux smiled shyly and extended his hand. "I'm thrilled to meet you at last."

Jani took in the brilliant blondness offset by brown eyes. The sharp bones, slim fitness, vague, indefinable accent. *So you're Anais's new Lucien.* His skin felt cool and smooth; he'd buffed his nails until they shone like glass. She likened him to a snake that had just shed its skin, then pushed the thought from her mind before it showed in her face.

"I thought we'd stop at a place I know nearby, grab some lunch." Derringer nodded to his driver; the skimmer pulled away from the curb. "Lord knows how long we'll be holed up at the embassy—we better stoke up while we can."

"*Excellent* thought, Colonel," Lescaux nodded as though someone had spring-loaded his neck.

Oh brother! Jani knocked the back of her head against the seat bolster.

"Fancy setup you've got." Derringer cast a sideways glance in her general direction. "I'd heard you'd taken a flat near the Parkway, but Armour Place? Now I know what happens to all those consultant fees we pay you."

Jani counted to three before answering. "The Registry employment adviser advised my renting at the best address I could afford. It instills confidence in the client." She wanted to add that since her flat overlooked the alley and commanded views of neither the Chicago skyline or the lake, she paid half the rent of her more scenically gifted neighbors, but she'd be damned if she'd justify her living arrangements to Derringer.

"It is a good address," Lescaux said, nodding knowingly. "All the Families have residences nearby."

Jani watched the passing city views, and waited. And waited some more. "Are you two going to tell me what's going on"—she swung around and glared at Derringer—"or are you going to make me guess?"

Derringer nodded again to his driver, who raised the privacy shield between his seat and the passenger cabin. "How much do you know about problems on Elyas?"

Jani flash-filtered all the scuttlebutt she had heard over the past weeks. "The problems I've heard about are confined to Karistos. It's a typical colonial capital, grown too big too quickly. The infrastructure hasn't kept pace. Skimways can't handle the traffic. Water treatment facilities are overtaxed. Last month, a majority of the population got dosed with a microbial contaminant that had infested the treatment system of the primary facility. Several people died."

"Twenty-two," Lescaux piped. Jani acknowledged the information with a nod, Derringer not at all.

"The plant needs an upgrade—that's a given. A new plant is the best solution, but you're talking two to three years down the road before that's completed." He thumped his thigh with a closed fist. "Take a wild guess who's volunteered to help the Elyans with their micro problems in the meantime. Just guess."

Jani blinked innocently. "The regular crop of Family-connected suppliers, the ones who designed the inadequate plant in the first place."

Derringer glared from Jani to Lescaux. "Tell her."

For an instant, Lucien's sharpness flashed in Lescaux's eyes. Then he looked at Jani, and the boyish aspect returned. "The Elyan Haárin surprised us all. They struck a deal with the Karistos city government for a microbial filter assembly with sufficient capacity to tide over the Karistosians until the new plant is built."

"The Haárin sold us a component that they use in their own water treatment?" Jani looked at Derringer. "The Rauta Shèràa Council will consider that a violation of their dietary protocols. The Oligarch won't allow it."

"You'd think that, wouldn't you?" Derringer deigned to glance at Lescaux once more. "Show her the big surprise."

Lescaux rummaged through the briefbag on the seat beside him. "It took several passes through the stacks of contract documentation before we realized what we had." The shy smile shone once more. "I'm sure I don't need to tell you how easy it is to overlook that one vital piece of paper." He fumbled through his files once, then again. His searching grew more agitated as the soft *patpatpat* of Derringer's fingers drumming on the leather upholstery filled the cabin. "*Ah!*" He yanked a document out of its slipcase—the high-pitched tearing noise of smooth parchment sliding over pebbled plastic made Jani cringe.

"Thank you." She took the document from him as though it was wet tissue, her thumbs and index fingers gripping the top corners. "Ease it out of the slipcase from now on—abrasion can play hell with the inset chips."

"Sorry." Lescaux wavered between sheepish apology and expectant anxiety as he watched Jani examine the document. "You see what that is, don't you?"

Jani draped the paper across her knees. "It's an analysis of the Karistos city council decision to contract with the Elyan Haárin." She ran her fingers along the edges once, then again. The paper possessed the substantial, almost fleshy feel of highest quality parchment. "Best grade of paper. Premium inks and foils." She reached for her duffel. "If you want me to scan—"

"Just read the bottom paragraph," Derringer growled.

"I'll read the entire thing." Jani activated her scanpack and set it beside her on the seat. "Neat little precis describing how the Karistos city government has come to depend on the Elyan Haárin for many things—shipping and receiving of goods and documents, design and maintenance of everything from devices and instruments to buildings." She shrugged. "It's the way of the colonies—human and Haárin doing business together. Some Haárin enclaves have been in existence since before the Laum-Vynshàrau civil war. They remained in place even during the postwar cessation of human-idomeni diplomatic relations. Over the course, the Haárin have sold us things that violated their dietary protocols. But they never wrote it down, and they sure as hell never drew up a formal agreement that required a buy-in from Shèrá."

"Keep reading." Derringer kept his gaze fixed on the view outside. They'd entered the far north region of the city, a place of narrower streets and smaller buildings separated by stretches of parkland, and he seemed to be savoring the early fall scenery.

You're not the sight-seeing type, Eugene. Jani turned back to the document. "The writer concludes the piece by stating that"—her voice faltered—"that the Haárin have set out purposely to win the trust and confidence of the human population of Karistos with a mind toward undermining colonial security. Acquiring control over utilities and infrastructure by supplying vital services and equipment will serve as the first step in this infiltration." She flicked at the document with her thumb and forefinger—the sharp crack filled the cabin. "That's bull."

Lescaux's chin jutted defensively. "Exterior takes these opinions very seriously."

"The reason the Haárin want to provide us with vital services and equipment is because there's money to be made." Jani thought back to some of the Haárin she had known. "They like money. They like the reputation they've garnered for sound business practices. Those things give them a freedom they don't have within the Shèrá worldskein—they're not going to do anything to screw that up."

Lescaux cleared his throat. "Exterior believes the Elyan Haárin were specifically ordered by the Oligarch to infiltrate Karistos. Exterior believes Karistos is a preliminary step in Morden nìRau Cèel's plan to weaken Commonwealth defenses from the outside in."

"By Exterior, you mean Anais Ulanova." Jani waited for Lescaux's nod. "Anais is prejudiced where the Haárin are concerned. She believes them responsible for the death of her good friend during the idomeni civil war. She also derives a substantial portion of her fortune from her ownership of companies with which the Haárin are competing. It's in her interest to stop their expansion."

Lescaux licked his lips and tried again. "Her sole interest is in protecting the Elyan citizens."

"Her sole interest is in maintaining an income stream," Jani countered. "Family companies have worked for years to stifle competition in the colonies. That water treatment plant was built to fail so that someone could rake in exorbitant repair fees. And if fond recollection serves, any deals that the Karistos city government tried to work with unaffiliated colonial businesses were countered with veiled threats of sabotage and sudden unavailability of vital parts. The Elyan Haárin were their last resort." She glanced at Derringer, who still looked out the window. His silence was uncharacteristic. He should have questioned her loyalty to the Commonwealth at least once by now.

"Anais's prejudice, as you call it, against the Haárin isn't unfounded," Lescaux said. "She showed me evidence linking them to the death of Talitha Ebben. That was her friend's name."

I know all about General Ebben. A sergeant named Niall Pierce killed her and two other officers during the human evac from Rauta Shèràa, and a colonel named Hiroshi Mako covered it up. Those are the bodies Mako needs to keep buried. Any investigation into Knevçet Shèràa would have uncovered them—that's why Mako arranged to medical me out of the Service rather than risk an open trial. Niall talks to me about Ebben . . . a lot. That's our shared experience, that we both killed officers. Only I paid my own bill, but Borgie paid Niall's and the guilt eats him alive, so let's not talk about Ebben, all right? "Let's get back to this precis," Jani said. "I assume it was written by an Exterior agent working in Karistos?"

"Well, we're here." Derringer rubbed his hands together as the skimmer docked in a secluded chargelot. "I can't bear to keep you in suspense, Kilian, so let me cut your legs out from under you while you're still sitting down. Your old teacher wrote that precis. His Excellency Egri nìRau Tsecha, the ambassador of the Shèrá worldskein. Only you still call him Nema because you two are such good friends." He shot her a cruel grin. "Now, shall we go to lunch?"

Derringer's restaurant of choice was located at the end of a tree-lined shopping street. He chose a table in the outdoor dining area; as soon as they sat down, waitstaff appeared, watered, appetizered, and vanished.

"You're awfully quiet, Jani." Derringer's voice, muffled by poppy seed bread and stuffed egg, sounded smug.

"Just massing my artillery." Jani picked through the assorted baskets and plates as John's ever-growing list of forbidden foods looped through her mind, searching for something to quell her roiling gut. She settled for a piece of flatbread; the taste lived up to the name. "If you're looking for an initial volley, I think you're both full of shit."

Derringer responded with a cocked eyebrow and a nod in Lescaux's direction. "Careful. You'll shock young Peter."

Jani looked at Young Peter, who stared fixedly at his water glass. "Do you have any idea the magnitude of the accusation you're leveling?" Lescaux's eyes, awash in full defensive smolder, came up to meet hers, but before he could answer, Derringer intercepted the conversational pass.

"It makes sense. Tsecha's the most pro-human idomeni alive. He thinks you're his heir, that we're all destined to become human-idomeni hybrids, and that our futures are as one." He broke bread, scattered crumbs. "Oligarch Cèel has had Tsecha's delusions up to *here* and has started blocking him at every turn. Tsecha's old and getting older, afraid he'll die before his dream is realized. That fear has made him desperate enough to give us a leg up."

The anger in Lescaux's eyes transmuted to shocked realization. "That's right! Anais told me that Tsecha started grooming you at the Academy. He thinks you're to succeed him as the next chief propitiator of the Vynshàrau!"

The silence that fell held a tense, after-the-thunderclap quality. Jani studied the diners at the other tables, the flagstones at her feet, the flowering shrubs surrounding the patio. Anything to avoid the two faces that regarded her, one with distaste, the other with rapt curiosity.

Waitstaff arrived to refill and take orders. That broke the tension somewhat, even though Lescaux looked uncomfortable when Jani declined to order any food. Derringer, however, let it pass. He knew about her dietary difficulties. Their relationship being what it was, he had taken special care to bring her to a restaurant that specialized in the dairy-drenched food she could no longer stomach.

While Derringer and Lescaux devoured the creamy, cheese-laced appetizers, Jani scanned what she had already christened The Nema Letter. She placed her palm-sized scanpack over the upper left-hand corner of the document and began the slow back and forth initial analysis. She had only gone a few centimeters when her 'pack display flared red and the unit squealed so loudly that a woman sitting at the next table dropped her spoon in her soup.

"That's what made Exterior Doc Control suspicious about the document's origins." Lescaux's face reddened as the soup-spattered woman graced them with a highbred scowl. "That letter was subjected to five full-bore scans and each time, seventeen separate incompatibilities registered."

Jani lowered the volume on her 'pack output and re-scanned the same spot; this time, the device emitted a barely detectable chirp. She read the error coordinates on the display, and frowned. "Did all the inconsistencies show up in the same places each time?"

"Yes." Lescaux fell silent as the waiter arrived with their main courses.

"Do you have a copy of your chief dexxie's report delineating the locations and types of errors?"

"Y-yes." Lescaux fidgeted as the waiter hovered.

"Better give it to her now, boyo. She's going to keep asking questions until you do." Derringer tore his attention away from his sauce-drenched steak just long enough to shoot Jani a self-satisfied smirk.

"Just doing my job, Eugene."

"I know, Jani. And nothing kicks your overofficious ass into high gear like a professional anxiety attack." He hacked the meat with a heavy hand, bloody juice spilling across his plate. "That's the initiator chip that's set your 'pack to bleating. All it does is tell your scanpack that it's about to scan a document. It's basic, a throwaway, a nonissue, and your 'pack can't read it." He shrugged off Jani's unspoken question. "I've been taking a crash course in chip placement, courtesy of your good friend, Frances Hals. It's been a pretty goddamn interesting last couple of days."

Lescaux removed a slim packet of files from his briefbag and handed it to Jani. "Here's our doc chief's report, along with her affidavit that she stands by her conclusions. She's worked for Exterior since her graduation from Chicago Combined. She has extensive colonial experience and she acted very carefully once she realized what she had." His chin came up again. "Yes, I guess you could say we all understand the accusation we're leveling."

Jani unbound the packet and riffled through the documents until she found the chief's report. *So, Roni McGaw, you think you know from idomeni paper.* She read the first few lines. "McGaw's basing her conclusion that this document is of idomeni origin on the fact that she and her staff can't read a few chips." She read further. "There's no discussion here of prescan testing of any of the 'packs, no record of paper analysis stating whether it's of human or idomeni origin, no mention of the conditions under which the documents were stored and transported or whether they were stressed by temperature or humidity extremes—"

"You're grasping at straws, Kilian," Derringer snapped.

"You realize that this level of subterfuge is alien to the idomeni mind-set?" Jani directed her attention at Lescaux, knowing Derringer a lost cause. "They despise lies and secrecy more than the crimes they're meant to cover up. That's why they accept me despite the fact that I was the first human to ever kill any of them in one of their wars, because no one ever tried to hide the fact that I had done it. That's why they refuse to acknowledge Gisela Detmers-Neumann and the other descendants of the instigators of Knevçet Shèràa, because they've denied to this day that Rikart Neumann and his co-conspirators did anything wrong."

"Human experimentation." Lescaux looked down at his own rare steak, and nudged the plate aside.

"Rikart and crew couldn't have arranged any experimentation without Laumrau participation." Derringer took a sip from his water glass and grimaced as though he longed for wine. "Seems to me they took to secrecy and subterfuge rather well."

"And they paid for it during the Night of the Blade. What was the last estimate you heard of the number of Laumrau who were executed that night? Twenty-five thousand? Fifty thousand? An entire sect, wiped out within hours." Jani pushed her chair away from the table and the stench of charred meat, the sight of blood, the memories of that final terrifying dash through the city. "That's how the born-sect idomeni punish secrecy and lies among their own. Does this give you some idea of how they would punish Nema if they discovered he had perpetrated such a deception, and do you believe for even a fraction of a second that Nema doesn't realize that?"

Derringer pointed his steak knife at her. "Spies have always risked death. It's part of the job description."

"You're basing your conclusions on human behavior. You've made that mistake before and damn it, you just won't learn!" Jani returned the chief's report to its slipcase. "The Elyan Haárin are outcast of Sìah and hard-headed as they come. They never had a great deal of patience with either Nema's plan for the universe or Cèel's distrust of us. They do, however, possess a deep and abiding respect for a signed contract. Karistos needs Haárin technology, and the Family-affiliated businesses are worried enough to try to upset the deal by defaming Nema. It all boils down to money, gentlemen, and it's going to take a hell of a lot more than one jazzed precis to convince me otherwise."

"Jazzed?" Lescaux's face flushed. "You mean *faked,* don't you? If you're saying that Her Excellency—"

Jani held up her hands in mock surrender. "I'm not saying who, Peter. I'm just saying what." She picked up The Nema Letter. "This arrived, I assume, with the rest of the contract documents in the regular diplomatic pouch from Karistos?"

Derringer bit down on a breadstick—it crunched like brittle bone. *"Yes."*

"Did any of the other docs in the pouch show the same faults? McGaw's report doesn't mention supplementary testing."

Lescaux hesitated just an instant too long. "No."

Jani nodded as though she believed him. *You didn't check. You found one anomaly and ran barking to Derringer, who got so jacked about the prospect of placing a mole in the idomeni embassy that he didn't run any confirmation either.* "To prove definitively that this document is what you claim, you'd need an idomeni to scan it with their scanpack and prove the chips aren't simply damaged or faulty."

Derringer shook his head. "We don't want any of them to even know this exists. Couldn't you just load an idomeni chip in your unit?"

It was Jani's turn to respond in the negative. "Chips are designed to operate in unison with the thought processes of the brain matter that drives the 'pack. Idomeni brains and human brains function differently in several key areas. An idomeni chip wouldn't work in a human scanpack."

"Not even yours?" Derringer didn't quite manage to keep the slyness out of his voice.

This time, Jani counted all the way to ten. "The brain between my ears may change over time. The brain in *this*"— she held her 'pack up to his face—"is a self-contained unit—it won't change unless I do a refarm-rebuild."

"I suppose I could have our labs analyze the chips."

Lescaux's voice sounded tight—the accusation that he peddled a fake document still rankled.

Jani waved him off. "This is a diplomatic-grade document. Therefore, if you attempt to remove the chips from the paper or try to analyze them with anything other than a scanpack, they will self-destruct. The only way you will ever know for sure if an idomeni assembled this document would be to get one of the embassy examiners to scan it."

"I thought you could just ask he who wrote it." Derringer plucked another breadstick out of the basket and snapped it in two. "During our embassy visit today, just before you ask him whether there are any other useful tidbits of information he thinks we should know."

Jani looked at Lescaux, who looked away. "What?"

"You heard me." Derringer pressed the two breadstick halves together lengthwise, and broke them again.

The noise around Jani faded. The babble of conversations. The clatter of plates and cutlery. The rustle of the breeze through the trees. "You want me to spy—"

"*No.* Tsecha's doing the spying. You just need to ferry the information from him to us. He wants to help us. We only have to provide him the opportunity." Derringer grinned. "You were the first person I thought of when this fortuity presented itself."

Lescaux tossed his napkin on his plate and rose from the table. "I need to clean my teeth." He held out his hand to Jani. "The precis, please." A look passed between them—on his part, it held fear, and dislike, but also a shade of uncertainty. "You can keep McGaw's report overnight, but I need it back tomorrow first thing." Jani handed him the letter—he slid it back into its slipcase and tucked it into his bag. "I'll meet you both back at the skimmer." His shoes clicked on the flagstones. He looked like a well-dressed prep schooler on his way to address student-teacher assembly.

Derringer watched him. "Think it's true what they say about him and his boss? He only did time in a couple of dinky colonial posts before he nailed the Chief of Staff job—I mean, he must have nailed her first, right?" He glanced at Jani. "Cheer up, Kilian. Tsecha bubbles like a fountain around you—once you get him started, you won't be able to shut him up."

"Don't you remember what I said would happen if Cèel suspected him of this level of duplicity?"

Derringer shrugged. "We disavow immediately. Standard cut and run."

"No, not what happens to your operation. What happens to *him!"*

"I could not care less."

"You bastard."

Derringer leaned toward her. "No. Not a bastard. A human being. Which is what you still are too, at least officially. I'm just offering you a chance to prove it." He pointed his fork at McGaw's report. "You take that home to your posh flat on posh Armour Place, and you study it as much as you want. Then you take a good, hard look at your posh walls and your rapidly growing credit account and your flash lieutenant boyfriend, and then you do what you are told."

Jani took a deep breath. She felt agitated enough for her augmentation to weigh in, and an aborted augie overdrive was the last thing she needed right now. "You are threatening a Registered documents examiner. You are trying to intimidate said examiner into making grave and important—I quote these words from the Registry Code of Ethics—*grave* and *important* decisions based on the conclusions drawn from a document that she does not trust. That's a Commonwealth felony, Eugene. I may lose my posh flat when all this settles, but you'll lose a lot more."

"You're crazy, Kilian. It's public record. No one will believe you."

"If that's the case, why would anyone believe anything I say I heard from Nema? That little blade cuts both ways."

"That little blade is supposed to get lifted from your slender throat by year's end. Employee assessments are going to have some bearing on whether that in fact occurs." Derringer sat back and hooked his thumbs in his trouser pockets, like a gambler who knew he held the winning card. "Do not cross me on this. Burkett's not exactly wild about you—if I push a recommendation that they yank your 'pack, he'll listen." He glanced at his timepiece and looked around. "Do it. You have no choice."

"Eugene, the last time someone thought they'd left me without a choice, I wrote a chapter in idomeni mythology."

"You wrote a few other chapters, didn't you? I read that white paper, Kilian—my, my, what a bad girl you were. Combine that with your present emotional state, I see someone who can't afford to say no." Derringer stood, removed his garrison cap from his belt, and set it on his head. "I'm willing to let you start slow. Grab a few minutes with Tsecha during a break in today's meeting, feel him out. He loves to talk to you—you're his pet. It shouldn't take much effort to get this rolling." He started walking in the direction Lescaux had gone. "Now let's go. We're keeping Young Peter waiting."

Jani watched Derringer stride away. In her ear, she heard her augmentation whisper about pressure points and methods of dismemberment and the best ways to dispose of body parts, but augie tended toward the direct approach when it sensed she was in danger and that wasn't what was needed right now. She wasn't sure what was, but she'd think of something. For Nema's sake, she had to.

CHAPTER 5

"And with this bite of ground, of soil, I—" Tsecha fell silent and stared at the slice of *faria* impaled on the end of his fork. *"Bite of ground . . ."*

The piece of purple-skinned tuber offered him no clue as to the words he needed to say to complete the prayer. No prompting scrolled across its glistening white surface, as it did across the broadcasters' eyepieces at the holoVee studio he had visited earlier that humanish week. Instead, it stared in death glaze, as white and blank as a humanish eye, leaving him to suffer the humiliation of a chief priest who had forgotten how to petition his gods.

"I have prayed such for years," Tsecha murmured in English. He often talked to himself in English. He found the language's hard sounds complemented his mood. "I prayed such only yesterday." But yesterday seemed an age ago.

"Now yesterday is today and all is hell." He shoved the slice of *faria* into his mouth and chewed without the benefit of prayer. The bitterness of the vegetable stung his throat—he coughed into his sleeve so his cook-priest wouldn't hear. He knew she waited near the outer door of his private altar-room, pacing the hall like a nervous beast as she prayed for his soul. She esteemed him—he knew that. She possessed the proper skein and standing. He sensed she might ask him to breed her, and if she did so, he could not refuse.

Then she would leave me to make her birth-house, and I would need to find a new cook-priest. One who didn't worry so much. Yes, that would be most pleasant. It weighed upon Tsecha, the way others worried after his soul.

He removed his handheld from his overrobe's inner pocket and entered the English word "weight." The aged device took some time to search and collate. It had been built for him many seasons before, prior even to the War of Vynshàrau Ascension, when humanish had first begun to visit his Shèrá homeworld. It contained his favorite humanish languages: French, English, and Mandarin, along with the many odd terms and definitions he had compiled during the glorious Academy days more than twenty humanish years before, when Jani Kilian and Hansen Wyle taught him so much.

Such days. He studied his handheld's scratched display. *Weight.* He shook the device gently as words appeared, then faded. *Ballast. Tonnage. Anchor. . . .*

Anchor. Yes, that was the word. The fears of others weighted him as an anchor. They immobilized him, kept him motionless, static, changeless, at a time when change meant life and stasis meant something quite different.

Tsecha sipped his water, warmed and sweetened with *veir* blossom. It soothed his throat, and quelled the burning on his tongue.

"Pain focuses the mind." He spoke softly, so his cook-priest would not hear his ungodly English. "With the pain I have experienced this day, mine should be the most focused mind in the universe." First, he awoke to the ache of age in his knees and back. Then he recalled his upcoming meeting, which like most such gatherings promised hellish depths of boredom and confusion. They were to discuss the Karistos contract today—such a ridiculous thing, and truly. Haárin and colonial humanish had entered into such agreements since before the last war, so many that one lost count. Why Anais and her allies objected so to this particular agreement, he could not understand.

He set down his cup, and picked with ungodly indifference at his food.

"They are assembling, nìRau."

Tsecha looked up from his reading. Sàñalàn, his suborn, stood in the doorway of his front room. She had already donned her own formal overrobe, and carried his draped over her arm. "Is it time already?" He folded the Council reports with heavy hands and inserted them back into their sheaths.

"The Exterior Minister arrived most early." Sànalàn lapsed into the curt cadences and minimal gestures of Low Vynshàrau as she fussed with the overrobe's folds. "She asked one of the Haárin to show her the allowed areas of the embassy, and he did."

Tsecha rose slowly from his favored chair. The frame had stabbed him in all the usual places, but even that discomfort had failed to sharpen his mind. "It is allowed that our Anais tour the allowed areas of the embassy, nìa." He let Sànalàn help him don his robe, since such was her temper that he did not think it wise to reject her assistance. "That is what the word means."

"It is unseemly." Sànalàn prodded and yanked as though she dressed a squirming youngish and not her aged dominant. "You must reprimand him. He should have directed her to me or to nìaRauta Inèa instead of taking charge of her himself."

"I must take care how I admonish any embassy Haárin, and truly." Tsecha adjusted his twisted, red-trimmed sleeves as unobtrusively as he could. "They maintain our utilities. Our air and our water, our fire and our foundation. I berate this one you speak of too strongly, and we may all freeze in our beds."

"Not this one. He is the tilemaster."

"Ah. You have complained of him before."

"And still you have done nothing."

Tsecha offered a hand wave of acquiescence. "I will speak to him. I will threaten him with the anger of the gods." He waited for Sànalàn to precede him to the door, then fell in behind her. "What is his name?"

"Dathim Naré." Sànalàn gestured abruptly. "He is unseemly."

"So you said, nìa. So you said." Tsecha tried to recall the last time he had witnessed such agitation in his suborn as he continued to wrestle with his sleeves. "Jani is here?"

"Your Kièrshia has just now arrived, along with Colonel Derringer and Lescaux, Ulanova's suborn."

"The one who looks as my Lucien? He did not arrive with Anaìs?"

"No, nìRau. With Derringer and Kièrshia, as I said."

"Ah." Tsecha slackened off his pace so that he fell a stride farther behind the aggravated Sànalàn.

He entered the windowless meeting room to find it as Sànalàn described. Humanish filled one side of the banked spectator seats, Vynshàrau the other, the murmurs of conversation stilling as all faces turned to him.

How different we look. The contrasts struck him particularly in these meetings. The humanish appeared stunted, truncated in every way. So short they were—even the tallest only reached Tsecha's nose, while the shortest . . . well, one had to watch where one stepped. Males and females both wore their hair in clipped styles that showed their ears and the shapes of their heads, and dressed in fitted clothing in dark, forest colors of leaf and wood and pool. Even his Jani, who sat in one of the banked rows of seats behind the tan-garbed Colonel Derringer, wore a green as dark as the depths of a well.

Against the multihued gloom of their clothing, their skins shone every color from worm-white to wood-brown, their pale-trimmed eyes glittering with feverish death glaze. Not an aesthetically pleasing people, humanish—Tsecha could admit this despite his affection for them. As ever, they seemed to war with their surroundings, rather than blend with them.

So different are my Vynshàrau. Gold-skinned and gold-eyed, garbed in flowing robes of sand and stone that complemented the muted hues of the walls and floor, long of limb and fluid of line and motion. Like him, most wore their hair in the braided fringe of the breeder; the few unbred, like his Sànalàn, wore theirs in tight napeknots. All wore shoulder-grazing hoops or helices in their ears. *We are the Gold People of the High Sands. A dène vynshàne Rauta Shèràa.* He never felt the surety of this more than in the contrast with humanish. Never more than now, the differences daunted him. So vast. So overwhelming.

He took his seat at the point of the arrowhead-shaped table, in a chair so low that his knees complained as he low-

ered into it. On one side of the arrowhead sat the secular
dominants who acted in Cèel's stead, Suborn Oligarch Shai
and next to her, Speaker to Colonies Daès, their chairs
pitched slightly higher than Tsecha's in deference to his status as their religious dominant. Tsecha stretched out one leg
beneath the table as surreptitiously as he could, and wished
that they had deferred to the status of his old joints instead.

He looked to his Jani again. She looked back, her eyes
half-closed as though her head pained her, her face as a wall.
He nodded, and she responded with a flick and waver of the
fingers of her left hand, a Low Vynshàrau gesture of agitation and the need for explanation. Then Derringer turned
around to speak to her, and she let her hand drop.

Derringer. Tsecha watched the man point his finger in
Jani's face, his expression stern. He scolded her constantly,
for reasons Tsecha could never comprehend and Jani refused to discuss. *But only when his dominant is absent.*
When General Callum Burkett attended meetings, he and
Jani talked as Derringer sat most quietly. Which was not to
say that Burkett never scolded Jani, or that Jani never
scolded him in return. In the end, Burkett listened. Derringer
never did.

I have used up all my dried pokegrass, Eugene. But the
Haárin who managed the ornamental gardens did grow leafbarb to discourage the feral animals that evaded embassy security barriers. A wondrous plant, leafbarb, and truly. Not
only did the blade-sharp yellow leaves poke through clothing admirably, but their clear juice contained a chemical that
caused humanish skin to erupt in a seeping rash. . . .

"Minister Ulanova." Suborn Oligarch Shai gestured toward the chair at her side. "Join us at table, so we may begin."

A miniature figure rose from her front row seat beside
Lescaux and walked to the table. Her hair and clothes were
as wood-brown, her face as sharpened stone, her steps as
minced as a youngish. "My gratitude is yours, and truly, nìa-
Rauta," Anais Ulanova replied in stilted High Vynshàrau as
she mounted the chair across from Shai. Her knuckles
whitened as she clenched the rim of the seat to keep her balance, her tiny feet dangling half an arm's length above the
floor.

Tsecha glanced at Jani, who bit her lip and looked away.

"In deference to Vynshàrau directness and openness, I will simply begin." Anais had returned to English, which sounded as forced as her Vynshàrau. Many of the assembled attached translator headpieces as she spoke, while others paged through their copies of the official Exterior report that had been provided them. "I wish to state for the record how much the Commonwealth esteems the Oligarch's candor in dealing with this unfortunate chain of events. I would also like to state that this idomeni custom of facing difficult matters in such a straightforward manner is one that humanish also esteem and appreciate, and one that we will seek to maintain as our diplomatic relations strengthen."

How glorious, Anais! Tsecha had to clench his hands to keep from erupting into humanish applause. *Somewhere in that speech was a point, I believe, although it would take a crew of deep-pit miners many seasons to uncover it.*

Anais continued. "The situation I speak of is, of course, this regrettable circumstance in Karistos, which is the capital of Elyas, one of our Outer Circle colonies. It is indeed unfortunate that Karistos city officials failed to explore all avenues of recourse available within the Commonwealth before taking it upon themselves to set precedent."

Out of the corner of his eye, Tsecha watched Shai tap her headpiece and gesture to Daès, who curved his right hand in supplication. "You should clarify your thoughts for we the direct and open, nìaRauta." Daès glanced at Anais's report on the table in front of him, which even now the Vynshàrau xenolinguists studied for the hidden meaning that existed in all humanish documents, the words between the lines. "You are angered that the Karistos dominants acted without consulting you. Except that they have consulted with you for many months, and pleaded for assistance in solving their water problems. Elyan humanish died, yet you told them to wait. Elyan humanish died, yet you told them to draw up plans and obtain estimates."

Anais raised a hand, palm facing up. A subtle variation of a plea, Tsecha had learned, a request for the speaker to rethink their words. Not her usual reaction to Daès's questions—she usually fluttered her hands and turned most red.

"A great tragedy, which occurred because the water treatment facility in question was built too hastily, from a design that had not been adequately thought out. We must take the time to think now, nìRau. We are most concerned that to act in haste again could result in even greater tragedy."

Tsecha closed the report before him with one finger, then pushed it away with such force that it slid to the middle of the table. "You are most concerned, you say. Most concerned. Yet when the Elyan Haárin offer a way to stop the dying *now,* you protest. Because your colonial business interests lose money, you assemble reports with graphs and charts and financial analyses, reports that could not be assembled when it was only your *people* whom you lost."

Anais's face reddened in a most gratifying manner as in the banked rows, whispered conversation rose. "Are you accusing me of allowing my people to die in the interest of financial gain, nìRau?"

Tsecha folded his hands before him. "Is there any question—"

"Tsecha."

The droning humanish conversation silenced. Jani sat up most straight, her gaze fixed on Suborn Oligarch Shai, whose shoulders had rounded in anger.

Shai gestured to her suborn, who reached to the table's center and removed Tsecha's copy of the report. "Allow nìaRauta Ulanova to finish," she said as she opened her own copy.

Tsecha barely restrained his laughter as he watched Shai study a triaxial graph as though she understood what it meant. "Shai—"

"Allow nìaRauta Ulanova to finish." Shai spoke to him without any clarifying gesture, which was most unlike her. "We are all most aware of your thought in this."

Anais inclined her head toward Shai. "Many thanks, nìaRauta." She bent her head over her own report, and read words that all in the room realized she knew, as humanish said, by heart.

As Anais yammered about cost estimates and medical ramifications, Tsecha caught a flash of palest platinum hair move into his periphery. His Lucien raised his hand in a subtle greeting as he stepped among the seated crowd. Unlike his fellow humanish, he did not seem stunted at all. His smooth movement and quiet arrogance reminded Tsecha of the cats he sometimes saw stalking across the embassy grounds, their contempt for the gardeners' leafbarb evident in their every motion.

"When it became clear—" Anais's voice faltered as she caught sight of Lucien. Her pale skin once more colored. "When it became clear," she repeated, her tone sharpening so that humanish eyes widened, "that the drafters of the contract failed to properly consider the many issues involved in this situation, we in Exterior felt it our duty to step in and take charge of the proceedings. We took this step despite the risk of angering the Elyan Haárin, who set great store in signed agreements, as do we all. We now formally request that the Shèrá worldskein accept our humblest apologies for this misunderstanding, as well as financial reparations well in excess of those lost by the Elyan Haárin in the cancellation of this contract."

As Anais ended her speech with wishes of good fortune for all, Lucien positioned himself against the wall directly opposite her. Their gazes locked. Her voice faltered once more.

Tsecha looked at Jani, whose face appeared as the wall against which Lucien rested. Then he looked at Lescaux, the youngish that seemed so poor a replacement for such a startling animal, and pondered the flush he saw on his face. Was it anger? Jealousy? Both? He could not tell.

Tsecha glanced around the room at the uncomfortable humanish, the confused Vynshàrau, and inhaled deeply of the suddenly charged air. Such a marvel, his Lucien, like a humanish shatterbox.

"The Elyan Haárin are indeed most dismayed at this action by the Exterior Ministry." Speaker to Colonies Daès entoned in High Vynshàrau, oblivious to the emotional maelstrom that surrounded him. "The assemblage had committed to a shuttle purchase on the strength of the contract affirmation. This pledge now needs to be cancelled, as well as the pledges made by the shuttle dealer for her own purchases. Broken agreement after broken agreement will proceed from this, a simple contract no different from many that colonial humanish and Haárin have entered into over many seasons."

Anais waited until the full translation of Daès's speech filtered through her headpiece. Then she bared her teeth—the expression barely widened her narrow face. "As I have stated, nìRau Daès, we are prepared to make generous reparations to all concerned—"

Tsecha flicked his left hand in curt dismissal. "Reparations." He knew his English to be most sound and easily understood, thus he ignored Derringer's aggravated tapping on his headpiece as though the translators erred. "Do you believe, Anais, and truly, that *reparations* are sufficient—"

"Tsecha!" Shai brought the flat of her hand down on the table. "Allow nìaRauta Ulanova to finish or leave until she does so!"

Humanish spoke of "shattered silence," as though an absence of sound could be as a solid thing, tangible and breakable. Tsecha often had trouble comprehending these strange meanings, but sometimes they revealed themselves to him with almost godly insight. *Shattered silence.* Yes, the quiet that filled the room now felt as corporeal, as stone and metal, waiting only to be smashed by more of Shai's words, by her strange behavior. *She silenced me?* Even though Tsecha knew this to indeed be the case, he felt difficulty accepting it. *She silenced me.*

How the humanish stared at Shai, even Anais. Only Derringer and Jani looked at Tsecha. Derringer glowered, his long face dark with the dislike Tsecha knew he felt, but until now had managed to hide.

But it was his Jani who alarmed him the most. Confusion, yes, in her furrowed brow and narrowed eyes, but anger, too.

Then he watched her gaze drift to Derringer, and the anger sharpen. *If looks could kill,* as his Hansen used to say. Tsecha felt the grip of wonder as the meaning of even more humanish imagery bore down on him. If his Jani's eyes had been knives, oh, the blood that would spill.

"I am finished speaking, nìaRauta." Anais once more inclined her head. "My concerns are more completely expressed within this report, copies of which were submitted to your xenolinguists ten days ago to allow them time to interpret the material contained therein."

"Ten days?" Tsecha looked out at his Jani, who stared back at him, the knives in her eyes gone dull. "I did not see—"

"I have conferred with nìRau ti nìRau Cèel on this matter." Shai addressed the assembled, seemingly oblivious to the fact that she had once more interrupted her ambassador and priest. "He agrees with nìaRauta Ulanova. There are issues of seemliness involved here. Our dietary protocols are most strict on the subjects of exchange of food and water and the possibilities of cross-contamination. The Elyan Haárin are expected to arrive here in a matter of Earth days. During their stay, they will be retrained in these protocols. They will also be awarded reparations for the broken contract." She gestured agreement to Daès, who tilted his head in the affirmative. "Cèel will be pleased that it has been handled so cleanly."

Tsecha flicked his thumb over his ear in disdain. "Cèel would be pleased if Haárin and colonial never bought any equipment from one another ever again. He would be happier still if the Elyan Haárin decamped from Elyas and returned to the worldskein. He would declaim in rapture if every Haárin enclave ceased to exist and every humanish returned to their Commonwealth. His opinion is not the most balanced on the matter, and I do not feel it can be applied here!"

Shai's back bowed in profound anger, a posture understood by even the most ignorant humanish. "Tsecha, you are Cèel's representative—"

"I am the ambassador of the Shèrá worldskein. Thus do I speak on behalf of all idomeni, not just Cèel. I am also chief propitiator. Thus do I speak the will of the gods when I say that you err gravely here."

"Tsecha." Shai pitched her voice higher than normal in respect, and directed her gaze above his head to indicate same. Her words, however, held a Haárin's intransigence. "The decision is made. The discussion is ended. The meeting is adjourned."

"With all due respect, nìaRauta ti nìaRauta?"

At the sound of the voice, Lucien started. Anais clenched her hands. Derringer scowled. The humanish rustled and the Vynshàrau stilled.

Tsecha bared his teeth as his Jani stood. She spoke English, but gestured as Vynshàrau, so that the tone of her thoughts would be clear to the Vynshàrau along with the translation of her words.

"I know of the Elyan Haárin, and have dealt with them on many occasions in the past." Like Lucien, she did not seem in any way short in height. She gestured as smoothly as any idomeni, even as the Oà, who spoke the most beautifully of any of the born sects. "They are outcast of Sìah"—she gestured toward the half-Sìah Sànalàn—"and the Sìah were the first to codify idomeni secular law and develop the documents protocols we all adhere to. They carry the highest regard for all that is written, and for all that is composed within the boundaries of law. They will most assuredly *not* understand the cancellation of this contract, and they possess ways of making their displeasure felt."

Anais waved a dismissive hand. "We are discussing a single contract—"

"I believe, Your Excellency, that if you examine various shuttle dock and infrastructure maintenance contracts signed by the Elyan colonial government in recent years, you will find you have more cause for concern as to the feelings of the Elyan Haárin than you might wish for. In addition, the immediate needs of the Karistosians must be met. The safety of their water supply is of paramount importance—"

"The contract will be put aside—"

"The cancellation needs to be examined—"

"It will be put aside," Anais snapped. "Thank you for your input, Ms. Kilian, but the matter is settled."

"Is it? How? By your words, which cannot even convince the only one here who knows the Elyan Haárin well!" Tsecha stood and pointed to Jani. "She knows the ways of the enclave and the assemblage as she knows the ways of these ridiculous meetings, and she knows that the Elyan Haárin will not understand. She is of us and of you. She is the hybrid who knows us all. She will wear my ring and robe after I die. If you have not convinced her of your argument, then it is as worthless!"

The translation filtered through. Shai resorted to banging her fist on the table to restore order so she could formally adjourn. The meeting dissolved into whispers and gesturing and huddled groups. Tsecha tried to push through the clusters to reach his Jani, but Derringer had grabbed her by the arm and herded her out the door before he could do so.

CHAPTER 6

Tsecha stalked the halls, alert for the sounds of argument that would signal the location of Jani and Derringer. He passed humanish along the way, dressed in gloomy Cabinet colors or the tan uniforms as the one Derringer wore, now sanctioned by the Service for their personnel to wear when they visited the embassy. It did not surprise him unduly that he could not recognize the postures and faces he passed—meetings frequently took place at the embassy of which he knew nothing, and for that, he offered the gods thanks.

After a time, he grew conscious of a presence at his back. He thought once more of cats, and put a name to the sensation. "Lucien. It is unseemly of you to follow me."

"I didn't want to alarm you, nìRau. You seemed so deep in thought." Lucien drew ahead of him in a few strides, even though he did not appear to quicken his pace. "You let Jani walk behind you sometimes. I've seen it."

"That is my Jani. You are not she."

"True." As usual, Lucien accepted the rebuke without a quarrel. Such behavior always caused Jani to remark that he was "conserving his ammo," whatever that meant. "You certainly know how to break up a meeting."

"If your people or mine cannot accept the truth, it is not reason for me to refrain from speaking it." Tsecha stopped before a meeting room door and listened, but the voices he thought he heard proved to be the whine of drills and the clatter of building materials that managed to seep through the soundshielding. "So much renovating. It is a wonder this embassy does not collapse from the pounding and banging. . . ." He herded Lucien ahead of him and continued down the hall.

"I saw her arrive with Derringer and Lescaux." Lucien tugged at his tan uniform shirt, spotted with the first dark dots of sweat. Many humanish still found the temperature of the embassy uncomfortable even though the Vynshàrau had lowered it earlier that summer, thus guaranteeing misery for all.

Tsecha opened another door and stared into the quiet dark. "Well, she has not left with them. I asked my Security suborn, and she told me that no one detected them leaving."

"NìRau." Lucien stopped in front of a narrow window that looked over a seldom-used veranda. "Over here."

Tsecha walked to Lucien's side. His ears heard before his eyes saw; he bared his teeth wide at the sound.

"He doesn't know anything about it—"

"—think you know every fucking thing—"

"—you've made a mistake—"

"*—when I tell you to do something, you do it!*"

"One day I will offer them the blades, and they will take them. *À lérine* they will fight, for such is the only way." Tsecha nodded to Lucien. "Such hatred must be declared openly, or it festers like a sick wound." He swept aside the portal and stepped out into the weak sunlight. "Colonel Derringer, you are needed in the meeting room. Anais Ulanova wishes to speak with you."

Derringer wheeled, his face reddened from embassy heat and undeclared anger. "Her Excellency? In the meeting room?" He looked from Tsecha to Lucien. "Is this true, Lieutenant?"

"Her Excellency wishes this matter resolved as soon as possible, sir." Lucien stood most straight and tall, his eyes focused on a point somewhere above Derringer's head.

Derringer looked back at Jani, who stood obscured in the shadow of a wall. Then he nodded brusquely to Tsecha in the humanish manner. "NìRau."

"Colonel." Tsecha stepped aside to allow the man free passage to the door. "I should challenge him for asking you if my words held truth, Lucien," he said when he heard the door seal catch. "I have never before been called a liar so openly."

"You're both going to get your heads handed to you when he figures out you sent him on a fool's errand." Jani stepped into the light. Anger stiffened her stride and made her face as painted sculpture. "But then, I don't know what other kind you'd send him on."

Lucien shrugged. "Ani will come up with something for him to do. That's what she thinks colonels are for." He took a step toward her. "We caught some of the shrapnel out in the hall."

"I caught the rest in the neck." Jani stood still as Lucien approached, but she did not bare her teeth or reach for him as some humanish females did when their males drew near.

They have an arrangement. Tsecha watched Lucien question, Jani twitch a shoulder in response. The breeding protocols of humanish confused him in the extreme, but he thought them a most seemly pairing. Except. . . .

The way they watch each other. . . . Was such the way with all humanish pairings? Tsecha did not have enough experience to know for sure. But whether or not such was indeed so, he needed to set his curiosity aside for now. "Nìa, we must speak."

"Yes, I think that we had better." Jani stepped away from Lucien without gesturing or speaking farewell, walking past Tsecha and through the door into the hall.

"She is very angry," Tsecha said, because he felt one of them should acknowledge what had happened and he knew from experience that neither Jani nor Lucien would. He raised his hand in salutation to Lucien, who regarded him in his particularly empty way that made even Jani seem expressive.

They walked the embassy grounds, as they often did. They both dreaded the coming cold, and savored the last warm rays of the sun.

Jani did not speak until they had walked one complete circuit around a Pathen-style water garden. She stopped before one of the stone arrangements, an upright hollow-center circlet through which one diversion of the stream flowed. "You think the Karistos contract is a good thing?"

Tsecha raised his right hand palm facing up, his equivalent of a humanish shrug. "Of course, nìa. Any such interaction between idomeni and humanish is greatly to be wished."

"You don't . . . consider it a threat to your dietary laws, or to anyone or anything here on Earth?"

"Nìa?" Tsecha bent nearer to study Jani's face, to no avail. He would have learned more from studying the stone circlet. "You have a reason for these strange questions?"

"Just confirming the blindingly obvious, nìRau." She twisted first to the left, then to the right—the bones of her spine made a crunching noise. "Shai interrupted you several times. That's not good."

"I have always angered her, nìa."

"You're her priest. You outrank her. She should let you finish speaking, then take your head off." Jani bent over and swept her fingers through the water. "She and Ulanova discussed this contract days ago. Shai shut you out of the final decision."

Tsecha watched her spray droplets at some insects that had clustered at the rim of the pool, sending them flying. He brushed away one of the fleeing creatures, which buzzed and hovered near his head. "She cannot do so, nìa—I am ambassador."

"NìRau, she just did." Jani straightened and dried her fingers on the hem of her jacket. "When is she returning to Shèrá? She came here months ago, right after Cèel packed up and pulled out. The Suborn Oligarch's role is to act as Council dominant, lead conclaves, monitor voting and debate. She can't do that from here."

"She . . . likes Chicago, nìa." Tsecha felt as though he stood under the questioning attitude of the Council tribunal, as he had so often in the past. But he had always been able to conjure answers for the tribunal, when the wrong ones would have meant his life. Why did he feel so confused now, when all he risked was a sharp rebuke?

Jani turned and looked at him, her green eyes shining as the water. "She isn't going back, is she? Cèel sent her here to replace you as ambassador." She bent and splashed water at the insects again, this time more vigorously. A few managed to fly away, but two failed to take to the air in time. They lay swamped in the puddle, their legs waving feebly.

Tsecha watched one of the black and yellow creatures shudder, then lay still. "You are killing them, nìa."

Jani threw more water, washing the stunned insect into the rivulet. "They're wasps, nìRau. I don't know anymore how I'd react if one stung me. I'd rather not chance finding out."

"If you left them alone, perhaps they would not bother you."

"If I get rid of them now, I don't have to worry about 'perhaps.' " Jani frowned as more wasps alit on the edge of the puddle. She backed away from the water garden and onto the lawn, working her shoulders as she walked. "Humanish diplomats attend classes on Vynshàrau behavior. We know that Vynshàrau study humanish, as well. Everyone knows you and Cèel don't get along. We humanish interpret that as disunity in the ranks, a sign of weakness. In cases like that, the leadership needs to act decisively to close the perceived schism, or they are seen as weaker still." She stretched out her arms toward the sun and swept them in wide circles. Then she let them fall to her sides, and tilted her head from side to side. "You do not work with Shai to present a united front. Every time you open your mouth in one of these meetings, you outrage everyone. You tell humanish and Vynshàrau that I'm your heir when you know that my condition scares them and that the idea of hybridization terrifies them." She turned to him, her posture as tense and troubled as it had been during the war, when she had worried for his life. "Every day, in every way, you make it more difficult for Cèel to allow you to remain here and more difficult for me to do my job."

Tsecha crossed his arms and shoved his hands into the sleeves of his overrobe. "And what is your job, nìa?"

"To keep you from wrapping yourself around a tree." Jani swatted at another insect that buzzed past her head. "To keep the wasps away."

"To keep the wasps away." Tsecha pronounced each word most distinctly. "You are my protector, in the way a suborn sometimes is?" He watched Jani's motions still, and knew they shared the same thought. He slipped close to her, grasping her right hand in his before she could move away. "Then

where is your ring, nìa? My suborn should wear my ring."
He straightened her fingers, so long and thin and brown,
then held out his beside them. His ring of station glittered,
cagework gold surrounding an oval of crimson jasperite. "It
looks much as this one, I believe. You have not lost it, have
you?"

Jani refused to look him in the eye, as she always did
when he inquired about her ring. "No." She pulled her hand
away, slowly but firmly. "It's in a bag, on the shelf of my
closet."

"In a bag. On a shelf in your closet. Perhaps I should ask
you to keep your concern there, as well."

"NìRau—!"

"Our Hansen died wearing his."

"His ring fit him out of the box. You didn't have his ring
made too small so he'd have to shrink into it. The fact that he
wore his didn't signify that he had become point man for a
new race!"

"Point man . . . out of the box . . ." Tsecha patted his
pockets and wished for his handheld. "You confuse me with
your words as no other."

Jani strode away from him, flexing her arms as a youngish
bird. "If you're so easily confused, maybe you shouldn't talk
so much."

"I did not risk my life and soul to come to this damned
cold place so that I could remain silent!" Tsecha rounded his
shoulders in irritation. Jani's constant twisting made his own
muscles ache. He closed in on her, his back hunched in
anger. "All I hear from you is censure! Lecture as to how I
should act. Why? There are no wasps. They cannot threaten
to kill me anymore."

Jani slouched in response, so quickly and smoothly that
Tsecha straightened in surprise. "Don't be so sure." She
slipped into Low Vynshàrau, her muted gestures hard and
swift. "If I told you it was as Rauta Shèràa, I would not be
far from wrong."

Tsecha looked up at the sky, its clear blue broken only by
the swoop of seabirds. "As Rauta Shèràa, is it? Then where
are the demiskimmers, nìa? Where are the bombs?"

"Explosives aren't the only things that can blow up in

your face." Jani must have sensed his abating temper, since she drew up straighter as well. "Will you behave until I tell you it is safe?"

Tsecha twitched his shoulder as he had seen her do so many times, when she wanted to seem to answer without actually telling him anything. He had gotten quite good at it, in his opinion. "No more disputation with Anais?"

Jani smiled. "On the veranda, or in your rooms, fine. But not during public meetings."

"No more musical gatherings with Colonel Derringer?"

"Good God, no."

"You worry after me."

"Constantly."

They regarded one another. Tsecha sensed fondness in Jani's relaxing posture, which he always knew to be there. He sensed exasperation, as well, which he had grown to accept. He turned to walk back to the embassy, beckoning her to walk ahead of him, as was seemly. If he needed to behave, now would be a good time to start. "You are well, nìa? I notice that you seem pained."

Jani looked him in the eye. The afternoon sun struck her full-face, lightening her green irises to the color of new leaves. But the bright light overwhelmed the diffusing ability of the filming—her pale green sclera showed beneath the hydropolymer the way a dark shirt showed beneath a pale overrobe. "I'm all right. Just a little achy." Then the shadow of a tree branch played across her face, sharpening bone and darkening skin to gold-brown. She lifted and cupped her right hand in a gesture of resignation, the movements as smooth as though performed beneath water.

Tsecha watched her move as no human could, and felt the clench in his soul. *You are as Rauta Haárin now, and truly.* She had become as he always knew she would, as he always wished she would. Why then did he feel sadness? Why then did he feel fear? "Winter comes," he said, because he could think of nothing else to say.

"Yes, nìRau. I can feel it in my bones." Jani's voice sounded as dead. As she turned her back to him, a wasp swooped near her face. She reached out and caught it in her animandroid left hand, then with a single swift movement opened her hand and smashed her palm against the grid of the pestzap installed alongside the entry. The wasp shot through the grid opening and vaporized in a flash of blue. Jani brushed her hand against her jacket and disappeared into the darkness of the embassy.

They heard the commotion well before they saw the cause: the babble of voices from around the next corner, Anais Ulanova's piping above them all.

"I told you, Colonel. Isn't it lovely!"

Jani looked back over her shoulder at Tsecha, then quickened her pace. Tsecha hurried, too. He recalled only too well the rooms located down that hallway, the clatter of renovation that perpetually sounded from them. The buzz of drills. The hum of sealers.

The shatter of old tile.

"I haven't seen work of this quality since I toured the Pathen Mosaica on Nèae. Flowers so well detailed, they looked real. The shadings! The hues!"

Tsecha broke into an unseemly trot, catching up with Jani just as she rounded the corner.

The crowd stood packed around the doorway of one of the rooms undergoing refurbishing. A secondary altar room, Tsecha recalled, the same one in which he had prayed with his Jani prior to her very first *à lérine*. The embassy workers had installed a small laving area for the washing of blessed vessels and cloths, but the final decorations had yet to be applied.

Jani pushed through the crowd. Tsecha shoved after her, his eyes locking on the anger-bowed back of Suborn Oligarch Shai, who stood just inside the doorway next to Anais Ulanova.

"It would not be seemly, nìaRauta." Shai gestured stiffly, her hands clenching when they should not have, her voice catching when it should have flowed.

"But it could serve as a gesture of good faith during a tense time." Anais nodded to Lescaux, who nudged to her side. "We would be most happy to arrange some sort of exchange. One of our finest craftsman could design something suitable for your embassy." She said something to Lescaux, who shook his head. "We must admit, though, that we will be hard-pressed to compete with this." She crossed her hands over her chest, glittery-eyed rapture softening the harsh planes of her face.

Tsecha looked past her into the altar room, where an Haárin male dressed in dull blue work garments wiped the surface of the freshly tiled wall that served as the back-splash for the altar sink. He wore a leaf-patterned wrap around his head to keep the grime out of his hair. He also kept his back turned toward the crowd so none could see his face or his attitude.

Tsecha looked at the wall on which the Haárin worked. The cava shell was only half-completed—the head and the horn-like flare of the opening had yet to be tiled, and shown in lead-sketched simplicity beside the finished portion. Nature scenes were common décor in Vynshàrau rooms—at first, the shell did not appear at all remarkable.

Then Tsecha studied the work more carefully. The lower half—the sand-colored body striped with darker brown, the pink-tinged curve where the shell opening began—at first seemed painted. Upon closer examination, the shell would devolve into precisely cut triangles and curved slivers of carefully colored ceramic. But for now, graced by distance, the fragments seemed to form a glorious whole, an emerging perfection, as though the shell itself had been buried within the wall and was now being slowly uncovered. A wondrous work, assembled by an artist of godly skill.

The Haárin continued his polishing, oblivious to the commotion behind his back.

Tsecha flinched as an elbow jostled him in the side. *"Dathim Naré,"* Sànalàn hissed in his ear, her Low Vyn-shàrau roughened by anger so that it sounded harsh as Haárin dialect. "I told you of him. I told you to speak to him! Now look what he has done!"

Tsecha glanced over the heads of the crowd, and sighted his Jani on the opposite side of the gathering. She stood between Lucien and Treasury Suborn Kern Standish, her arms folded, watching the Haárin.

"I do not know what your craftspeople can bring to us,"

Shai said. She, too, watched Dathim. Her back had unbent, but her voice still held the guttural sharpness of anger.

Anais waved a small, bony hand. "Precedent exists in the colonies. I know of several instances in which humanish craftspeople worked in idomeni buildings, and your tilemaster mentioned several more when he escorted me through the public portions of the embassy."

Dathim the tilemaster, having now lost his ability to mention, tossed his polishing cloth aside and resumed insetting bits of tile.

Tsecha pushed past Derringer and Lescaux so that he stood at Anais's shoulder. "How easily you accept our Haárin's presence when they have something you want, Ana—"

"We will discuss this in private, Minister Ulanova," Shai interrupted. She backed out of the altar room, pushing the crowd behind her as if they formed one body. "In my rooms." She beckoned in a humanish manner for Anais to walk with her. Tsecha watched in befuddlement as they proceeded down the hall, humanish and Vynshàrau alike trailing after, until only he and his Lucien and his Jani remained.

"What did I tell you? They've shut you out. You need to take care, nìRau." Jani did not look at Tsecha as she spoke. Instead, she watched Dathim Naré tap and arrange.

Only once did Dathim look at her. Their eyes met for only the briefest time; he then returned to his work, taking care to position himself so that she could not watch his hands, or see over his shoulder.

CHAPTER 7

Jani trudged up the access road that ran along the idomeni embassy property. The blue-green groundcover that the Vynshàrau had imported from Shèrá gave way to terrestrial grasses and shrubs as she entered the "demilitarized zone" that served as boundary between the embassy and the Exterior Ministry. Her back ached. Her stomach growled. The L station lay a few hundred meters ahead, elevated tracks and silver bullet cars glinting in the afternoon sun.

The Exterior Minister's disruption of the afternoon's agenda had released Jani from an afternoon's diplomatic servitude and prevented another confrontation with Derringer. With luck, Anais's determination to have the Haárin tilemaster redecorate her annex would keep the colonel occupied for several days. That probably wouldn't give Jani enough time to figure out why someone tried to set up Nema as a traitor to his people, but it would let her do some initial fact-finding.

Shai's had it with him. Jani didn't believe Shai had arranged the faked precis—that would have scaled heights of Byzantine treachery beyond the reach of most humans. *But if she suspected that he had betrayed the idomeni, she would send him back to Shèrá in restraints.* And there Cèel would be waiting, eager to mete out the justice that had been denied him so many years before, and repay Nema for bringing humanish into their lives. Nema had talked his way out of execution once. He wouldn't be allowed to do so again.

Jani stepped onto the grassy berm when she heard the

hum of a skimmer approaching from behind, and turned as it slowed to a stop beside her. A deep gold sedan, lightened to gilt by the sun.

The passenger-side window lowered. "Jan!" Kern Standish called through the gap. "You need a ride?" He jerked his head toward the woman sitting beside him in the passenger seat. "I'm dropping off Dena at Commerce—I can swing by Armour no problem."

"We tried to catch you after the meeting, but Gene tackled you first." Dena Hausmann, the Commerce Finance chief, raised her hand to shield her eyes from the sun. She was a straw blonde with skin almost as pale as John Shroud's— even the weaker autumn light overwhelmed her. "He didn't look happy. Did you have a falling-out?"

"Eugene thinks I should be seen and not heard." Jani strolled up to the skimmer, mindful of the two pair of politically astute eyes watching her. *This road heads north— they'd normally use the south exit to return to the city. They tracked me on purpose.*

Kern snorted. "Ivy said she heard you two barking at one another all the way down the hall." Ivy was his Admin-slash-spy. "So what do you think about what happened?"

Jani didn't need to ask which *what* he referred to. "I think the idomeni study us as much as we study them. They've figured out that Nema contradicting everyone in public makes them appear disorganized. Shai may be trying to reel him in."

Dena squinted up at her. "Rumor has it that Shai's been sent here to replace him—think there's anything to it?"

Rumor's been getting up to no good, hasn't he? Jani hesitated. Kern and Dena were two of her supporters in the Cabinet purview—she owed them some sort of answer. "Nema will remain an influence, no matter in which capacity he serves."

"But he's the most pro-human of all the idomeni. If he loses any influence, we're in trouble." Kern waited for Jani to speak—when she didn't, the pretense of good humor fell away. His voice sharpened. "Jan, we should be working hand-in-glove with Anais on this, but whatever she knows, she refuses to share. Our Outer Circle Annex is on my back because of this Elyan thing. I've got Commonwealth–Shèrá trade and GateWay licensing agreements to examine. I've asked Anais for help, I'm not getting it, and frankly, my idomeni expertise could be inscribed on the head of a pin."

Then what the hell are you doing in this job? Jani thought of the piles of paper on her desk, and sighed. "Shoot 'em over—I'll see what I can see." She returned Kern's smile, as much as she could. "Any word on what she had to say about the white paper?"

"About what you'd expect." Dena grinned. "You're the Antichrist whose appearance signals the end of the Commonwealth, didn't you know that?" She glanced at her timepiece, and gasped. "Staff meeting in an hour—"

"Gotta run." Kern nudged the skimmer out of standby. "Jan, I owe you. I'm going to ask Jorge to kick you up to permanent retainer status."

"He won't do it."

"Bet you lunch. You'll keep us updated on Tsecha?"

"If I find out anything worth a damn, I'll let you know." Jani waved after the skimmer as it pulled away. "If I live that long." She kicked at a tuft of grass, then resumed her trudge to the L. "No. N-O. It's a very simple word—why the hell can't I learn to use it?"

She veered onto the berm again as another skimmer approached. A dark blue four-door this time, the mainstay of the Fort Sheridan vehicle pool. The driver's-side gullwing popped up, and Lucien poked his head through the opening. "Get in. Nema ordered me to drive you home." He disembarked and walked around to the passenger side. "He thinks you're not feeling well."

"I'm fine." Jani hitched her bag and bent low to enter the skimmer. "I—" She fell silent when she spotted Lescaux sitting in the backseat.

Lescaux held his briefbag up to his chest as though he expected her to grab him by the lapels and drag him out. "Lucien's giving me a lift into the city."

"How nice of Lucien." Jani glared up at the nice Lucien, who regarded her blankly as he pushed the door closed.

They rode in silence. Jani sensed Lucien's sidelong examination. He knew he'd dropped a small bomb, however unwittingly; she knew he relished the resulting tension.

As they swept up the ramp onto the Boul artery, a throat-clearing sounded from behind. "I guess we're going to have an Haárin laying tile at the annex sometime soon. That should prove a joy to organize."

"I'll be surprised if Shai allows it." Lucien spoke with the cool assurance of one who had taken a class on the subject. "If what I've seen in the colonies is any indication, that Haárin was advertising his services. He wants to do more than tile one wall in the Exterior Annex—he wants to start a business. Once Ani realizes what happened, she'll retract. She can't block the colonies doing business with Haárin, then turn around and do so herself. That would be ballsy, even for her."

"Nothing she does would surprise me anymore." Lescaux paused to ponder. "Does the shell have any significance? I saw it on a lot of Haárin walls during my colony years."

"The Vynshàrau like representations from nature," Lucien replied when he realized Jani wouldn't. "Shells, flowers, scenery. The Laum preferred symbols—geometric tracery and scrollwork. I don't think any of the born-sects go in for faces or figures, do they?" He looked at Jani and arched his brow in question.

"The Oà like portraiture," Jani mumbled.

That was all the opening Lescaux needed. "You made quite an impact at the meeting."

"Not enough," Jani replied eventually.

Lescaux grasped her words like a rope, pulling himself forward until his head poked between the front seats. "But do you really feel that a colonial government should contract with Haárin at the expense of their own people? Wouldn't it be better if we streamlined a way that the Karistosians could obtain materials and services from businesses on Elyas or elsewhere in the Outer Circle?"

"Yes, but what do they do for water while they wait for a half-dozen merchants' associations to argue whether the intercity dock tax should stand at a quarter or a third percent of sales price?" Jani exhaled with a grumble. She had sat in on those sorts of meetings over the summer, and had barely restrained the urge to throw her chair through a window. "If the Elyan Haárin have a filter system that works, Cèel should allow them to sell it to the Karistosians, and they should be allowed to install it. If a new plant comes two or three years down the road, let it come. But let's take care of *now* what needs taking care of now."

"But we have systems in place to handle these situations." Lescaux shook his head between the seats like a colt worrying in his stall. "You can't just ride roughshod over the process."

"Why not?" Jani ignored Lucien's frown. "The system is supposed to serve the people, Mr. Lescaux, not the other way around. If the system stops working, you change it. If the Karistosians can't obtain the equipment necessary to re-fit their water filtration system from their own people, they should be able to get it from the Haárin. And I'm not saying this because I'm pro-Haárin or anti-Commonwealth or a troublemaker or unrealistic. I'm saying it because the people at the sharp end of the stick come first and that's one thing that always gets lost in any trade discussion that I hear."

"But that's what I'm saying—"

"No, you're not. What you're arguing for is yet another variation of the same old song we've heard in the colonies for years. NUVA-SCAN affiliates. Sanctioned businesses. Preferred vendors. It's just one more way of forcing us to keep it in the Family. That's Family with a capital F, in case you missed it." Jani pounded her fist against the door. "Paid-for shipments that never arrived because they were diverted to somewhere with a bigger line of credit. Manufactured shortages. Buildings and skimways and equipment that were built to fall apart so that the vendors that sold them in the first place could collect premium prices for repairs and re-placements. That's what this colony kid remembers growing up. From what she hears, it's getting worse. Well, not in one little corner of the Commonwealth. Not if she can help it. Sorry."

Lescaux released the conversational line and eased back in his seat. When they drifted to a stop at an intersection near Armour Place, he muttered "Merci" to Lucien and slipped out.

Jani watched Lescaux circle in front of the vehicle and merge with the lunchtime bustle on the tree-lined sidewalk, then turned to Lucien to find him regarding her beneath his lashes. "What?"

"You *are* pro-Haárin and anti-Commonwealth. And a troublemaker." He re-merged with the midday traffic. "Not to mention flagrantly disrespectful. Estranged and unassimilated—"

"You read the white paper."

"Only a summary. I'm not high enough up the ladder to read the actual report." Lucien sighed his regrets. "But knowing you as I do, I can imagine the details. That being the case, do you really think ticking off the Exterior Minister's Chief of Staff is a good idea? Peter loves brushes with greatness—a few nice words from you and he'd sprain his arm throwing Exterior business your way." He tapped the steering wheel as the seconds passed. "So why don't you like him?"

Jani made it a point to sigh just as loudly as he had. "I never said that I didn't like him."

"I thought you were going to toss him out of the skimmer."

"I was just surprised to see him. I would have assumed you to be the one who wouldn't like him."

"Why? Because of Anais? I was well out of there before he came to take my place."

"You upset him at the meeting. He's jealous."

"Perhaps." Lucien shrugged as though he heard that every day. "But I'm a veteran of the war he's fighting. When he asks for advice, I give it. When he wants to talk, I listen."

"How understanding of you."

"I also find out some of the most interesting news that way." He turned the corner onto Armour Place. "You arrived with him and Derringer today. Change of pace for you—you always come alone."

Jani toyed with her duffel, taking care not to look Lucien in the face. "Lescaux had provided Derringer with some information about Elyas. Derringer thought I should have a look at it before the meeting."

"That was uncharacteristically nice of him." Lucien steered the skimmer into the garage—the interior darkened to night as they drifted inside. "What sort of information?"

"Trade propaganda—the kind of thing Peter talked about

here." Jani popped her gullwing as Lucien drew alongside a charge station. "He tried to lobby me. It didn't work."

"You're lying." Lucien slammed down his gullwing, then yanked the connect cable from the station and jacked it into the skimmer battery access. "I've watched Cabinet staffers lobby you all summer—you brush them off like mosquitoes. You don't get angry, and you're angry with Peter." He pulled his garrison cap out of his belt and put it on. "I called you an hour before the meeting. You didn't answer."

Jani headed for the exit ramp that led out to the street. "I'd already left." She limped up the incline, her knee griping with every stride.

"It only takes a half-hour to get to the embassy. Did they pick you up early, or did you take another *break*?"

"Are you keeping tabs on me?" Jani pushed open the access door, but before she could step outside, Lucien reached over her shoulder and grabbed the door pull, blocking her passage.

"I just wanted to talk to you. Is that a crime?" He stepped out onto the sidewalk in front of her, then held open the door, the sunlight sparking off his hair.

Jani watched a pair of women turn to gape. "It was certainly uncharacteristically nice of you." She tugged at the front of his sweat-splotched desertweight shirt. "You look wilted—are you going to change?"

"Change. Shower. Crawl in your cooler." Lucien sucked in a lungful of crisp fall air. "The heat at the embassy really doesn't bother you?"

"Nope."

"It's not fair."

"Want me to talk to John? He can have you throwing up inside a week."

"You make it sound so inviting."

They crossed the street, their steps punctuated by a series of sharp reports as pinpoint charges detonated within the renovation. Lucien patted his holster as the shooter-like noises continued to sound. "Doesn't that noise get to your augie?"

Jani hurried past the doorman into the quiet of the lobby. "If I avoided everything that got to augie, I'd spend the rest of my life in a soundshielded cell, no blinking red lights allowed."

"I thought you couldn't handle red at all."

"John brought that under control this summer." Jani nodded to Hodge as she crossed to the lift bank. "Much to my relief. You wouldn't believe how many people I know think red is a good color for a wall." She didn't notice that Lucien lagged behind her until she had entered the lift.

"Oh, damn." He had pulled up, gaze fixed in the direction of the lobby sitting area.

A young woman stood in the middle of the space, poised as though unsure whether to retreat or step forward. Her face was small-featured, a series of wispy upturns, the delicate effect complemented by clipped light brown waves. Slim and of medium height, she wore a wrap shirt and trousers in darkest burgundy.

"Roni." Lucien doffed his cap and tucked it in his belt. "It's been a while."

"Yeah," the young woman replied, in a tone that hinted that the while hadn't been long enough.

Roni? Jani stepped out of the lift. "Roni McGaw? The Exterior Documents Chief?"

Wide-set, slanted eyes narrowed further as they fixed on Jani. "Jani Kilian." McGaw's was the accent of privilege, twangy Michigan provincial. "I wanted . . . to talk to you." She looked again at Lucien, and her voice deadened. "If you're busy, we can meet another time."

"We are, as a matter of fact." Lucien tried to herd Jani back into the lift. "Sorry, but—"

"Wait." Jani stepped around Lucien and beckoned to McGaw. "I can spare a few minutes, if you don't mind a ride upstairs."

"I'm in a hurry myself. Late for a meeting." McGaw boarded the lift, taking care to stand as far away from Lucien as possible. "Forgive the informality, but I wanted to ask your advice and such requests are better made in person."

In other words, you didn't want to risk anyone from Exterior intercepting the message. Jani studied Roni more closely. The muted light of the cabin combined with the too-dark Exterior uniform to accentuate shadows beneath eyes and cheekbones and tinge ivory skin with blue. It was a picture Jani recalled well. *She's like Yolan—worry deadens her face.* It surprised her to think of her late corporal at a time like this, in the quiet of the vault. She usually only thought of Yolan Cray during the day, when she walked outside, and heard the *boom* of the charges.

McGaw's eyes widened when she entered Jani's flat, but she kept her interior decoration commentary to herself. "Nice place," she said as she walked to the window. "Nice view, too."

Jani joined her. "Yes, it is. You can see the intersection, and Armour Place all the way to where it veers onto the Boul Sidebar." She lowered her voice. "Do you think you were followed?"

"No." McGaw made as if to say more, but the sound of Lucien's footsteps silenced her.

"How's Miryam, Roni?" He wedged between them, his voice laced with petulant bite. "I heard she moved back to Lyon."

"She's fine. She . . . did leave, last month, yes, she started a consulting business with some friends." The blush crawled up McGaw's neck, then fingered along her jaw. Yolan had reacted the same whenever Neumann goaded her, her pale skin broadcasting her every emotion.

Jani interrupted Lucien's baiting, just as she had Neumann's years before. "Would you like a drink?" She headed for the kitchen, gesturing for McGaw to follow.

"Please." McGaw hurried to catch her up.

Jani swept through the door and yanked open the cooler. "Is this about The Nema Letter?" She removed a dispo of fruit drink and handed it to McGaw.

"Nema?" McGaw stared at the dispo, her expression clouding. Then her head came up. *"Yes,* I—"

The kitchen door slid aside once more. "Are you ladies avoiding me?" Lucien asked as he sauntered in. "Ron, is that any way to treat an old friend?" He joined Jani in front of the cooler and put his arm across her shoulders, pulling her close.

Since when? Lucien never put his arm around her—he wasn't the drapery type. Jani looked at McGaw to find her staring at Lucien, eyes hard and shining.

"All this increased business with the idomeni is highlighting the deficiencies in my staff's training. We could use input from someone with your experience." McGaw cracked the dispo seal and took a sip. "If you'd agree to conduct a seminar, I can guarantee a room packed to the roof."

"Ron, where have you been?" Lucien gave Jani a squeeze. "Ani will never allow Jan to set foot on Exterior grounds."

"Anais and I have a deal. She doesn't interfere with documents, and I keep my nose out of politics." McGaw took another swallow from the dispo, wincing as she did so. "Please think about it and get back to me, won't you?"

"Sure." Jani slipped from under Lucien's arm and followed McGaw out of the kitchen. "Lescaux doesn't know you're here."

"God, no." McGaw handed Jani the juice dispo. "It's so sour."

"Sorry."

"Anais will be in the city all day tomorrow. Stop by the Annex."

"Shouldn't we meet somewhere else?"

"I've mentioned you to my staff. They'll expect to see you. It's all right." Disgust rippled across McGaw's face as Lucien approached, intensifying when he once more slipped his arm around Jani. "I'll see what I can arrange," she said more loudly. "I will certainly appreciate your help." She stuck out her hand. "Call me when you have the time."

"Sure." Jani took McGaw's hand, shook it lightly, dropped it. It felt warm, not cold. Alive, not dead. So why couldn't she bear to touch it . . . ?

McGaw looked at her hand, then at Jani. "Is something wrong?"

Jani looked into her eyes. At least they were hazel, not pale grey like Yolan's. That would have been too much. "You . . . just remind me of someone I used to know."

"Oh? I can't tell from your face whether that's good or bad." McGaw backed out the door. "Until later." She ignored Lucien's weak wave and hurried down the hall toward the lift.

"Well, that brought back memories." Lucien's arm fell away as soon as the door closed. "She's trouble. Always sticking her nose where it doesn't belong. I lost track of the number of times I asked Ani to fire her."

Jani stepped around him to her desk, taking a drink from the nearly full dispo along the way. "Why didn't Ani listen?" She swallowed, then glanced at the dispo label. *It's just lemon tonic.* She'd always found it sweet.

"Roni's mother is Ani's cousin. Ani lets family get in the way. That's family with a small 'f,' in case you missed it." Lucien tossed his garrison cap atop the desk, then pulled his rumpled shirt out of his trousers and undid the fasteners. "I'm going to shower."

Jani sat and pulled a file off the top of a stack. "Have fun."

"I could use someone to wash my back."

"First rule of the Service—never volunteer."

"And a soldier's life is a lonely one." Lucien pulled off his shirt as he walked down the hall toward Jani's bedroom, allowing her an unimpeded view of his back before the door closed.

Such an admirable view. Thoughts of it warred with the upset that McGaw's surprise appearance had caused, but before either thought could claim precedence, the buzz of Jani's comport spooked them all back to their burrows.

"Documents, Mistress," Hodge imparted in hushed tones. "Treasury courier."

Boy, Kern—you didn't waste any time. "Send them up." Jani counted to twenty, then pushed away from the desk. By the time she reached the door, the entry bell sounded. Hodge passed the gold carrier across the threshold with solemn ceremony; Jani cracked the seals, sighing inwardly when she saw the amount of paper contained therein. *Retainer? Try a damned deputy ministry.* After Hodge departed, she hefted the case back to the desk, pulled the top file out of the portable bin and tried to concentrate on the tables and charts.

Only a few minutes had passed when she heard the bedroom door open, but Lucien seldom dawdled when he showered and dressed alone. She glanced up. "Are you going straight back to Sher—?"

"Straight back to Sheridan? I don't know." He smiled as he padded toward the desk. He had showered, judging from his damp hair and the stray drops of water glistening on his shoulders. He just hadn't bothered to dress.

Long thighs. Flat stomach. Just enough muscle—breadth

without bulk. *Blond all over—well, we knew that, didn't we?* Jani struggled with an "animal in the skimmer headlamps" feeling. Hypnotic view—inevitable outcome. "Forget something?"

"My cap." Lucien reached across the desk and picked it up, allowing her to catch the scent of musky soap arising from his bare arm. He studied the cap absently, then planted his elbows on the desk and jerked his chin at the Treasury carrier. "Those are new."

"Yeah." Jani dragged her attention back to the documents. "Kern asked me to have a look at them. Idomeni issues. Anais is supposed to be helping him, but she's ignoring his pleas."

"That means his boss ticked her off. It's Kern's job to heal the breach, not pass off the mess to you."

"I said I'd help."

"You're always helping. The more you help, the more they ask. What's Kern offering in return this time?"

"Permanent retainer."

"Did you get it in writing?" Lucien leaned closer. "Roni. Kern. Yesterday, it was someone else. Tomorrow, it'll be someone else again. They all want your help, but what do *you* get in exchange?" His eyes darkened in frank invitation. "With all you've been through, you still haven't learned the difference between people who earn their keep and people who don't."

Jani inhaled. The musky scent seemed to envelop her now, but McGaw's visit had unsettled her too much to consider the inevitable outcome. She nodded toward the clear windows, through which the afternoon sunlight streamed. "The privacy shields aren't up. Someone's getting an eyeful."

Lucien looked toward the unimpeded view of the nearby buildings. "Perhaps that someone will show an interest. I'm certainly not getting any in here." He straightened, then opened up the cap and set it at a jaunty angle atop his head. "My desertweights were rancid. I stuck them in your cleaner and set it for an hour."

"I'll take them out when they're done." Jani watched his perfect form recede down the hall, taut muscles working under tanned skin. Many thoughts occurred, none of which would have given Lucien any pleasure.

He's trying to distract me. But from what? Not work—he never interfered with her job except to opine that she didn't charge enough for her services. *Peter?* Possibly. It did strike her as odd that they got on well enough to confer about the care and feeding of Anais Ulanova, especially considering Peter's reaction when Lucien interrupted Anais at the meeting. *They're rivals, oh yes they are.* But allies of a sort too, apparently, inasmuch as circumstances and Lucien's misshapen personality allowed them to be.

What about Roni McGaw? His former coworker. *They despise one another.* Were they ex-lovers? No. *He'd flaunt that, not hide it.* Besides, Jani had sensed no heat between them, only the acrid odor of profound dislike.

He kept interrupting us. Why?

Lucien reemerged from the bedroom, this time fully clothed in a fresh set of dress blue-greys. "I'm off." His black tietops clipped on the bare wood. "I'm not sure if I'll be by again this week—my schedule's a little choppy."

"Whenever you can spare a few moments." Jani reached for the Treasury carrier to pull out another file, but before she could, Lucien flipped the lid closed.

"If I never came back, would you care?" His voice held the deadness he reserved for people he had no use for, which meant he wasn't real happy with her at the moment.

"I don't know." The words slipped out before Jani could stop them, driven by Lucien's odd behavior, the memory of Roni McGaw's agitation, and her own rising sense of disquiet.

"You. Don't. Know." Lucien slipped his hand behind her head and pulled her to him, kissing her hard enough to hurt. He'd rinsed his mouth with a peppermint concoction—the sharp taste filled Jani's sinuses and made her eyes water.

"Tell Kern he better come through with that retainer," he whispered as he broke away. The door had closed after him before Jani thought to breathe.

She spent the balance of the afternoon alternating between Kern's files, Devinham's dock data, and the other Treasury reports. As the sky darkened, she prepped a strange supper of Neoclona Chicken Surprise washed down with lemon tonic. The chicken did indeed surprise her by tasting good. She buried thoughts of how a fully human mouth would perceive the tangy wine-herb flavor she enjoyed, and sopped up the sauce with bits of bread.

Late evening found her restless, brain churning with Nema's troubles, Lucien's actions, Roni McGaw's trepidation, and her own white paper-lined collision with her past. She tried to decompress by flipping through a holo album her parents had sent her the month before. First came scene-shots of north Acadian wilds near Oncle Shamus's tourist compound, the moors and the rolling hills. Then came the more personal images. Her mother, Jamira, grey-edged black hair twisted into a loose knot, holding up a rainbow-hued sari she bought for Jani to wear during her expected visit home. Her father, Declan, sleeves rolled up to expose sinewy arms, displaying with self-conscious pride the oaken salmon he had machined to hang over the mantel of Shamus's lodge fireplace.

Jani stilled the rolling image and studied her father's face—the turned-up nose, snub chin, straight black hair—and saw the face she had worn before Evan van Reuter's bomb blew her out of the Shèrá sky. Her chest tightened. She slammed the album closed and shoved it back in her desk drawer, then pulled a Service-surplus field coat from her front closet.

The urge to bolt, which never lurked too deep beneath her surface, broke through several times as she walked to the lift. She could pack in minutes, catch any of a dozen trains or 'movers to O'Hare, lift off for Luna within the hour, be halfway to Mars before anyone realized that she had left Chicago.

No, I don't do that anymore. I've signed a rental contract. I have clients, obligations. I'm a free and functioning member of society.

Then why did she feel more trapped now then she ever had as a fugitive?

The air held a hard, brittle quality, as though it would sing like glass if Jani brushed her fingers through it. She pulled up her collar and stuffed her hands in her pockets, her internal thermostat having decided now was the time to freeze her to death. She trudged down the empty sidewalk and across the deserted street, past the tarpaulined silence of the renovation and down a side lane, until she came upon a small park nestled between two Family townhouses. She wiped an unseasonable dusting of frost from a slatwood bench, and sat.

Despite the cold, she savored the night silence. She hadn't been entirely truthful with Lucien—the blasts and clatters of construction did bother her. Not her augmentation, no. What they did was uncover memories. Of the bombs. The stench of smoke and char. The rubble, and what lay beneath.

Yolan Cray died during the first round of shelling at Knevçet Shèràa, when the Laumrau shatterboxes wrought their first wave of destruction. Windows had sharded. Safety doors had blown. Walls collapsed, and killed. Buried. Entombed.

Jani closed her eyes as once more, Borgie's sobs filled her ears. She could see him, clear as relentless remembrance could be, as he lifted Yolan's broken body and buried his face in her wispy blonde hair.

Silence. Silence felt like heaven. Jani tensed as the distant scree of a ComPol siren broke through. She thought of a seat on an outbound shuttle, and clenched her hands into fists. She forced herself to sit still as silence, and watched the shaded windows until the last light faded.

CHAPTER 8

Jani awoke with a start to find she had worked her way over to Lucien's side of the bed. She buried her face in his pillow, filling her nose with his scent as fragments of a rather pleasant dream drilled heat-tracks through her brain and down her spine.

I'm not in love. She struggled into a sitting position. *I know what love is, and this ain't it. This* was lust, the enthusiastic appreciation of a beautiful body and all the wonders it could perform. It worked beneath her skin like a constant prickling, as though nerves that had never felt before had suddenly come alive. It was ridiculous. It made no sense.

It was profoundly human and she would cherish its every ache and throe for all the human time she had left.

Love had nothing to do with her feelings for Lucien. Nor trust. She didn't trust him to give her the right time, but she had never felt that was part of the deal. She allowed him access to Nema, and a chance to build his career; he took her out of herself for a little while, and accepted her at face value. In the series of deals and trade-offs that had comprised her life for over twenty years, this one worked better than most.

Love, on the other hand, felt like a calm refuge in the midst of a raging storm. Nasty thing about love—it let you get comfortable, then threw you a curve. She'd loved Evan van Reuter once, with the handed-down-from-heaven certainty of a twenty-one-year-old who thought it all started with her. That ended when she realized what giving herself over to a Family member really meant. When she learned that the public Evan and the private Evan were two distinctly different men, and that while he didn't think that mattered, she did.

She tottered to the bathroom, collecting clothes along the way. *And then there's John Shroud.* A few weeks before, she had made the mistake of spending a day in the Neoclona documents archives to research a last-minute project. Funny how John needed to look up some data that very day. They'd spent hours discussing, bickering, and laughing over everything from the results of the latest Cup match to *exactly what color are Val Parini's eyes, anyway?* And when they didn't talk, they worked at their respective tasks, or read, or daydreamed, content simply to be in each other's company.

Jani didn't realize until she'd returned to her flat that she had once again *given herself over.* That she'd let John choose the chair in which she sat, the food she ate, the color of the folder she used to bind her report, and that she'd set her conscious will aside and allowed it to happen. She didn't blame him. Not entirely. They were inextricably bound, as only creator and created could be. He had saved her life, rebuilt her to the best of his ability, sheltered her from Service justice until she dug deep and found the will to shake him off.

He was the first thing I saw when I opened my eyes. Her mutant eyes, as green as the edge of a pane of glass. The harbinger of what was to come, the point man for the changes her body was going through.

Jani arranged her clothes and showering gear in the over-mirrored bathroom, all the while avoiding her myriad reflections. She bent over the sink to brush her teeth—the strong mint odor of her tooth cleaner irritated the inside of her nose. She sneezed, then groaned as she felt the telltale loosening over her right eye as the film fissured. She peeled away the ruptured hydropolymer and rummaged through the drawers for her filmformer. Bottle in hand, she made ready to *apply and let dry,* then stopped herself. "I need to look in the mirror to make sure it spreads evenly." Her filmed eye could wind up looking like a fried egg if the polymer didn't coat properly. *One . . . two . . .* She took a deep breath, and looked at her naked eye.

The iris had increased in size and darkened profoundly over the summer, thanks to her accelerated hybridization. Half again as large as a human iris, a forest green shattered marble accentuated by the lighter hue of her visible sclera. She pulled down her lid, exposing the edging of slight darkening that inscribed the border between green and white. *Sweet baby jades*, Val had dubbed them, as though giving them a nickname would help Jani accept their inevitable change.

John did this because he loved me. Because he didn't know how else to save me. Because he had convinced himself that he possessed the know-how to construct a human-idomeni hybrid that combined the best of both species but left the unwanted effects behind. Because he felt that since he did what he did with the best of intentions, for love and for science, that the law of unintended consequences didn't apply.

"That's love for you." Jani shook the drops of filmformer onto her eye and counted off the setting time.

She adjusted the shower to a pounding spray that massaged the constant stiffness from her muscles. She dressed for comfort, in a white Service surplus pullover and dark blue fatigue pants, since she had no appointments until her dinner with Steve and Angevin that evening. *Not unless Derringer drops by.* She didn't look forward to that. He'd pick up their argument where it left off at the embassy, and she'd have to employ every duck and dodge she knew to keep him from breaking out his particular set of thumbscrews.

She was in the midst of toweling her hair when the bedroom comport squawked.

"Good morning, Mistress Kilian," Hodge entoned formally. "Colonel Pierce is here."

"Good morning, Hodge. Send him up."

Hodge glanced off to the side, and nodded. "If you would, Mistress, attend here please. Colonel Pierce would prefer to discuss the matter in another venue."

In other words, Niall wanted to talk outside. "Tell him I'll be right down."

By the time Jani entered the lobby, she found Niall had already adjourned to the sidewalk in front of the apartment house. He wore fallweights—dark blue trousers cut by a mainline red stripe, paired with a long-sleeved grey shirt. He set his dark blue garrison cap on his head, then dug into his shirt pocket. When Jani saw him remove the nicstick case and shake out a 'stick, her stomach roiled.

"Pretty Boy up there?" He spoke without turning around, his eyes fixed on the street activity.

"No." Jani pulled up beside him, and caught a whiff of the astringent smoke. Her nose tickled ominously—she circled around Niall in search of clean air and started up the walk.

Niall fell in beside her. Luckily, the light breeze blew his smoke in the opposite direction. "Plan to see him today?"

"No. He does occasionally show up out of the blue, though. He's keyed into the flat, and he keeps things there." Jani stopped at a kiosk and purchased a packet of crackers. Her stomach was letting her know that skipping breakfast had been a dumb idea, and tasteless with a little salt had proved safe in the past. "Is there a point to these questions?"

"Yes." Niall glanced around uncertainly, then reached into his shirt pocket again.

Jani watched him shake out and ignite another 'stick. "OK, Niall, what don't you know how to tell me?"

They had come upon a small playground. Niall leaned against a low fence and watched two small boys launch a tiny pondskimmer in the shallow pool of a fountain. "It's your parents." His eyes widened. "I began that badly. I'm sorry. They're fine. They're—they're on their way here. They hit MarsPort tonight. They touch down at O'Hare the day after tomorrow."

Jani ran the words over in her mind once, then again. She knew what she'd heard, but it made no sense to hear it from Niall. "Repeat what you just said."

"Jani, you heard me."

"Why didn't they let me know?"

"I don't know. I have a few guess—"

"What happened?"

"I don't know. I got a bare bones Misty earlier this morning from a buddy in Guernsey. Ares Station called to confirm that they're on their way."

The boys argued over which of them should control the skimmer. As their high-pitched quibbling intensified, they lost track of the craft. Jani watched it veer off-course, bounce off the side of the fountain, and spin in tight circles. "Does this have anything to do with the white paper?"

"I don't know." Niall leaned out over the fence as the toy popped out of the pool, catching it before it clattered to the cement. "We're going to debrief them during the trip from Mars to Luna." He held up a hand to silence her protests. "They're coming here under very strange circumstances. We have to find out what compelled them. Were they told something about you that made them fear for your safety? What? From whom?"

"From whom?" Jani waited. "Spit it out, Niall."

Niall ran a finger along the pondskimmer's bow, and scraped a thumbnail over a colored decal. "Ever hear of a group called *L'araignée*?"

"Spider?" Jani shook her head. "Sounds like one of those trumped-up gangs that takes over a loading dock and calls itself a syndicate."

"This is a little more than a trumped-up gang." Niall flicked the skimmer's safety switch, then tossed it back in the water. "It's a well-organized alliance of colonial businesses. Their stated goal is to 'maintain standards and markets throughout the Commonwealth,' whatever the hell that means. The problem, according to my Guernsey friend, is that the membership wasn't very well vetted. They range in legitimacy from rock-solid to ones like you mentioned, gangs taking over loading docks. Unfortunately, the gangs seem to be taking over *L'araignée,* as well. My buddy says that in the months since its inception, *L'araignée*'s been responsible for all sorts of interesting incidents. Money laundering. Diversion of goods. The odd hijacked transport." He watched the bickering boys, still oblivious to their dead-in-the-water ship. "They're based in the Channel. That's why I wondered if you'd heard of them, if your folks had ever mentioned them."

"No." Jani backed away from the fountain, her hands pressed to her ears—the boys' screeching made her head pound. She envisioned her parents disembarking at Mars-Port, surrounded by uniforms. Did Spec Service receive training in making smalltalk with parents? Could Niall snag her a seat on a shuttle so that she could meet them at Luna? Were they afraid? "Does Mako know they're coming?"

"Of course Mako knows they're coming." Niall herded her up the street. "He assigned me to head up the welcoming committee." His weathered face set in grim lines. "They've become his new special project. He knows you'd ring the curtain down on him if anything happened to them."

"I'd never do anything that could take you out."

"You say that now. I've watched you look through holo albums for the past four months."

"Niall."

"Yeah." Niall pulled out another 'stick. "I told you I would check on who had been involved in compiling the information in that white paper, right? Well, matters got interesting in one hell of a hurry." He snorted smoke like a Tsing Tao dragon. "Guess who spent the first six months of this year zipping to most of the same cities covered in your report? Guess who met with agents based in the locations that he didn't manage to visit in person? Go on, guess."

"The Service was looking for me at the time, Niall." Even as she spoke, Jani felt a chill flood her limbs that had nothing to do with her wonky internal thermostat. It was augie, she knew, clamping down on the blood flow to her extremities, prepping her for the dash to safety that she couldn't afford to make. "It made sense to send Lucien after me. He did know me and he is in Intelligence."

"Intelligence." Niall gave the word a gamy twist. "Speaking of trumped-up gangs." They pulled up in front of Jani's building. "I'm going to be a little hard to get hold of until your folks arrive. I'll keep you posted, and I'll notify you as soon as we have them."

"I want to be there."

"Not a good idea. Save the reunion for the safe house. I want them in plain sight as little as possible, and I don't want the three of you together in public." He touched her arm, a brush of the fingers only. "I've got them. They'll be fine. You have my word. We have them sighted. We know when they'll arrive at MarsPort. We have people there to take charge of them. They'll be under close guard until they get here. I will meet them at O'Hare personally and place them in protective custody immediately."

* * *

Niall escorted Jani back to her flat. She tried once more to talk him into letting her come along to O'Hare, and he again stated reasonably and firmly why he felt that wasn't a good idea. He then took his leave, his the light step of someone who had an order of mission and a timetable and all those other things that kept the hours from hanging over your head like a sword suspended by a steadily unraveling thread.

"We also serve who only sit and go mad." Jani walked to her desk and fell into her chair. Her comport incoming message light showed dark for the first time in weeks, and she had her for-hire projects under control for the moment. She dug McGaw's affidavit out of her duffel and tried to examine it, but couldn't muster the concentration she needed. The image of two figures huddled in a ship's cabin had formed in her mind and refused to yield the floor.

Her stomach grumbled, and she went into the kitchen to shut it up. Her throat clenched with every swallow of the Neoclona premade, and she expected at any point to expel into the sink everything she had just swallowed. But augie ran her now, and his orders were always simple and to the point. Eat first. Sleep. Study. Evaluate the facts. Then act.

She lay down on her side of the bed. Lucien's scent didn't interest her now. The problem with Niall's quick and dirty assessment of the source of the white paper was that she could indeed imagine Lucien compiling it. "I can't see him leaving anything out, though." He enjoyed creating anxiety. Jani could imagine him dropping details of her deed-copying for months, then savoring her every start and display of unease.

She struggled to forget about Lucien by performing thought exercises that she'd developed during her years on the run, when augie threatened to blow out the top of her head unless she acted and she knew action was the last thing she should do. She inhaled slowly. Exhaled. Visualized her limbs sinking into the mattress. Concentrated on a mental image of Baabette, a storybook character from her youth. In her conception, the white sheep with the black face sat at a workstation and assembled a hologram landscape, an absurdity that for some odd reason Jani found calming. She had just reached the point where sleep seemed possible when her comport screeched.

"Mistress? I couldn't stop him." Hodge blinked rapidly, his equivalent of an emotional breakdown. "Colonel Derringer, Mistress. He's on his way up."

"It's all right, Hodge. I've been expecting him." Jani swung her legs over the side of the bed. Stood. Counted. By the time she reached her front door, the entry bell rang.

"Anais Ulanova should be shot," Derringer muttered as he stormed in. He wore dress blue-greys and clutched his brimmed lid in his hand like a weapon at the ready. "Fifteen hours I spent at the embassy discussing tile specifications! Delivery dates! I felt like a goddamn building contractor." He stopped in the middle of the floor and looked around. "What the hell?" He turned back to glare at Jani. "Where's your furniture?"

"Don't believe in it. Makes visitors think they're welcome." She folded her arms and leaned against the wall.

Derringer's scowl altered to a frown. "Are you feeling all right, Kilian?"

"No, sir."

Derringer flinched at the "sir." He knew she didn't mean it. "One of your many ailments, I assume." He backed farther into the room. "You slipped out from under yesterday. We never had a chance to *talk*." He offered a superior half-smile. "Tsecha. Information." He walked to the window and sat on the sill. "Report."

Jani fought the urge to stand at attention. "He knows nothing about that letter. He reaffirmed his belief that any and all interactions between humanish and idomeni are desirable."

Derringer's hand tightened around his hat brim. "And you accepted this at face value? You didn't try to dig deeper?"

"All there is with Nema is face value. There is no deep to dig into." Jani let her arms drop and stepped away from the wall. "He's being set up by someone with an interest in getting him out of the way. I have reason to believe that his position at the embassy is tenuous and that even the appearance that he is involved in subterfuge of this nature will result in his recall and possibly his execution."

"You said that at lunch yesterday. I don't buy it." Derringer sounded bored. Callum Burkett, his CO, had spent ten years working with the colonial Haárin. Derringer had heard all his stories and felt that he now knew all there was to know about the idomeni. "Tsecha's still invited to the meetings. I've received no official notification that from such-and-such date on, he no longer speaks and acts for the Shèrá worldskein."

"Didn't you see Shai's posture at yesterday's meeting? How she interrupted Nema when he tried to reprimand Ulanova about the tile?"

Derringer brightened. "Wish he'd succeeded. Would have saved me a lot of trouble."

"Shai *cut* Nema *out*." Jani's voice rasped as her throat tightened—she waited until the worst of the clench abated. This was her best shot at convincing Derringer to leave Nema alone. If she lost her temper now, he'd never give her another chance. "Shai"—she paused—"Shai took over the discussions with Ulanova herself. She's acting in Nema's stead, preventing him from acting as the worldskein's voice."

Derringer's gaze moved from Jani's face to some point above her head. "Why is she doing this? She's always deferred to him before. Why the sudden change?"

Jani spoke slowly, pacing her argument. "I think the Vynshàrau are studying us the way we study them, and they've realized that their habit of open disputation doesn't play well with us. We see it as a sign of weakness, a crack in the united front. Shai knows Nema will never change his ways, no matter how it looks to us, so she's trying to shut him out. If she does this, he's little use as ambassador. Cèel has been looking for an excuse to shut down Nema for years. The least misstep on his part could mean recall, and if there's a suspicion that he's betrayed his people, the penalty will be much greater. We can't afford to lose him. He's our best friend. He's the one who badgers Cèel to open up idomeni Gate-Ways to our shipping, to permit technology exchanges. He's the doorway—we don't want that door to close. You've visited idomeni factories and military bases. You've seen their technologies. Do you really want them to shut themselves away, to develop and expand where you can't see them? You don't trust them? You think they're the enemy? Well, what's that old saying—keep your friends close—"

"—and your enemies closer." Derringer's gaze dropped. He fussed with his lid, brushing invisible specks from the crown and running the cuff of his tunic over the brim.

Jani watched him ponder, and offered up a prayer to Ganesha, the favored god of her youth. The Remover of Obstacles. *Please, Lord, make this idiot see sense.* She thought of the shrine she had meant to construct for months. *Tomorrow—I'll build it tomorrow.* No. If the Temple store on Devon Avenue was still open, she'd build it today.

Then, slowly, like a clouded sunrise, Derringer's head came up. "Sorry, Kilian, I don't buy it. If the Vynshàrau are so averse to subterfuge, they wouldn't have let Tsecha come here in the first place. He pulled a few tricks of his own during that last war of theirs. Hell, I heard he helped plan your evac from Interior the night van Reuter was arrested." He shook his head. "He's their boy, like it or not. The gods chose him, so the idomeni are stuck with him. He's chosen us, and I have no intention of letting the opportunity go to waste." He stood up, tucked his lid under his arm, shot the cuffs of his tunic. "Since your meeting with him got cut short, I've arranged another visit for tomorrow. Some documents transfers that just won't wait."

Jani stepped out to the middle of the floor. The chill had flooded her limbs again—standing too near the wall made her feel trapped. "I will not go."

"You have no choice."

"I will not endanger Nema's life."

"You will do as you are told." Derringer started toward the door. "I'll send a skimmer for you. Save you having to hike to the L. End of story."

Jani remained silent. Her throat ached too much to try to talk. She stepped to one side as Derringer brushed past her, her hands clenched, nails gouging her palms. She fought to ignore augie as he urged her to strike, and stood frozen until she heard the door close.

CHAPTER 9

Jani remained standing in the center of the room for some time after Derringer left. She performed her breathing exercises, then tried to concentrate on Baabette and her landscape design. Derringer's face, however, kept superimposing itself over that of the sheep's. The image of him coated in white wool quieted Jani's wire-drawn nerves, much as envisioning a naked audience calmed an edgy speaker.

The ploy didn't work for long, though. Her throat soon ached again. Her stomach hitched along for the ride. She dragged her feet loose from their invisible moorings and paced the perimeter, her mind veering from thoughts of dockings at MarsPort to how she could pry Derringer off Nema's back to—.

I have an appointment with Roni McGaw. Lucky thing. The walking, riding, working out of her route would give her racing mind a track to ride on.

She lowered to the floor beside her desk and checked the contents of her duffel. Her scanpack and other devices she had inserted into the scanproof compartment she had rebuilt into the duffel's bottom. She fingered two torn edges where she had attached compartments that had been hacked out by over-officious investigators. *My history in the bottom of a bag.* One torn edge marked her detainment just prior to Evan's arrest; the other served as reminder of her capture by the Service that summer. *Bad things come in threes,* Jani thought as she tugged at one of the polyfilm fragments. She struggled to her feet, hoisted the duffel, and grabbed a Service surplus jacket from the entryway closet on the way out the door.

*   *   *

Jani disembarked the L at the station located just outside the entrance to the Exterior Ministry, and took some time to examine her target from the elevated platform.

The Outer Circle world of Amsun served as the true home of the Cabinet office to which fell the job of administering the Commonwealth's forty-six extrasolar colonies; to that placement belonged the sprawl one normally associated with a Ministry HQ. Therefore, since it was considered an annex only, the Chicago compound paled when compared to the other Cabinet installations that stretched from just north of Chicago to the lower tip of Lake Michigan. Unlike the neighbor Interior Ministry, which was comprised of an immense Main building, a score of subsidiary structures, and a private estate for the minister, Exterior consisted only of a smallish office tower and a few security and utility outbuildings. Instead of grounds measured by the square kilometer, it possessed a yard of mortal scope, easily traversed by skimmer in a couple of minutes. And as for the estate, Anais Ulanova solved that problem by residing in the Family home that was located a block or so east of Jani's own flat.

Jani shaded her eyes and looked to the south, where the sudden shift from the grey-green of native scrub grass to the bluish tint of the Shèrá hybrid species marked the boundary with the idomeni embassy. Only that southern boundary possessed any significant security presence—Jani could just detect the top of one of the boxy concrete booths that dotted the border from the western line of the Ministry access road east to the lakeshore.

That's not my problem. If Jani ever needed to infiltrate Exterior grounds from that direction, she need only ask Nema how he did it. He had, after all, penetrated the boundary regularly that previous winter, hiding clothing and makeup in one of the booths and using it as a jumping-off point for disguised forays into the city.

He blended right in. Well, truth be told, he must have looked rather strange. *So tall and stick-thin.* Cracked amber eyes obscured by filming. *But excellent clothes, and lightly accented English.* People must have taken him for one of Chicago Combined University's more eccentric professors.

The more Jani thought about it, the more she realized how well that particular shoe fit. *He does understand subterfuge, you know.* And plotting. And planning. *He's not the naïf you think he is.* So why did she feel so bound to protect him? What made her think he couldn't talk himself out of this jam as he had out of so many others?

Because at times, he is as blind and deaf here. At such times, I become his Eyes and Ears. I watch his back. I kill the wasps. A duty long-evaded, reclaimed. *My job.*

She switched her attention to the Exterior Ministry entrance. The long, curved drive was filled with double- and triple-length skimmers. Chauffeurs stood in groups, chatting and smoking, while security guards walked among the vehicles, scanning Registrations and making notes in recording boards. Of course, the skimmers had already been identified, cross-matched, and effectively searched when they turned onto the drive and passed through the sensor fence, but that was invisible and therefore had little effect on the nerves. Better for potential infiltrators to see the burgundy-clad guards, holstered shooters hanging on their belts, walking from vehicle to vehicle, opening boots and huddling in low-pitched discussion.

Jani brushed a hand over her jacket front and started down the stairs.

"Name?"

"Jani Kilian." Jani handed the lobby desk her ID, then waited as the young woman scanned her eyes. A distinct change of pace, announcing herself to a guard using her real name.

The guard checked her workstation display. "Ms. McGaw will be right out, ma'am. Please have a seat." She handed Jani back her ID, professional seriousness framed by a Service short-back-and-sides and the brilliant white collar of a fallweight "A" shirt.

"I'll stand, thanks." Jani strolled across the marble tile floor and pretended a pointed examination of the lakescapes on the walls. *I wonder if the Haárin tilemaster will be retiling this particular floor?* If Lucien's assessment proved accurate, and Jani felt it would, such a public display of his singular artistry would lead to more requests. *And after the tilemaster will come a painter, or a woodworker, or a skimmer designer. Anais, you do realize that you opened the door you wanted to keep shut?* Unfortunately, months or years would pass before open trade sank its roots in Chicago, and that would be much too late to do the Karistosians any good.

Jani turned as she heard the brush of a door mech and the high-pitched clip of thin-soled shoes.

"I wondered when you'd show." McGaw tugged at the pockets of her wine-red trouser suit. She looked even more drained and restive today than she had at Jani's flat. "My office."

McGaw closed the door, then touched an inset pad that Jani hoped activated an anti-surveillance array. "It's funny. Anais has been taking your name in vain on a regular basis ever since you started working closely with Tsecha. All I could think of was, 'Wow—Jani Kilian. She studied at the Academy. She walked the streets of Rauta Shèràa.' "

Jani sat in the visitor's chair on the opposite side of the desk. "Except for the night the Vynshà ascended to rau and their Haárin overran the place. Then we ran."

"You know what I mean." McGaw eyed her peevishly as she sat behind her large desk, which was covered from side to side with stacks of documents. "Must be something to turn to the face page of the Registry and find your name there."

"I don't really think about it anymore."

"You aren't going to give me a break, are you?"

"What break? You've romanticized it. I lived it. It loses a lot in translation, believe me." Jani's thigh muscles twitched as her news-from-home nerves finally abated and post-augie tremors settled in. Afterward would come post-augie languor, a muddle-headed state that would spell the end to her field-work for . . . how long? *Minutes? Hours? Days?* Her physical condition, once so reliable, had become more and more unpredictable. She could no longer time her augie stages as she used to—her increased hybridization had altered the old, familiar progression to a stop-and-start dissonance.

"Hansen Wyle and Jani Kilian, the senses, the infiltrators," McGaw continued, determined to shoulder on regardless. "Gina Senna and Carson Tsai, the musicians. The pacifiers. Dorothea Aryton and Ennegret Nawar, the Family members. The muscle." The recitation did some good—her calm seemed to reassert itself as she discussed Jani's history. "One of Six for Tongue of Gold, Two for Eyes and Ears, Three and Four for Hands of Light, Five and Six for Earthly Might."

Lives there a dexxie anywhere that doesn't know that damned verse? Who would have thought that the rhyme the six of them had concocted during a late-night study burnout would dog them for life? "Ms. McGaw, I thought you were in a hurry."

"I admire you. You helped mold my profession."

"You're confusing a set of circumstances with the person who lived through them. That's a common mistake, a dangerous one, one that a woman in your position can't afford to make."

"I—" McGaw sat back, the blear in her eyes slowly sharpening. "Angie Wyle's a friend of mine. We had a long talk about you last winter, before she headed off to Guernsey. She said you were different from the others." She shifted uncertainly. "Please call me Roni." It sounded more a plea than a request. She sat forward, elbows on desk, and covered her face with her hands. "Hurry. Yes. Where does one start? Audits brought me the letter a week ago and asked me to scan it. The first time my 'pack balked, I figured the mirrors needed cleaning, so I cleaned them. The second time it balked, I switched out filters and lenses. The third time, I thought the brain had suffered some sort of tissue damage, so I called in a friend from Commerce to check it out. My 'pack was fine, of course, so I asked him to scan the letter. That's when all hell broke loose."

"Why?" Jani spread her hands in question. "You should have let Labs check it out. A chip can hang up for many reasons. Oxidation. Degree of protein crosslinking. You always have some, but sometimes you can exceed the critical limit, and you're left with a worthless chip that scans like garbage."

Roni's head came up. "That's what I wanted to do, but Pe-

ter Lescaux wandered in. He had heard I had called in someone from Commerce on a consult, and he thought I was giving away the Family jewels. He hates to share." She snorted.
"I told him not to fly off to Derringer until I had time to go
over the letter with Forensics, but he saw a chance to make
points with Service Diplo. God knows why." She lowered
her hands, then let them drop to her desk. "He's always
jumping the starter, always trying to come off like the big
shot Exterior mover-and-groover. Little bastard sows chaos
wherever he goes."

Jani thought of Lescaux's wide-open face. The earnest
questions. *Save us, Lord, from simple, uncomplicated ambi-
tion.*

"I don't believe he let you scan it. He made us all look
like *fools.*" Roni fell back in her chair; the ergoworks
hummed and squeaked. "I'm still waiting for the quality
records for that batch of initiators. If they were manufactured near the upper cross-link limit, and the document
resided in an uncontrolled environment for too long, that
could be the answer."

"There's another possibility." Jani paused to look around
the large office. Expensive hardwood furnishings, befitting a
department chief. The requisite potted plants inhabiting the
corners. Windows facing the lake. Holos adorning the walls.
Roni's diploma from Chicago Combined. Nice, normal surroundings, inappropriate to the discussion. *We should have
met someplace else—I should have insisted.* She hated the
walls, and what could be hidden within. "What if the errors
weren't accidents? What if they were purposely put in place
to toss a stinkbomb in the midst of human-idomeni relations?" She took a deep breath, and opened a door she would
have preferred to keep closed. "Why didn't you want to talk
in front of Lucien? He's been out of Exterior for months,
and he left under a cloud. You've nothing to fear from him."

"He works for the competition. He probably knows about
this letter."

Yes, well he might. The fact that he didn't mention the fact
to Jani . . . well, Lucien adhered to his own pattern of consistency. "Peter apparently consults him on a regular basis."

Roni rolled her eyes. "That's a pair—the ventriloquist and

his dummy. Peter opens his mouth, and Lucien's words pop out."

Jani examined Roni's face for some sign she joked, but saw only tight-lipped disgust. "I didn't realize they had known one another that well."

"Lucien met Peter during some colonial assignment a little over a year ago. He's the one who introduced him to Anais. Groomed him to succeed, as it were." Roni's gaze moved to her windowed view. "Lucien may have departed Exterior officially last winter, but in too many ways, it's as though he never left. If you told me that he had something to do with this letter, I wouldn't be at all surprised."

Jani pulled her duffel onto her lap and fiddled with the straps to give her hands something to do. "One thing I know beyond doubt is that Lucien finds the idomeni fascinating, and anything he finds fascinating he lets live." She spoke as much to convince herself as Roni. "I don't believe he'd do anything to damage our relations with the Shèrá worldskein."

"I think he'd break anything just to see what would happen." A touchlock clicked as Roni opened one of her desk drawers. "I tried to research his life once. He had . . . come between me and someone I was very fond of, and I wanted to do something, *anything,* to sabotage his relations with Anais."

Jani nodded. She had done a little research into Lucien's background herself. Her reasons were less personal, nothing more than the fact that turning over rocks had become her habit long ago. "He was born in Reims, in the northern French province." Given the nature of the documents she had uncovered, she had gotten to the heart of the matter rather quickly. "His bioemotional deficiencies began causing real problems as he entered his teens. Luckily for him, that's when Anais came along and persuaded his parents to consign him to her care."

Roni's jaw dropped. "You found out a hell of a lot more than I did!"

"Friends in high places." Jani paused, recalling Val Parini's shouted description of the penalties for cracking sealed juvenile court records.

"I came up against brick wall after brick wall. Anais finally called me into her office one day and ordered me to cease and desist. Even she acted nervous." Roni hesitated. "What I'm trying to say is . . . he has a past worth hiding, and that begs the question of what he's gotten up to in the present." She held up a documents slipcase. "And, unfortunately, all I have to go on is this letter, purportedly from the idomeni ambassador, and I don't know how to make it tell me what I need to know."

Jani eyed the slipcase, which had a smooth finish rather than pebbled. "That's The Nema Letter."

Roni nodded. "Peter commented that you took exception to the rough finish of the slipcase you saw yesterday. You were correct, of course. We've been using them for, oh, two months now, and our Doc Repair hours have tripled. You can't stack the damned things—the pebbles push into and damage any insert they touch. I memoed Purchasing about them myself, but we buy them from one of Her Excellency's companies. I may as well spit into a hurricane." She pushed aside a pile, then extracted the letter and placed it in the cleared space. "I've taken to switching them out myself on the sly."

"I didn't get the chance to scan farther than the initiator chip." Jani removed her scanpack from her bag and activated it, then set the bag and the scanpack on the desk as she dragged her chair closer. "I want to—"

The office door opened, helped along by several Security guards. Two entered, splitting off like demiskimmers in formation and circling to either side of the desk. Two remained outside, bracketing the door like statuary.

Then Lescaux strode in, hands locked behind his back.

"Peter!" Roni shot to her feet. "How bloody dare you!"

Lescaux walked up to the desk and rooted through Jani's duffel. "How bloody dare you let this woman on the premises without clearing it with me." He picked up the top file, read the title tab, then shoved it back inside.

"You have no jurisdiction here!"

"I have every jurisdiction when I feel the security of the Commonwealth is at risk."

"Anais is going to hear about this."

"Anais is behind me one hundred percent."

As the argument waged around her, Jani eyed the letter, sitting like a holiday plum in the middle of Roni's desk. She then glanced at the guards, who deserved note mostly for their height and musculature. *If I made a grab for the letter, it would be a race to see which one broke my arm first.* Odds were square that they'd break her left arm, and she'd be inconvenienced only for the time it took John to switch out a new limb. Even a right break would put her out of commission for no more than a few hours. *Wouldn't solve the essential problem, though.* Namely, how to get the letter off Roni's desk and into her duffel.

"—trumped-up little bastard!" Roni's breathing had gone ragged from rage. "Aryton at Registry will hear about this, you can be damned sure!"

Dolly? Yes, Five of Six did work at Registry, didn't she? Registry Inspector General, so her title went. Pretty much ran the place. Jani hadn't tried to contact her since she'd settled in the city. They had gotten along well enough at Academy, but between work and health, there just hadn't been time.

"Dorothea Aryton is a good Family woman. She will not involve herself in matters of state"—Lescaux shot a disgusted look at Jani—"unlike some documents examiners I could name."

Roni braced her hands on the edge of her desk and leaned forward. "Listen, Beddy Boy—"

"It's all right, Ms. McGaw." Jani stowed her scanpack and rearranged the files Lescaux had muddled. "Just return me my sample docs, and I'll be on my way."

Roni proved at that moment that she could have guarded the third baseline for any professional baseball team in the Commonwealth. Her eyes lit with anger-fueled glee. "Of course, Ms. Kilian. I appreciate your . . . understanding." She plucked a few random documents off the top of one of her piles, then stacked them together with The Nema Letter and tucked them into the substitute slipcase that Jani hoped and prayed Lescaux hadn't seen before. "I appreciate you taking the time to consult with me on this matter." With steady hand and steely countenance, she held out the case to Jani.

Jani took her time tucking the slipcase into her duffel. She made sure the guards could see everything she did, and didn't move too quickly or stealthily. She shut the bag and shouldered it. Her heart beat slowly. Her hands felt dry. The twitchiness in her limbs vanished as augie took the controls.

She turned, and walked to the door.

"Hold it!"

Jani pulled up. *Oh well.* Roni had shown unexpected nerve, which probably signaled the end of her career at Exterior. But she'd find another job—Jani would help—

Lescaux stepped between her and the door. Anger firmed the line of his jaw and chilled his eyes, strengthening his resemblance to Lucien. "The affidavit, if you please."

Jani looked down quickly. "Of course, Mr. Lescaux." She undid the clasps of her duffel and picked through the files until she came upon the familiar pebbled slipcase. She removed it from the stack, handed it to Lescaux, and closed her bag.

"I should have expected this from you, considering our last conversation." He tucked the file under his arm and stepped to the side. "This was not the time for cheap dirty tricks."

Jani departed the office. Two of the guards preceded her. Two brought up the rear. She waited for the pound of footsteps from behind, the shout for her to once more *"Hold it!"* But the only steps she heard were those of the guards, and her own easy stride.

She walked through the lobby. Out the door and down the drive. Her heart tripped as she approached the sensor fence and it struck her that Exterior might lock-chip its documents and that third baseman McGaw hadn't had the chance to perform an unlock. But she passed through the sensors with nary a blip or beep.

The rear guard peeled off as Jani mounted the steps to the L platform. The lead pair stayed, bookending her silently as she waited, and remained on the platform until she boarded and the train pulled away.

Jani sat, still and silent, duffel cradled in her lap. She studied the other passengers, on the alert for someone who sat too close or looked at her for a little too long. After a time, she lowered her bag to the floor and opened it. Using the blip scanner she had secreted in the scanproof compartment, she checked the letter and slipcase for any tags, collars, or leashes. The testing proved negative, to her relief. She would have hated to ditch the valuable document beneath the seat if she had found an attached sensor, but she also had no intention of allowing Exterior to track her every waking move.

She then checked the soles of her shoes. Roni's office had been carpeted, and carpets could transfer all kinds of nasty things. Most people knew enough to search their pockets, the cuffs of the trousers, their hair. But they seldom checked their shoes.

After assuring herself of bug-free status, Jani disembarked at the next stop. She then waited for three trains to depart before boarding the fourth, a local that stopped at every lamppost. She rode it past her Armour Place stop, into the heart of the shopping district, getting off with the bulk of the passengers at the station across from a large mall.

She used the main entrance, taking care to stay with the crowd. Boarded the lift, hit the pad for the fourth floor, and got off on the third. Hurried to the nearest bathroom and shut herself in a stall. Only then did she sag against the wall, and pound her fist into her open hand.

CHAPTER 10

Jani wandered the mall to kill time, and surprised herself by actually committing *purchase*. She visited a religious shop, and pored over the shelves of figurines until she found her Lord Ganesha. The statuette she chose stood about ten centimeters high. The four-armed elephant sat upon a lotus throne, a mouse at his feet. He held a lasso in one hand, and wore a gold-weave snake around his waist.

Remove the obstacles that impede my mission, Lord, I pray. Jani cradled the Ganesha in her arms as she roamed the store. She picked a brass bowl to hold offerings, and a teakwood pedestal to serve as an altar. The size and weight of the pedestal precluded her carrying it with her, so she arranged to have everything delivered unto Hodge's sterling care.

She bewildered herself even more with the next items she bought. She didn't like shopping for clothes. Her business attire copied the uniform style she'd grown used to in the Service—conservative in color, severe in cut. Casual clothes were anything she could talk Lucien into scrounging for her from Service stores.

And then there were *nice* clothes, the evening dresses that John Shroud sent her in the unfulfilled hope that she would wear them in his company. Murderously expensive confections all, perfectly fitted and exquisitely shaded. She had yet to wear any of them, despite Lucien's assurances that he was more than willing to act as dresser.

I don't like to dress up. Even so, she couldn't tear away from the display of saris. The one that claimed her attention shone blue-green as sunlit seas, bordered in a chainlink pattern of gold and silver threads. She finally entered the shop to inquire as to the sari's price, gasped, and bought it anyway, escalating the damage by adding the platinum-dyed short-sleeve top, wrap trousers, and slippers that completed the outfit.

I need something to wear for the folks. Her mother, Jamira, always dressed in bright colors—she said they cheered her in the Acadian cold. *This will make her happy,* Jani thought as she fingered the turquoise silk. She then followed her newly acquired habit and had everything sent to Hodge.

Just remember to scan it before you bring it inside the flat. Jani made that note to herself as she settled into a comport booth in one of the public stands that dotted the mall. She'd determined by her many passes through the area that no one had followed her from Exterior. Now she dug an untraceable credit chit—the sort one could buy from a vend machine—from her pocket, ran it through the comport pay slot, and punched in a code.

A prim young face appeared on the display. "Registry?"

"Aryton, please."

The young woman stared. "You're—"

"Yes." Jani forced a smile.

"I'll . . . tell . . ." The desk emitted a tight little sigh as the display blanked.

Jani picked through the files in needless confirmation of the presence of The Nema Letter. "Bet she knows the words to that damned poem, too."

The display came up again, more quickly than she'd hoped.

"Jan?" Dorothea Aryton looked out at her with the solemn quizzicality that Hansen Wyle had christened "Juno rising." "My God." She still wore her thick black hair bound in a head-wrapping braid. Sharp Family bones, broadened more than usual across the cheekbone and brow, served as frame for clear blue eyes. Her skin had tanned red-brown from a summer of outdoor activity. Sailracing, if Jani remembered correctly. A risky sport for the seasonal amateur, but Dolly had always been willing to skirt the edges when they lived on Shèrá. Apparently, that still held true.

Apparently.

"You look . . . a different sort of person." Dolly squinted, grooving the skin around her eyes. Her voice still emerged in its own good time, drawled Virginia Provincial. "Impish, before. Now . . ." She sat back and folded her arms. "Solemn." She touched a hand to her chin. "I don't believe it."

"That it's me?"

"That you've grown solemn to match your face." Dolly pushed papers about her desk. "We've waited for you to call. Carson and I. He heads NUVA-SCAN Fraud, you know. Right down the street from Registry. We're the only others in town. Ennegret manages the Family money in London, and Gina consults out of Jo'burg." Her hand stilled. "You're calling from a public place."

Jani exhaled with a rumble. She'd forgotten Dolly's charming habit of approaching from all sides at once. "Yes."

"You always did." Dolly smiled, a minute shallowing along the corner of her mouth. "And I'm doing all the talking, as ever and always."

"I received a notice that there's a problem with one of my position filings." Jani tilted her head to the left as she held out her right hand, palm open and facing down. A Laum gesture, signifying grave worry. "If you have the time, I'd like to discuss it with you."

Dolly's eyes narrowed. The pleading inherent in the gesture didn't match the sort of routine document dispute Jani described. "I have some time now, as it happens."

"Allow me fifteen minutes." Jani gathered her gear, then paused and looked back at the display. "How's Cairn?"

"She's well, thank you." Dolly smiled again, winter-cool. "Social niceties discharged, Jani Kilian. You can come out now." The display blanked, leaving Jani to stare at the fading blue-to-grey.

Afternoon commuters filled the train—Jani switched her duffel from one shoulder to the other so she could change her grip on the overhead strap. Her back bothered her enough that she would have preferred sitting, but the standing view served her better. She stood near the rear of the car and monitored every embark and debark, watched every head and action. She imagined Nema's letter growing heavier in her bag with each passing minute, and wondered how well Roni could lie when pressed. If Lescaux possessed any wit at all, he would have wanted to reassure himself of the letter's presence immediately after ordering Jani off Exterior property. That meant Roni would have had to stall. *Straddle that third base line, McGaw.* What Jani planned to do, she could complete in a few hours. After that, let Lescaux track her down.

The train slowed. Stopped. Jani pushed along with the crush, shifting her duffel so she could guard it by holding it against her chest, grabbing at the handrails to keep from falling as her right knee grew wobbly.

The Registry resided on LaSalle Street, in a silvery glass tower that possessed the smooth, featureless surfaces of refrozen ice. Jani pushed through the nonscan front entry into the skylit lobby, then immediately veered to the right and palmed through another set of doors that funneled down a narrow hallway. As the doors swept aside, she saw Dolly Aryton standing at the hall's far end, distant smile still in place.

"Prompt, as always. Hansen always said he trusted you more than any timepiece." The reserve cracked as she watched Jani walk toward her. She folded her arms and touched a fist to her chin—the contact turned to tapping that became faster and faster as the distance between them shortened. "My God."

"You already said that, Doll."

"Then I'll say it again. My God." Dolly looked Jani up and down, ticking off the differences between the woman with whom she'd schooled and the one that stood before her now. "It suits you, though. It hides. Gives the impression that you are what you're not." She took a step back—she wore trousers and wrap shirt in an autumnal shade of melon, and the flowing material swept around her wrists and ankles. "Collected. Contained."

Jani suppressed a sharp comment. Her back griped from the walk, and she was in no mood for Dolly's pronouncements. "I *am* collected and contained."

"If you insist." Dolly took a step closer, her gaze fixed on the top of Jani's head. "You're taller than I am now."

"*Yes.*" Jani stared until Dolly arched her brow and backed away.

"As I said, Carson and I have been waiting for you to call." Dolly turned and walked up the hall toward the lift-bank, gesturing for Jani to follow. "Now you have. Since we both know you're not the sentimental sort, to what do I owe this reunion?"

Jani realized protest would be futile. Dolly had pegged her during their comport conversation—it was one of her more disconcerting talents. *Business. I'm here for business. That's all I ever had in common with you and Carson, and Gina, and Ennie.* Only the long-dead Hansen had been a friend. *You others are just people I used to know.* She followed Dolly into the lift car and waited for the doors to close. "It's Nema."

Dolly frowned. "I understand he's having a hard time working with Shai."

"It's gone beyond that. I believe Shai and Cèel are trying to force him from office."

"That's *our* style. The idomeni don't operate that way."

"I think they're starting to learn."

Dolly appeared to stare at the floor indicator, but Jani could detect the far-off look in her eyes, the telltale sign of a wicked turn of thought. "You think Nema's in danger."

"Yes, I do—" The lift decelerated, and Jani grabbed the railing as her head rocked and a wave of chills shook her. *What the hell's wrong now!* Maybe she should have eaten at the mall. Maybe her second dance with augie neared its finale, signaling the end to her ability to concentrate. Or maybe yet another new wrinkle had developed in her ever-changing physical state.

"Are you all right?" Dolly moved toward her, voice mellow with concern.

Jani hurried out of the lift as soon as the door opened and ducked into a furnished alcove. "Dolly, I may not have much time." She lowered into a chair and dropped her bag over the side. "I need a vacuumbox, a full set of tools, and access to paper and chips. I need . . . a copier."

Dolly crouched in front of her. She pressed a hand to Jani's forehead, then to her cheek. "You're *freezing.* You need a doctor."

"I'm used to it—it will pass!" Jani grabbed Dolly's wrist and yanked her hand away from her face. She didn't think she squeezed that hard—why did Dolly wince? "I have a lot to do and not much time in which to do it. Someone is depending on me—I need to get started now."

Dolly straightened smoothly, like the athlete she was. "You want to copy a document, then alter the copy." Her dulcet voice hardened. "You want to fake—"

"The thing I've got is a fake. I just want to make another fake with a few differences. Then I want to feed it back into play and watch where the alarms sound."

Dolly turned away and walked across the alcove to the picture window behind them. She considered the view as precious seconds ticked by. "I look out this window, eighty floors above the streets of Chicago, but what I see is the Rauta Shèràa Consulate courtyard. I can feel the summer's raw heat through the glass. I expect to see Laumrau skimmers float into view, and watch the Laumrau walk and gesture again. Hear their loopy voices." She pressed her palms against the pane. "All because you show up in rough clothes with a bag on your shoulder and a wild story about Nema. You look different, yet the same, and anyone who doubted your identity would know you as soon as you opened your mouth. Always scamming. Always feeding back. Always looking for alarms." She turned. Her face held sadness and frustration. "That war is over, and this one, if this is indeed one, is none of your business."

Jani hoisted her duffel onto her lap. It dragged like lead. "I need your help."

"This is Registry. We're supposed to *stop* what you want to do."

"I only have a few hours."

"You're not listening."

"*Neither are you.* I want to replace what I believe to be a fake with another fake. A double-reverse. Registry investigators do it all the time when they suspect documents fraud and they want to trace-back."

"You have no jurisdiction."

Jani tried to stand. Her head rocked. "Maybe Carson will help me. You said he's down the street at NUVA-SCAN?" She tried to grab the chair arms for balance, missed, and fell back.

Dolly's hands flew to her face. "You never grew up, did you? You just got older!" She cut around furniture and hurried to her side. "What is the matter with you!"

Jani struggled to a half-crouch, then slowly rose. "I need a vacuumbox, tools, a copier, and access to supplies. I came here because I knew that you'd have it all at the ready."

Dolly grabbed her arm to help support her. "You're in no condition—"

Jani pressed a hand to her stomach, and felt as well as heard the grumble. "Get me food. Chili. Curry. Something spicy. No milk or cheese. Bread—bread is good, but no butter. And coffee." She looked into her old schoolmate's eyes, and saw the anger and the aggravation. *"Dolly. Please."* She tried to get the sense of the sailracer, to find the wedge that would win her the opening she needed. "One thing you must admit, Dorothea Aryton, grubby, raving thing that I was—"

"I never said grubby or—"

"—is that on those hot summer days at the Rauta Shèràa Consulate, the one thing I never did was waste your time."

Something flickered in Dolly's eyes. Not a softening—never that, not between them. A touch of memory, maybe. Of jobs done well, and more importantly, of those left undone. She gripped Jani's arm more firmly, positioning herself so that they could walk side-by-side. "The Registry cannot support you if this backfires."

Jani almost sagged with relief, but stopped herself. Dolly wouldn't be a sure sale until the job was done, and she couldn't allow her any excuse to back out. "Of course not."

They started down the hall toward the workrooms. As they passed a sealed door, Jani caught the sulfurous rank of the nutrient tanks, where the new scanpack brains grew and developed. Her empty stomach turned.

With moves practiced on sailboards throughout the Commonwealth, Dolly countered her sag and struggled to hold her steady. "I'm taking you to the hospital."

"Fine. But not until I'm done."

Jani braced her feet on her lab chair crossbar and balanced her plate on her knees. The curried chicken with peanut sauce had cleared her head marvelously. She sopped up the remains of the sauce with bread, then washed it down with coffee that rivaled John Shroud's for punch and depth. She looked down to the far end of the lab bench, where Dolly leaned in skeptical examination, and raised her cup. "My compliments to your kitchen."

"Thank you." Dolly straightened as the door opened and two techs entered pushing laden skimcarts. "Put them here." She led them to benches on the opposite side of the large laboratory, and helped them unload the cart contents onto the benchtops.

Jani set her plate aside and eased off the seat. Her internal choppy seas had calmed—no more lightheadedness, and she felt stronger. She picked up her duffel and walked across the lab to where Dolly oversaw the unloading. "Got anything that can scan idomeni paper?"

Dolly shrugged halfheartedly. "We have some prototypes, but nothing I'd stake my rating on. Every document we get from them self-destructs when we try to crack it." She gave Jani a look of calculated disinterest. "We've begun to work with Neoclona to develop a scanpack that can read both types of chips. John's been very helpful."

"Has he?"

"Yes. We talk about you on occasion. I'm surprised you have trouble with him—I've always found him quite easy to work with."

He doesn't perceive you as a professional threat and he doesn't love you. Congrats—you've got the best of both worlds. Jani dropped her duffel onto a benchtop and opened it. She removed The Nema Letter, but left it in its slipcase as the techs unloaded the last of the equipment, killing time by leafing through the other documents Roni had given her in the hope they might prove interesting. Unfortunately, they turned out to be face pages and forewords from unrelated reports, dross and decoy only.

After the techs departed, she slid the heavy parchment out of the protective cover and lay it on the counter. "Some factions in Service and the government think Nema composed this document, which warns us against allowing the Haárin to continue to infiltrate the colonies. They take it as a sign that he'd like to serve as our agent."

"I gather I should keep this information to myself?" Dolly removed an elegant pair of wire-rimmed magnispecs from the pocket of her wrapshirt and put them on. "I don't believe it. Nema couldn't keep his mouth shut long enough to pull off a subterfuge like that." She picked up the document by the barest edges and eyed it from all angles. "Humans did this."

"Agreed. I'm worried, though, that if Shai and Cèel learn this letter exists, they'll use it as an excuse to recall Nema whether they think he compiled it or not. If they choose to regard it as a Laum–Knevçet Shèràa-scale treachery, they may take a more drastic step than mere recall. They may just kill him and be done with it." Jani removed the letter from Dolly's grasp, then moved down the bench toward a large rectangular instrument that looked like a handscanner with a lid. "So this is the devil's device?"

"The latest iteration." Dolly pushed her magnispecs atop her head, then slid aside the copier lid and pondered her reflection in the black glass surface. "Officially, it doesn't exist. Unofficially, we don't talk about it." She cast Jani a hard look. "And you treat it like just another tool in the tray."

"That's because it is." Jani nudged Dolly aside and laid the letter ink-side down on the copier surface. "How long does the duplication take?"

"Anywhere from fifteen minutes to five hours, depending on the complexity of the document." Dolly lowered the lid, then touched the side panel. Slivers of white light shone through hairline gaps in the seal. "First pass, it types the paper strata. Then it moves to inks, then foils. Those are easy—five minutes, tops."

"Then comes the fun." Jani watched as the color and intensity of the light slivers changed. Blazing blue. Dark red. An almost invisible green. "Reading the types of imbedded chips and identifying their settings."

"Assuming they'll let themselves be read." Dolly dragged over a lab chair and sat. "Proprietary paper locks this thing up like a dream. It knows a chip is there, but it can't read it, and it pitches a fit. Buzzes. Jams. Lights start blinkin'." She smoothed a well-manicured hand over the sleeve of her shirt. "I christened it 'Jani' some time ago."

"Thanks." Jani pulled over a chair, positioning it so she could watch the copier's every flash and flutter. "What would you say if I told you that the chips embedded in this document contain seventeen separate discrepancies, all of which make scanpacks scream aloud?"

"This copier is capable of error analysis. It should be able to untangle the snarl and define the problem when all a scan-pack can do is tell you you're outside variance. What that implies to me is that whoever constructed this document never believed it would see the inside of Registry, which I find interesting considering the magnitude of the matter." Dolly plucked a pair of pinch-grips from the tool tray, and regarded them thoughtfully. "If you were out . . . in the field, how long would it take you to manufacture a copy like this?"

Euphemisms, euphemisms. "The class of criminal I worked with—" Jani stopped as Sasha's face formed in her mind. *You were never better than you had to be, Kilian—never forget that.* "I wouldn't have been able to. I couldn't access gear like this. I didn't work at the organized crime level. An exact copy of even a simple deed could take me weeks. Exact placement of chips and inserts is a bitch without a 3-D field array marking the positions. I'd have to do my best with my scanpack and a handheld measuring device. That's why low-level scams involve altering existing paper. Building a document from scratch is hard enough. Making an identical copy is beyond the capacity of most forgers unless they have access to something like this copier."

"Interesting." Dolly still concentrated her attention on the pinch-grips. "Carson mentioned to me just last week that your varied experiences made you a valuable resource. He asked that if I ran into you first, I should tell you that there's a position at NUVA-SCAN with your name on it."

Jani tried to visualize herself in a staid corporate confer-ence room, surrounded by Family types. "Hmm."

"Here, too."

That brought Jani up short. She turned to Dolly to find her still enraptured by the pinch-grips. "Really?"

"We here at Registry nurse a fondness for the criminal mind. Saves training." Dolly looked up as the colored lights dimmed and a length of tissue-thin fiche spun out of the copier. "Well, that was fast. It's already time for the second act." She picked up the fiche and studied it. "Colony-sourced paper." She glanced at Jani. "Does Acadia tie into this at all?"

The home of L'araignée. "It might." She joined Dolly benchside. "Commercial or government-class?"

"Commercial. Fairly recent dating—early summer." Dolly walked across the lab to one of the wall-spanning cabinets, fiche in hand, and opened it to reveal shelf upon shelf filled with niche after niche of virgin paperstock. She pulled down her magnispecs so she could read the printed labels on the topmost shelves, then reached up and removed a single piece of parchment from one of the niches. "I doubt it would be government. Even if a Ministry is behind this, you wouldn't expect them to play quite so obvious a hand as to use their own paper, would you?"

"I would have expected them to cut to the chase and use idomeni paper. Nema would have used idomeni paper. Whoever planned this tried to be too clever." Jani stood up to watch as Dolly fed the sheet into a slot on the copier's side.

"The chips and foils are stored inside—saves on oxidative wear and tear." Dolly watched the paper disappear into the slot. Then she handed Jani the fiche with the air of a stern teacher returning a below-average grade. "In a few minutes, you will have an exact copy of your not-very-complicated letter." Her voice dropped an accusing half-tone. "Then it will be your turn, to do whatever it is that you do."

Jani perused the discrepancies the copier had listed. "Looks like Jani Junior had problems with the initiator chip, just like my scanpack did. Can't define the error, though. Same with the others."

Dolly leaned back against her seat and folded her arms. "If those *are* idomeni chips loaded in that paper, then Jani Junior won't be able to read them. It will know that something is awry with the coding, but because of the differences between the idomeni proteins and ours, it won't be able to define the differences. I have no idomeni standards to load into Junior—I can't give it anything to compare to."

"That's been the problem with this all along." Jani picked

through the UV styli scattered throughout the assorted trays. "The only way to prove this is indeed an idomeni document is to have an idomeni documents examiner scan it, and no one I've been working with wants that to happen because they don't want Shèrá to know what's going on."

"Convenient, that. You can construct as loopy a document as you want because no one who knows which end is up is ever going to get their hands on it to check it out." Dolly shifted restlessly. "So what are you going to do?"

"It shouldn't take long." Jani held the styli in her fist like a child gripping her coloring pens, and waited for the freshly imprinted document to emerge from the copier. "A shot here. A shot there." She let the paper slide onto her open palm, then walked down the bench to the vacuumbox. "The time-date stamp is still untouched. So's the counter chip that records the number of scans." Jani glanced at Dolly. "Would it count the copy as a scan?"

Dolly nodded. "Possibly."

"Then it fries." Jani slipped the document into the vacuumbox slot, tucked the styli in the box's access drawer, then stuck her hands in the gloves that would allow her to manipulate the materials in the vacuum. "And I bake the Environmental Variant."

Dolly's eyes slowly widened. "You're going to make the discrepancies look like a Brandenburg Progession."

"Yup." Jani positioned the document in the center of the vacuumbox platform, then looked through the lens array so she could visualize both the chips she needed to hit and the beams of UV light she needed to hit them with. "A prionic mutation that's initiated by broad-spectrum UV damage and eventually spreads throughout the document, rendering it unscanable."

"Those are extremely rare." Dolly closed in beside her. "And the mutation proceeds at a well-defined rate, hence the name."

"How many dexxies have seen one, do you think?" Jani chose one of the styli and activated it. "A real Progression, not the idealized deterioration they teach in school." She directed the thread-thin beam at the time-date chip. *Light . . . hit!* "After this gets out, you may get a few panicked calls.

Professional reputations at stake, and all that." She activated the second stylus and directed it at the counter chip. *Light . . . hit!*

"I can stall, I suppose." Dolly's voice held a dubious edge.

"They'll fall all over themselves for a few days in the excitement of it all, before one of them cottons on that they may have been had." Jani zeroed in on the environmental chip. *Light . . . hit!* "And a few days should be more time than I need."

"For?"

"For 'Gotcha.' " Jani pulled out of the vacuumbox, then removed the styli and documents from the transfer drawers. "That special moment that we who have never grown up enjoy so much." She slid the faked Nema Letter into the smooth Exterior slipcase with the other documents and tucked the slipcase into her duffel. She felt wonderfully vigorous and alive now, in a way that seemed improbable only a half-hour before.

Then she turned to Dolly, found that grave countenance regarding her sadly, and felt the joy crack.

"I think I should keep this. It'll give me a chance to run some of the hybrid prototypes through their paces." Dolly slid the original letter into a Registry slipcase. The silvery surface caught the room light and flashed back stars. "Unless I find something, we won't be able to prove beyond doubt that those chips are not idomeni in origin. Nema may have worked out something like this to make sure all roads led back to him—are you willing to bet your 'pack that he isn't involved?"

Jani shouldered her bag. "I think . . ." The new letter felt as heavy as the old—she imagined Roni's growing panic weighing it down. "I think that if Nema realized how Shai and Cèel are working to cut him off, he would try something like this. And he'd fail. And he'd be executed by year's end." She checked her timepiece—she needed to go. But an explanation was owed, and she needed to provide it. "He suspects something is wrong. That's one reason I'm working so fast. I've made him promise to behave until I tell him it's all clear, but you remember how he was."

"Yes." Dolly fingered the edge of the slipcase. "I never liked him."

"I know." Jani turned to leave. "Therein the insurmountable difference between thee and me."

Jani deflected Dolly's insistence that she go to hospital with vague noises about an appointment to see John. Dolly threatened to follow up with a call of her own to her new work partner. Jani knew she'd be well away before her lie was discovered, so she responded with a cheery "go ahead."

She traveled home via the usual assortment of Ls and people-movers. She had overshot her self-allotted few hours, and knew Roni must be feeling the brunt of all Lescaux could bring to bear. *Whatever that is.* She didn't like him and that alone made her wary of him, since she seldom disliked a person without reason. *Even if that reason is that he's Lucien's twin, seen through a distorted mirror?* She clucked her tongue. *My, aren't we the philosophical one?*

She disembarked the last 'mover two blocks from home because her thigh muscles had cramped and she knew exercise would loosen them. She kept a brisk pace, and turned onto Armour Place to the loud pops of fastener guns and the hum of machinery as the construction crew within the renovation continued their labors.

She spotted Roni McGaw near the renovation entry, standing apart from the small crowd that had gathered to watch workers unload metal framework from a flatbed skimmer. As soon as Roni saw Jani, she turned in the opposite direction and walked, a slow, relaxed pace. She proceeded for half a block, then entered a small bookstore, successfully resisting any urge she may have felt to look behind to see if Jani followed.

By the time Jani entered the bookstore, Roni had already settled in front of a rack of audio wafers. Jani fingered through a bin of new releases until she found a collection of pop songs. She added a holozine so that they would be forced to give her a large sack to carry them in, and headed for the checkout.

Roni got in line behind her. She held an audio wafer as

well, supplemented with another holozine the same size as Jani's.

Jani paid for her purchases with a nontrace chit. As she walked through the store to the exit, she picked through the outer pockets of her duffel as though she searched for something. Finally, she crouched on the floor and opened her duffel, picking through the folders. She tucked the sack in amid the folders, sliding the slipcase containing the faked Nema letter deftly between the pages of the holozine. Then she pulled the sack out again, as though she'd changed her mind.

As she straightened, she felt an elbow impact her shoulder. She dropped her duffel and bag to the floor.

"Oh Christ!" Roni didn't even look her in the face as she bustled about picking up bags. Jani barely caught the switch, so deftly did Roni obscure matters with the flaps of her jacket and general dithering. Then she was gone, out the door, the bag with the faked letter clutched to her chest, leaving Jani with a holozine about birds and, she was pleased to see, a copy of the Mussorgska she'd been meaning to buy for weeks.

Jani felt the adrenaline ebb for the third time that day as she trudged back to her building. She recovered her deliveries from Hodge, and scanned everything in the hall before opening her door. Even the parcel from Roni. Even the soles of her shoes.

She yawned as she entered her flat. She set everything aside but the Mussorgska, which she inserted into her audio system. Then she stretched out on the floor beside her desk, and shoved her duffel under her head to serve as a pillow. A nap before dinner with Steve and Angevin was a necessity if she wanted to avoid pitching face-forward onto her plate. As the strings swelled around her, she closed her eyes and pondered Roni's surprising competence, and the possibilities of alarms.

CHAPTER 11

Tsecha walked the embassy grounds, in the hope that exercise would soothe him. He felt disquiet when he remained in the embassy, a sense that things went on of which he did not know. So many humanish whom he had never before seen. So many meetings that he heard of *after* they had taken place.

It was one thing to refuse to go to the damned meetings. It was another to know you were not wanted.

But my Jani wishes me to wait. For what? *Until it is safe.* And what did that mean? *She does not trust me to tell me.* No one trusted him anymore, so it seemed, and truly.

"I am Égri nìRau Tsecha. Representative of the Shèrá worldskein and Chief Propitiator of the Vynshàrau." So he spoke to the grass and the trees, which paid him as much attention as did any in the embassy. Even his Sànalàn had not wished him a glorious day, as she had each morning since her investiture.

He strode past the main building, the annexes, the row upon row of greenhouses and food storage facilities. Gradually, his step quickened and his stride widened, as though he could outdistance his worries if he tried. The pound of his feet striking the ground jarred along his spine and shook him to the teeth. His old joints protested the abuse, but he denied their plea, and picked up his pace even more.

Across the brilliant blue-green hybrid ground cover. Past the utilities huts. Through the barrier parks that sheltered the embassy property from the view of the neighboring Interior Ministry.

Tsecha broke through the last line of trees and stopped

atop the rise to recover his breath. Below him lay the boundary area just inside the perimeter security stations that served as the dividing line between Vynshàrau and humanish. He surveyed the scattering of lowform structures that dotted the sequestration. *Our own place between the lines.* The compound where the Vynshàrau Haárin lived.

Tsecha took a step forward, then hesitated as a male emerged from one of the houses carrying a large bucket.

It is Sànalàn's tormenting tilemaster. Dathim Naré had removed his head cover. He had also exchanged his dull work uniform for a shirt that blazed blue as clear sky and trousers as green as humanish lawns, colors of the sky and sea more common to the southland-dwelling Pathen than the desert Vynshàrau. In spite of the chill, he wore no overrobe. He had rolled up his shirtsleeves and turned down the cuffs of his black boots—perspiration darkened his clothes as though he had run through a rainstorm.

Tsecha watched him upturn the bucket into a debris barrel. Shards of white tile clattered into the bin, flashing sunlight like the teeth of demons.

Dathim banged the bucket against the rim of the barrel— the clang of metal on metal filled the air as white dust clouded about him like smoke. He did not see Tsecha until he turned to walk back to the house. When he did, he stopped in mid-stride, the empty bucket dangling at his side.

"Glor-ries of the day to you, Tsechar-rau!" he shouted in trilled English, as though his Chief Propitiator's appearance was a common thing, worthy of the informality.

"Glories of the day to you, ní Dathim." Tsecha strolled down the rise toward him. "A cold day, and truly. How can you tolerate such?"

The male looked down at his bare forearms. His *à lérine* scars shone dark gold-brown and waled, as though parasites burrowed beneath his skin. "Today I retile a laving room, nìRau." He reached for his belt and took an ax-tail hammer from his tool-holster. "Removing the old is hard work. Hard work warms the blood." He swung the tool through the air— the sharply pointed hammer cut the air with a whistle, while the polished blade-end slivered white light into rainbow glisten.

Tsecha watched the back and forth of the hammer with tense fascination. As the Laumrau–Vynshà civil war had neared its bloody conclusion and weapons had grown scarce, the traditional tool had helped the forces of Morden nìRau Cèel capture the dominant city of Rauta Shèràa. They had, of course, not been used during the final battle, when the Vynshà had confirmed their ascendancy to "rau" and order had again been restored to the Shèrá worldskein. The Night of the Blade had been reserved for classical swords and knives, masterpieces of godly workmanship.

But there had been other nights. . . .

"You are on patrol, nìRau?" Dathim cocked his head in the direction of the Interior Ministry as he returned the ax-hammer to his holster. "The Interiors patrol many times a day. Four, five, six times or more. They watch us as the Laum did. I think myself in the High Sands when they pass in their skimmers."

High Sands. As much as he enjoyed his English, Tsecha did not like the postureless, gestureless translation of Rauta Shèràa. It left out so much. The prayers and the blood and the pain. "You are of the Shèràa, ní Dathim?"

"Yes, nìRau." Dathim tipped his bucket and clapped the bottom, forcing out the last puff of tile dust. "We lived in the city since my body-father's body-mother's outcast. Her Haárin name was Par Tenvin. My body-father's name was Naré Par." He reattached the bucket handle, which had loosened at one end because of his pounding. "And you know who I am."

Tsecha basked in the Haárin's arrogance. After the collected silence of the embassy, it felt as the warm winds of home. "Three generations? That is not so long."

"It is for Haárin. So many have gone to the colonies that three generations is a very long time indeed." Dathim bared his teeth. "No longer three, since I am here now. In She-ca-gho."

Tsecha studied Dathim—something about his appearance bothered him, but he could not say what. Then it struck him. Dathim wore his brown hair in neither the tight napeknot of an unbred or the braided fringe of a breeder. Instead, he had sheared it as short as some humanish males, his golden scalp bare above his ears and visible beneath the spiky, brush-like growth. A stunning thing, and truly. Tsecha had heard that some colonial Haárin had taken to shearing their hair, but he never expected to find such rebellion in the embassy itself. "You like Chicago, ní Dathim?"

"Like?" Dathim offered a perfect imitation of Jani's infuriatingly vague shrug. "It is a place like any other. Humanish are strange. But where humanish are is a good place for Haárin. To them, we are as born-sect. We are all we need to be." He bared his teeth again, though not so broadly. "Unless we are not careful, and take too much of their money. Then they will find a reason to hate us. I have read of humanish, so this I know, and truly."

As they spoke, they walked down the narrow stone path that led to Dathim's house. Like the other structures in the sequestration, the smooth-sided whitestone dwelling had been built along godly lines. All the doors and windows faced the tree barrier so that no inadvertent glimpse of humanish could be seen. The yellow polywood door had been polished to smooth glossiness, the only decoration a line of cursive carved across the top. A prayer to Shiou, the goddess of order.

As Dathim pushed the door aside, Tsecha noticed a walled-off area set along the lake-facing side of the house. "You have rebuilt your veranda, ní Dathim?" He walked around the side of the house and fingered the edge of the wall. The allowed paints transported from Rauta Shèràa had been formulated for desert climates—constant exposure to the lake-tinged air caused them to mottle. Dathim's once-white wall had already stained streaky grey, but as Tsecha recalled, it took a season or more for the discoloration to form. "You rebuilt it some time ago, from the look of it, and truly."

"Yes, nìRau Tsecha." Dathim's amber eyes focused above Tsecha's head, as was seemly.

"I only gave permission for the verandas to reopen for meditation last month."

"The humanish had deeded us the Lake Michigan Strip months ago, nìRau." Dathim gestured toward the water. "All ours, lake below and sky above, from here to the eastern

Michigan province. They have not been able to transport foodstuffs across that area since they made their pledge. The place became clean as soon as they made their promise."

Tsecha gestured in emphasis. "Yes, but the final purifications were only completed during the last days of the blessed heat. Oligarch Cèel decreed the verandas could not be reopened until I pronounced those closing prayers." He raised his gaze until he could see into Dathim's eyes, and savored the hard light he saw there. Different than humanish. Most easy to read.

"Oligarch Cèel is overcautious, as always," Dathim replied. "We felt it safe to rebuild." His speech had slowed so every word sounded crisp and sharp.

"We?"

Dathim pointed to the other houses, one by one. "We." His gaze dropped until he looked Tsecha in the face.

The thrill of rebellion warred with the need for order in Tsecha's soul. He pressed his hand to his stomach to quell the battle. "Someone in the embassy must have known of this. So strange, and truly, that they did not tell me."

"Shai's suborn came here. We spoke." Dathim shrugged again. "But what can they do? What can you do? We are already outcast. We have lied and stolen, behaved in ways ungodly, seen more of humanish than you ever will, and for such have already paid with our souls."

"There are other punishments, ní Dathim."

"Yes, nìRau. You can send us back to the worldskein. But if you do, you will need to find more English-speakers who can mend the plumbing and tend the lawns and go out into ungodly Chicago when poison is needed to kill Earth insects or solder is needed to bind our godly but most leaky metal conduits. No matter how much you ship and how well you think you prepare, there will always be needs to go out into this city, and that is what we are for."

Tsecha crossed his open hands, palms up, in strong affirmation. "Such has always been the contract between Vynshàrau and Haárin. As when we were of Vynshà. As it has always been."

Dathim smiled with his mouth closed, an oversubtle expression that, combined with his haircut, made him look eerily humanish. "Yes, as it has always been. In whatever life you choose, in war and in peace, we are your glove, your mask, your shield. By doing that which we do, we allow you to be what you are. Such is our cost. But in exchange for having us do what we do, you must allow us to be as we are. Such is yours."

Tsecha's shoulders rounded as his enjoyment of Dathim's insubordination gave way to irritation. No Vynshàrau knew better than he of the defiant nature of Haárin, but he had done nothing to merit this outburst. "*I* have always known this, ní Dathim. Such is no surprise to *me*."

"No," said Dathim, his shoulders rounding in response. "No surprise to you. Avrèl nìRau Nema always knew how to use his Haárin well."

Tsecha slumped more, until he had to twist his neck to the side to look up at the taller male. He should have dropped his gaze, should have stared at the center of Dathim's chest. Such was much more seemly, but such, he sensed, would not meet Dathim's challenge. And Dathim challenged him, most assuredly. *But he has no right! He has no reason!* No, yet he did so. "That name has no place between us." Tsecha's voice emerged as a low rumble. "I did not give you leave to use it."

"No." The light in Dathim's eyes brightened. "Such is for your favored humanish and those in Council and Temple who have declared themselves against you. For all else, you are called by your Sìah Haárin name. Tsecha. Fool. But you do not live as a Haárin fool." He gestured toward the tree line. "You live a most godly life on the other side."

"I am still Chief Propitiator of the Vynshàrau. As such, I live where I must."

"Convenient, is it not, and truly?" Dathim straightened his shoulders and walked to his doorway. "I am unworthy to stand before you, nìRau Tsecha. Still, I beg you to enter this place and witness my labors." He looked back. "To bless them and remove all traces of ungodliness."

Tsecha watched the tilt of Dathim's head, his open-handed gesturing. He could detect no outward sign of disrespect—the male had learned to reserve such for his speech. *How humanish of him.* "I will bless your home, ní Dathim."

He followed his refractory host into the house. *Whether the gods acknowledge the request is their decision.*

As he passed through the short entry hall, Dathim touched his left hand first to a small, black-stained wooden box that hung at eye-level on the wall, then to his stomach.

A reliquary? Dathim did not seem the type. Tsecha raised his hand to mimic his host's actions, but stopped just before his fingers contacted the box's surface. The front of the device held only a single decoration, but it was most distinctive. A clenched fist, gnarled and bony, the crumbled remains of some object barely visible between the fingers.

Caith. The goddess of annihilation. The least or the most of the Vynshàrau's eight dominant deities, depending on your point of view.

"It is a most blessed relic." Dathim stood in the center of the small main room and watched Tsecha with still regard. "It is from the crater at the Sands of Light's Weeping. At the site where the asteroid impacted so long ago, the heat melted the sand to glass. That reliquary contains a shard of the glass."

"Sands of Light's Weeping." Tsecha could barely force out the English words. "Knevçet Shèràa."

"Yes, nìRau. A blessed place, and truly."

"You worship Shiou on your doorway and Caith in your home. Such opposing views are most unusual. So unusual that it is a question whether one can trust them."

"All the doors here are the same. It would make more sense to say the builder of these houses worships Shiou." Dathim thumped a fist against his stomach. "The reliquary is mine."

And this is supposed to mean what *to me!* Tsecha pressed a hand to his own stomach, not to soothe his soul but to quell the growing ache. "You vex me, Dathim."

"I do what I do, nìRau." Dathim walked to his tree-facing window and swept the curtain aside, but the northern light did little to brighten the room. "As she did what she did. Your humanish. Twenty-six Laumrau died at the Sands of Light's Weeping. Twenty-six Laumrau with no Haárin to guard them—your Kièrshia shot them as they took sacrament in their tents."

"She did so to save her suborns. The Laumrau would have killed them if she had not acted."

"But yet they died, as well. Her suborns." Dathim tilted his head in enquiry. "We have heard that van Reuter killed them. The Family member who is now much as Haárin, out-cast among his own. Do you believe such was the case?" He shrugged again when Tsecha remained silent. "Sands of Light's Weeping. The Laumrau had attained many triumphs over the Vynshà until that point. After the slaughter, the tide of the war, as the humanish say, turned." Dathim stood still and silent by the window. Then he brushed his hands across the front of his shirt as though to clean them. "Come with me, nìRau. See what I labor upon."

Tsecha trudged forward, taking care to keep his eyes focused on Dathim's back so he would not see something he should not. He had never lived in such a house, where rooms and screened barriers served the same function as entire wings did in the embassy. He had no wish to look into Dathim's kitchen. It pained him to think what he might find there.

After only a few steps, he found himself a reluctant occupant of the laving room doorway. He allowed himself a small relief as he bore witness only to cloth-covered flooring, expanses of stripped wall, and stacks of colored tile.

Then he looked at the wall behind the small sink, and stared.

The sand dunes rolled across the space as they did in his memories of home. The colors warmed him by their very presence—the pale gold of the sand, the red-brown of the shadowed troughs between the dunes, the ivory of the peaks where the relentless sun drove all color away. All manner of tile shape, from square to circle to splinter, combined to form the scene, resolving into a whole as he drew away, then fracturing into discrete scenes as he drew close. Here, a scatter of stones. There, the curve of a bird in flight.

"I will replace the glaring white of the walls with this." Dathim picked up a square of lightest sand and held it out for inspection. "And I will edge near the ceiling and the floor with the red-brown of the shadows."

As when he first saw the cava shell in the embassy, Tsecha

found himself groping for words to describe the beauty of the scene. "You do not reuse the tile you broke?" he finally asked, because he did not want Dathim to know how the magnificence of his work affected him.

Dathim shook his head. "That tile was inferior. It would not take a break well—it shattered into irregular pieces. And the color was too stark. I could not make it blend with the rest. And to blend is a good thing, is it not, nìRau?"

Tsecha picked up one of the sand squares and turned it over. "There is no purity mark." He pointed to the blank surface. "No cursive signatory of the maker. This tile is not of idomeni."

"No, nìRau. It is humanish. I purchase it in this city."

"How ungodly." Tsecha spoke as to himself. "You go into the city often?"

"Yes, nìRau. After I finish my work at the embassy. I do work for others here"—he gestured in the direction of the other houses—"repairs and alterations."

Tsecha set down the tile, his gaze drifting again to the desert scene. "It is a creation of great beauty, and truly. One who conceives such deserves the blessing of the gods."

"To serve well is its own blessing, nìRau." Dathim picked up an abrading cloth and wiped it across an area of the wall still rough with old grout. "I serve this task as I do my others. Every morning, before the sunrise, I join my skein-sharers in the common room behind the central utilities array." White powder spilled at his feet, greying his trousers and coating his black boots. "It is a good place. Quiet. Not a place where born-sects deign to gather, but I am still grateful for the small shelf where I store my tools and the section of bench where I can sit."

Damn you, Haárin! Tsecha grappled with the urge to kick at the stacks of tile and send them clattering across the room. How Dathim could beckon and repel with the same words. Offer, and then take back. *But offer what?* He did not understand. *It is the way Dathim speaks.* Yes, that was the reason for his confusion, and truly. "How did you learn your English, ní Dathim?"

"I learn by listening, nìRau." Dathim continued to abrade the wall as he turned and looked Tsecha in the face. "I am a most accomplished listener, and truly." The words hung in the air, then filtered down as the dust. "You call your Kièr-shia 'nìaRauta Haárin.' "

Tsecha sighed. "Yes."

"It is said that she is hybridizing, changing into a not-quite-idomeni, not-quite-humanish." The soft rasp of the cloth filled the tiny room. The stone smelled of the powder. "You have said you believe we will all be as she is, that the worlds will command us to change, that our bodies will listen to the order of the worlds, and all will be the same."

Tsecha thought of his Jani. Their discussion in the garden. The way she moved and the strangeness of her eyes. "The commands have sounded in some colonies. They take different forms. In some worlds, a sickness in the bones, in others, an ache in the soul or an inability to eat blessed foods. But our physician-priests deny the will of the gods. They name it 'environmentally induced chimerization.' They attack it as illness and drive it away."

"Environmentally induced chimerization," Dathim repeated. "The annihilation of that which is." He removed the ax-hammer from his belt. "So often have I seen you walk this place, as fast as if demons chased you, pondering your 'that which is.' " He tapped the pointed hammer end sharply against a remaining expanse of white tile. "The Elyan Haárin will no longer be allowed to do business with humanish. So says my facilities dominant." The tile cracked like thin ice—Dathim pried it from the wall with the edge of the ax-blade, and the pieces tumbled to the canvas. "But that is not what you would have, is it, nìRau? You wish that this business continue. You would even allow it to grow, would you not? You would allow us to trade freely with humanish."

Tsecha watched Dathim work, and pondered their strange conversation. The Haárin's unwarranted challenges. The way he changed subjects, which made his words as difficult to follow as Jani's at her most obscure.

Only three generations as Haárin—I would have thought many more, if this one's attitude is as that of his forebears—

Tsecha's memory opened. Dathim's words served as key.

The emotions of disputation. The smell of the dust. The beauty of the sand dunes. Together, they took him back to Rauta Shèràa, and the time when he answered to his born name, and many were the Haárin who came to him.

Memories. They revealed to him how to rework Dathim's words into the old patterns, the old vows.

I, Dathim Naré, outcast by way of Naré Par, who was outcast by way of Par Tenvin, offer myself in service to you, Avrèl nìRau Nema. I am skilled in tilecraft. I know facilities, and the ways of the embassy. I can go out into the city unimpeded, because such is my purpose and my way.

I know how to speak between lines.

I know your beliefs. I, too, await the annihilation of the old ways. Cèel and Shai are of the old ways, and I owe no loyalty to them.

I know you have walked this way many times. I have seen you. I planned to call out to you, boldly and openly, the next time you walked. And so I did.

I have been waiting for you.

Tsecha felt aspects of himself that he lately set aside, rejoin. Unlike the shards on the floor, never to be mended, his own fragments reshaped, his hope, fear, and anger. His pride. The glue that held them was the awareness that he had not felt for so long. That he was Vynshàrau of Shèràa, and that a Haárin who wished to serve well had offered him his aid. "Yes, ní Dathim, I would allow you to trade freely."

"As you say, nìRau." Dathim tapped and pulled. More tile tumbled to the covered floor. "Tomorrow is my first visit to the Exterior Ministry. I must study the room in person, assess the light and the space, and decide which scene will suit Her Excellency best."

Once more, Tsecha felt the cold of the air and heard the silence of the trees. "Shai agreed to allow you to work in the Ministry?"

"Yes, nìRau. Did she not tell you?" Dathim continued to work, his back to Tsecha, his sheared head silvered in the light. "Most unseemly, that she did not inform you of such. Of course, she did not wish to let me go. But nìaRauta Ulanova can be most persuasive." More tapping. More pulling. "You would have me deliver any message, nìRau?"

The soft thud of shards hitting the cloth floor cover. "You would have me do anything?"

Tsecha again struggled with the inability to think clearly. *They have shut me out.* He pushed back one sleeve, and ran a finger along his many scars. *I should challenge Shai.* In Rauta Shèràa, there would be no question that he should offer *à lérine.* But if he did so here, would she accept? Would she even reply? Would Cèel consider such behavior unseemly, and recall them both? *No. He will not recall Shai.* Jani's truth struck him as a blow. *He will recall me.* Not openly, with challenge and argument and directness of idomeni, but quietly, for reasons other, as the humanish did. *Cèel and Shai have watched. They have learned.* To say one thing and mean another. To use their blades in his back. "I will decide later, ní Dathim." He took one last look at the rolling dunes. "Glories of the day to you."

Tsecha left the house to find the stone-paved street no longer empty. Other Haárin now walked, or talked in doorways. As he passed, the elders straightened in respectful greeting. Youngish stared after him more boldly, small hands clutching the overrobe hems of their house-parents. He gestured blessings to all of them, lifted his chin in gratitude at the offered thanks.

When he reached the treeline, he looked back to find Dathim standing in his doorway, ax-hammer in hand, watching him. Tsecha paused to offer a blessing, but before he could, the Haárin turned his back and disappeared into the darkness of his house.

CHAPTER 12

Jani passed the tables of an award-winning holoVee actor, the prima ballerina of the Capital Ballet, and the team captain of Gruppo Helvetica as she followed the maitre'd through Gaetan's mirrored main dining room. The ballerina, a favorite of Niall's, wore something wispy in black that was held together by thin silver straps and prayer.

Jani tugged at the snug bodice of her own gown. According to Gaetan's unwritten code, long dresses were *de rigueur* for women, which meant that one of John's gifts would at last see candlelight. At least the silver-green holosilk didn't pose any sartorial challenge—it was long-sleeved and floor-length all the way around, and lacked any slits or plunges that could have proved embarrassing if she moved like a normal human. *Unlike that copper thing.* The next time she saw John, she would have to ask him what the hell he'd been thinking when he bought *that*.

Her mood lifted when she caught sight of two familiar heads visible above the leather bolster of a corner booth. Auburn and carrot, straight and curly. Carrot-curly saw her first.

"*Jani!*" Angevin Wyle scooted out of her seat and circled around the table, handling her taupe satin with enviable ease. "You won me my bet!"

"Glad to hear it." Jani bent down to accept a neck-wrenching hug. "What was it?"

"Didn't think you'd wear a dress." Steven Forell stood, ever-present nicstick dangling from his lips. His hair and black dinner jacket had absorbed the clove-scented smoke—

Jani stifled a film-threatening sneeze as he pulled her close. "You let me down, gel," he said as he released her. "Ange is gonna ride me 'bout this for a week."

"Two." Angevin looked Jani up and down, her pert face alight with approval. "I like it."

"Posh," Steve added. "Guess the fancy consulting life agrees with you."

They returned to the table—Steve grinned as he watched the maitre'd help Jani with her chair and spread the linen napkin across her lap. "World's not ready for this," he said after the man left. "You've gone all civilized."

"I've done a turn or two through society in my dim and distant past." Jani tucked her flowing skirts around her legs. "You make me sound barbaric."

"Nah. Streamlined, more like." Steve beckoned for the wine steward and waiter, who stood off to the side. "Like it were beneath your notice." He announced his own surrender to the status quo by extinguishing his 'stick before ordering the wine.

Glasses were filled and orders taken. Jani sipped iced water with lemon and nodded as Steve waxed rhapsodic about the Interior posting from which he and Angevin had just returned.

Angevin, however, refused to cooperate—for every bit of praise Steve tried to heap on his homeworld, she responded with a leveling aside. "I blame selective amnesia," she said as she extracted a steamed mussel from its shell. "Yes, Guernsey's pretty—"

"Gorgeous," Steve muttered.

"—and I got along with his family—"

"They fookin' adored you."

"—and yes, on paper, going there was a good career move." She regarded the sea-born morsel doubtfully before popping it in her mouth. "But nothing gets *done* out there. It takes weeks to process transactions that can be handled here in days. I thought Interior Main was bad—Helier Annex made them look like a Misty relay station."

"Colonies are more *relaxed,* Ange." Steve tore grilled shrimp from a skewer. "They don't take life rush-rush."

"Oh, belt it! You'd chewed your nails down to the second

knuckle by the time we pulled out. The project teams we were assigned to missed *five* deadlines because paperwork we submitted for approvals disappeared down a rat-hole." Angevin attacked her butter-sauced fingers with a scented dispo. "Two of those were equipment requisitions for construction projects. The crews are sitting around waiting to work and nothing's been shipped in for them to work *with*. Those were Steve's—you can imagine how well those little mix-ups went over with his department head."

"Thanks for the reminder, love," Steve grumbled around a piece of green pepper.

"Paperwork probably got through all right. The equipment just got resold to a higher bidder." Jani stirred her soup. Beef consommé, protein-based and bland, the culinary equivalent of hot water.

"Folks been complainin' for a while." Steve's voice emerged small and slow, like a young boy confessing he'd stolen cookies. "When I send things home, gifts and suchlike, I use an Haárin courier service that has its own docks and staff." He frowned. "Except they're getting squeezed by the crooks."

Jani shivered and rubbed her upper arms. Either the dining room was set to "freeze" or her own thermostat misbehaved again. "Did your folks mention when the squeeze started?"

"Life's always been a free-for-all in Helier, but me folks said things started getting really bad early this year." Steve chewed on the deshrimped skewer. Like Niall, he needed something in his mouth when the going got bumpy.

About the time L'araignée *formed.* Jani stirred her soup. "Helier government doing anything?"

Steve snorted. "Yeah. Sitting about with their fingers up their bums."

"Wait a second." Angevin looked at him. "You knew about this, and you didn't bother to tell me what we'd be in for?"

Jani pushed her still-full soupbowl away. "When he left Helier, the problem hadn't grown to the extent that it affected the Cabinet annexes. No one ever dared tamper with them before. Times have changed."

"Tell me." Steve took the wooden skewer from his mouth and snapped it in half. "Lost a friend while we were there. Barry went to Oxbridge Combined, same as me. We both started at Interior right off—he left after the van Reuter dust-up. Nabbed a job with Commerce, doing dock audits out of the Helier Annex." He fell silent—it seemed to take a lot for him to start talking again. "He called me one morning. He were auditing one of the bigger receiving companies. Whole box of scanpack chips gone missing. He thought he'd found an erase and reentry in the incoming log—he asked me questions about loading and unloading procedures 'cause I worked my way through Oxbridge on the docks." He frowned at the broken sticks in his hand, and tossed them on the table. "Security found his body that afternoon. He'd been stuffed in a supply closet, covered with a drop cloth."

Jani felt a twist of nausea at the thought of her parents. Of Niall. "Was it a professional killing?"

"Might've been." Steve tapped the back of his neck. "Snapped. Could've been a pro or just someone strong. Last I heard, ComPol were still investigating. Doubt they'll find anyone. It's been six months and they've come up with nothing."

The three of them sat in moody silence as the waiters removed, replaced, and refilled.

"Jan?" Steve's voice, gone soft again. "What's going on?"

"Later." Jani forced herself to eat. "At my flat."

"The concept of furniture!" Angevin had consumed most of the wine Steve had ordered. The alcohol lifted her mood and liberated her sense of drama—she strutted the center of Jani's main room, gesturing broadly. "Chairs! Couches!"

"Streamlined." Steve nodded his approval. "I, for one, am not surprised."

"I'm appalled." Angevin walked to one of the windows. "Views could be better, but parties are still a possibility."

Jani strolled to her side and looked out at the rainbow-lit park beyond. "I don't have time to throw parties."

"Don't think you should, with all this crap you got goin'." Steve picked through one of the piles on her desk. "Guess business is poppin'." He looked at her, eyes sharp with question.

Jani stepped away from the window and walked a tight circle. "How much have you heard?" She glanced at Angevin in time to see the guilty flinch.

"Trash report floatin' round with your name on it. Stolen equipment. Altered paperwork." Steve plucked a half-smoked 'stick from his jacket pocket and chewed it. "Bitty stuff, Jan—that's what we're hearin'. Earn you a slap on the hand from your ol' schoolie Aryton at the Reg, maybe." He tossed the old stick in the 'zap and ignited a fresh one. "Anything else goin' on that we should know about?" He walked back around the desk and perched on the corner. "Safety in numbers, an' all that."

"There are . . . problems with the idomeni."

"Oh, that's news. What else?"

"It's better if I don't say."

"Don't you trust us?"

"It's safer for you if I don't say. In fact, it would be in your best interest to leave here now."

"If I recall correctly, you invited us."

"That was a mistake. I'm sorry."

Steve regarded Jani steadily, then beckoned to Angevin. She walked to him, her step steady, her wine euphoria vanished. He pulled her close; she nestled against him as he rested his chin atop her head. "Jani Kilian, I'll say it once and then no more. You believed I were innocent when no one else did. However much trouble you got, it'll never be enough to drive us away."

Jani fidgeted beneath two worried stares. *They're so young.* And yet, older than she had been at Knevçet Shèràa. *They can handle this.* Indeed, they might not have a choice. Despite the cover of night and the care she took in bringing them in through a side entrance, odds were good that someone had seen them. "If nothing else, my bad reputation could rub off on your blossoming careers."

Steve blew smoke. "Well, that's a load of tripe, innit?" He released Angevin, who began her own root through the paper on Jani's desk.

"Not to change the subject." She waved one of Jani's client logs in the air. "You have a report due tomorrow and all you've done is tabulated the data."

"I was going to finish it after you left." Jani hurried deskside before Angevin uncovered any more half-completed work. "I just need to write a conclusion."

"It's an easy one." Angevin hiked her skirt and boosted atop the desk chair. "Just your standard summation. 'Here's your list of numbers, fool—if you'd had half as much sense as money, you could have done it yourself in ten minutes.' "

"Looks like you could use some help here, Jan, seein' as you'll be otherwise occupied salvaging yer tarnished reputation and all." Steve removed his dinner jacket, then wandered the room looking for a place to hang it. "We've got a few days before we clap on the Interior irons again. We'd be glad to help you out—right, Ange?" He opened the closet door with a grunt of triumph and stashed the jacket within, then resumed his ramble.

Angevin looked up from her summation. "We need to get typed into your workstation."

Jani stood back from the desk, hands on hips. "Do I have any say in this?"

Angevin shook her head. "No. And I hope you have a credit line in place," she added darkly, "because first thing in the morning, I'm leasing you some furniture."

"She's got plenty of furniture in here! And a few other things, besides." Steve stormed out of Jani's bedroom carrying a pair of Lucien's shoes. "So who do these belong to, then?" He waved one of the trainers in a threatening manner. "You think we're going to let some cad swank in and outta here without a thorough vettin', you got another thing comin'."

Oh, damn. Jani hadn't personally witnessed any confrontation, but according to what she had heard from her Dr. Montoya, Steve and Lucien had despised one another on sight. "You're not going to like it."

"I don't like it already." Steve continued to wave the shoe. "I'm standin' in for your dad, I am, and if you think—" The sound of the door mech cut him off, and he smirked. "Now, we'll get this business straightened out."

Lucien entered, attired in dress blue-greys, brimmed lid tucked under his arm. "Jan, we've got twenty minutes to get to the idomeni embassy. I've got a skim parked—" He slid to a stop and surveyed the scene. "Hello." He smiled warmly at Angevin, who grinned back in silly rapture.

Steve was much less impressed. "What the fook are you doing here?"

"Those are Lucien's shoes you're holding, Steve." Jani fielded his glare and threw it back. "He lives here when he visits the city."

"Twenty minutes." Lucien eyed Jani's dress. "I'll brief you while you change." He grabbed her elbow and steered her toward the bedroom. "What the hell are they doing here?"

"They're working for me for the next few days."

"What!" Lucien forced the door closed, then activated the lock. "Was it something I said?"

"I could use the help." Jani stopped in front of the dresser mirror to check her hair and makeup. "You said yourself that I've taken on too much."

"That's what employment services are for." Lucien moved in behind her and finger-combed his hair. "If you weren't so damned picky, you could have had someone here months ago."

"Thanks for the personnel advice."

"You're welcome."

"They're friends. I like them. They're staying." Jani walked to the closet to hunt for embassy-suitable clothes. She looked over a black trouser outfit from John, but vetoed it because of its plunging neckline and pushed it aside.

"Mind if I ask a question?"

Jani sensed Lucien standing behind her. She riffled through the hangers once, then again. "If you must."

"Why don't you ever look at yourself in the mirror?"

Jani forced herself to turn to him. "I don't know what you mean."

"You'll check your face for two seconds. Three, tops. Just to make sure you haven't smeared colorstick on your chin or something. Most women catch themselves in any reflective surface they can, but never you." Lucien leaned against the entry. "Don't you like what you see?"

You bastard. He could spot a weakness the way a carnivore scented prey. "I try not to get too wrapped up in what I look like." Jani studied a dark blue trouser suit, and voted it suitably somber. "That way, when I change, I won't know what I missed." She yanked at the gown's shoulder fasteners, but they remained stubbornly fixed in place.

"Is this one of John's gifts?" Lucien stepped closer. "I think I know how it operates." He tugged lightly at the places Jani had pulled without success. The seaming released with a sigh—the silk slid down Jani's body and puddled to the floor. His fingers followed close behind, down her arms, cupping her breasts, roaming over her stomach.

"What's happening at the embassy?" Jani could hear the hoarseness in her voice, and damned her weakness.

"SOS." Lucien nuzzled her neck, then gripped her shoulders and turned her around to face him. "Same old same old. . . ." He pulled her close and kissed her.

Jani savored his taste, pressed her naked skin against rough polywool. Shocks spread across her body as though the cloth held static. Her weak knee sagged as Lucien backed her against the closet wall—the sight of the blue trouser suit shook the sense back into her. "Twenty minutes," she gasped in his ear.

Lucien released her abruptly. He walked out of the closet and straight to the dresser. He braced his hands on the edge, his breathing irregular.

Jani resumed dressing eventually. When she walked to the mirror to check her face for smeared makeup, she ignored Lucien's pointed stare. "So what's the story?"

Lucien paced by the bed, lid in hand. "There are issues with Ani's tile. Believe it or not, some of the materials used in the manufacture could be classified as edible, and Shai's trying to use that as an excuse to can the project. Colonel Derringer ordered you called in."

"Derringer's going to be there?" Jani hefted her duffel. "That will be the highlight of my evening."

Steve and Angevin sat side-by-side at the desk, their heads bent together over an open file. They looked up as one when Jani and Lucien entered. Angevin smiled. Steve didn't.

"The idomeni embassy." He slipped off the chair. "That's the only place you're goin'?"

"Yes," Jani answered, because she knew Lucien wouldn't.

"Take some time, ya think? Couple hours?"

"Probably."

"He's drivin'?" Steve followed them into the hall.

"Yes, Daddy."

"We'll be waiting here for ya, Jan." Steve trailed them down the hallway and watched them until the lift doors closed.

Lucien watched him in return. *"Âne-recolteur—"*

Ass-picker. "Be quiet." Jani watched the floor indicator move. "Stop speaking French as though I don't understand."

"I hate that little bastard."

"Well, he hates you, too, so wallow in it."

Except for the assistant desk, the lobby proved empty at that late hour, the street devoid of traffic.

"I'm parked in the garage."

"I have trouble walking up and down that ramp."

"The battery was low—I needed to charge it."

"You just did this afternoon."

"I drove a lot today, ran it down." Lucien strode ahead of her at first. Then his step slowed until she caught him up. He slipped his arm around her shoulders and pulled her close.

What the—? Jani tried to shake off the unfamiliar embrace, without success. "What's with the bear hug?"

"Just trying something different," Lucien said sourly as he pulled his arm away. "No one else seems to mind." He stepped aside and let her precede him into the garage. "You know, the last time you received a summons like this, we were at the embassy for two days."

"Don't remind me." Jani edged down the steep ramp, her knee sagging with every stride. She felt Lucien's hand on her shoulder again, then her knee buckle. "Will you—!"

"I'm just trying to help—!"

A flash seared from the bottom of the ramp. A crack like a whip. Jani hit the ground and rolled behind a pillar. Tossed the bag aside. Reached for the shooter she hadn't carried for months, and cursed her empty hand.

I'm here for you, augie told her. He spoke to her with the slowing of her pounding heart, the quenching of the sour taste of fear. *You'll never die as long as I'm around.*

Jani heard the clatter of running, into the depths of the garage.

There they go, augie cried. *Get them!*

She rose to give chase—

"Jani!"

—but the outer voice stopped her. She turned, and saw Lucien struggle to sit upright, his tunic smoking.

He reached out to her. "It's not a graze—it's a full-front hit." He tried to bend his legs so he could rise, but they shot from beneath him as though he sat on wet ice.

Jani scooted to his side, her attention torn between assessing his wound and the dark interior of the garage. She reached inside of his tunic, and felt the tingle of residual charge as she dug out his handcom and flicked the emergency call. "I can't tell if it's dead or not—the display is fried." She tossed it to one side and pushed down on Lucien's shoulders as he tried to rise. "Lay back! Stop fighting!"

"Why don't my legs work!"

"Nerve disruption. You just got hit by a bolt of lightning." She had to push with all her strength to keep him down— augie had him by the throat and the pain had yet to break through.

She pulled away his belt, the metal buckle still hot enough to sting. The shooter holster cracked in her hands, the weapon within burned like a live coal. She tossed the belt and holster aside and tucked the shooter in her pocket. She could feel its heat through her clothes as she continued to work.

The smoking polywool came next. Jani searched Lucien's disintegrating trousers, removing a charred wallet, vend tokens, and a mini-stylus and pocketing them as well. The stink of burnt fabric burned her throat and made her eyes tear. She pulled away fragments of shirt. Underwear. "Oh—"

"What!" Lucien tried to raise himself on his elbows to look.

"Get down." Jani pushed him back. "You're burned. It's bad. Stop moving around." She swallowed hard as the odor of charred flesh filled her nose. The burn covered the lower quarter of Lucien's abdomen—his right, her left—a sprawling oval of red-white blistering centered with charred, leathery black. Second- and third-degree burns, com-

pounded by whatever internal damage the impact of the pulse packet caused and aggravated by Lucien's moving around.

"Jan?"

"Yeah."

"Am I still there?"

Jani glanced beneath the remains of Lucien's underwear. "Yup. The burn didn't spread that far."

Lucien laughed. "Probably not a jealous spouse then." The happy expression froze as sweat bloomed on his face. "It's starting to hurt."

"Stop moving around."

"Is that me that I smell? Medium or well-done?"

Jani rolled her duffel into a pillow and tucked it beneath Lucien's head. "Quiet."

Lucien stilled. Then the pain broke through in earnest. He gasped and stiffened. *"Ça ne fait mal!"*

"I know it hurts. I know. *Je le sais.*"

"Ça ne—!"

"Paix, paix." Hush, hush. Jani pushed his damp hair off his forehead, whispering thanks when she heard the wail of an ambulance siren. She checked her timepiece. Only a few minutes had passed. Seemed like hours. Then she heard running. Instinct compelled her to reach for the shooter.

"Where are you!" A woman's voice.

"Down here!" Jani waited until she saw the skimgurney and Medibox before slipping the shooter back in her pocket.

The woman knelt beside Lucien as two other techs readied the gurney. She took in his uniform, then looked at Jani. "Augment?"

"Yes."

"Ab-scan," the woman said to one of the other techs. She probed Lucien's abdomen—he moaned and tried to push her away. "He's not rigid, but we could have shooter belly." A male tech knelt at Lucien's other side—together, the two of them adjusted a portable scanner over Lucien's stomach while the second man applied restraints to his hands.

Jani walked down to the end of the ramp, to the spot where she'd seen the flash. In the background, the techs talked in their own language. *Cardio-scan. Fluid replacement. Percent BSA. Debride.*

She found the shooter in the shadow of a pillar. A late-model Grenoble, dull blue and ugly, but powerful from mid-range on in. *The ID tags will be etched away. The markers embedded in the metal will point to a middleman-broker who went out of business five years ago.* And the professional who had pressed the charge-through would be halfway to O'Hare by now.

In the distance, she heard the nasal sing-song of a ComPol siren.

CHAPTER 13

"NìRau? NìRau?"

Tsecha's eyes snapped open. He blinked into the dark. At first, he thought the Laumrau had begun bombing again, that Aeri had awakened him so they could flee to the shelter of the Temple cellars. His heart skipped. He gripped the sides of his bed and braced for the blast.

But the face that bent over him was not Aeri's. Similar in shape but finer-boned, and much, much younger. Tsecha tried to look into its eyes, but it turned away.

What are you? Where is Aeri?

Then he remembered. That Aeri was dead. That the Laumrau were no more. That the war had ended long ago, and that he had not slept in his Temple rooms in Rauta Shèràa for a long time.

"NìRau, you must come to the meeting room." Sànalàn, Aeri's body-daughter, addressed Tsecha's footboard to prevent any more unseemly eye contact. "Suborn Oligarch Shai bids you attend."

"Nìa—?"

"There has been a shooting. Any more, nìaRauta Shai has forbidden me to say."

Tsecha rose too quickly for his old bones, and dressed as though he indeed heard the shatterboxes singing outside his window. Fear drove him. That, and the triumph he heard in Sànalàn's voice.

Tsecha edged about in his low seat and leafed through the scant few pages that lay in front of him. When he leaned forward to study the words more closely, the table's pointed edge caught him in his stomach, forcing him to sit back.

He looked one by one at the others who sat on either side of him, along the table's two arms. Suborn Oligarch Shai sat in the slightly higher seat to his left, as she had the previous day; Sànalàn's seat placed opposite hers on the right arm. The two lowest ranks in the room, Diplomatic Suborn Inèa and Communications Suborn Lonen, occupied the tallest seats at the ends of the arms.

Tsecha found the upward slant of the table disquieting. He felt dazed, as he had the night when the bombs fell and Aeri had not come for him. The night when he learned that Aeri would never come again.

He pushed thoughts of his dead suborn from his mind, and studied the others again. They had dressed hurriedly, as he had, their hair disarrayed, their overrobes bunched and creased. *As though they, too, flee the bombs.* He looked down at the paper once more. His soul ached from tension, but he dared not let it show. "This is all we know?"

"The Service has thwarted our attempts at message interception, nìRau." Lonen held on to the arms of her elevated chair as Tsecha had the sides of his bed. "They use cryptowave, and change the cipher with each word."

"Cryptowave for standard communication is most unseemly." Shai's roughened voice and harsh gestures defined her impatience. "This Pascal is known to us—we are entitled to be told of his condition, not to have to grab it from the air."

Tsecha reread the few words Lonen had been able to decrypt. *Jani Kilian . . . Lieutenant Pascal . . . shot upon entering . . . burned . . . other injuries.* "Has any formal explanation yet arrived?"

"No, nìRau." Diplomatic Suborn Inèa sat easily on her high seat. A perfect posture, of the sort Hansen had always called *angel on a pin.* "We have contacted Prime Minister Cao's offices for information. All they say is that"—she slipped into English—"*the situation is beneath control.*"

"*Under* control, nìa." Tsecha suppressed a gesture of berating. He reread Lonen's report once more, in the hope that what he did not see was there to be found, and that he could avoid the question that he knew the others waited for him to ask. But such, he decided as he turned the final page, was not to be. "Nìa Kilian was not hurt?" He heard Shai grumble in Low Vynshàrau and shift in her seat.

"We could not learn if she was, nìRau," Lonen replied with a hand curve of bewilderment. "We could not learn if she was not."

"This secrecy for no reason is repellant. This repellency defines the difference between humanish and idomeni more than any other thing." Shai elevated the language from formal Middle to formal High Vynshàrau, so that her every feeling would be clearly revealed. "Our forthrightness in the midst of this secrecy leaves us at a disadvantage. If we request openly, we will only be told what Li Cao wishes us to know. Our interest will be taken as further reason to withhold—this I know from studying humanish, and truly."

Tsecha could see the tension in the posture of Diplomatic Suborn Inèa, much more so than in Lonen's or Sànalàn's. As if she knew what Shai would say next. *So, it happens.* He remained silent, and waited for what he knew must come.

"Much of our behavior leaves us at a disadvantage in dealing with humanish. We speak as we feel. We act in honesty. We offer everything. Humanish take all of it, and return nothing." Shai sat back in her chair and stretched her right arm out before her on the table, palm up. A gesture of pleading. "And so in the end are we left with nothing."

Tsecha toyed with the ends of his overrobe cuffs, rearranging them so as to expose the very edges of his many scars.

Shai understood the challenging nature of the gesture—her hesitancy before she spoke indicated such. Yet still she spoke. "We do not deserve *nothing*. We deserve to know all that the humanish wish to withhold from us." She turned her palm facedown, a sign of an unpleasant decision having been reached. "Morden nìRau Cèel sent us here because of our strength, because he knew that we would nurture and protect all that was as idomeni in the middle of this chill unholiness. In doing so, we have sacrificed much, including that which we sought most to protect. Our sovereignty." She drew her hands together, one atop the other, again palm down. The decision confirmed.

"I have consulted with Cèel these past weeks, and with our xenolinguists, and our behaviorists. Our conclusions concur. The humanish think us weak when we act as our way demands. They see our open disputation as disunity, our godly challenges as discord. They do not think us strong, and because of this, they feel right to hold back information from us, to break agreements and disregard contracts."

"But you wished breakage of the Elyan Haárin contract, Shai, and truly," Tsecha muttered without gesture, so low that only Shai could hear him.

Shai responded by raising the pitch of her voice, as in prayer. "Thus will we act strong as the humanish understand strong. Thus will we withhold our opinions, and keep our arguments amongst ourselves. Thus will we behave as one before them, as they behave as one before us."

Lonen crossed her left arm in front of her chest in supplication. "NìaRauta Shai, we will damn our souls if we behave as false."

"Then we will petition Caith to protect us, nìa Lonen, for only in this annihilation will we remain whole." Shai bared her teeth for an instant only, a truncated expression that signified as much as a humanish shrug. Or as little. "We are the stones that form the Way. Although we are as nothing, other Vynshàrau will tread on us, and thus make their way along the Bridge to the Star."

Tsecha remained quiet as the last tones of Shai's speech drifted through the air and settled, like Dathim's tile dust. He looked from figure to figure, searching for the subtle changes that would signal their agreement with the Suborn Oligarch. The elevation as they sat up straighter, to show their respect. The lifted curve of their left hands, to show their certainty of agreement. He saw them in Lonen, and of course, in Sànalàn, and in Inèa. He kept his own hands clasped before him on the table. He had reached his own difficult decision many years before—this night saw only the laying of another stone in his own long Way.

"Humanish secrecy defines itself not by what it does but by that which it leaves behind." Tsecha heard his own voice, low and measured. He petitioned no one with his words. "Trails of blood, and humiliation. Former Interior Minister van Reuter would attest to this, I believe." He bared his teeth wide, in the truest idomeni fashion. "I have read of the humanish writer Sandoval, who wrote that secrets bind with their own weight, that to carry many secrets is to wrap oneself in a chain of one's own making." He rounded his shoulders and slumped in his chair, a most obvious display of his displeasure. "You have bid us don our chains, at a time when we must move as free. You damn us, Shai."

Shai tossed her head and fluttered her right hand once, a gesture of the greatest disregard. "I seek to save us, Tsecha. It is you who will damn us with your beliefs and your false predictions. You announce them before the humanish, and thus give them reason to fear and mock us. You claim to speak for the gods, and in the gods' names you will dilute and dishonor us!"

Tsecha sensed the mood of the room, the acceptance of Shai's words in the postures of the others. "You speak as you do, Shai, because nìa Lonen and nìa Inèa and nìa Sànalàn give you leave with their every movement. In this room, at this time, you know how each of us regards you, and use such as a basis to decide how you will next act. No indecision. No uncertainty. Yet you will take that away from us all and call it strength, and you dare to accuse me of dishonor!"

"It is settled, Tsecha!"

"It was settled days ago. Before yesterday's meeting, when Anais commended the idomeni for their forthrightness, you already knew of this plan. You have studied the hiding lesson well, have you not, Shai? We both know that there is more to this than contracts." Tsecha tilted his head to the left until his ear touched his shoulder, and let the anger wash over him like the cold season air to come. "Say her name, Shai! In the name of annihilation, say the name of the one whom you will keep from this place, in the name of your new-found secrecy!"

Shai's voice lowered in menace. "Until we have received sufficient information regarding the condition of Lieutenant Pascal and the reason for the attack on him, we cannot allow your Kilian within these walls. Nor can we allow you to leave the embassy compound. It is a precaution—"

"*It is cowardice!*" Tsecha shouted now, his voice reverberating off the polished stone walls. "Wanton disregard of the truth you have denied since we lived at Temple. And now you will take this new truth that only you and your behaviorists see and use it as a way to separate me from my Kièrshia!"

Shai tensed, then raised her hands in argument. "Your Kilian—"

"My Kilian, my Jani, my Captain. My Eyes and Ears. My student. My teacher. *Mine.*" Tsecha forced himself silent. His heart pounded; his face burned. So unseemly, to rage in such an uncontrolled way. "You have learned well, Shai. In a few months, you have become as Anais or Li Cao. You will shut me up in this place, for my *safety.* You will keep me from my Jani and my Jani from me, for my own good. When has protection ever destroyed so utterly that which it was supposed to defend? Tell me, Shai, and damn your soul if you lie of this!"

Shai sat still. Then she rested her arms as Tsecha did. As a secular, her sleeves lacked the red banding that complemented *à lérine* scars so well. Her pale scars seemed to fade into the sameness of her skin.

Tsecha studied Shai's exposed arms for the ragged red of fresher lacerations, but could see none, not even the self-inflicted hack to the forearm that signaled the end of a bout. *It has been a long while since your last challenge.* He looked down at his own arms, and the spare scattering of red. *It has been a long time since mine.* How they would slash and stab at one another, the smooth parries of youth replaced by the deceptions and strategems of age. *I await your challenge, nìa.* It would no doubt prove an interesting encounter.

"You may well pronounce my soul damned, nìRau ti nìRau. You are my Chief Propitiator, my intercessor with the gods, and such is most assuredly your right. In the ways of the gods, no Vynshàrau is your dominant." Shai pushed away from the table, whatever challenge she felt to make put aside for another time. "But when you act as ambassador, you become a secular, and all seculars in this place answer to me. I have ordered that you will not leave this place. You will, therefore, not leave this place until I lift the order. For your safety." She stood, her overrobe falling in wrinkled folds to the floor. "Glories of this too-late night to you, Tsecha." She swept out the door behind Lonen and Inèa, and finally, his Sànalàn.

Tsecha gestured in easy agreement as the door closed. "Yes, nìa." He thought again of his Hansen. How he would pace and rail at times like these, when the Laumrau or the humanish Consulate had acted in some stupid manner and he knew nothing could be done to stop them. Tsecha tried to recall the comment Hansen used in those situations, which twinned so well the one he found himself in now. *Pissing into the wind.* Yes, that was it, and truly.

Tsecha tried to sleep, and failed. Tried to pray, and failed again.

He dressed. He walked. Throughout the embassy, and the altar room where he would soon pass his days, much to Shai's rejoicing. Out on the lake-facing verandas, where even in the dim of night, Vynshàrau contemplated, wrote, discussed.

Across the lawns. Past the buildings. He knew where he went, though what good it would do, he could not say. He wondered if Shai now had him watched, or if she felt her confinement order eliminated the need.

He had just reached the treeline when he heard the sound. He paused to listen to it, such a contrast to the rustle of leaves and crunch of undergrowth. The high-pitched *sweep sweep* of stone against metal. Odd to hear it in this place, at this time. It was a sound of the quarries, the weapons forges, and during the time of war, the hallowed courtyards of Temple. The steady hasp and scrape of a Vynshà sharpening a blade.

Tsecha followed the sound to a small clearing. Why did it not surprise him to find the crop-headed figure seated on a stump, stone in one hand, ax-hammer in the other? "You work so early, ní Dathim?"

"As do you, nìRau." Dathim did not look up. He had hung a lampstick by a cord around his neck; the yellow light illuminated the work of his hands. "Did the noise awaken you, as well?"

Tsecha lowered to the ground beside the stump. He

looked up at Dathim's face and tried to discern his feeling, but all was obscured by the odd shadows cast by the lampstick. "I heard no noise in the embassy. My suborn awakened me." He debated telling Dathim of his house arrest. The Haárin had declared himself to him, and for that reason alone he had a right to know Tsecha's status.

But Tsecha decided against doing so. *I must fight secrets with secrets.* Dathim would find out from the guards or the embassy staff soon enough, and he would understand the reason for silence. If Shai discovered that the Chief Propitiator discussed such matters with an Haárin, confinement to the embassy for one could become confinement to rooms for both. "What noise did you hear, ní Dathim?"

"The ComPol sirens. Other sirens as well, for the skimmers that transport humanish sick and injured. But then, one hears those every night." Dathim set the stone aside, and held the ax-hammer blade close to his face. "Tonight has been most different." He tilted the blade end back and forth, then ran a finger along the edge. "Interior Security has been most active tonight, nìRau, and truly. Constant passes up and down our borders. Along the lakeshore, as nearly as they could approach. Overhead, in demiskimmers." Something about the blade made him frown. He lowered it and once more ministered to it with the stone. "I saw all this. Then I saw the embassy lights, and the activity of our guards."

Tsecha looked through the trees, and watched the green and blue lights of Vynshàrau and Interior lakeskimmers shimmer and reflect over the water. "My Lucien was shot."

"He is the youngish, the pale-haired soldier?" Dathim nodded in the humanish way, which signified that his head moved up and down. "I have seen him walk with you. I have seen him walk alone, in the public areas. Even though he stays within the allowed boundaries, the guards follow him most closely. He watches as someone who remembers what he sees. Not always a wise thing, for humanish." He lowered the stone to his lap and pointed to another tight formation of lakeskimmers that flitted on the Interior side of the Michigan Strip boundary. "The last time I saw this much activity was in the winter, when they took the dominant van Reuter away. For the entire season afterwards, when I traveled into the city, I heard the talk about that night. And now I see it again, for one humanish lieutenant who walks where he is allowed and remembers what he sees."

Tsecha thought back to the night of van Reuter's arrest. The incomprehensible cold. His Jani's rescue from Interior, which he had planned with Lucien. The pursuit. The fleeing. "My Jani was with Lucien. Any more than that, no one knows."

"Did she shoot him?" Dathim lifted his hand in question. "She shoots, nìRau. Such is her way."

"She would not shoot *him*!" Tsecha heard his own voice raised too loud, and berated himself. Such a shout, an avalanche of sharpening stones could not have drowned out. "They are friends," he added, much more quietly.

"As you say, nìRau." Dathim turned the stone over. The surface changed from rough to shiny, from honing to polishing. "But friends often turn on friends. This I know from reading humanish history."

"I, too, have read humanish history, ní Dathim."

"Have you, nìRau?" Another sweep of the stone. "No wonder you walk the night."

Tsecha clenched his hands at the Haárin's assured tone. "You vex me, ní Dathim."

"I am unworthy to sit in your presence, nìRau." Unworthy though he was, Dathim made no move to rise. Instead, he set the ax-hammer and stone on a nearby log and looked out once more toward the water. "I must return to sleep. Tomorrow, I visit the Exterior Ministry for the first time, to examine the space which Anais Ulanova wishes me to tile." The dimness played tricks with the bones of his face, filling in hollows with seeming substance, combining with his hair to make him appear even more humanish. "They will show me, among other places, a *lobby,* and a *conference room.* I am to look over each location very carefully, and pick the one that will highlight my stunning work the best—this was I told, and truly." Ready as he claimed to be to leave, Dathim made no attempt to gather his tools. "I am to look. And look." Instead, he sat slightly forward, hands on knees, perched to stand, yet waiting . . . waiting. . . .

Tsecha waited, as well, for the most seemly offer he knew to be forthcoming.

"Is there anything in particular you would have me look *for,* nìRau?"

Tsecha felt his heart catch, as it had all those times in Rauta Shèràa when his Hansen had made the same request. How Dathim had come to know of the behavior of spies, he did not think it wise to ask. Better to simply accept, and quickly. "Anything of this shooting, ní Dathim. Anything you see of my Jani." He picked up a twig and used it to poke beneath some fallen leaves. "Although I do not know how you will remove it from Exterior grounds."

"I know of facilities, nìRau. So I told you." Dathim grew still as an idomeni demiskimmer skirted the shore. "You should believe your fellow Haárin when they tell you of matters, and trust them to do as they say."

"Fellow—?" Tsecha's shoulders sagged as fatigue suddenly overtook him—he could muster no anger at Dathim's impertinence "You claim to share skein and station with me, ní Dathim? You claim me as equal?"

"No, nìRau." Dathim stood slowly, long limbs unwinding. "I am able to leave this place, and you are not. You are a prisoner, and I am free. In such an instance, we are most unequal, would you not say?"

Tsecha twisted his head so quickly, his neck bones cracked like dried leaves. "You know of that? So soon?" Even the darkness could not obscure his shock—that he knew, though little did he care.

Dathim looked down on Tsecha from his great height. "Yes, nìRau—I know of your restriction. Thus did I hear from an embassy Haárin, who overheard a conversation between your suborn and Diplomatic Suborn Inèa. After your meeting, when you were informed of your imprisonment in the interest of your safety." He bent to pick up his tools. "Such listening is the way of Earth, nìRau. The way of humanish. Of your Eyes and Ears. It shocks me that you have not learned it better." He strode off, sharpening stone clenched in one hand, ax-hammer in the other, leaving Tsecha alone in the dark and the leaves.

CHAPTER 14

"Look at the light, Jani."

Jani glanced out the corner of her eye at the red illumination that fluttered just beyond arms' reach.

"You know better than that." Calvin Montoya stepped out from behind the lightbox. "I need to assess the activity level of your augmentation so I know how to treat you."

"*I'm* not injured. *I* wasn't shot."

"*Look at the light.*"

Jani kept her eyes fixed on a point above the lightbox. Then, slowly, she dropped her gaze until she stared at the red head-on. "See? I told you I was fi—"

Suddenly, the light twinned. Once, then again and again. The pinpoints skittered across the source surface and throbbed in programmed patterns.

The examination room spun—Jani had to grip the edge of the scanbed to keep from toppling to the floor.

"That's what I thought," Montoya said smugly. "On the downward slope, but still firing. Augie had enough of a jolt to initiate normally—I think we can let you settle on your own without a takedown." He shut off the source, and the red dots faded to black. "Show me an augie that doesn't kick in when its owner's shot at, and I'll show one worthless bundle of brain cells."

Jani struggled to maintain her equilibrium. The walls of the examining room billowed out, then in, as though the room breathed. "I can show you another worthless—"

"*Testy,* aren't we?" Montoya pushed the lightbox to the

far corner of the examination room. "Lieutenant Pascal will be all right."

"He didn't look all right in the ambulance." Jani watched Montoya fuss with a tray of instruments. He still wore the trimmed beard she recalled from the winter; his band-collar dinner jacket mirrored its rich black color. Together, they made him look like a cleric in a historical drama. *Bless me, Father, for I don't know what the hell's going on.* "How much longer will he be in Surgery?"

"They've only had him for half an hour." Montoya's voice still chided, but more gently. "He suffered serious injuries in addition to the burn. A shooter blast is like a kick in the gut—you know that as well as I do. Along with internal bleeding, add a ruptured peritoneum and a bruised kidney." He pulled a stool in front of the scanbed and sat. "He's young, strong, and augmented—he'll heal quickly, but he'll still need to *heal*." He fingered the scuffed knee of Jani's trousers. "Now, you said you fell after the shot blitzed out."

"My right knee gave out when I walked down the ramp." Jani massaged the injured joint. It had begun to ache soon after she arrived at the hospital—now that her augie had backed down, it hurt every time she flexed it.

"Let's see what we have here." Montoya braced her foot atop his thigh and pushed up her trouser leg. "Oh, my." He probed the egg-sized bruise below the patella. "You've got some nice soft-tissue damage there. Augie quelled the worst of it, but I'll still fit it with a chillpack to ease the swelling."

Jani cupped her hand over her knee so Montoya couldn't probe it anymore. She could feel the heat radiate from the injury like a localized fever. "Can't you inject it with something so it heals faster?"

"No." He glanced up at her and smiled his regrets. "If I give you anything while augie is still active, your healing cascades will go into overdrive. A month from now, we'd have to remove tissue and bone growths, or worst case, have to rebuild the joint entirely." He pulled open a drawer in the base of the scanbed and removed a packet of gauze and an aerosol canister. "And there are just some risks we can't afford to take with you right now."

Jani leaned her head back and stared at the ceiling. "Meaning?" As if she didn't know. As if she hadn't heard the same excuses from a multitude of medical faces over the last few months.

"Meaning that you could react adversely to one of the accelerant proteins. If you did go into anaphylaxis, the only thing we could treat you with is adrenosol and your therapeutic index and toxic threshold overlap. In other words, a dose sufficient to help you could just as easily kill you." He pulled her hand away from her knee, sprayed her bruise, and wiped the freezing foam with the gauze. "We need to develop desensitizing proteins specific to you. We're close, but we're not there yet." He continued to spray the cooling, cleansing foam, then dab it away. "On the other hand, there's a chance you won't need them. If your response to past injury is any indication, your body is a healing accelerant factory on its own."

Jani looked at the *à lérine* wounds on her right arm, and compared them to the faint scars on her animandroid left. The real had caught up with the counterfeit—the wounds had already healed to silvered threads, as though she'd had them for years, not months. The residual weakness in her right knee served as the sole reminder of her most recent health disasters. According to every physician she spoke with, both Neoclona and Service, anyone else who had gone through the myriad adversities she had would be bedridden. Or dead.

John tells me I'll outlive everyone I know. All she'd lost in exchange was the right to call herself a human being. *I am a hybrid. A race of one.* The idea hadn't bothered her so much when she lived on the run—when all that matters is getting through today, who thinks about tomorrow?

But as her body continued to change and the inevitability of the process dawned, she'd come to resent every aspect of the transformation. That her life had become the eggshell walk of the chronically ill. That she couldn't put anything in her mouth without wondering whether it would sicken her. That she couldn't think an odd thought without worrying whether it was just a passing weirdness or the sign of a brain that didn't process things the same way anymore.

Add to that the reactions from others—the orderly who switched duties whenever she came in for a check-up because he thought hybridization contagious. The nurse who crossed herself when Jani looked her in the eye. The doctors who called her names when they thought she couldn't hear. Goldie. Pussy cat. *John would kill them if he knew.* But to what purpose, when others would take their place who felt the same. Even the kindest remarks, from Niall and Dolly, aggravated and worried her. She changed, and everyone could see that she changed. She couldn't hide it anymore.

She looked down at Montoya, who had finished with the foam and gauze, and now adjusted a padded coldpack around her knee. "Calvin?"

"Yes?"

"I'm tired of being a medical miracle."

His hands stalled. He didn't look up. "I'm sorry, Jani."

Jani studied the top of his head. The first traces of a bald spot had formed on his crown, a thumbnail-sized imperfection in his thick cap of straight black. *I spit in the eye of the inevitable,* he had told her when she asked him why he didn't correct it. His refusal to tweak his own little defect colored his judgment regarding hers. He was one of the few white coats who treated her like a woman named Jani, not a cross between a freak and the publication opportunity of a lifetime.

Jani tapped Montoya's bald spot to get his attention, then pointed to his jacket. "Where were you when you got the call?"

He grinned at her and sat up straighter. "My parents' fortieth wedding anniversary. Brothers, sisters, children, grandchildren." The grin wavered. "The party had just started to wind down. The call came at just the right time—I didn't have to help with the clean-up." He looked down again, but not soon enough to keep Jani from spotting the longing in his eyes.

"Guess it's my turn to say I'm sorry."

His head shot up. "Did you plan this?" He waited for her to shake her head. "Then don't apologize." He looked down again and fiddled with the coldpack. "So, I heard buzz that it was a robbery attempt."

"More than likely." Jani had no intention of discussing her certainty as to the professional nature of the attack. She placed a hand over her left shoulder, on the spot that Lucien had touched just before the shot. *Touched.* She winced as she pressed her fingers into the area. Make that *grabbed.* She'd find a bruise there in a few hours, augie or no.

"What's wrong?" Montoya stood up and kicked the stool back into its niche beneath a bench, then pushed back her T-shirt and probed her shoulder with the same uncomfortable thoroughness with which he'd examined her knee. "A robbery, huh? I've lived in this city awhile, you know? Robberies in garages happen. Not in the Parkway area, though. Too many Family members. Too much high-priced security." He took a scanner from the top of a nearby table and pressed it to her shoulder. "Bit of a wrench," he said as he read the display. "I don't need to reseat the arm, but it will be sore for a few days."

"Is this another 'augie will provide'?" Jani got down off the scanbed and tested her knee. Thanks to her internal factory, the sharp pain had already receded to a dull ache. Unfortunately, the motion aggravated her Montoya-induced vertigo—she had to keep one hand planted on the bed frame as she adjusted her trouser leg. "Why wouldn't criminals come to the Parkway? That's where the money is."

Montoya eyed her with professional scrutiny as she walked across the room. "A Chicago robber would not attempt to kill his victims. Bad for business. His colleagues would nail him before the ComPol did." He walked to her side. "Speaking of the ComPol, they're here. A detective inspector and a detective captain. John deposited them in a lounge down the hall."

"Really?" Jani recalled the green-and-white skimmer that had dogged the ambulance. She waved away Montoya's offer to help with her jacket, since he'd have detected the small but weighty presence of Lucien's shooter and personal effects in her side pocket.

"I wouldn't advise talking to them for at least two days. Not until we're sure augie has settled down." Montoya blocked her way to the door. "You're not yourself. That feeling of invincibility isn't the thing to take with you when you deal with authority."

Jani patted his shoulder. "Calvin, I was dealing with the ComPol back when you still had a full head of hair."

"That's cold."

"I'll be fine." She stepped around him and out the door.

The Outpatient wing was deserted at that late night hour. That made it easier to hear the raised voices emerging from the lounge where the ComPol awaited. Three voices—two women and a man.

"Ms. Kilian has nothing to say!" the man shouted. His voice was cultured Michigan provincial flavored with Earth-bound Hispanic.

"Why don't we let Ms. Kilian tell us that!" one of the women countered.

"No!" the man responded. "Absolutely not. She is on bio-emotional restriction and cannot be questioned at this time!"

Jani sneaked into the lounge entry so that she could gauge the combatants before stepping into the fray. The women appeared to be her age, and wore the professionally dour dark green of ComPol detectives. The man was older, a brown-skinned walking wire dressed in casual trousers and an expensive pullover. He spotted her first, and turned his back on the women's verbal barrage.

"Jani." He hurried over to her, his expression at once tranquil and alert, the way Val looked when he felt he needed to calm her down. "You shouldn't walk around." His face was shallow-boned and dominated by an aquiline nose, his hair a grizzled cap.

Jani took a step back. "Who the hell are you?"

"Joaquin Loiaza." He pulled up short and bowed from the waist. "John has asked me to represent you in this matter."

"You're a *lawyer*?" All the reply that elicited was a slow affirmative blink. "What the hell do I need a lawyer for!"

"That's our question too, Jani," one of the detectives piped.

"Did you see anything?" the other asked. "The garage's monitoring system was knocked out by the construction—you're our only witness."

Loiaza turned on them. *"Ms. Kilian has nothing—!"*

"Jani?"

Silence fell as everyone looked to the voice, a rumbling bass that made any word sound like a command from on high.

John Shroud stood in the hallway. He looked a study in ice: bone-white hair, milk-pale ascetic's face, an evening suit of palest blue. "Should you be walking about?" He turned his attention to Loiaza, who stiffened. "I asked you to see to this, Joaquin." As usual, John had filmed his eyes to match his clothing—the crystal blue glare moved from the lawyer to fix again on the reluctant client. "I'll see you back to your room." He walked toward Jani as though one quick move would dislodge his head. Spine straight, stride long and smooth. A weighty step, but fluid, like mercury.

Jani tried to dodge, but two ice-blue arms snaked around her and held her fast.

"You will come quietly." John spoke in her ear, sounding like Death come to collect his due.

"I don't need your lawyers, or your goddamned help!" Jani gripped the arms of the visitor's chair, supporting all her weight on her hands as she struggled to sit without bending her knee. The furniture in John's office was all ebon wood instead of battered metal, the floor covered with Persian carpets instead of cheap lyno. Yet still she sat, and still she argued, as she had so many times before in the basement of the Rauta Shèràa enclave hospital. "I could have found out what they knew. Who they suspected. Right now, I have *nothing!*"

"Any information they have, Joaquin will obtain through proper channels." John fell into his chair. The ergoworks screeched in protest. "Now are you going to tell me what happened tonight, or are you going to make me guess?" He slumped forward and worked his hands through his hair.

Jani counted slowly in an effort to quell her ire, using her throbbing knee as a metronome. "A robbery attempt." She watched John's hair catch the light like finely drawn platinum. She could still feel the pressure of his arms where he'd held her. "How long have you had that headache?" She imagined pressing her fingers into his nape and massaging the tension from the knotted muscle.

"I got it right about the time some misinformed idiot told me you'd been shot." John lifted his head. His melanin-deficient skin showed every crease and shadow of fatigue. "A robbery attempt." He sat back in his chair. "Well, time's passage has taught you consistency—that jibes with what Calvin said you told him. He and I managed to exchange a few words before I found you wandering the halls looking for trouble." He sounded all-business now, which meant his bullshit detector was activated and calibrated. "We agreed that it was utter garbage, of course, and that you're hiding something. So, what are you working on that could have precipitated this attack?"

"I push paper." Jani heard her voice rise, and tried to lower it. Her hand went to her left shoulder again. "I write reports. Those are not shooting offenses, even in this town."

"How do you expect me to lie for you if I don't know what the truth is?"

"Who's asking you to lie? This is Chicago. Things like this happen all the time."

"A robbery attempt gone awry? Jani Moragh, who do you think you're talking to?"

Jani flexed her knee. It scarcely hurt at all now. Either her little factory ran full-tilt or she was too angry to feel the pain. She rose shakily. "You started this interrogation right off the bat. Back in Rauta Shèràa, you'd at least offer me coffee first." She limped to the door. "Good night." She checked her timepiece. "Make that good morning."

"Wait a minute!" John hurried after her. "One of those detectives asked me whether Pascal carried a weapon in the course of his duties and if he still had it when he arrived in Triage. I told her I had it locked away in my office, and I know damned well she's going to show up inside the hour with a Request to Cooperate warrant and demand that I produce it."

Jani leaned against the doorway. Her stomach rumbled. She felt lightheaded. "I can hold it for him just as easily as you can." She dug Lucien's shooter out of her jacket pocket, taking care to leave his wallet and other things behind.

John plucked the shooter from her hand and walked to a large armoire that loomed like a monolith in the far corner of the room. "The bioemotional restriction on your MedRec prohibits you from carrying a dischargeable weapon." He opened a door and activated a touchlock. A small panel slid aside, and he inserted the shooter in the niche. "If you behave, it can be lifted by year's end. If you're caught carrying, it's an automatic two-year extension, and there's not a thing I can do about it."

"Who's asking you to do anything about it!" The shout rang in Jani's ears. The room spun. She slid down the wall, gasping each time her heel grabbed on the thick carpet and forced her to bend her knee.

John hurried to her side and knelt in front of her. He checked her eyes and pulse, then removed a sensor stylus from his pocket and pressed it against the tip of her right index finger. "Your blood sugar's in the basement," he said as he checked the readout. "When did you last eat?"

"Dinner." Jani rested her head against the doorjamb. The sharp wooden ridge dug into her scalp, but she didn't have the strength to move. "I met some friends at Gaetan's."

"Oh?" John loosened her jacket collar, then straightened out her leg. "Who?"

"Steve Forell and Angevin Wyle." Jani felt her mouth move, but the words sounded hollow, as though they came from another room. She hugged herself as a wave of the shivers overtook her.

John rose with a rumbling sigh. "Just sit quietly." He walked to the wall and slid aside a floor-to-ceiling panel, revealing an inset kitchenette. "Don't move," he warned as he disappeared within. Water ran. Something ground and gurgled. Soon, the weighty aroma of brewing coffee filled the air.

"What did you wear?" John's voice growled above the sputter of the brewer.

Jani took one deep breath, then another. Her head cleared. She didn't think caffeine could diffuse through the air, but this was *John's* coffee. "The green thing."

"The mermaid dress." John emerged bearing a tray, looking like heaven's headwaiter. "It's very pretty, but I rather wish you'd have tried one of the others." He handed her a cup. "The copper column is nice, I think. Off the shoulder—"

"Everybody's been out on the town tonight." Jani gestured toward John's suit, slamming the door on any further discussion of her shoulders. "Where were you?"

John eyed her in injury as he set the tray on the floor, then worked into a cross-legged position beside it. "A chamber music recital at the Capitoline. Calvin was—"

"His parents' fortieth. I know." She sipped her coffee. Make that *tried* to sip her coffee. She stared into her cup at the few centimeters of dark foam that filled the bottom.

"I want you to leave here in a relatively alert frame of mind, not in orbit." John handed her what looked like a brightly wrapped chocolate bar. "And not under arrest. Or under sanction, observation, or any other of the legion of oversights possible in this town. Removing Pascal's weapon from the scene was remarkably stupid—you should have handed it to one of the emergency techs immediately."

"It felt good to carry again." Jani examined the bar skeptically. "I hadn't been without for over twenty years."

"I find that a sad commentary on your life." John drew one knee up to his chest and draped his hand over it. His spine remained straight, though, his manner formal. Even after all these years, he still hadn't gotten the hang of *casual*, and the fact that he tried to pull it off under such tense circumstances raised warning alarms. "You don't need to live like a fugitive anymore. You have freedom, and with freedom comes alternatives." His voice dropped until it sounded like a whisper from inside her head. "There's no need for you to live here just because it's the only place on Earth that you know."

Jani nodded vaguely as she tore away the bar's purple and green wrapping. Her mouth watered as she inhaled the scents of chocolate and caramel. "What is this?"

"A meal bar," John snapped. "Now, as I was saying, there's no need for you to stay in Chicago. You could live anywhere."

"I have lived anywhere. Anywhere and everywhere. It's nice being able to stay in one place for a change." Jani broke off one end of the bar, catching the filling on her finger just before it dripped down the front of her jacket. She touched her finger to the tip of her tongue, and tasted the buttery gold of the richest confectionery. "S'good." She popped the piece in her mouth.

"It's a calorie bomb. The way your post-trauma metabolism seems to be kicking along, you should eat two or three of those a day for the next week. That's in addition to your regular meals, *not* in place of." John set his cup on the tray with a clatter. "Are you going to stop changing the subject?"

Jani pulled off another piece of the bar. "I like it here. The work's interesting. And I have *friends*." It sounded strange to say that, considering she'd spent half her life fleeing any sort of connection. Strange, but nice. "There's Frances Hals and her husband. Steve and Angevin. And let's not forget Nema."

"Oh, let's, please." John picked up his cup, but instead of drinking he stared into it. "Work and friends can be found in every city. Seattle, for example, is filled with friendly people."

Most of whom are on your payroll. "I doubt they're any friendlier than they are here."

"I can guarantee no one would shoot at you." He looked up, filmed eyes glittering. "Jani, what hap—?" The entry buzzer interrupted him. *"Yes?"*

The door slid aside and Valentin Parini, John's partner in bleeding-edge science, entered. "It's only me." He looked down at John, then at Jani. "Somebody steal all the chairs?" His evening suit was dark brown, a color that complemented his ash brown hair and hazel eyes perfectly. He had strong bones and a brushed-back hairstyle that accented a widow's peak—devilish handsome described him well.

"Where were you when you heard the good news?" John asked sourly.

"Dinner with the latest love of my life." Val winked at Jani and touched the tip of his chin. "You're dripping caramel."

"We've just been working through a bout of the stubborns." John handed Jani a dispo napkin, then rose to his feet. "If I ever decide to switch to Pediatrics, the behavioral courses should be a snap." He picked up the tray and headed back to the kitchenette.

Jani stuck out her tongue at his receding back, then dabbed caramel from her chin. She swallowed the last bite of meal bar and washed it down with the scant remainder of the coffee. "How's Lucien?" From out the corner of her eye, she saw John step to the kitchenette opening and stand still, listening.

Val saw him too. "He's out of surgery." He walked across

the room and seated himself on the edge of John's desk, within full view of his partner in crime.

Jani watched as an unreadable look passed between the two men. *Ah, this brings back memories.* It was a given that they kept something from her. Her job was to find out what it was. "Can I see him?"

Val shook his head. "Not until later today. A crew from Intelligence showed up—they've got him surrounded. Besides, we had to take him down before we could prep him, and between that and the post-anesthesia, he's not discharging on all battery cells. Better to leave him alone for now." He glanced at John, who nodded once and slipped out of sight.

"I'll stop by this afternoon, then." Jani rolled onto her left knee, waving off Val's offer of help as she struggled to her feet. "I need to wash my hands." She tested her right knee as she walked to the kitchenette, first by putting all her weight on it, then by flexing it as she stood in front of the sink. Both times, she elicited only the barest twinge. She dried her hands, then reached under her trouser leg and removed the coldpack.

John emerged from a walk-in pantry holding a plastic sack full of meal bars. "You should leave that on until you get home."

Jani tossed the gel-filled pack into the sink. "My knee's numb. It feels a lot better." She accepted the bag of bars, taking care to avoid his eye. He'd start making suggestions if she didn't move quickly. Dinner, with another gown thrown in as an inducement. A chamber music recital or two. The rest of their lives. "I had a duffel when I arrived here—where is it?"

"The Triage desk." John stepped in front of her, blocking her path. "I'd feel better if you told me you'd visit Seattle sometime soon. As in immediately."

"I'm sure you would." Jani dodged him easily. "How's your headache?"

"It had eased up, but now it's back. I'm worried about you."

"I'm sure you are." She brushed past a doleful Val, who had taken up sentry duty at the kitchenette entry.

"Seattle's a very nice city," he chimed in support.

"I'm sure it is." Jani stuffed the sack under her arm and darted into the solitary freedom of the hallway.

CHAPTER 15

Jani picked up her duffel in Triage, and refused the desk's offer to arrange a ride home. She walked out into the darkness, mindful that she wouldn't remain alone for long, that John would send a team of his Security officers after her to make sure she arrived home intact.

Sure enough, when she glanced back into the lobby, she saw the aide talking to her comport display, the rigid expression on her face announcing to all that she spoke to A Superior. Jani slipped out of sight and circled around the less-inviting region of the complex. Past the busy receiving docks, the medical waste treatment facility, the utilities outbuildings, all those places where someone in dark clothes carrying a bag and plastic food sack would blend.

She crossed State Street, and continued to veer south and east in the hope that John's Security would assume she had headed north toward the Parkway. Her left shoulder ached enough that she had to sling her duffel over her right; that in turn aggravated her iffy balance and hampered her stride. Her knee griped with every step, the shock of impact zinging down her shin. The damp chill seeped through her jacket. She walked in the shadows, avoiding the light of the streetlamps, all but invisible to the other pedestrians who trudged the early morning hours. Workers on mealbreak, on their way back to third shift jobs. Nightowls, prowling the twenty-four-hour clubs and shops.

Hired killers, hoping to finish what they started.

John's coffee and the meal bar worked magic on Jani's fatigued mental processes. Images that hadn't touched her at the time returned *en force*. The flash of the shooter. Lucien's pained rictus as the agony of the burn clamped down. The fear-driven quickness of John's actions as he aided her after her collapse. His urgings to leave Chicago.

Jani hopped a 'mover as soon as she reached the Boul. She nestled in a rear seat, her eyes on the few haggard faces that shared the ride. No one looked like a hired shooter. No one paid much attention to her. The men looked at her face, then gave her body a quick once-over. The women looked at her clothes and manner and relaxed, counting her another member of the working wounded and therefore safe to ignore.

She disembarked two blocks south and east of her building and approached it so she could see the front and side entrances. Skimmers drifted past—she edged away from the curb to discourage interested parties from offering her a lift.

She cut down a wide, well-kept alley and entered the garage through the entry opposite the one she and Lucien had used. From there, she surveyed the entire tableau. The ramp she'd walked down. The pillar from which shadow the shot had emerged. She studied the area for several minutes, imprinting its layout on her brain. Then she cut across the scancrete floor, her steps echoing in the empty space, and revisited the scene.

Scant remnants of ComPol presence littered the area. A few scraps of barrier tape. A skid mark from a holocam tripod. Jani touched the floor where Lucien had lain, situating in her mind the location of his wound.

She walked to the top of the ramp and switched her duffel to her left shoulder, wincing as the weight settled over the bruise. She stuffed the sack of meal bars into the bag so her hands would be free, as they had been at the time. She then walked down the too-steep incline, matching step for step where she had walked before, her knee complaining with every impact.

She stopped at the place where she had fallen.

Fallen.

I fell. She touched her left shoulder, probed the perimeter of the contusion. *I slipped. Lucien grabbed for me as I fell, to help me up.*

Standing upright, she faced the spot from where the shot

had come. Imagining Lucien still behind her, she reached around and marked in the air the place where his right hip had been.

I fell . . . he tried to help me up.

His right—her left. Contorting her arms, she marked the place on her back that lined up with Lucien's wound. The place the shot would have hit if she hadn't fallen. She then drew an imaginary line through her body, marked the point where it emerged with her hand, and looked down—

He tried to help me up.

—to find she had placed her hand over her heart.

"Looks like you reached the same conclusion I did."

Jani wheeled, nerves keening as augie pricked up his ears.

"I was in my office when the word came." Niall emerged from the shadows. "Half of Intelligence is parked at Neoclona. Shroud must be having a fit." He wore dress blue-greys—the entry light splashed over him, highlighting his packed shooter holster. He strolled down the ramp, his knees taking the impacts with enviable ease. "How's Pretty Boy?"

"Groggy from takedown and anesthesia. They wouldn't let me see him, but I'm told he'll recover completely." Jani stepped down the ramp to the comfort of the level floor. She wandered to the column where she'd found the Grenoble, and saw only a yellow ComPol marker where the weapon had lain. "It is possible that he was the intended target."

"You willing to bet your 'pack on that?" Niall wandered a circle at the foot of the ramp, eyes locked on the scancrete floor. "You willing to bet that whoever wanted you dead knows they missed, and are blowing the dust off their back-up plan?"

Jani leaned against the column to take the weight off her right knee. "You would have to bring that up."

Niall dug into his tunic; a nicstick soon saw the light. He eyed Jani with weary patience. "What did you do?"

Jani pushed off the column and gravitated toward the rear of the expanse. "Nothing."

Niall hurried after her. "This was a messy attempt. Somebody is spooked about something, and they didn't have time to plan. What happened in the past twenty-four hours?"

Jani opened the door that led to the garage stairwell. "I found out my parents were on their way here. I ticked off Anais Ulanova." *I faked a document*—She paused in mid-climb, then sped up before Niall noticed. *I faked a document, and waited for the lids to pop.* "Something popped, all right."

"What did you say?"

"My knee popped. I fell on it during the attack."

Niall unholstered his shooter and moved to one side so that Jani no longer stood in his line of fire. He drew even with her on the stair, then waved her back as they approached the landing. "Stay behind me, and keep your head down." He pushed the door open and went in low, arms extended, shooter gripped in both hands.

Jani scooted around him and ducked behind a waist-high trashzap. "I don't see anything out of the ordinary." She sprawled flat on her stomach and searched for unusual shadows beneath the scattering of skimmers that populated the space.

Niall had darted behind a column. "I'm scanning, and I don't sense anybody." His rough whisper emerged from shadow. "We're alone." He stepped into the light and pocketed his small box-like scanner. He also reholstered his shooter, but took care to leave the clasp undone. "Is this just an attack of nerves, or did you see something?"

"Nerves." Jani walked around the level, glancing through skimmer windows and placing her hand on battery casings, feeling for the residual warmth that indicated a recent trip. "You think *L'araignée*'s behind this."

"You don't want to know what I think." Niall checked the download time on a charge unit. "Where were you two going?"

"Idomeni embassy. An ongoing project had blown up, and they needed my input."

"Did you call to confirm?"

"No. It was a common occurrence." Jani crouched low to explore the shadows beneath a skimmer. Her knee griped accordingly. "You're heading somewhere with this. Spit it out." She straightened to find Niall standing beside her. He made as if to say something, hesitated, then took a deep breath.

"My Guernsey buddy—he has connections in the Channel commercial sector, which is how he found out about *L'araignée*. He couldn't find out many member names, but one of the ones that he heard a lot was Le Blond."

"You think that refers to Lucien? Le Blond happens to be a very common surname in the Channel."

"Le Blond helped organize *L'araignée*, Jani. He was one of the driving forces. He used his Family connections to arrange sweetheart vendor and maintenance contracts for some of the less cultivated members. Now I don't think Pascal is half the genius he thinks himself, but he's no dummy, he has Family connections, and he was in the area during the time in question." Niall's voice had turned cold, hard, like his facts. "He set you up. *L'araignée* knows you promote Haárin business interests in the colonies and they see you as a threat. They yanked his string, and he complied. Only you fell. Pretty Boy tried to pull you back into the line of fire, but he got hit instead."

Jani kicked at the bare floor, then strode to the wall opposite. She felt better when she walked, even when she had nowhere to go.

Niall fell in behind her. "Jan, if it fit any better, you could wear it to Gaetan's."

Jani examined the wall, standing so the beam from a safety light fell over her shoulder and highlighted the area. "Does this surface look right to you?"

"That's my Jani. When in doubt, change the subject." Niall moved in behind her and sighted down. "No." He stepped around her and brushed his hand over the wall surface. "There's an area that looks dull. The rest of the wall is shiny coated scancrete. But there's an area that doesn't reflect."

Jani stepped in front of the dull portion and examined the boundary. "It's a sharp line." She scratched the matte surface with a fingernail. Fine grey powder fluffed—she backed away to avoid inhaling it and risk a film-splitting sneeze.

"Probably just a patch." Niall leaned against a scancrete portion of the wall and folded his arms. "Maybe there used to be a passage between the renovation and the garage."

Jani dropped her bag to the floor at her feet, placed both

hands against the matte panel, and pushed. Lightly first, then harder as the squeaking of shifting polyfill sounded.

Niall grumbled as he moved in beside her and set his hands against the panel. "On three. One . . . two . . . *three*!"

The panel gave with the screech of a startled rodent, then toppled backward into the blackness with a soft, floaty *thuk*. Jani stepped to the side and the shelter of the solid wall, then looked across to Niall to find he had done the same *and* pulled his shooter. "I don't think it's that serious."

"No?" Niall glared across the open space. "You know that just by looking, do you?"

"Hodge said that the construction crew figured out a way to circumvent their parking ban." Jani stepped into the space, taking care not to trip over the narrow gap where the two buildings met. "They're supposed to park their skimmers in the trade lots three blocks away, but they don't find that amenable."

"So they park here and use their ready-made door? So much for high-priced Family security." Niall's voice held aggravated wonder as he followed Jani through the gap. "Holy—!"

They entered a vast skeletal coliseum. No trace remained of the living areas and office space that had filled the former manse. The ten-story interior had been carefully demolished—all the flooring and interior walls had been removed, leaving only the structural supports and the exterior walls with their historic marbles and sculpture. Rings of scaffolding marked every floor, joined by hoists and rack ladders and the occasional portable lift.

"They're supposed to finish this by Thanksgiving." Jani reached out and touched a scaffold support. "Does this look anywhere close to done to you?"

"It looks like a goddamned shooting gallery." Niall stood hands on hips and surveyed the space. "Anybody coming through this opening is a clear target for anybody hunkered down on one of those levels."

"You look at the world differently than the average person, Niall." Jani climbed partway up a ladder, then shook it to test its solidity.

"This is true." Niall sauntered over to a workbench,

brushed off dust with the flat of his hand, and sat. "You going to talk to me, or are you going to keep ducking the issue?"

Jani jumped down from the ladder, taking care to land on her left foot. "I don't know what you mean."

"The hell you don't." Niall eyed her impatiently. "Pascal's going to be in the hospital for a while?" He waited for Jani's affirmative nod. "Leave him there." He looked around the desolate interior again, and grimaced. "This place gives me the jim-jams. Let's go."

"In a second." Jani rummaged through an equipment bin until she freed an aerosol dispenser of lubricant. "Heard anything about my folks?"

"Nothing new to report. Everything proceeding as planned." Niall watched her activate the dispenser. "What the hell are you doing now?"

"When you find a door, first thing you do is see where it goes. Then you fix what needs fixing and remember where it is, because you never know when you may need it." Jani sprayed the lubricant over the sides of the polyfill panel, then returned the dispenser to the tool bin.

Niall helped her drag the now-silent panel back into place. "You look at the world differently than the average person, Jani."

Jani shrugged, catching herself as her left shoulder bit. "This is true."

Niall accompanied Jani to her building entry, offering a not-so-subtle recommendation that she avoid further explorations for the balance of the night. Then a Service sedan drifted out of the darkness and up to the curb.

The passenger-side gullwing popped up; Lt. Pullman bent low to look through the breach. "Good morning, ma'am. Glad to see you're OK." He stopped just long enough for Niall to climb in, then swung the vehicle around and disappeared into the dark.

Jani entered the lobby to find the night desk waiting for her. The ComPol had been by . . . several times . . . they had left messages . . . this was highly irregular. . . .

So's being shot at. Jani left the agitated woman behind for the quiet of the lift. On the way up, she uncased a meal bar.

Chocolate-caramel wasn't her first choice for an early morning snack, but she felt light-headed again and the last thing she needed was another trip to Neoclona to hear John rumble "I told you so."

She keyed into her flat, and slipped through the open door and into the path of a redheaded hurricane.

"Where the hell have you been!" Angevin had returned to her own flat in the interim—she had exchanged her evening-wear for a pullover and trousers in a lived-in shade of yellow. "We've been waiting for *hours!* Don't you know what a comport is!"

"How much do you know?" Jani extracted her arm from Angevin's grasp and headed for the kitchen to find something to wash the taste of meal bar from her mouth.

"Not a fookin' thing." Steve emerged from the kitchen, soft drink dispo in hand, wearing a darker version of Angevin's outfit. "Fifteen minutes after you leave, we hear sirens. Run down to the lobby just in time to see you tumble into the ambulance after Blondie. Then before you can say Bob's yer uncle, we're up the spout with fookin' ComPol."

"We tried to tap friends for news, but nobody knew anything and there was a comlock on calls going in and out of the Ministries." Angevin wedged herself between Jani and Steve. "Are you all right? How's Lucien?"

"I'm fine." Jani tried to circle around the pair, but they moved as one to block her. "Lucien took a shooter blast in the stomach. He suffered burns and impact injuries. He had just come out of Surgery when I left Neoclona. They wouldn't let me see him, though—he was too woozy. But he'll be fine."

"So everyone's *fine.*" Steve raised the dispo like a toast. "So all's bright and sunny and we kin go home, then?" He pushed Angevin aside as gently as his temper would allow and stepped up to Jani. She stood taller than he, but that didn't seem to faze him. "What. Happened?"

Jani squirted past him and darted into the kitchen. "Robbery attempt. Idiot fired before we could give him what he wanted." She yanked open the cooler and scrabbled for a dispo of lemon tonic. She cracked the seal and drank half the container, then turned to find Steve standing in the entry, choirboy face clawed by fatigue.

"I told Ange yer shook and I sent her to bed." He stepped inside and let the door close. "We're sleepin' here, in one of the spares. Brought bedrolls from our flat, until we can order proper furniture. We're movin' in—we're not leavin' you alone."

"That's not necessary."

"Bullshit."

"You could be leaving yourselves open to some sort of retaliation."

"So it warn't no fookin' robbery, were it? It's like what happened to Barry."

"It—it's possible."

The unsureness of Jani's response touched Steve. His anger softened to aggravation—he patted her arm and backed off. "Get some sleep. You look all-in." He took a final swig of his drink and poured the remainder down the sink.

Jani trudged to her bedroom. Undressed. Showered. The egg beneath her right knee had shrunk to a marble, and the joint itself didn't hurt at all when the spray hit it. Her shoulder did, however—if she twisted her neck just so, she could just glimpse the tender, purple-red swelling.

She carried her trouser suit to her closet to hang it up; as she did, she caught sight of the green holosilk. She felt the release of the seams, the slide of the material down her skin. She stood in the middle of the closet, clutching the trouser suit. Then she hangered it and closed the door.

She pulled a pair of sleep shorts and a T-shirt out of her dresser. In her effort to avoid the mirror, she found herself looking at the painting of the costumed couple. It proved a more complicated scene than she had initially thought. The gowned woman stood in the center of the ballroom, amid a swirl of dancing couples. She looked toward the veranda where the young officer, clad in brilliant white, stood, but her expression held more worry than welcome. She may have planned a tryst with him for later that evening, but someone had gotten his signals crossed.

"Is that what happened, Lucien?" She sketched an outline around the young officer with her finger. "Niall thinks you tried to set me up. John and Val think something's up, too. They sure don't want me talking to you." She flicked her finger against his painted brim, as if to knock it off.

Then, for the first time, Jani noted the man with whom the woman had been dancing before the officer made his appearance. A dour, older sort in a staid evening suit, he watched the woman with the same intensity with which she studied the officer. "What do you know that I don't, John?" Jani asked the figure. "Hard fact? Rumor? Or just jealousy?"

She piled into bed. Sleep came eventually. At one point, she dreamed a shooter crack. The imagined sound shook her awake—she opened her eyes to find herself clutching her T-shirt over her pounding heart. She managed to fall asleep again, but it took time. Her head ached, and she flinched at every sound.

CHAPTER 16

"And the plan fer the day is what, then?" Steve sat opposite Jani on the sitting room floor near the window, the remains of a makeshift breakfast scattered between them—tea, bread and jam for Steve, coffee and a meal bar for her. "Talk to the ComPol, get them off yer back?"

Jani braced against the wall and struggled to her feet. "I need to go to Sheridan." She picked a fleck of chocolate from the sleeve of her dark brown trouser suit and massaged away the miniscule smear. "Besides, I have a lawyer. His name is Joaquin Loiaza—let him talk to the ComPol."

"Ah, yeah?" Steve locked his hands around his knee and rocked back. "This is what you want me to tell the green-and-whites when they call for the eighty-seventh time, or better yet, stop by in person?"

"I'll talk to them." Angevin sat at Jani's desk and screened through comport listings for furniture companies. "I know exactly what to say."

"You know exactly what to say to get us all arrested." Steve expelled a healthy billow of smoke. "Ange and I will get started on your paper mail," he said to Jani as he rose, "just to kill time before the ComPol rounds us all up."

"I'm ordering furniture first." Angevin hit the comport pad. "If I have to sit in this chair for one more hour, I'm going to get a nosebleed."

"You found any catalogs?" Steve planted himself in front of the desk. "So's we know what we're orderin'? So's we don't wind up with three purple couches?"

"I know how to furnish a flat."

"Oh yeah? Well, *I* remember—"

"Have fun, kids." Jani pulled her duffel from beneath the desk and waved good-bye as she slipped out the door.

"Foreign Transactions, please." Jani held out her Fort Sheridan ID to the front gate check-in desk.

"Yes, ma'am. Wait here please." The desk corporal disappeared with the ID into the communications alcove.

Jani wandered the tiny lobby. Outside the front window, the main archway of the Shenandoah Gate glistened in the morning sun, its whitestone surface etched with the names of those killed in the Greatest War, the conflict that defined the Commonwealth and her colonies generations before. Tens of thousands of Earthbound names.

Along with a few colonial. Her ever-remembered dead, inscribed in the only memorial they would ever have. *Borgie. Yolan. Felicio. Stanleigh.* Eleven others. Their names didn't belong in the Gate—Jani reentered them by means various after the Gate monitors excised them during their weekly checks. It was a losing battle on her part, she knew—sooner or later, implacability and cryptography would triumph over guile and bloody-mindedness. *But until it does, I'll keep plugging them in.* All the dead merited remembrance, especially those everyone wished forgotten.

"Ma'am?"

Jani turned.

"Colonel Hals is expecting you." The corporal held out Jani's ID, along with a day pass to clip to her jacket. "She says you know the way."

"Lt. Ischi, of course, knew almost immediately it happened. That young man has connections from Base Command to the vehicle pool. He called me at home. 'I hope you don't mind, ma'am,' he said." Frances Hals turned away from her office window and frowned at Jani. She looked prim and collected in her fallweights, wavy brown hair tucked into a tight french roll. "I'm disappointed that you didn't call me yourself."

"I didn't have the time." Jani had settled into her regular

place in the visitor's chair near Frances's desk. "I spent most of the night at Neoclona. When I finally got back to my place, it was all I could do to fall into bed."

"Hmm." Frances walked slowly back to her desk. "All our regularly scheduled dealings with the idomeni embassy have been cancelled until further notice." She lowered into her chair. "Looks like Shai's using this little misfortune as an excuse to reel in Tsecha's lead."

"That doesn't surprise me." Jani crossed her legs with care. Her right knee no longer hurt, and she wanted to keep it that way. "I think she wants to shut him out completely."

"Are they allowed to do that?"

"I think they've started listening to their xenobehaviorists too. I also think the term 'loose shooter' has been explained to them *ad nauseum*."

"Hmm." Frances's round face turned a study in downward curves. She didn't appear as eager to discuss Nema and his quirks as she normally was. "So." She sat forward, cupping her chin in her hands. "What happened?"

"Everybody keeps asking me that."

"You were shot at! Lucien was gravely wounded. Heaven forbid we should care."

Jani picked at the thin band of upholstery covering the chair arm. "I don't know for sure. I think it was a blown robbery attempt, but I just don't know." She held back a "damn it!" One thing she missed about her former life was that she had never let anyone get close enough to ask questions she didn't want to answer. The fact that she lacked a complete answer to this particular question aggravated her even more.

"You'll tell us when you know?"

"Yes."

"All right." Frances held up her hands in surrender, then toyed with the edge of her leather desk pad. "I hate to admit this, but I do have a selfish reason for bugging you." She gave the pad a last, irritated shove. "We've become quite involved with the doings at the embassy since your discharge. In just a few short months, Foreign Transactions has gone from being a glorified colonial shipping office to playing a major role in the determination of Commonwealth–Shèrá policy."

Jani nodded. "You put your bird on the line to make that happen. It was a gutsy move, and you pulled it off."

"You helped." Frances's brown eyes flared a "don't give me that" warning. "The problem is, now that we're perceived as an arm of Diplomatic, we no longer handle the sort of work we performed during your short but eventful stay here. In other words, without the idomeni, we don't have anything to do. And you know what happens when the Service finds out some of its own don't have anything to do?"

Jani tugged her duffel onto her lap. "Reassignment."

"It's not a given, but it has crossed my mind." Frances smiled knowingly. "So, given that I know how much you dislike having people fuss after you, consider my inquiry into your affairs completely self-serving."

Jani let her head drop back against the headrest. "I appreciate it, really."

"No, you don't—you hate it. You're a born lone operator. You prefer that people disappear until you need them."

Jani lifted her head and stared into a quietly attractive face softened with weary humor. She enjoyed Frances's spot-on character assessments . . . except when they were directed at her. "You're the second person to tell me that in the past two days."

"Who was the other one?"

"Dolly Aryton. I went to see her yesterday about some . . . stuff."

Frances had paused to take a sip of tea. She held a hand over her mouth as she grabbed for her napkin. "Dorothea—?" She coughed, then tried again. "The Registry Inspector General?"

"I went to school with her."

"I know that." Frances dabbed at her shirtfront. "Which one was she again?"

"Five of Six. Earthly Might. Family connections." Jani eyed her timepiece as surreptitiously as she could. "Mind if I ask a question?"

"Oh, for heaven's sakes, Jani." Frances's face tightened with aggravation.

Why do I seem to possess such talent in that regard? "Do you think I'm immature?"

"Immature? My word, what did Aryton say to you?" Frances folded the napkin into a neat square and set it next to her cup. "If it makes you feel better, no. My take on the Kilian psyche is that you don't have much use for the social details other people think are important. No one's going to get a 'Good morning, and how are the kids?' from you—you just jump right into the business and that tends to ruffle folks. You're also intensely private, and when someone probes, the walls fly up. Sometimes, that knocks people off-guard, and sometimes it makes them angry." She shrugged. "And sometimes they find it attractive." She studied the folded napkin, her lips pursing. "Like your fine Lt. Pascal. I can't think of another man of my acquaintance who has less interest in the everyday, and he follows you like a moth follows a flame."

But Niall would tell you that he had his reasons. Jani heard a mild bumping against the office entry, like someone moving furniture.

Frances sighed. "That's Ischi's latest version of a ten-minute warning. He thinks it's less rude. I wish he'd use the intercom like everyone else." She tapped her workstation touchboard and checked her calendar. "And I do have a meeting in twenty minutes at North Lakeside, so I had better get my tail in gear." She gathered some files from a slotted rack. "Did you come here for a reason, or was this an actual social call?"

"I felt restless." Jani forced a smile in an effort to practice one of those disregarded details. "I just wanted to talk." She fingered the day pass, which would allow her to walk unimpeded anywhere in the South Central area of the base. Not that a visit to her former CO had been an onerous price to pay to obtain it. She liked Frances, and enjoyed her company. She called her a friend. That made it OK. No harm, no foul.

South Central Bachelor Officers' Quarters were situated atop the highest in the series of rises that served as an informal boundary between the business side of the base region and the sports facilities that took up most of the West Central area. Twelve floors of white cement, unadorned and sparsely landscaped, it seemed designed with the intent to persuade its tenants to either marry or move out as soon as possible. An interim place for the newly commissioned, it contained nothing to recommend it as a long-term domicile.

Lucien's lived here for four years. Jani entered the empty lobby. *Officially.* In reality, he had spent most of the time on Anais Ulanova's Security team, and had lived where her orders demanded. A good part of that time, he had offered during one pillow confession, had been spent running down rumors of Jani's existence. And Jani had believed him. That's how they had met, after all, when Lucien served undercover on the Interior ship that ferried her to Earth for the first time.

But did he spend all his time looking for me? Or had he worked double-duty laying the groundwork for *L'araignée? Are you Monsieur Le Blond, Lucien?*

She darted past the open entry of the rec room, from which the raucous sounds of a Cup match emanated. Up the stairs to the mezzanine. Down the hall to the lift.

Fifth floor, Number 5W1. Jani watched the floor indicator flick upward. She had obtained the address months before from the Base Directory. She had never visited Lucien's rooms, though—he had never invited her and she felt that there were some things about him she didn't want to know.

My mistake. She disembarked the lift. Turned left. Right. Left. Stopped before the middle door in the short hallway.

L. Pascal. The name had been etched on a rectangle of unpolished metal, the sort of seat-of-the-pants doorplate meant to be disposed of in a few months. Jani gave the door a sharp rap, because no one ever heard loud sounds, only quiet ones. Hit the entry buzzer twice. Knocked again.

Then she dug into her duffel for Lucien's wallet and picked the meager contents, looking for a key card. *Although God knows what good it will do.* The lockmech consisted of a handpad as well as a card reader, and since Jani had never visited, Lucien had never had a chance to key in her print. She dug out the key card and ran it through the reader anyway, then touched her hand to the plate with a sigh of acknowledged defeat. *I should have asked Niall to crib me access, but then he'd know I suspect Lucien of something and he'd take that ball and run with it—*

She froze as she heard the *whirr* of the lock. The slide of a bolt. The whisper of polywood surfaces sliding over one another as the door swept aside.

Jani stared dumbly at the opened door, hopped over the threshold as the sound of approaching footsteps startled her, then damned herself for her stupidity as the door slid closed behind her.

He's trapped me. He had rigged a system that let people in, but didn't let them out. Base Security was no doubt bearing down on her location at that very moment.

Then I had better get a move on, hadn't I?

Jani looked around. The sitting room contained a couch along the near wall, a table with two chairs along the windowed far wall. A narrow desk stood in the near corner by the door, its work surface filled by a comport and a stylus holder.

Jani walked to the desk. The comport's incoming message indicator showed still and dark. She hit the command pad anyway, in case it malfunctioned, but the device remained silent.

She gave one of the drawer pulls a ginger yank—like the entry, it opened to her touch. *I know how he did it.* An Intelligence gadget expert like him would have had no trouble obtaining her scan from her ServRec and coding it into his room network.

She checked the drawer's bare interior, feeling along the top and the underside in case he had stuck anything in the runners. *A* L'araignée *expense chit. A nameplate reading "Le Blond."* She closed the drawer and opened another, riffled through the blank parchment pads, picked through the small dish containing salvaged parts from old styli. Examined the last drawer to find it empty.

As she gave the bare white walls a visual once-over, Jani dug into her briefbag for her own devices. The bugscan to check for monitoring appliances, the sniff to nose out whatever toys Lucien had stashed away for later use. She examined the couch cushions, the furniture frames, the baseboards, the lighting fixtures. She even peeled up a corner of the thin carpet to check for a floor cache. The flooring, however, proved to be solid poly, a material that prevented such a hiding place.

Jani moved on to the bathroom, which, like the sitting room, contained very little of its occupant. The shelf above the sink held only a stack of dispo cups and a toiletry kit. She unclasped the kit and rummaged through the compartments. *Shaver . . . soaps . . . hairwash . . . toothbrush . . .*

She probed the innermost pocket, flinching as her fingernail struck something hard. She pushed further, looping her finger around the small, stone-like object and pulling it out into the light.

. Red and blue painted clothes reflected as though still wet. A tiny face, its eyes closed in sleep. The missing piece from the matryoshka. The innermost one.

The baby. Jani examined the tiny figure, on distracted lookout for any grooves or pinholes into which a bug could have been inserted. She skirted around any thoughts as to what the presence of the doll in Lucien's kit *meant*—that was the sort of question to toss at Dolly or Frances. *He put it here for me to find.* She held that thought close as she stuffed the doll back in its recess and set the bag back on the shelf, then scanned the bathroom as she had the sitting room.

The bedroom, to Jani's complete lack of surprise, was the one place where Lucien let his personality show. Instead of standard issue white polycottons, he'd made his bed with silk-like linens in the same rich, chocolate shade as his eyes. His pillows were overlarge and encased in paisley-patterned covers of burgundy, brown, and dark blue. Jani scanned them, then commenced a hand-search. She probed under one pillow, then inside the case itself. Her hand closed around something silky.

"What the hell . . . ?" She pulled out a favorite bandbra that she had given up for lost a month before. It had been laundered and carefully folded, and exuded the peppery aroma of an expensive cologne. She stared at it, her mind stalling as it did over the doll. *He . . . wanted me to find this.* It was the only reason that made sense. She tucked the bra back where she found it, then continued her exploration. She found nothing else of note, except for a few long strands of red hair.

She scanned the closet with its neat row of uniforms, the walls and fixtures. She then moved on to the dresser, which proved as sparsely decorated as the desk. Sparse, yes, but oh so tasteful. A brush-comb set in heavy sterling silver. A catch-all dish of antique china. A head and shoulders portrait of a young boy, framed in silver and leaning against the mirror.

Jani picked up the sketch. The boy appeared in his early teens, androgynous beauty just beginning to segue into masculine handsomeness. He wore an open-necked white shirt. His silver-blond hair fluttered in the artist's breeze.

"Portrait of the lieutenant as a young man." Jani pondered the familiar line of jaw and chin, then set the picture down and turned her attention to the drawers. There were three of them—she tugged open the top one.

Uh . . . huh. She lifted out a weighty silk scarf adorned with the bold scrollery popular with the Family women she had seen in her building. *I'll bet my 'pack this once belonged to Anais.* Several more bandbras and a couple of men's T-shirts, all laundered and scented.

Jani sorted and counted. Eight items in all, belonging to six women and two men. She wondered absently whether the redhead rated a souvenir, or if she hadn't yet worked her way into that special category. *And then there's me.* She wondered what she had done to rate the pillowcase of honor.

The next drawer contained a more mundane assortment—Lucien's underwear, socks, and gymwear.

Jani pulled at the bottom drawer, then pulled again. Repositioned her hands and yanked hard, without success. She set down her briefbag, crossed her legs at the ankle, and lowered to the floor. Tried to remove the drawer above to see if she could go in over the top, and found that one fastened to the runners in such a way that she'd need a metal saw to hack it out.

"This drawer, you lock. Why?" A snatch of childhood story surfaced in her memory. In it, the husband told his new bride, "You may open every door in the house but this one."

"And we know what she did, don't we?" Jani dragged her bag onto her lap. She pulled on a pair of dispo gloves, the sort she wore to keep skin oils from contacting delicate paper. She didn't care that she had left hair, skin, and fingerprints throughout the suite. She and Lucien had been seen together around Sheridan, and it would be his word against hers that she had never before visited his rooms. However, she hadn't yet left anything in a place no one would expect, and while her hair and skin cells could waft about and wind up anywhere, her prints would stay where they were put.

Gloves in place, she searched through her miscellaneous tools for a suitable pry, and uncovered a knife that she used to open particularly stubborn envelopes. "Yes, Lucien, I'm playing into your hands. I'm doing just what you want me to do. Well, you can needle me about it later." She stood, pulled the dresser away from the wall, and wedged the blade into the paper-thin gap where the dresser's back panel met the frame. Trying to lockpick or pry open the drawer from the front would have taken hours and tools and devices she didn't have. Besides, the drawer fronts were too thick and well protected, while the rear panel usually proved, as in this case, to be only a thin sheet of poly. *They never expect you to go through the back.* That lapse of judgment on the part of the furniture manufacturers of the Commonwealth had served her well for many years.

It took her thirty-two minutes to pry the side of the panel away from the frame to the point that she could fit her hand through the gap. She walked around to the front of the dresser, pulled out the drawer above the locked drawer as far as it could go, then returned to the rear. As it turned out, the drawers were separated by more thin layers of poly. An inconvenience, but not an insurmountable one. Jani wedged her knife into a corner and pried some more—after a few minutes, she had freed the edge sufficiently that with the help of a stylus-light, she could see into the locked drawer's interior.

She had to lie on her stomach and prop herself up on her elbows to see into the tight space. Her lower back cramped as she boosted her torso; the points of her elbows ached from supporting her weight. She flicked the light beam between tight and wide angle—tight was brighter, but wide illuminated a larger space. She had no idea what to expect. More valuable gifts? A long shooter, broken down into easily stored sections? Sex toys bizarre enough for even Lucien to hide?

Instead of any of those, she found . . . an arrangement. Neat rows of folded cloths, either napkins or scarfs, lined the bottom of the drawer. Centered atop most of the squares were small objects: a shot glass, a marker disc of the type handed out by casinos, a stylus, a small hairclip, and other items, their only commonality their small size and their ordinariness.

Jani counted. Lucien had folded twenty-four small squares, of which fifteen held objects. She tried to push her hand into the small breach so she could reach the casino marker, the closest object in the strange collection. Failing that, she crawled around the front for her bag and mined for the long-blade forceps she used to pick up delicate documents.

It was an easy pickup. She'd had practice at that sort of thing.

Jani stood up. Uncricked her back. Pocketed the marker. Smoothed the poly separator back into place and straightened the rear panel until only a minor bend at the corner betrayed her invasion.

He'll know. But that had been the point of the entire game, hadn't it? He'd know she looked, and he'd know she knew. *That he keeps souvenirs.* Of his special sexual conquests. *And other . . . events in his life.* Whatever they were.

Jani pushed the dresser back against the wall. Gathered her bag. Did one final sweep to make sure things looked as they had when she entered.

The front door opened for her, releasing her into the quiet of the hallway, negating her concern about reverse alarms. Three halls, three turns. The lift down to the mezzanine. The lobby, and the sounds of football matches. Outside, and the bright sun, cool breeze, and the bump and jostle of normal life.

Her nerves nipped at her—she braved the long hike to the Shenandoah Gate to dull their edge. She felt the casino marker in her pocket, weightless yet leaden, filled with information that she had always known existed, but hadn't needed until now.

CHAPTER 17

Tsecha leafed through the latest Council reports transmitted from Shèrá, combing through the phrases for his name. He did not see it, of course. Unless his workstation search of the machine versions of the documents had faltered badly, he did not expect to. *But I look anyway.* Because he had nothing else to do. Because he felt well on the Way to madness, and the turning of pages calmed his disjointed mind.

After he finished reading exactly three pages, he looked up to the timeform on his work table and counted backward, converting to humanish chronography as he did so. *Five hours since the sunrise.* Five hours since Dathim had departed for the Exterior Ministry to search for the most propitious place to lay his tile. Among other things.

Tsecha once more forced his gaze upon the Council report. After three more pages, he would look at the timeform again, count backward again, convert time again. He felt this pattern served him best. If he looked at the timeform more often, it appeared as though no interval had passed at all, as though all was *now* and nothing had happened. If he checked it less often . . . well, he could not check it less often. *Then I would go mad, and truly.*

He pressed his sleeve to his mouth to stifle an unseemly yawn. He had not slept. His encounter with Dathim had agitated and thrilled him. He had passed the night staring at his ceiling and remembering Rauta Shèràa during that final Laumrau season. The nights, long and sleepless as the one he had just spent, when he and his Hansen plotted and planned and searched the humanish enclave for his missing Jani.

Unfortunately, we did not find her. But they had battled John Shroud, for whom lies and deceit were as speaking and breathing, and to win that bout would have been most difficult. He and Hansen had no assistance, no information—the Consulate preferred to believe his Jani dead, therefore dead she was.

It seemed as though I fought only humanish then. His own Vynshàrau, he had not counted as adversary until the war's end. *Then when our time came, I fought them as they were meant to be fought.* Openly, with well-tuned argument and honorable disputation, not with the stealing of documents, the plundering of offices and laboratories, the treachery, and the lies. He and his many esteemed enemies would all have preferred to be slaughtered in the streets as the Laum had been rather than to stoop to such behavior in the sacred halls of Temple.

Now it appeared the time had changed, and with that change came confusion and difficulty in believing what had happened. *It was much easier to do this subterfuge when I was the only one who knew how.* Now everyone possessed such knowledge, from the Oligarch to the Haárin. *And I am left behind.*

Three more pages. Another evaluation of the timeform.

Tsecha leaned back in his chair. He felt the frame stab him in the usual places, the sole constancy in his life over the last days. *What do you do now, Dathim?* Which room did he stand in? Whose desk did he search? *Where did you learn such things?* Who had served as his Hansen, his teacher?

Three more pages. After he assessed time's passage, he paused to watch the shadows commence their meander across his wall. A worthless exercise, and truly. Most appropriate to his new station at the embassy.

"NìRau?"

Tsecha twisted in his chair, gouging himself in the side.

Sànalàn stood in the entry. She wore an informal overshirt and floor-length skirt in the color of wet sand, which meant she had been about the business of the altar room.

"The altar cloths should be changed. I have brought these for your approval." She stepped into the workroom and extended her arm, over which she'd draped several folded oblongs of brown and dull green. The cloths had been freshly laundered, the hems newly rolled. Hem-rolling was a tedious duty, and as such allowed for contemplation.

Ah. Tsecha took the top cloth from the pile and pretended to examine it as he awaited the outcome of Sànalàn's meditation. She offered no formal indication that she wished to discuss something with him. But she had been his assumptive daughter and suborn since Aeri's death, and he had long ago learned to recognize her informal signs. "These are most sound, nìa, and truly." He handed the cloth back to her, and waited.

Sànalàn took the cloth and slapped it atop the pile. She then stood as though captured in place, as though a serpent crawled past her and she dared not move until it had passed.

Tsecha glanced back at his timeform. Dathim would no doubt spend most of the day at Exterior. Perhaps until sunset, or even beyond. This meant that Tsecha could offer Sànalàn as much time as she needed to discuss her meditations.

"We must speak, nìRau."

And so it began.

Tsecha closed the cover of the Council report. "Yes, nìa." He stood and walked to his window, which looked out over the embassy grounds, landscaped with the grasses and shrubs of Shèrá. "Say what you will." He fixed his gaze on what little of his homeworld that he recognized, and waited.

"You have stated repeatedly before idomeni and humanish that I am not to succeed you." Sànalàn's voice emerged level, with none of the elevated tones or inflections of supplication. "I have spoken of this with nìaRauta Shai. She tells me I should not be concerned, that I am your suborn by ordination of Temple and Council, and that more than your word is needed to remove me from this station."

Tsecha turned his hands palms-up and raised them to waist level, a gesture of profound agreement. "Such is true, nìa." He rounded his shoulders, but only by the smallest deviation from vertical. A hint of displeasure to come, rather than a warning of existing anger. "But you should consider that a suborn requires the complete confidence of her dominant in order to train effectively. You should also consider that, after the events of these last days, such confidence no longer exists."

"Did it ever?"

Tsecha turned to find Sànalàn standing beside his work table, one hand gripping the edge as though she needed support to stand. "For as long as I remember, you searched for her. From the time I first studied the scrolls and laved the altar stones, I listened to you talk of her to friends and enemies alike as though she served you and not me. I wondered for so long who this Kilian was, this strange humanish that you felt merited your place. Then I learned." She released her hold on the table, standing still and silent as though she needed to regain her balance. Then she pulled the cloths one by one from her arm and stacked them atop one another on the table.

After she finishes, she will pick them up, one by one, and place them again across her arm. Such actions, Tsecha knew as he knew his robes and his rings. "You learned only what Cèel and Shai wished you to know, nìa, that my Jani slaughtered the Laumrau as they took sacrament. They left it to me to tell you of the betrayal of our Way by the Laumrau, and the treachery of Rikart Neumann. By then, it was too late. Cèel's half-truths suited your ambitions better, thus you preferred them."

"My *ambitions*?" Sànalàn's voice deepened as her shoulders rounded. "I did not choose to serve as your suborn, nìRau, I was chosen. As was my body-father. As were you. As are all who serve the gods. We are given no choice." She clenched the topmost cloth she held, crumpling it as paper. "The gods marked me, nìRau, by birth and examination. Are you maintaining that they did not know what they did? Are you saying that you know better than they who should serve them?"

Tsecha turned away so that he could not see Sànalàn's posture. Only if he ignored her form and concentrated on her words could he divorce her from his memories of her youth, when she argued with him over lessons and made him laugh. When she spoke in ways that brought back her body-father. When he had esteemed her. *You have come here to betray me, nìa, to make me utter blasphemies that you can report to Shai.*

"You must provide me an answer, nìRau." The voice,

stripped of respectful inflection, goaded him. "I am deserving of one, and truly."

The ground cover outside Tsecha's window captured the sunlight and returned a blaze of blue. *My Jani warned us all of the Sìah, and your love of rules. Now you will punish me for breaking rules by causing me to break more.* "You would perform adequately as Chief Propitiator if times were as normal, nìa. I have no doubts in that regard." Tsecha remained focused on the view out his window. "But as we change, as the times become not normal, adequacy will not serve. We will need the strength of one who knows how to fight, who knows death, who knows . . . loyalty." He heard a roaring in his head, as he had on the night Aeri died. The Laumrau had bombed the Temple, and all Vynshà knew that the next battles would attain a level unlike any ever fought by idomeni. "Even as she acts as toxin, even as she brings pain and change, my Jani protects those she calls her own." He offered silent prayer, and turned to face his traitor. *You may deny your truth in order to save it. I am Vynshàrau, and I would sooner die than corrupt it so.* "I predict great change, and with it, great pain. Those who claim my Jani as their dominant will need the protection that only she can give."

Sànalàn had once more gripped the edge of the work table, but whether she did so out of anger or fear for the steps she took, she did not make clear by her posture or gesture. "You deny the will of the gods?"

"I interpret what I believe their will to be. Cèel and Shai deny my interpretation because it does not suit their beliefs. They defer to me as propitiator, yet deny me the right to act as is my duty. So humanish are they in their conflict between words and actions, it is as though they have already hybridized." Tsecha savored the anger that leached into his words, and rounded his shoulders fully in gratifying announcement of the emotion. He wished his Jani in the room, so he could hear her yell at him to wait until it is safe. *It will never be safe, nìa. It will only . . . be.*

"You dishonor the Oligarch and his suborn with your words. You spread disorder as the winds strew sand." Sànalàn's own posture bowed to match his. "I should challenge you."

"Yes, nìa. You should." Tsecha fought back the impulse to shout aloud in joy. Only a little while before, he sat at his work table contemplating shadows. *And now I have this glorious declaration!* "But before you do so, consider the certain result. Consider that never in the history of the Vynshà Temple have declared enemies served as chief and suborn propitiator. Chained by tradition as Cèel is, do you believe and truly that he would allow such a thing?"

"Cèel is not so chained, nìRau." Sànalàn straightened in respect as she uttered the Oligarch's name. "He is the one who commands us to act as walls before the humanish—it is *you* who seek to shackle us by your interpretations of tradition. To scare us with your talk of hybridization, when we all know the blending will never be!" She bowed her shoulders again, in a hunch only possible in one so young. "You are disorderly! You are unseemly! I do challenge you!"

Tsecha could hear Hansen's voice in his head. *You get them where you want them, and then "Gotcha!"* Hansen spoke of the Consulate humanish, of course, but if idomeni were determined to behave as such, let them learn what it meant. "You must petition your dominant for the right to offer challenge." He slumped in grave dignity. "Do you petition me, nìa?"

Sànalàn's spine wavered as a young tree in the wind. "Yes, nìRau, I do petition you." Her voice lilted with uncertainty as the gravity of her action bore upon her.

Tsecha nodded in humanish nothingness. "Petition is conveyed. Right is granted. Challenge is accepted. Which of us will inform Suborn Oligarch Shai, nìa?"

The joy of challenge left Sànalàn's posture. Her left arm crossed over her soul in dismay. *"NìRau?"*

"Yes, nìa?" Tsecha bared his teeth.

"NìaRauta Shai will take no joy in this!"

"You are quite correct in that, nìa, and truly." He tried to imagine his Jani's reaction when she heard of what had transpired and felt his own soul clench, for his Jani scared him more than Shai ever did. "You have taken steps against me that no other suborn has ever taken against their dominant. In your fear of change, you have changed beyond belief."

Sànalàn's arm dropped to her side as her anger revived. "It is your Kilian's fault! I do this because of her!"

My toxin. "Yes, nìa. So you do." He jerked his shoulders in a maddening humanish shrug. "So do I." He turned away from his newest enemy toward the blue lawns of home. "So do we all."

"This is a desecration and a denigration! This is anathema!" Shai paced before her work table, a humanish trait that she had acquired during the War. "This cannot be!"

"Challenge cannot be retracted after it is accepted by the challenged, Shai." Tsecha stood in solitary censure in the middle of the Suborn Oligarch's private workroom. Sànalàn had long since been escorted to her rooms by Diplomatic Suborn Inèa, who had pledged to serve as her support, much to Shai's consternation.

"You knew this would happen, Tsecha." Shai lapsed into the short sentences and truncated gestures of Low Vynshàrau, as was her habit when angered. "She is as youngish, and your constant public declarations of Kilian have dishonored her. She sought to discuss the matter with you, and you lured her into the worst show of disunity that we have ever displayed!"

"You sent her to trap me into blasphemy. Your attempt failed. See the price of failure when you play as humanish?" Tsecha pressed a hand to the point where his left leg met his hip, and winced. "I am sitting down, Shai." He limped to a low seat set against the wall opposite Shai's desk.

Shai stopped in midstride. "You are not . . . ?"

"No, I am not *ill,* Shai." Tsecha stressed the word for sickness because he knew Shai disliked such things discussed openly. "I am only tired."

Shai swept her right hand across her face as though she brushed away one of Jani's wasps, a gesture of profound displeasure. "I did not send your own suborn to trap you."

"Do you think me stupid, Shai—of course you did."

"Do you call me a liar?"

"Does that shock you? I have called you worse." Tsecha maneuvered a cushion so that it padded a particularly sharp metal prong. "Have you learned anything of my Jani?"

Shai hesitated. "You will be most happy to hear that she is apparently most well. She roams the city. Lt. Pascal remains in the Neoclona facility. He is to leave soon, I understand. His injuries were not insignificant, but humanish augmentation precipitates rapid healing." She gestured in confusion. "How openly they speak of their illnesses. It stuns me continuously."

Tsecha sat so his left leg stuck straight out. A bizarre posture, complicated by the unfamiliar irritations of Shai's furniture. "It is wise to get past an enemy's ability to stun before imitating them in everything they do." He lapsed into Low Vynshàrau as well—the roughened language complimented his physical discomfort. "One of our soldiers would have explained such to you if you had asked."

"You are arrogant, Tsecha."

"I am arrogance itself, Shai. So I have been told many times." Tsecha felt the pain ease in his hip, a muscle cramp only. "When will the challenge be allowed to take place?"

"There will be no challenge." Shai walked again, this time to the far end of the long room and back. She had arranged all her furniture against the walls so nothing impeded her loping stride. "I will return you to Shèrá before I allow such."

"But you plan to do such anyway, Shai." Tsecha bared his teeth. "This is the excuse for which you have searched! Most excellent, Shai, and worthy of the most deceitful humanish."

"This challenge would devastate us. It will not be allowed to take place."

"As I am the challenged, it is for me to relinquish the right, and such I will never do."

"I will tell Cèel of this."

"Yes, Shai, you will tell. Such is your way." Tsecha rose and walked to the door, holding onto the heavy wood of the entry before pushing himself away and into the hall.

The news of Sànalàn's challenge had already traveled into every corner of the embassy with the air and the light. The greetings Tsecha received were delivered with gestures of perplexity and question, surprise and anger. He looked forward with thankfulness to the solitude of his rooms. Now, the prospect of turning pages held the promise of rest, which he needed most surely.

His step quickened as he approached his door. He did not notice the shadow across the hallway until it stepped forward into his path.

"You will walk with me, nìRau." Dathim wore the drab colors of a crafts worker, a dark green cloth wrapped around his shorn head. He spoke in statement, not in question, as though the possibility of refusal did not exist.

Tsecha again pressed a hand to his hip. The ache had returned, dull but persistent. Idomeni philosophers made much of the mind-focusing abilities of pain, but he had lost patience with such, and truly. *I must sleep.* And take sacrament—it had been seasons since he recalled a true longing in his soul for such.

Then he caught sight of the weighty sling pouch hanging from Dathim's shoulder, of the sort used by craftsworkers to carry their tools. "Yes, ní Dathim." He took a step forward and suppressed a groan as pain shot down his leg. "I will walk with you."

"The Exterior Ministry is a most strange place." Dathim's stride covered ground as rapidly as a skimmer. His speech came too quickly for his gestures to keep up—his posture altered so quickly he appeared in spasm. "Storage rooms next door to work rooms instead of in separate wings. Humanish sitting at work tables out in the open, in the middle of hallways!"

"They are called *receptionists*, ní Dathim." Tsecha struggled to match the Haárin's stride, but finally surrendered to pain and fatigue. "Or sometimes, they are just called *desks,* like the furniture at which they sit." He limped to the first bench he saw, and sank gratefully onto the sun-warmed surface. The radiant heat warmed him through his robes, a gift from the gods, and truly.

"Remarkable!" Dathim circled the bench, head down, like a youngish inscribing a games boundary. "NìaRauta Atar advised me to seek you out, nìRau Tsecha, for absolution. Such were the things we saw that she felt it necessary." He stopped in place and glanced at Tsecha. "This is why we speak here, nìRau. Because I seek absolution."

"Wise, ní Dathim."

"In case we are asked why we speak so frequently. It is because my soul is troubled by so much contact with humanish."

"I understand, ní Dathim."

Dathim turned full-face. His gold eyes altered to molten yellow in the bright sunlight. "You are not well, nìRau." Again, he spoke in statement, not in question.

"I am tired, ní Dathim." Tsecha shivered as a lake breeze brushed him. "I have not slept since we spoke amid the trees."

"I slept most well." Dathim sat, legs splayed in the sprawl of a humanish male. "It is wise to do so at times such as these." He lowered the sling pouch to the tiles at his feet and freed the closures. "Humanish are strange."

"Reading of and hearing of does not prepare one for the reality, ní Dathim." Tsecha paused to untangle one of his side braids, which a gust of breeze caused to entangle in an earring. "At times, the disorder is enlivening. Other times, it is most vexing, and tru—" His words expired to nothing as Dathim opened the sling pouch, and he saw what lay inside.

"They have no idea, nìRau." Dathim reached into the pouch and lifted out a documents slipcase. Beneath it lay more slipcases, folders, and wafer envelopes. "None."

"*Dathim.*" Tsecha leaned forward and ran a finger over the slipcase.

"They meet us outside, the humanish. Minister Ulanova is one of them. She laughs too loudly. Her hands flutter as a youngish. I do not like her." Dathim sat back, hands in tense rest atop his thighs, yellow eyes watching the water. "They lead us inside. Me. NìaRauta Atar, who does not belong but she is my facilities dominant, so I cannot argue. Ní Fa, who is suborn to me. The young pale-haired one, who looks as the lieutenant who was shot—?"

Tsecha visualized an angry red face. "Lescaux."

Dathim nodded. "Lescaux. He takes over. He precedes us, which is odd, considering his station. He should walk behind, and let one of his suborns lead, but such are humanish." He nudged the sling pouch with his booted toe, so that the gaping opening closed. "He is despised."

"Despised?"

"Beddy-Boy, they call him when he cannot hear." Dathim raised a hand and let it drop, a gesture that meant nothing. "Ulanova has elevated him. She touches him when she thinks they are alone, the way humanish do. Why do the others laugh?"

Tsecha flicked his right hand in puzzlement. "Humanish make mockery of such, I have learned. The difference in age and station bothers them. It makes no sense. Such elevations are most seemly. Most orderly."

"Maybe humanish get it wrong. Like Lescaux leading us. I have noticed that humanish often get it wrong." Dathim sat in silence, his gaze still on the water. "They show us the lobby first. It is an open space with many windows. Most appropriate for a wall mural or a floor work. Not *both*. Nìa-Rauta Ulanova wants *both*." He reached up and tugged the cloth from his head, exposing his sheared scalp. "A smaller space, I tell them. Otherwise, it is too much. So they take me upstairs, to the conference room."

Tsecha grew aware that he held his breath, and forced himself to inhale.

"The room they show me is in the same wing with the dominants' rooms. The *offices*. I watch the humanish walk from one to the other as if what belongs to one belongs to all. No hand readers. No ear scans. They label the doors with the names of the residents. It is as walking into my workroom and taking a tool from its hook!" Dathim's breathing rasped, as though he ran. "They take me to the conference room. It is beside Ulanova's office, connected by an inner door."

Tsecha closed his eyes.

"They take me inside the conference room. It is large, with a window. I say I can tile the wall opposite the window. Ulanova says she wants the floor, as well. I say, too much. She says, what of the short wall? Perpendicular to the wall I will tile. Opposite the wall with the inner door." Dathim's breathing slowed. "I needed to sight. Several times. I say I need room to do such. Lescaux opens the inner door. I sight. Several times. The first time, I walk by Ulanova's desk. I look at what is there. I cannot tell what concerns your Kilian. The second time, I take a file from the middle of a stack, and put it in my pouch. The third time, another file from the top of a stack. Four, five, six times I sight. Each time, I take a file from a different place, except for the last time, when I take the wafers from a holder beside Ulanova's comport."

"But you do not know what you took?"

"It is on a dominant's work table. It must therefore be important."

"Yes." Tsecha opened his eyes, then squinted as the glare of the sun off a lakeswell pained him. "Ní Dathim?"

"Yes, nìRau?" Dathim sat forward in another humanish posture, elbows on knees, legs still open, hands hanging inward.

"When humanish steal, they follow certain protocols. Either they ensure that the thing they take will not be missed, or not be missed until they are well away." Hansen's rules played through Tsecha's memory, in his Tongue's mellow, musical voice. "It is best that the thief not be around to be linked to the thievery. Nìa Ulanova will realize quite soon that these files you have taken are no longer in her office. It may not take her long to determine that you took them, and you and I will still be here in this damned cold place when she does so."

Dathim held up his hands, then let them drop, yet another variation on the ubiquitous humanish shrug. "They would not think a Vynshàrau could do such things, nìRau."

"You are Vynshàrau *Haárin*, ní Dathim."

"How well do the humanish know the difference, nìRau?"

"They will soon learn." Tsecha rose slowly and trod the short path that led from the bench to a stand of shrubs. His hip no longer ached, but his head pounded.

"I did as you asked, nìRau." Dathim's voice pitched low in anger.

"I asked you to look for documents about my Jani."

"I did not have time to read, nìRau, only to take!"

"Yes, and now you must get rid of that which you took quite soon, and truly."

"How?"

"If I admit I have them . . . the humanish call such an *incident,* ní Dathim. Humanish do not like incidents." Tsecha turned and walked back to the bench, kicking at the pouch with his booted foot as he passed it.

"An incident?" Dathim's voice held a tension beyond anger. "As your suborn challenging you—that is an incident, also?"

"So, you have been listening to conversations in hallways again. Yes, ní Dathim, that is also an incident. I am quite good at them, and truly." Tsecha kicked at the pouch again. "I can think of only one way to get rid of these."

Dathim passed a hand over his clipped head. "Tell me, nìRau."

Tsecha told him.

CHAPTER 18

Jani returned to her flat to find a great deal less open space than when she left.

"Now this is more like it." Steve sprawled across one end of the room's new centerpiece, a large couch upholstered in ivory polycanvas. "And there's a table in the dining room now. With chairs yet. One can actually sit and eat and not have to chow over the kitchen sink—*that's* a concept I can live with."

"You've gone soft in your old age is your problem." Jani sat at the opposite end of the couch, picking through the leafy innards of her Neoclona vegetable sandwich as she surveyed her new furnishings. A pair of off-white chairs now sat in the far corner. Adding to the new decor were a few strategically placed birch tables, brushed steel floor lamps, and a huge oval rug in shades of sapphire, cream, and tan.

Jani popped the last bite of lunch into her mouth, then thumped the cushion on which she sat—it was thick and firm and buffered her back marvelously. "I'm going to miss that wide-open feel."

"Blow yer wide-open feel. Every time I talked, I heard an echo." Steve stuck an unignited 'stick in his mouth, and chewed reflectively. "So, what'd ya do at Sheridan?"

Jani plucked at the cushion edge. "Visited Frances Hals. I figured she'd heard about the shooting, and I knew she'd worry until I checked in."

"Could have called her. Saved a trip."

"Some things should be handled in person."

"Jan the Goodwill Ambassador. Will wonders never cease?" Steve lay back his head and stared at the ceiling. "I figured you'd have stopped by Intelligence, asked a few questions about Blondie. Found out whether that embassy thing he came to take you to were a load or not."

It was. Jani reached into her jacket pocket and felt for the casino marker.

"Did ya hear me, Jan?"

"I heard you." She slipped out the plastic disc and examined it under the light of one of her new lamps. It was a hard, bright green, like a cheap gemstone. Three centimeters in diameter, smooth surfaces trimmed with a ridged rim.

"Gone gamblin', did ya?" Steve's brows arched. "Must've felt lucky—greens run five to ten thousand Comdollars, depending on the casino."

Jani held the marker directly up to the light source, squinting as she tried to see through it. "These things come loaded."

"With what? A chip?" Steve scooted down the couch, his clothes hissing against the polycanvas. "Might, since it's a big denomination. Casino might register them."

"They do." Jani lifted her duffel onto her lap. "Plastic this thick can be hard to scan."

"I can scan plastic. I used to have to log in equipment in Helier, so I had my 'pack source boosted." Angevin rounded the couch and sat on the floor at Jani's feet—she held a juice dispo in one hand and her scanpack in the other. "So how do you like my decorating?"

"Nice." Jani handed her the casino marker.

"She misses the wide-open feel," Steve added helpfully.

"Blow." Angevin worked through her 'pack start-up checks, then held out her hand for the marker. She passed her scanpack reading surface over one side, then the other. Once. Twice. Again. "It's colony. Beyond that, I can't tell anything."

"Too thick?" Jani took the marker from her and again held it under the lamplight.

"I don't think so." Angevin glowered at the disc with the suspicious eye of a thwarted dexxie. "Could be the dye in the plastic. Some of them emit at wavelengths that interfere with scanmechs. I'd need a sheath that filters at just the right hairline of the spectrum in order to read further."

"Could be sending blocking signals, too." Steve reached for the marker, but Jani batted his hand away.

"Blocking dyes and signals are controlled out of Registry." She held the marker by the edges and tried to flex it. "Legal casinos can't use them and the illegal ones don't bother. The only problem with this thing is it's too thick." She felt it bend, very slightly, and eased off. "It's a marker—they're never meant to leave the casino." She held it up to the light again to see if she could spot the whitened stress cracks. "Bets are tracked by other means. All this should contain is the name of the casino and the pit registry code." She gripped the edges again and flicked her wrists down. The marker snapped like an overbaked cookie.

"What the hell ya do that for!" Steve pulled the nicstick out of his mouth—it had suddenly developed a distinct bend in the mouthpiece. "You just—gah!" His hand flew to his mouth. He ran into the kitchen.

"Bit right through to the scent core." Angevin watched her lover's flight with a distinct lack of anxiety. "With his temper, he does that about once a week. Stings like hell for a few seconds, then his tongue goes numb. You'd think that would teach him not to smoke those damned clove things, but he's got a memory like a stalk of celery."

Jani dug tweezers out of her tool kit and probed one of the marker's newly exposed inside edges. "You don't seem concerned."

"Shuts him up for hours. Sometimes I appreciate the peace and quiet." Angevin grinned and hunched her shoulders as though she'd said something naughty. "But sometimes I ask him questions that he can't answer with a yes or no, just to see that Guernsey glower." She moved into a kneeling position and studied the marker half that Jani examined. "I hope you didn't screw up the chip."

Jani used the sharp points of the tweezers to work a groove into the broken edge. "In a casino, you pay for everything with markers. Officially, purchases and bets are tracked with handprints, but as part of the tradition, you go through the motions of paying with markers. They're made breakable so you can get change back. Because of that, the chips are offset in one of the quadrants, well away from the break-axes." She eased up on the pressure as she poked into a miniscule open space. "Get that antistat out of my bag."

Angevin pulled out the square of charge-dissipating black cloth that sat atop the muddle and spread it across Jani's knee. "Those chips don't self-destruct like doc insets, I gather?"

"No." Jani removed the chip from its home and placed it on the cloth. "They can, in fact, be reused. Like I said, all they contain is the casino and the reg number." She pulled her scanpack from her bag and activated it.

"Why do you need to know where it comes from?" Angevin managed an expression of disinterest, but her hands betrayed her, fingers curled and clenching.

"Just a data point." Jani held her scanpack over the chip, and watched the information scroll across her display. "Andalusia. That's a high-end club in Felix Majora, Felix's largest city."

"You're speaking from experience?" Angevin tried to smile, but the corners of her mouth twitched.

"I made a few business calls. Peeked through the trade entrance a couple of times." Jani recalled the black and yellow uniformed waitstaff, the vast expanses of spotless stainless steel in the kitchen. Andalusia was the sort of place that ran a credit check before letting a customer in the door. "Steve would call it posh and full of nobbies."

"He wouldn't call it much of anything at the moment." Angevin uncurled to her feet and gazed down at Jani. Her skin was clear cream, untouched by worry and a stress-shortened night spent in a bedroll in a strange flat. Only her eyes, mossy green and large, held the dull light of concern. "You're not going to tell us why you think this marker is important, are you?"

"It's just my curiosity." Jani tucked the chip back into its slotted home, then enfolded the two marker halves in the antistat and tucked the bundle into her duffel.

"You're a real good liar," Angevin snapped. "You're as good as Evan van Reuter. Around Interior Doc Control, we used to say that he could sell a potluck dinner to the idomeni."

Jani's head shot up. *"Don't ever compare me with him."*

Angevin took a step backward. "I'm—I'm sorry, I—"

"Just *don't.*"

"All right." Angevin glanced over Jani's head, and did a

game job of wiping the upset from her face. "How are you feeling, darling?"

"Mmph." Steve circled around the couch and flopped back in his old seat. The skin around his mouth was reddened from scrubbing, the front of his pullover splattered with water.

"Well, I should get going." Jani stood and hoisted her duffel to her shoulder.

"But you just got here!" Angevin threw her hands in the air. "You haven't even seen the rest of the flat!"

Jani made a show of checking her timepiece. "I need to get to Neoclona. Val told me I could visit Lucien this afternoon."

"Nrrm." Steve got up just as Jani walked past him, bumping into her in the process.

Jani felt his hand slip in her jacket pocket. She maintained her path to the door without breaking stride, and exited into the hallway two steps ahead of Angevin.

"We need to go through your paper mail," Angevin called after her, "and you've got fifteen comport messages and you're going to miss a deadline on—"

Jani stopped short and turned around. "Angevin, someone shot at me last night. Now whether they meant to hit Lucien, or me, I don't know and I don't care. Pulse packets discharged in my vicinity make me edgy, and I mean to find out who fired that particular one and why."

Angevin planted in the middle of the hall. "I have spent half the morning taking calls from people asking where you are, and what happened last night, and are you under suspicion of anything. One son of a bitch had the nerve to ask if your past had caught up with you."

"Devinham, probably. His report is sitting atop the far right-hand stack. Call NUVA-SCAN Courier and tell them to come pick it up." Jani walked back to Angevin and placed a hand on her shoulder. "I'm caught up on my most pressing projects. I need to do some work tonight, which I will. And if any clients bail on me because they're afraid my grubby little past will rub off on them, I will deal with it." She walked backward toward the lift. "Right now, though, I'm going to visit someone who had half the skin of his lower abdomen seared off, and who feels like a elephant stepped on his lower back. OK?"

Angevin cringed at the description of Lucien's injuries. "Tell him I said hello."

"I will."

"Steve doesn't like him a bit."

"I am aware of that."

"I'll do what I can with the rest of your calendar."

"Thank you. I mean that." Jani stepped aboard the lift; just as the door closed, she caught a glimpse of Steve in the entry, hands buried in his pockets, angry stare focused on her.

Jani reached into her pocket and removed what Steve had stuffed there. It proved to be a folded piece of dispo towel. She opened it and read the hurried printing, made blurred by the way the stylus fluid bled through the cottony material.

> *Why are you protecting that bastard when he tried to set you up?*

Jani touched her left shoulder, still bruised and tender from Lucien's grip. It seemed to be taking a longer than normal time to heal. As though the damage was worse than she thought. As though it believed she needed a reminder.

The main branch of the Capital Library loomed over its neighbor buildings like an overbearing professor, its stern stone and metal lines and forbidding entry inviting the information seeker while promising them a difficult search. Jani didn't know whether the stacks really were as daunting as their shelter made them appear—she had acquired a membership in order to access the free workstations reserved by the Library for the use of its patrons.

She entered the lift. Since she was the only occupant, she hit the pad for all twelve floors and got off at the fourth. She stalked the aisles until she found an unused carrel, and fed her rental card into the entry reader. An anonymous card, paid for with an anonymous vend token. What she lost in a business expense tax deduction, she gained in privacy.

She locked the carrel door and activated the privacy shading in the doorside window. Then she opened her duffel and removed all the things she needed to initiate a proper search. Notepad. Stylus. Dispo of lemon tonic. Anti-trace jig. She activated the palm-sized jig and attached to the workstation core, so that no one would be able to monitor her search.

Jani sat at the desk. She ratcheted the touchboard into a more comfortable position, then hesitated just as she made ready to initiate systems. "Would I feel better if I didn't know?" Maybe. "Would I feel safer?" There was only one answer to that question—she gave it by activating the station and wading through the Library's arcane search driver to the vast reaches of Colonial Archives.

Casinos—Felix Majora.

The Felicianos had a well-earned reputation for enjoying life. Felix Majora contained forty-seven casinos within its metro limits, with Andalusia topping the alphabetical list. Jani, however, didn't zone in on that target immediately. Instead, she keyed into the archives of the Vox Nacional, Felix Colony's most popular newssheet. She pondered the keyword request, entered *death* and *accident*, set the time limits to the months Lucien spent in the colonies earlier that year, and initiated the search.

She sipped her tonic as the display faded and the device went about its business. After a few seconds, it brightened to active blue, then darkened to the deep gold background and red arabesques of the Vox Nacional screens. A flicker, then a flood of print as a formidable list filled the display.

Five hundred eighty-seven names. Jani didn't know whether that number was high or low, incorrect or skewed by her search terms. She entered various and sundry codes and passwords she had acquired by means fair and foul during her years living "out." Then she entered the reg code she had gleaned from Andalusia's chip and initiated a cross-sort of credit checks requested by Andalusia against the names of the deceased.

Within minutes, she had sifted out fourteen names. She whittled it by more than two-thirds after she discarded net worths below one hundred fifty thousand. No casino manager wanted to gut a new customer on the first go-round, therefore they never approved a credit line greater than ten percent of the customer's net worth. Steve had guessed low—green markers in Felix Majora signified a fifteen thousand Comdollar investment, therefore everyone worth less than one hundred fifty thousand fell by the wayside.

And then there were four . . .

Four names. Jani discarded that of the woman who choked on a sandwich at her family reunion. She also tossed out the man in his twenties who had decided to raid the Fort Constanza ordnance depot for Dia Felicia fireworks and fried himself on the security fence that ringed the Service base's outer perimeter.

And then there were two . . .

After a little more thought, she rejected the ninety-four-year-old man who had fallen in his bathroom and struck his head with killing force against the corner of his marble bath. He had been a cornerstone of the Majoran import-export cartel, which made his exclusion difficult. But it was the wrong sort of death. The wrong manner, wrong method.

And then there was one . . .

Etienne Palia. Killed when the racing-class skimmer he drove veered off Felix Majora's infamous Camino Loco and slammed into a scancrete abutment. Massive systems failure, according to the on-site investigator. A rare occurrence with that particular model skimmer, but not unheard of. Accidents did, after all, happen.

"The article says Palia was a businessman." No particular business mentioned, not even something vague like import-export. *A businessman.* Well, they all were, weren't they? No one ever admitted to an inquiring reporter, yes, I am a high-level soldier in a brand-new Commonwealth-spanning criminal organization. It was always, *I am a businessman,* said with a cool smile as unblinking eyes gazed directly into the holocam.

"Palia—member of *L'araignée*?" Jani doodled a looping question mark on the top page of the notepad. That's what she kept the writing materials for—any pertinent facts she would store in her head and her head only. She backed out of the search driver and powered down the workstation. Disengaged the anti-trace jig and tucked it away, along with the pad and stylus. Tossed back the last swallow of tonic, consigned the dispo to the sparky maw of the trashzap, and departed the carrel. Her stomach growled as she hit the walkway. She dug a meal bar out of her bag and consumed it in a few untasted bites.

Massive systems failure. The right sort of death. An assassination that a professional adept at gadgetry might pull off.

CHAPTER 19

As Jani negotiated the final turn leading to Lucien's hospital room, the sounds of a familiar voice raised in anger reached her. She opened the door slowly, poised to back away and flee around the nearest corner if the occasion demanded. Val Parini didn't often lose his temper. When he did, it paid to be elsewhere.

Unfortunately for Jani, Val also possessed the hearing of a nervous cat—he turned as soon as he heard the door mech. *"Damn it, Jan—you talk to him!"* He stood at the foot of Lucien's bed, recording board in one hand, stylus in the other. The stylus performed double-duty as a weapon—Val used it to stab the air with malice aforethought. "Only a certifiable idiot would sign himself out of here in the condition he's in!"

"I'm fine, really." Lucien stood bedside, looking as far from fine as Jani had ever seen him. He wore winter base casuals—grey pull-on pants and a loose blue pullover that hung untucked. His faded tan looked sallow, the overhead illumination highlighting the sheen of sweat that coated his forehead. He packed a plastic sack with the few items of clothing that had come through the shooting unscathed—his lid, his tietops, and socks. He moved in slow motion, turning with his whole body to avoid bending or flexing at the waist.

Jani saw him wince as he leaned forward to insert a sock into the bag. "Lucien, I think you should listen to Val."

"Damned right he should listen to Val. Now get back into bed before you pass out." Val circled to Lucien's side of the bed and reached for the sack, but Lucien stuck his arm straight out to the side to stop him.

"I've signed myself out. I'm not your problem anymore." He lowered his arm, then resumed folding his other sock with a slowness that was maddening to watch. "Leave me alone."

Jani edged closer. "Do your superiors know you've done this?"

Lucien smiled as she approached, but exhaustion damped the usual four-alarm blaze to a dying ember. "It's easier to obtain forgiveness than permission." He closed the bag, tried to lift it, then gasped and let it drop back to the bed.

"This is *bullshit!*" Val headed for the door, open medcoat flapping. He stopped long enough to make a hurried entry into the board. "I'm countermanding that release right now." He pointed the stylus at Jani. "Don't you dare take him out of this room. I'm getting John. Maybe he can talk some sense into him." The stylus swung around toward Lucien. "Then I'm calling your CO."

Lucien waited for the door to close before speaking. "Jani, please get me out of here."

Jani hesitated. Then she walked around the bed to his side because she knew he expected her to come close and he'd wonder why if she didn't. "You can't even stand." As soon as she drew near, he leaned toward her and tried to kiss her, but she ducked him easily and grabbed his arm so she could steer him back to the bed. "And you sure as hell can't do *that,* so lie down."

"I love it when you order me around." Lucien slipped his arm around her waist and lay his head on her shoulder. Then he groaned. His weight shifted.

Jani widened her stance for stability and helped him lower onto the bed. She hoisted his legs, then supported his shoulders as he lay back, felt the sweat soak through the thin pullover knit as she held him. His face had paled to chalky ochre. "Asking if it hurts is a dumb question, isn't it?"

Lucien shook his head. "They implanted a pain med diffuser. I just feel pressure. Weight. Like I've got a cannonball lodged against my hip. But I'm so goddamned *weak!*" He gripped her wrist as soon as she let go of him. "I have to get out of here. Shroud does *not* like me."

Jani tried to ease out of Lucien's grasp, but as soon as she pulled one wrist away, he grabbed the other. "He won't allow his personal feelings to affect his treatment of you."

"Oh yeah? Are these the same personal feelings that didn't affect your treatment?" Blood rose in Lucien's cheeks, warming his pallor.

"You're just another patient—I'm the incredible ongoing experiment." Jani worked her wrist free, but she had to bend close to Lucien in order to do so, which gave him a chance to grab the hem of her jacket. "Damn it—will you knock it off!"

"I've missed you." Weak as he was, Lucien still pulled with enough force to drag her down beside him on the bed.

"Let me go!" Jani tried to work his fingers loose, but he outmaneuvered her once more by releasing the jacket and capturing both her wrists in a surprisingly strong grip. "I thought you were ready to faint."

"See? You're here five minutes, and I'm already feeling better." He slid his hands up her arms until he caught hold just above her elbows. "Take me home with you, and I'll be back to full strength in a week." He pulled her down to him. Because of the angle, his lips found her throat first, leaving a tracery of fire behind as they moved over the underside of her jaw and her chin, then settled over her mouth.

And then there was one . . . Jani tried to pull away, but Lucien's grip tightened. She'd have to wrench free and retreat to the middle of the room to ensure that he couldn't grab anything else, and that would make him wonder why she didn't want him to touch her. Then he'd start asking questions, like why hadn't she tried to visit him sooner, and what had she been doing since the shooting?

He let loose her arms. One hand moved to the back of her neck to guide her closer, while the other slid over the front of her jacket and settled over her breast, massaging it with a light, experienced touch.

Damn it! Jani's body reacted in fits and starts, warming to Lucien's taste and feel and her own arousal, then chilling as the memories intruded. Of the bottom drawer of a dresser, and fifteen objects nestled in their displays.

And then there was one . . . She braced her hands on either side of Lucien's head and tried to push away. But her hands wouldn't listen to her thinking brain—instead they worked through his hair, then under his head, embracing him, holding him closer—

"My apologies for the interruption."

Jani broke away from Lucien and twisted around to find John looming in the doorway, his long face a stern blank. Val peered from behind him, eyes widened in a *what the hell do you think you're doing* glare.

"I disagree with your assessment, Val. It appears Mr. Pascal may be fit for release after all." John closed in on the side of the bed. His eyes, filmed tiger's eye brown to match the day's tan shirt and trousers, never left Lucien's face. "How are you feeling today, Mr. Pascal, aside from the obvious?"

"John." Jani worked Lucien's distraction to her advantage, easing off the bed and into the nearby visitor's chair.

"Sorry." John didn't look apologetic. He didn't look at Jani, either, instead alternating his gaze between Lucien and the recording board that Val had shoved into his hands. "And the impediment to discharge is what?"

"Well, for one thing, the doctors and nurses are all *here,* not on Armour Place." Val shot Jani another aggravated look. "He suffered renal trauma. He's showing blood in his urine—"

"His hematuria's microscopic. The trauma proved relatively minor—the point of impact was too low to cause much damage." John glowered toward the bed. "That being said, Mr. Pascal, I really would *not* move around any more than absolutely necessary if I were you."

Lucien, who at that point had been trying to sit up, sank back against his pillows like a deflating balloon.

John returned to studying the board display. "He is receiving regular standard monitoring. Dressing changes—they're not as necessary as you think, Val. With his augmentation helping to speed things along, his wound has undergone a week's worth of healing in a day. He won't even need a dressing by the day after tomorrow—enough new skin cells will have bonded to the support to make it unnecessary."

"But John, his peritoneum—"

"The rupture was small—Osgood sealed it completely—"

Jani sat quietly, ignoring Lucien's attempts to catch her eye. *I don't want him in my flat.* But if she came right out and said that, Lucien would know she didn't want him near her, that she suspected him of something.

On the other hand . . . keeping Lucien in plain sight had its advantages. *Think of this professionally, not personally.* As the object of both Angevin's admiration and Steve's animosity, he would be carefully watched. In hospital, or as an outpatient at Sheridan, he could get up to anything. In her flat, his activities would be limited.

What did I tell Derringer . . . keep your friends close and your enemies closer. It only remained to be determined on which side of the line Lucien belonged.

"John, he's not one hundred percent ours to discharge." Val had wandered to the opposite side of the room and hoisted himself atop the lowboy dresser. "Service Medical has a say in when he leaves and where he spends his post-discharge recovery."

"So cart him out to Sheridan and get their buy-in. He can't be approved for active duty yet—he may as well stay in the city for a few days." Before Val could argue out from under, John pulled a stylus from his medcoat pocket and impressed his scrawl onto the board input. "Have Liu arrange an ambulance to Sheridan. While they've got him, Croydon and the set-up team can install all the necessary equipment at Armour Place. He can be settled in a couple of hours."

Val dismounted the dresser. "I don't think it's a good idea. I—" He glanced at Lucien, whose look at him had grown more focused, and fell silent.

"It's done. In the works." John walked to the door, handing off the recording board to Val on the way. "You wanted him so badly, you've got him. He's all yours."

It took Jani a few seconds to realize that John had directed the comment at her.

"This is the most ridiculous bloody thing I ever heard." Steve had fully recovered from his nicstick mishap and had been making up for lost talk time ever since Jani had returned to her flat to break the news. "He belongs at Sheridan—let them haul his freight till he's cleared fer active."

Jani peeked around the open doorway into the newly furnished spare bedroom, where "Croydon, Outpatient Services" and her team outfitted the French Quarter-style bed with detachable rails and a mattress that folded up like a chair or flattened at the touch of a pad. Rails had also been added to various points in the adjoining bath, attached with specialty bondings that would dissolve when exposed to ultra-high frequency vibration, leaving the walls "as clean as you please, ma'am." They had also installed a comport that patched through directly to Neoclona by touch or voice, and a small cooler stocked with nutritionals.

"It's possible that once Service Medical gets their hands on him, they won't let him leave." Jani stepped to one side as Croydon and crew bustled out of the bedroom, skimdolly of tools and equipment in tow. "I doubt he's been debriefed yet, and I'm sure Service Investigational has initiated their own inquiry into the shooting."

"Live in hope." Steve shoved an unactivated 'stick in his mouth and fell in behind the installers.

Die in despair. Jamira Shah Kilian used to pluck that saying out of the air at the damnedest times. Her daughter Jani hadn't liked it any better back then than she did now.

She entered the main room to find Angevin standing by the desk, holding a recording board.

"More calls. First, Colonel Derringer."

Jani stopped in the middle of the floor and covered her face with her hands. *You sent the skimmer for me this morning, and I wasn't here. Now you're going to get me.* "Shit."

"That's what I thought. What a creep. He said sorry that he missed your appointment this morning, but all hell had broken loose at Diplo because of the shooting. He wants to meet tomorrow. He said the idomeni embassy's locked Tsecha down, again because of the shooting. Says you and he need to 'rethink,' whatever that means."

The relief of reprieve evaporated. "They've pulled Nema out of the public eye?" Jani walked to her desk and sat heavily. "Did Derringer say for how long?"

"He didn't say much of anything. He said he'd prefer not to deal with *staff*. I almost told him what he could do with his *staff,* and his gold eagle, but I didn't want to get you into trouble."

Oh, you couldn't make matters any worse, trust me. Jani wondered if Derringer had heard any interesting news about The Nema Letter, or whether she'd have to prompt him herself to rescan it. *Oh look! The pattern's changed. It's not an idomeni document—it's just deteriorating.* She would have given a great deal to receive a call like that. A great deal.

"Jani?"

"Hmm?"

"Devinham said thanks for the report but that it wasn't what he wanted and he won't pay the delivery half of his bill." Angevin looked up from her board and crossed her eyes.

"It's exactly what he asked for and I have the comport recordings to prove it." Jani ran a hand over the curiously uncluttered surface of her desk, the result of Angevin's organizing. "But I knew he'd be trouble. That's why I charged him double my usual rate and made him pay half upfront."

"So you aren't going to file a complaint against him with Registry?"

"No. I'll just spread his name around. Within a month, not even the deregistered dexxies will take his business."

"Good." Angevin nodded agreement as she continued down her list. "Niall Pierce called to say he would have been by today, but he couldn't get away from Sheridan. He said you'd understand."

"I do." Jani checked her timepiece and wondered where her parents were. Still in transit from Mars? Docked at Luna, and checking their timepieces as well?

"He also asked me how you were. I told you you had just squirted out from under and were out and about, so you must be OK. That made him laugh." Angevin studied the display a little too carefully. "He seems nice."

Jani crumpled a sheet of notepaper and slow-motioned a throw at Angevin's head. "He has a girlfriend."

"Hmm." Another tickmark on the board input. "Kern Standish from Treasury. Allow me to quote. 'I heard what happened. If you think you're going to get away from me that easily, think again.' " Angevin glanced up. "Is he serious?"

"Yes and no." Jani grinned. "That's just his way of letting me know I'm still clean and green as far as he's concerned."

"As if you wouldn't be." Angevin frowned at the display. "You did have two cancellations, both from AgMin."

"If I recall, they're looking into negotiating food transport rights through newly leased idomeni GateWays. If they don't need me now, they sure as hell will later."

"Confidence. I like it." Angevin hoisted her stylus in an "up theirs" gesture. "Last and definitely least, Roni—"

Jani felt a jolt. "She called?"

"You know her?" Angevin shrugged. "She wasn't real talkative. She said she mispunched, that she had been trying to reach a bookstore down the street, that the code's only one character off."

"Did she say anything else?"

"She just started nattering, like she sometimes does. Said she had to get to the bookstore tonight before it closed at seven. Then she cut off." Angevin made another entry into the board, then shut it down. "That's it."

Jani directed her splintered attention to her desktop. "I have two analyses due tomorrow."

Steve chose that moment to emerge from the kitchen, half-eaten sandwich in one hand, juice dispo in the other. "I done a draft fer one of them. Since it were about Guernsey doc protocols, I figured I were qualified." He took an extra-large bite in answer to Jani's look of surprise. "Well, I had to do something today, didn't I? 'Sides furnishing the place fer visitors who belong *elsewhere.*" He grimaced around a mouthful of 'cress and chutney. "Don't get yer hopes up. I left you the other one to do all by yerself. Wouldn't try to analyze Pathen Haárin contract practices on the best day I ever had."

Jani slipped off the seat and walked across the room to the window. She could see the bookstore from there. *One character off—does that mean six o'clock instead of seven, Roni, or does it mean eight?*

A soft jostle of her elbow made Jani flinch. She turned to find Angevin gazing up at her with the look of worry that had become her baseline expression over the last twenty-four hours.

"I pulled all the pertinent data together. If you want to get started . . . ?"

"Is that really what Roni said? One character *off*?"

Angevin's eyes narrowed. "What is it with her?"

"I just want to know what she said. *Exactly* what she said."

"Why—?" Angevin pressed a hand to her forehead. "She said the code was one character off—one character off—one—*high*!" The hand dropped. "High. Like I wish I was right now." She grabbed Jani by the arm. "Now let's do some work before you lose all your clients and I have to send all my beautiful furniture back."

It felt good to work. Afterward, Jani even took the time to make herself her first hot meal since Gaetan's. She knew she strove to stay busy in order to keep her mind off all the things rattling around in her head. Her parents. Nema. Lucien. Her eight-up meeting with Roni. The ploy even worked to an extent. Unfortunately, it couldn't work forever.

"Jan?" Steve stuck his head in the kitchen door. "He's here." No need to say who "he" was.

Lucien made his entry in a skimchair pushed by Val Parini, who was in turn backed up by two Neoclona orderlies. "I'm here through the weekend. Then I have to report back, and they may decide to keep me."

"Live in hope," Steve muttered again. Jani wanted to ask him if he knew the rest of the damned saying.

As Val crossed the floor, his brow arched higher and higher. "And furniture finds Armour Place. Which room?"

"Down the hall, second right." Jani took note of Val's careful eyeballing. Full report to be submitted to John, she felt sure, along with the singular item that Lucien had been put up in his own room, not hers.

The skimchair wouldn't fit through the narrow doorway, so the orderlies took over. They hoisted Lucien as though he was a small boy and not a grown man and deposited him on the bed. They then checked the Outpatient installations while Val evaluated the patient's condition and made notes in a handheld.

Surrounded by medical bustle, the patient himself looked worn and a little bewildered. Lucien had exchanged his cast-off casuals for Main Hospital-issue pajamas and robe—he sat in bed looking like the heir apparent who had just been awakened and told *the King is dead, long live the King.* His eyes met Jani's, and he smiled warmly.

Le Blond. Jani forced herself to smile back.

Then Val tucked away his handheld and herded everyone out. "The patient needs his rest." He put his arm around Jani and steered her toward the door. "Let me give you the rundown." He prodded her into the hallway ahead of him, then grabbed her arm to stop her as she tried to follow the orderlies to the lift. "We can talk over here." He directed her to the window at the hallway's end, and pulled her down next to him as he took a seat on the sill.

"He can walk around a little, starting tomorrow. This place has a roof garden—he could putter around up there. His appetite's going to be voracious due to the rate at which he's healing. His temper may be short, too, because of the fatigue and assorted chemical imbalances." Val grinned at her, and shook his head. "I don't know why I'm telling you this—when it comes to augie cascades, you wrote the book."

Jani took his hand and squeezed it. "Thanks, Val." She flinched when he squeezed back hard enough to hurt.

"Be careful." The humor left his face—he looked nervy, his temper bubbling just beneath the surface. "And if you need anything, and I mean *anything,* just call."

Jani laughed, partly from stress and partly from the surprise at having a firmly held conviction blown out of the water. "Funny. I always thought you liked Lucien."

"Like?" Val chewed his lower lip. "He floors me. I could watch him forever. I'm not dead, Jan. Neither are you, apparently. That's some face to wake up next to."

"But?"

"But I've been *the* Valentin Parini for almost twenty years, and I've been dodging stuff like him since I banked my first million." Val's chiseled face took on a sad cast. "They tell you everything you want to hear, and they know how to show you the face you want to see. Even when you know in your bones that you can't trust them, you still try, because you can't accept the fact that they can't feel and that there's nothing, *nothing,* that they won't do to insure their survival. All I ever had at stake was some money, and maybe my heart." His eyes clouded as some buried memory surfaced. "But never my life." He raised her hand to his cheek. "If I thought I could convince you to move in with me for a few days . . . ?"

Jani freed her hand, then brushed a finger under Val's chin. "And leave Steve and Angevin alone with him?"

"He might torture them a little, like the cat he is. But they're not what he wants." Val sighed and scrubbed a hand through his hair. "John is so eaten up with jealousy right now that he can't see straight. Otherwise, he'd tell you what I'm telling you. We're just a call away. We can do everything the big boys do, but in the end, we're not as . . . accountable."

Jani sat back against the window bracket and regarded her old friend through a new filter. "Val? I always thought you were the nice one."

Val stood. "If anything ever happened to you, John would tear this city apart." He looked down on her with a fondness that had developed improbably and withstood separation and medical disasters and the passage of time. "But he'd have to beat me to it." He bent over and kissed her, then turned and walked with a heavy step toward the lift.

Jani waved good-bye. Watched the lift door close and the numbers flicker as the car descended. Enjoyed the silence. It didn't surprise her to see the car start to ascend almost immediately. She knew she lived in a busy building, despite the façade of calm.

Then the car stopped at her floor. She sat up.

The lift door opened, and Niall Pierce stepped out. Instead of a Service uniform, he wore civvies—a dark blue shirt and black trousers. It struck Jani that while he roughened the edges of any uniform he wore, he lent a strange grace to civilian clothes. A sense of mystery. In either garb, he looked the hatchet man, but in civvies, you couldn't tell whose hatchet he swung.

He spotted her and stopped in the middle of the hallway, hands patting his pockets without diving in because the Spacer in him despised the sloppiness. "Jani?"

He didn't say anything else. He didn't have to.

CHAPTER 20

"Nervous?"

Jani look at Niall. He appeared at first glance to sit easily at the skimmer controls, but closer examination revealed the whitened knuckles, the tension along the jaw. "About as much as you are." She grinned when he glared at her. "Maybe a little more." But the smirk soon died, leaving her with the twisty gut and tripping heart. This wasn't augie's sort of strain. He had crawled off to recover his strength, leaving her to manage this emotional assault on her own.

"Shocked the hell out of me when Pull called to say they'd be hitting O'Hare in an hour. Lots of balls got dropped on this one—if it takes me a month to nail all the hides to the wall, I'll do it." Niall steered down a tree-lined Bluffs side street, then another, before veering onto the ramp leading to a Boul artery. He had driven with evasion in mind since they left Armour Place, but he changed directions and speeds so smoothly that for scattered moments Jani felt herself on a private guided tour of the capital and the Bluffs.

"How are they?" She almost coughed the words. Her throat had taken to tightening intermittently, with a pain that felt as though someone attempted her slow strangulation. She'd known someone who died that way, and the memory of being one of the first to find the body piled atop the rest of her jumbled emotions. She could feel the pressure build inside her head, making her feel one raw thought away from exploding.

"They seem fine. Exhausted, like the rest of us." Niall emphasized the point with a yawn. "Lots of questions about you. How you were. When you'd be visiting." The corner of his mouth curved. "Your mom talks more than your dad. Asks a lot of questions."

"Your point?"

"Just making an observation." He settled back in his seat, smiling quietly.

Jani let the silence carry them for a few kilometers, but as they continued north on the Boul, her nerves nagged again. "Where is this place?"

"I told you before. On the base."

Jani looked out the window at the homes they passed. Nice, anonymous homes with easy access to the Boul and the lake. "Why not a safe house in the Bluffs?"

"Not secure enough." Niall's voice tightened. "At Sheridan, they're shoulder-deep in steel blue. No one is going to get to them there."

What about the ones that are already there, Niall? Like the ones who dropped the ball on forwarding you the news that my folks arrived ahead of schedule. Jani sat forward, hands on knees, and willed the skimmer faster.

Dusk had settled by the time they reached Fort Sheridan. The western skies had colored with streaks of pink and purple, backed by the last light of the setting sun. To the east, the darker sky served as backdrop for the base sprawl, the single and multi-story buildings that stretched in street-split clusters to the horizon and beyond.

Instead of entering the base via the well-peopled Shenandoah Gate, Niall drove farther north and entered through an unmanned control point reserved for emergency vehicles. Once inside, he ignored signs and skimways, gliding over lawns and around buildings and trees at speeds that had Jani muttering a proxy version of the Pedestrian's Prayer and hoping the Grounds crews had been diligent in pruning low-hanging branches.

They settled to a stop in front of a nondescript two-story whitestone box. Only one other skimmer sat parked nearby—the place had the deserted look of an office annex in the middle of second shift meal break.

Niall popped both gullwings; they slid out of the vehicle and hurried up the short flight of steps.

The lobby consisted of a chip-sized entry, with barely

enough room for the solemn Spacer who snapped to attention as soon as she saw Niall.

"Anyone else come here?"

"No, sir. You're the first, sir."

Jani felt her legs grow heavy as they entered the lift. She hugged herself as the shivers hit.

"What's wrong?" Niall took a step toward her.

"I'm fine. It's nerves, I think." Then her stomach growled. "Damn it!"

"I heard that from here." Niall leaned against the cabin wall as his alert stage dropped from red to orange. "Want me to get you something?"

"Yeah. If I'm going to be here for a while, I'll need it." The door opened and she stepped into a short hallway consisting of bare white walls and a floor of speckled grey lyno. "God, this is grim."

"Don't worry—what we saved on the hall, we spent on the rooms." Niall took a step back when Jani turned on him. "That was a *joke*." He rummaged in his shirt pocket and pulled out his nicstick case. "Steady on, Jan, you're rubbing off." He shook out a 'stick, bit the bulb, and watched the smoke curl. "Third door on the left. Do you want me to come with?"

"No."

"You're fine. You look fine. You'll do fine."

"Yeah." Jani tugged at her jacket as she walked to the door. Why did she wear brown? *Maman hates brown.* She should have made Niall wait while she changed clothes. The sari would have been ridiculously inappropriate, but she had a wine red suit that she didn't wear often because she never knew when she'd get a call to the idomeni embassy and under the right light, it looked *almost* bright—

She stopped in front of the door, then looked back at Niall, who offered a grin and a thumbs-up. She pressed her hand to the entry pad. The doormech hissed and the bolts slid. The panel moved aside, and she stepped into the breach.

Niall had been partly correct about the rooms. The walls were still white, but the bareness had been cut with some unimaginative but pleasant landscapes. The depressing lyno had been covered with a green carpet patterned to look like leafy groundcover. The garden motif carried over to the couch and chairs that furnished the sitting room, with their frames of light brown woodweave and cushions awash with red and yellow flowers.

Declan and Jamira Kilian sat close together on the couch, a magazine spread across their knees. They had looked up as one as the door opened, and stared at Jani as she stepped into the room.

Jani stared back. Her mother's napeknot, as ever the poor containment for a thick waistfall of hair, had come undone and now hung over one shoulder in a stream of grey-tipped black. Jamira Shah neared seventy, yet her bold face looked little different from that of the woman whom Jani had last seen almost twenty years before. As always, she wore clothes designed to fight back the storm and wind of the north central islands. Today, bright yellow trousers and a patterned shirt in yellow, white, and orange that carried with them the warmth of a motherland she had never seen and the light of a sun she had felt for the first time that day.

"Jani-girl?"

Jani looked to her father, who studied her like a puzzling schematic. Declan the fixer. Kilian, who never met a system he couldn't crack. His was the seven-decade version of the impish face Dolly remembered, the face Jani had once shared. Upturned nose and apple cheeks ruddied by wind, framed by jet hair, cut by green sea eyes. He wore Channel colors, dark green and darker blue. Like his wife, he showed little of twenty years' passage. It took a special endurance to live on the islands, and more than time to age her natives.

Jani waited for her father to say more, for her mother to say anything. *Do I look that strange to you? Did the Misty distort my image—is that why you don't recognize me? Or is it because you don't think I look like I could be your daughter? Or anyone's daughter.*

Is it because you don't think I look human?

Jamira raised a hand to her mouth. Let it fall. Then she shoved the magazine onto her husband's lap. Rising quick and smooth, she legged across the fake greenery floor, strides growing shorter as she picked up speed. *"Ma petite fille!*" She knocked Jani back a step as she collided with her, wrapping her arms around her waist and pressing her face against her chest.

"*Oui,* Maman. It's me." Jani's throat clamped down hard, her voice emerging high and thin like a little girl's. She gripped the rope of hair, held it fast. Smelled jasmine perfume and makeup and the barest hint of incense from a distant shrine.

A heavier step approached. Stronger arms embraced. Sharp herb soap and hair like wire and a face rough with new beard. "Jani-girl."

"Papa." Jani heard the roar in her ears and called it the wind and tasted the salt on her face and called it the sea.

Felt a rent in her heart heal, and called it home.

"—and then Shamus returns from the stores and tells us that a man is looking for us." Jamira lifted her spoon from her cup and raised it like a question. " 'What man?' I asked. 'No one knows we are at Faeroe.' "

Jani sat back in her flower chair and watched her mother resume stirring her tea. "No. No one. Only Tante Smruti so she knows to keep an eye on things, and Cheecho so he knows to take care of the birds, and Jones the Grocery so she should stop the deliveries, and then all the people you asked to keep an eye on those three to make sure they do their jobs."

"Tell Smruti anything, may as well tell ChanNet." Declan frowned into his coffee, ignoring his wife's glower. "So, Shamus being Shamus, he raised his tail and pelted home. Just as he's gasping the details, I look out and see a skimmer in the circle. Dull green two-seater. Old. Sort of model you see around Faeroe. And out comes the man. Also the sort you see around Faeroe, at least these days. The kind that looks like he's just waiting for you to turn your back."

"He said he had a message from you, Janila. That you needed us and we had to come to Chicago." Jamira lifted a sandwich from the tray on the table in front of her and took a small, examining bite. "He gave us billets, and money for expenses, and a note in your handwriting. The note read just like you—to the point, with no explanation."

Jani looked across the room, where Niall perched atop a low cabinet. "They got hold of samples of my writing and knew enough about me to copy my style."

Niall nodded. He took a pull on his 'stick, then held his breath to leech the last molecule of nicotine from the smoke. "My Guernsey friend thinks *L'araignée* planned to waylay them at Helier Transfer Station. Busy place like that—who'd notice if two travelers disappeared? But the white paper had made the rounds out there, and the name Kilian was on everybody's mind. When it showed up on the passenger manifest of an Acadian cruiser, it was a footrace to see who'd get to the station first. We won."

"White paper?" Declan peered over the rim of his cup at Jani. "Did someone write you up, Jani-girl?"

"I work for the government, Papa. Someone decided to investigate me." Jani picked at the makeshift supper Niall had scrounged for her. Slices of kettle chicken soaked with Chinois hot sauce. Lemon wedges and a cup of red pepper for dredging. "When I was in hiding, I did what I had to. I helped smugglers. Tampered with documents. Some people think that makes me a security risk."

"Then there are those of us who think that makes her a consultant." Niall paused to blow a perfect smoke ring. "The white paper is a smear attempt. Your daughter is an important player in our dealings with the idomeni. Because of that, some very powerful economic forces who want to destabilize our relations with Shèrá would like to see her discredited."

Declan nodded. "I've tried to work with some of those forces. Make that *in spite* of them." The lines of his puckish face drew down. As always, sadness made him look angry. "Those people tell you, 'We want this and this and that.' And if you don't give it to them, well . . ." He drew a shaky breath. "I've buried four good friends in the past months. They died because they wouldn't give up what they'd spent their lives building, because they wouldn't hand over this and this and that."

"Who?" Jani's hand tightened on the arm of her chair as she braced for the answer.

"Jani?" Niall leaned forward, voice and posture tense.

"People seldom leave Ville Acadie," Jani replied to his implicit concern. "I probably knew them."

Declan blinked as he spoke, as though he couldn't believe what he said. "Simone. The Fuel Cells, not the Butcher. Echevar and Samvoy, the cousins in construction, not their parents whom you knew." A pause. "Labat."

"Labat?" Jani looked again at Niall. "He ran the off-track near our house. He took bets that I wouldn't make it through OCS."

"He didn't count on your stubbornness, Jani-girl. He didn't always think things through, and he paid the big price." Declan's weak grin subsided. "The day after Labat's funeral, I shuttered my business and left my home, took my wife away from her family. I fled because I install and re-work systems and they look for people like that. I knew one day, the shop door would open and I would look up and see two or three well-dressed, soft-spoken people standing there, and I would know the questions before they uttered them." His voice grew small. "And I'd think of four dead friends, and the answers I would give . . . would not be worthy of them."

Jamira reached out to him. When he didn't respond, she gripped his hand and laced her fingers through his. "They have always been in Ville Acadie, but they kept themselves to themselves. Now, they dine in the best clubs, build the largest homes. Send their children here to university. There are no brakes, no walls. Nothing stops them."

"Why didn't you tell me?" Jani watched her parents hold on to one another, and felt her freshly closed wounds ache anew. "I asked you why you left home, why you went to Faeroe. Why didn't you tell me!"

"We didn't want you to worry, Janila. We thought we would come here in the spring to visit, and not go back." Her mother forced a smile. "But spring came early."

"Doesn't the Acadian government do anything?" Niall didn't sound angry, only tired, as if he already knew the answer.

Declan snorted. "Oh, it does *something*. Takes its cut and turns its back." A gloomy silence settled, hanging over them until the room entry buzzer offered respite.

Niall pushed off the lowboy and opened the door. When he saw who stood in the hall, he beckoned to Jani. "We need to discuss logistics."

Jani rose awkwardly, hampered by her knee. Before she joined Niall, she leaned over the table and touched her father's shoulder. "You are worthy of every friend you ever had. The fact that you left La Ville means nothing. Everyone pulls back. Regroups. That doesn't make you a coward and it doesn't mean you're a sell-out. You don't belong to them."

"Yet." Declan made no move to touch her, no effort to meet her gaze. "That's what they do to you, Jani-girl. They plant that 'yet' in the back of your mind, and it grows until it eats you alive."

Jani waited for her father to look at her. When he didn't, she turned her attention to her mother. Jamira sat as her husband did, her shoulders rounding, her eyes focused on the floor. They both seemed drained of energy. Beaten. Old.

"I'll be in the hall with Niall," Jani said quietly. She watched the carpet as she made her traverse to the door, and found that she could pick out each individual leaf, discern every shade of green. She could thank augie for the heightened senses—it detected her growing rage and responded accordingly.

She walked out into the hall to find Niall surrounded by a circle of uniforms. Lt. Pullman was the only one she recognized—he smiled weakly at her, then returned his attention to the heating discussion.

"This is no time to be arguing jurisdiction, Major." Niall stood within a handbreadth of a red-faced woman in rumpled fallweights. "Your team lost them at MarsPort, and didn't pick them up again until they had almost boarded the wrong ship!"

"They were out of our sensor range for a grand total of ten seconds, and out of our physical sight for less than thirty." The major closed the distance to two fingers. "That does not, sir, in my estimation, qualify as lost!"

"I've seen people disappear in the time it took to turn a corner." Jani wedged in between a lieutenant in fallweights and a captain in dress blue-greys. "The time it took to turn around. Glance at a timepiece. Blink." She stepped inside the circle, shouldering Niall to one side and taking over his position in the major's face. "Ten seconds is enough time to hustle two people into a lift, or out a side door, or through an airlock." She saw the uncertainty in the woman's bloodshot eyes, and rode it. "Who lost them? I want names."

"I can't give you the—"

"Those were my parents they almost lost. You will give me their names."

"She will be reprimanded—"

"She?" Jani heard Niall groan. "Let me get this straight. You had one operative with a handheld sensor escort two people through one of the busiest transfer stations in the Commonwealth by *herself*!"

The woman rocked from foot to foot, then edged back a half-step. "It's . . . standard practice. Ma'am."

Jani closed the distance the major tried to open. If she left too much space, she'd have room to use her hands; that wasn't a risk she wanted to take with augie worrying his bit.

Then a glint of gold on the major's collar caught her eye. Augie liked flashes of light, and the overhead illumination playing off the woman's rank designators drew his attention. Bursts of gold from the oak leaves, and from the twin letter I's. "Intelligence?" Jani heard her voice like a shout, but no one flinched so she knew she couldn't have spoken that loudly. "When did you horn in on this?"

The major drew up as tall as she could, which meant that she hit Jani at shoulder height. The disadvantage seemed to bother her. She reversed another half-step and bumped into Pullman, who looked like he wanted to toss her back. "Since the case involves intersystem flight of colonials, it's standard practice for us to be included."

"No, it's not." Jani put a handlock on Niall's elbow and pulled him out of the circle and partway down the hall. "Why were they doing the tracking? You said your people were handling it."

"That's one of the things I'm trying to find out." Niall's face reddened with anger, embarrassment, or a combination of both.

Jani glanced back at the major, who was engaged in intense conversation with the dressy captain. "I'm taking them out of here. My folks. I'm taking them out."

"*What?*" Niall circled in front of her, blocking her view. "What are you talking about?"

"You said Intelligence helped compile the information in the white paper. That means they delineated the corruption in the Channel Worlds, then and now. They knew what the conditions were on Acadia. They knew better than any of you the risks my parents faced, and still they almost lost them at MarsPort." Jani stepped out to the side so she could watch the major, and found the major watching her as well. "Now you expect me to leave my parents here under their care?"

"Not under *their* care." Niall bent close. "I'm in charge."

"You may be in charge, Niall, but you're not in control. For every door you slam shut, they'll find two more."

"Are you saying you don't trust me? Is that what you're saying!"

"I trust you, Niall, but you're not the entire Service. You and Pull can't oversee everything. You can't vet everything. You can't see inside their heads."

"What?" Niall's brow drew down. "You think Intelligence screwed up on *purpose*?"

"They give *L'araignée* my folks now, *L'araignée* gives them something later. A crooked colonial governor. A bent general." A thought lasered through Jani's augie-cleared mind, like the reflection off the major's designators. "Your Guernsey buddy wouldn't happen to be Intelligence, would he?"

Niall grew still, his breathing irregular. He believed in his Service—its discipline and rigor had helped him pull himself from the Victorian gutter. He believed in his friends, too. "That's *coincidence*. Corin's different—I've known him for twenty years."

"I'm hearing that, from you of all people. There's no such thing as coincidence, Niall. You start believing in coincidence, you're *dead*!" Jani headed back down the hall toward the group, which had fractured into Pullman and the lieutenant on one side and the major and the captain on the other. She beckoned to Pullman, who hurried to her side. "I need a skimmer from the vehicle pool. A four-seater. Not the one they want to give you, but one you pick out yourself. Have it at the far-northwest automatic entry in fifteen minutes."

"Ma'am?" Pullman looked at Niall, who had dogged Jani's steps. "Sir, I thought—"

"Do it, Pull." Niall spoke with Declan Kilian's voice, drained and old.

Jani waited for Pullman to leave before speaking. "I'm sorry, Niall. But sometimes it's hardest to see what's closest to you." She turned her back so she wouldn't have to look at his face, and palmed into her parents' room.

"Papa? Maman?" She looked to the couch, and found it empty. The chairs. The bench seat by the shielded window. "Papa!" She stalked a quick circuit of the room, looking for an entry she had somehow missed the first time. Her heart slowed, then tripped, then slowed again. "Maman! *Pap*—!"

"Why you be shouting, Jani-girl?" Declan stuck his head through a gap between two panels in the far wall. "We're in the lave. Your mother tried to eat some of your chicken."

"Oh, shit!" Jani dodged around furniture and into the tiny bath to find Jamira bent over the sink, cupping water repeatedly over her mouth and chin. "Maman, I told you in all the Mistys that I eat strange food!"

"You did not say that you ate fire, Janila." Her mother straightened slowly. Her eyes teared as though she wept. Her nose and mouth had reddened and swelled. "Is that what Dr. Shroud did to you?"

Jani felt the strength of her mother's eyes, even through their mirrored reflection. "He did the best he could."

"Did he?" Jamira coughed, then tore a dispo towel from the sinkside dispenser and dried her mouth.

Declan looked from his wife to his daughter, as he had so often in the house on Rue D'Aubergine when he felt the drag of the undercurrent but couldn't decide which way the harbor. "You were calling us, Jani-girl?"

"*Oui*, Papa." Jani tore away from the sharp brown examination. "We're leaving."

"But we've just arrived."

"I have another place in mind. Where's your luggage?"

"The young major took charge of it at O'Hare, Janila." Jamira's eyes had stopped running, but she had to keep pausing to cough and blow her nose. "She said it would be brought to us after our talk with you."

"You have to leave that stuff here. Anything you need, I'll buy you."

"I packed equipment, Jani-girl." Declan nodded toward Jamira. "Your mother brought family things. And your dowry."

"You lugged fifteen kilos of jewelry?" Jani pressed her fingers to her tightening scalp. "It will be safe here. I just want Niall to check everything first." She waited for them to leave the bath ahead of her. Her father walked out right away, but her mother stopped to pull a handful of dispos from the dispenser and tuck them up her sleeves.

"Where are you taking us?" she asked, concentrating on her tissues.

Jani hesitated. "To—to someone I trust."

"To someone you trust. You do not trust Fort Sheridan, or the whole of the Service, or your scarred colonel. Yet there is *someone*." Jamira Shah tugged down her sleeves and walked to the door. "I must meet this person, Janila." She swept out, leaving behind a trail of softest scent.

By the time Jani returned to the hallway, all the uniforms had departed. Niall stood against the wall, unlit 'stick cupped in his hand. His eyes softened when he looked at her parents. Unfortunately, they chilled when they focused on her.

"Pull went to get the skimmer. Are you going to tell me where we're going, or do I have to guess?"

Jani told him.

And when he turned red and threatened to stop her, she told him again.

CHAPTER 21

Pullman proved his worth and wit by obtaining a skimmer equipped with an ultra-secured comline. Jani made one carefully worded call as the night scenery whipped past and offered the occasional bracing smile to her parents, who sat in hand-holding silence in the rear.

Niall didn't speak much, either. The efforts Jani made to draw him out by asking specific questions about timing and transfers elicited terse replies spoken around one nicstick after the other. By the time they reached Chicago, the skimmer cabin looked as though a smoke bomb had detonated. Jani hunted down the ventilator switch, but even though the influx of fresh air soon cleared the space, the damage had been done. Her eyes stung. Her films felt tight. *Don't let them break now.* That wasn't how she wanted her folks to find out how far down the hybridization path John Shroud had taken her. Judging from her mother's still-inflamed mouth and focused glare, the encounter with Jani's version of pleasantly spicy had been telling enough.

Niall turned off the Boul and steered them up and down midtown side streets before turning onto a short alley that was blocked at the end by a five-meter-high fence. The skimmer headlamps illuminated the security guard that opened the gate and waved them through, along with the trademark name that studded the top of the gate in letters half a meter high.

"Neoclona, Janila?" Her mother touched her shoulder. "Why did you bring us here?"

Jani ignored Niall's grumble. "They're private, Maman. Outside official channels." Val's words returned to her.

"They're not as accountable, so they can do as I ask without needing to explain to anyone."

They turned sharply, then drove down the same wide utility road that Jani had walked the previous night. The road was as deserted now as it had been then, except for the lone figure standing in front of the water treatment station, his silver sport skimmer hovering alongside.

Niall slowed to a stop, reset the vehicle charge-through to "standby," and popped the gullwings. He alit from the skimmer and scanned the roofs of buildings, the sky overhead, on the lookout for holes in Neoclona security.

Before Jani could get out, Val hurried to her side and offered his arm. "Excuse the attire." He tugged at the neck of his stretched-out pullover. "I was having a quiet night at home when Security forwarded your call."

"So they're the only ones who know you're here?" Niall called out as he scanned an adjoining alley. "I trust they know how to keep their mouths shut."

"Yes, Colonel." Val looked at Jani, brows arched.

"Cautious." Jani let him help her out. Her back ached in earnest and a knifeprick of pain stabbed behind her right kneecap every time she flexed it. "I decided to take you up on your offer."

"I'm glad you did." Val slipped behind her and slid the seat forward. "Sir. Ma'am." He helped Declan and Jamira alight, then stood back, an over-wide smile frozen in place.

Well, well. Jani bit her lip to keep from grinning. Like Val angry, Val nervous was a rare event, worthy of note. "Maman. Papa. This is Dr. Valentin Parini. You received messages from him this summer, when I was sick. You'll be staying with him for the next few days."

Val and Declan muttered greetings and shook hands, then broke apart in that trailing way of men who had nothing to say to one another besides "Hello." The Parini charm worked a little better on Jamira, who lost some of her tension in the shelter of his quiet concern.

"I live in a building near the lake. I've got the entire top floor—you'll have your own wing." Val nodded toward Jani. "Jan said you had to leave your things behind at the base—some of the best shops in the city are within walking distance—"

"They can't leave the flat, Val," Jani broke in. "Not until Niall or I give a personal OK."

"Then I will send someone to get you anything you need." Val smiled gamely. "Clothes. Books. Anything."

Jani groaned quietly as the word *books* rang the memory bell. Had Roni McGaw given up on her yet, or did she still wait for her in front of the bookstore? Her mind spun in tight conspiracy circles—did Roni know Niall would be coming for her? Did she have any knowledge of Service Intelligence's double-dealing? Had she contacted her in order to warn her, or to get her out of the way?

"Heads up."

Jani turned to find Niall standing next to their skimmer, his attention focused up the road.

Jani followed his gaze, and saw the growing headlamps of a rapidly approaching skimmer. *It's not going to be able to stop.* Judging from the rate at which the headlamps increased in size, the only thing that would bring it to a halt would be the side of a building. Or their skimmer.

"Get into that doorway!" Niall shouted. *"Now!"*

"No!" Val knew enough to approach Niall around the back. "I think I know who that is!"

"Thinking's not good enough, Parini." Niall reached to his belt and came up with his shooter. "You said no one knew you were here!"

Jani grabbed her mother's arm and herded her toward the doorway of the treatment plant. Jamira reached for Declan, and they daisy-chained into the sheltering dark.

"Janila, what is happening!"

"I don't know, Maman!" Jani swore under her breath, her hand aching for a weapon. She watched in helpless rage as the skimmer kept coming. Closer. Closer. *"Niall!"*

Niall ignored her. He raised his weapon.

Sighted down.

Fired.

The pulse packet impacted the driver's-side bumper, forcing the skimmer offcourse. Proximity alarms screamed. The vehicle spun halfway around in one direction, then another, as the driver and the balance arrays fought to keep it from careening into a building. The whine of reversing directionals joined the alarms in a night-splitting howl as the skimmer shuddered to a halt a scant few meters from Niall, who closed in, weapon raised. *"Get out of the vehicle! Now! Hands above your head!"*

"It's John, goddamn it!" Val circled to Niall's side, reached for his arm, and barely ducked his fist. *"Put that goddamned thing down!"*

Lights flashed around the corner. Emergency vehicles. Guards on foot, weapons drawn.

Jani shook off her mother's restraining grip and ran into the road, her knee threatening to buckle with every stride. *"Niall, stand down!"*

The driver's side gullwing of the damaged skimmer swept up. The telltale white head emerged.

"That was really stupid, John!" Val waved back the Neoclona guards. They obeyed grudgingly, glaring at Niall as though they wanted to toss him in the back of a security van and drop him on his head a few times on the way.

Niall slowly lowered his weapon. "I disagree with your friend, Dr. Shroud. Stupid doesn't even get it started!"

John struggled out of the skimmer. *"What the hell are you trying to do!"* He looked from his blistered bumper to the guards, then to Niall. His face slackened as the realization of what might have happened punched through his anger. He raised a hand to his mouth, and stared at the charred bumper.

"Janila?" Jani's mother came up behind her and tugged on her jacket. "Is that *your* Dr. Shroud?"

"Maman, how many other one-nine albinos do you think are out there?"

John grew still as the sight of Jani broke through his angry daze. Then he saw Jamira, and his hand dropped to his side. *"Val. You should have called me directly."*

Val aimed the same look at John that the guards had toward Niall. "I left a message," he said flatly. "You told me specifically that you didn't want to hear any more about Ja—"

"You should have called me directly." John undid the closure of his evening suit jacket and slid a hand in his pocket. In the next breath, he removed his hand from his pocket and refastened the closure. He'd chosen one of his more striking outfits, dark ivory and rigorously tailored.

Wonder what color he filmed his eyes? Jani ran down the list she had compiled over the summer. Light brown wouldn't raise any eyebrows. Gold or pearl would earn her the parental fish-eye she'd won as a youngster whenever she brought a particularly unsuitable friend home to visit. "Dr. John Shroud." She reached behind her and beckoned. "My parents, Declan Kilian and Jamira Shah."

John had recovered his composure by the time Jani finished her introduction, and stepped forward with the easy assurance of a man who walked on his own land. The light from a safety illumin fell across his face, highlighting amber-brown eyefilming that looked distinctive but not bizarre.

"Père Kilian. Mère Kilian." The polite Acadian titles and throaty French R's flowed, as though he'd been practicing. "I am at your service." He shook Declan's hand, then drew a collective gasp of surprise by bending over Jamira's and applying a haute formal not-quite-kiss on her knuckles.

"Dr. Shroud." Jamira reclaimed her hand with a cool smile. "So much kindness after such a raucous welcome."

"It's not kindness, Mère Kilian. It's a joy."

"Is it? Well, then, I should take advantage while I can, should I not?"

John's eyes sparked. He could reek charisma under the right circumstances, and the opportunity to bestow brought out the gallant in him. "You could never take advantage, Mère Kilian. Anything I have is yours." His deep bass flowed like warmed molasses. "You have but to ask."

"Really?" Jamira's brow arched. "Any*thing*?"

Jani leaned against the treatment facility wall and pressed fingertips to forehead. Twenty years had passed since she'd heard that questioning flick at the end of a word. Like the approaching skimmer headlamps, she realized what was happening, but knew she risked a good bashing if she tried to step in and stop it. She glanced at her father, who widened his eyes and looked at the ground.

"Anything, Mère Kilian." John's sugar synthesizer was running at full capacity now. "Name it."

Jamira patted her palms together in almost-silent clapping, her "decisions, decisions" gesture. Then it stopped, and her face lit. "I should like Luna, Dr. Shroud. Your moon. In a gift box. With a large red bow."

"Then you shall have it, Mère Kilian." John crossed his arm over his chest and bowed deeply, then straightened and spread his arm wide.

"So readily you promise me the moon, Dr. Shroud. Like a god." The lightness had left Jamira's voice. She looked pointedly at Jani, then back to John. "Who made you a god, Doctor? Who allowed you the right to promise what isn't yours to give?"

John froze in mid-flourish, his self-satisfied smile ebbing. Val mouthed an "ouch." Niall grinned for the first time since they left Sheridan.

Jamira brushed past John, eyes averted, and walked up the road toward Val's silver skimmer.

"We need to get going, folks. Our little noise and fireworks display must have attracted attention." Niall sauntered over to Val. "Is your in-vehicle comline secure?"

Val nodded, his attention focused on his business partner. John stood where Jamira had left him. He avoided everyone's gaze, and seemed preoccupied with the state of his jacket lining.

"We split them up," Niall continued, "and take separate routes. Do you have access to a private lift in your building?"

"Of course," Val said, eyes still on John.

"Well, don't use it. From here on in, it's the service lift only." Niall pulled Val to one side so they could continue their discussion.

Jani gave John a wide berth and rejoined her parents, who stood in huddled argument beside Val's skimmer.

"—need his help!" Declan's cheeks flared as though he'd been struck. "Couldn't you wait?"

"Non! Why should I?" Jamira's voice rasped. Her eyes brimmed. "That *bâtard* turned my daughter into an *anormal,* a mutant!"

The words stopped Jani in her tracks. A sudden ache

flared in her gut and spread to her chest. "Is that what you think I am?" Her jaw felt wooden. "You thought I needed you, and you came. If you felt that way, why did you bother?"

Jamira's face paled to clay. "Janila, it is not to you that I say this."

Jani raised a hand to her eyes. She wanted to rip off the films, reveal the truth behind the lie, let her parents see. Let Niall see. "But who else could you say it to? *I'm* the freak, Maman. The abnormal." She tried to lift the right film away, but she couldn't slide her thumbnail underneath it far enough to get a good grip. "Before you left Acadia, you should have had one of the priests fashion you a charm to protect yourself from me." She dug the sliver of carved-away film from under her nail and flicked it away.

Jamira pressed a hand to her cheek, then took a step toward Jani and reached out. "Janila?"

"Time to go, folks." Niall stepped into the breach unseeing, jaunty grin still in place. "Jan, which skim' are you riding in?"

"I think it's better if I don't go with you." Jani turned her back on her mother's outstretched hand. "You never know." She saw the comprehension dawn in Niall's eyes, and turned away from that as well. "You just never know." She started to walk, although she had no idea where she should go.

"Janila!"

Jani's feet dragged to a halt as her mother's shout filled her ears, even as her will tried to propel her forward. She gasped as Jamira's arms snaked around her waist and squeezed until her ribs ached from the pressure, yet she couldn't bring herself to touch her hands. Heard her sobs, yet felt no urge to comfort her. *Freak.* Yes. Only a monster could remain untouched by such a firestorm of emotion. Only a wretch could be so cold. She pried her mother's arms loose. "You have to go. I'll visit . . . when I can." She forced herself to turn around, to stand still as Jamira again embraced her and whispered her name over and over, begging her forgiveness. "Go with Niall, Maman." She patted her mother's shoulder, then prodded her toward a shaken Niall. She watched them get into the Service skimmer, watched the skimmer bank and glide and disappear around the corner.

It took Jani some time to realize that she was being watched, as well. She looked around to find her father still standing beside Val's skimmer. He massaged his knuckles one at a time, a tic he took down from the shelf whenever his emotions threatened to get the better of him.

"Your mother loves you more than her own life, Jani-girl." Declan's voice emerged dead calm, as it did when he was the most angry. "You always fire at the wrong target. When you were mad at Cheecho, you took it out on his sister. When you were mad at your schoolwork, you took it out on your games, and I took the calls from the parents with the bruised children. When you were mad at van Reuter, you took it out on everyone but him." He walked around the skimmer to the passenger side and popped the gullwing. "Wrong target." He lowered inside the low-slung cabin and yanked the door closed, sitting in stiff-faced rage as a visibly distressed Val hurried over and inserted himself into the driver's seat.

Then Declan said something, and Val's head bobbed up and down in overwrought agreement. Declan opened his gullwing, struggled out of the skimmer, and strode back to Jani.

"Man his age driving that ridiculous thing. Looks a twit." He pulled Jani to him. "Be careful."

Jani hugged him hard, wishing part of the embrace travel to wherever Niall's skimmer was. "*Oui*, Papa."

"Don't stay away for days. She doesn't deserve that."

"I know, Papa."

"She loves you. I love you. You're our girl."

"I love you, too."

Declan released Jani and returned to the skimmer. The vehicle sped away—just as it cornered, Jani caught sight of her father's furiously waving hand. She raised her own in response, even though it was too late for him to see. Then she let it fall, and felt the numbness settle as she turned to walk up the road toward Neoclona Main.

"Where do you need to go?"

Jani wheeled to find John leaning against the treatment facility wall, jacket once more unfastened, hands shoved in trouser pockets. As distinctive as he was, he had a talent for fading into the background that she always found unsettling. "I don't know. Back home, I guess."

John pushed off the wall and ambled toward her. "I'll take you."

"You don't have to."

"Jani, just get in the goddamned skimmer."

As Jani opened her mouth to argue, her right knee started to ache, a low-level twinge that promised to become a higher-pitched misery if she kept walking. She limped after John, stood aside as he opened her gullwing for her, fell into her seat, and sat with hands folded in her lap as he closed her in.

John sat heavily himself, and punched the charge-through four times before it engaged. They maneuvered down the street and through the same gate Jani had entered seeming days ago.

The streets contained more people than they had earlier now that Chicago's night had begun in earnest. Jani glanced at John's dapper suit, and added two and two. "I blew another evening for you, didn't I?"

John was either too beaten or too angry to deny the obvious. "Dinner. With a very close friend."

"If she was that close, you shouldn't have left her."

"First I get the forward from Security with the notation that you'd called Val from a military line, then I get Val's message. What the hell did you expect me to do, waltz back to the sorbet!" John swerved too close to the skimmer in the next lane. Proximity alarms blared, and he jerked the wheel to return to his track. "I never said my friend was a *she*."

Jani watched the passing scenery, and thought of all the famous females she'd seen over the summer in the *Tribune-Times* or on the 'Vee. John's "very close friends" tended to fall into very specific categories. "Anybody I've heard of?"

John hesitated, then shrugged. "She sings at the Lyric occasionally."

"Hmm." Jani yawned. "Niall could probably recite her every role."

John struck an uneven beat on the steering wheel. "You really don't care, do you?"

"I abrogated the right to care the night I fled Rauta Shèràa. You asked me to stay. I said no. End of story."

"No. It never ends. We keep writing new chapters." The skimmer windows filtered the city light. The resulting semi-dark of the cabin offered the perfect backdrop for John's voice. "I love you."

"I love you, too." Jani answered automatically, but some truths were easier to admit than others. "Not that I had much choice. You were the first thing I saw when I came out of the coma, and you always did make a strong initial impression."

"Funny how some things never change. You used the same excuse back then." John wore the glower of a statue that had found a crack in its pedestal. "Maybe there's something to it. You were the first thing I saw when I opened my eyes, too. Figuratively speaking. I didn't have much . . . experience with women before you came along."

Didn't I know it. "You bury me with your regard, John, until I can neither move nor breathe. To save me the trouble of making choices, you make them for me. I can't live like that."

John snorted lightly, but didn't speak. The traffic jam that ensued as skimmers maneuvered around a double-parked people-mover gave him something to concentrate on for a time. "I really got off on the wrong foot with your mother," he said as the squeeze cleared. "Mind telling me what happened?"

"Niall got me some food while we were at Sheridan. Maman tried it, and the pepper almost did her in." Jani blinked away the ache as the image of her mother bent over the bathroom sink returned. *Anormal. Mutant.* "Your folks used to call you a freak, didn't they?"

"No, they had the Christian Fallback Council of Elders declare me Marked by God. Amounted to the same thing, though." John's lip curled. He had never offered more than the occasional remark concerning his youth. That reticence alone told one all they needed to know. "How would my life have changed if they had approved my *in utero* genetic adjustment? Would I have grown into the man I am? Built Neoclona? Would I even have studied medicine? I don't know. But as I told you back in the basement, by the time I was old enough to request adjustment on my own, I didn't want it. Being unique has its advantages." He glanced at

Jani, and raised a hand in grudging admission. "It has its disadvantages, too, but overall the good outweighs the bad."

The skimmer turned onto Armour Place, and Jani leaned forward to stretch her back in preparation for the trudge across the lobby. "At least you could make a choice. Refer to my previous comment on the matter."

John edged the skimmer curbside, then waved away the doorman who hurried toward them. "Well," he said after a time, "that was an interesting interlude."

"Niall reacted to a perceived threat—"

"I'm not blaming him. If I'd seen a skimmer bearing down on you, I'd have shot at it myself." He focused his broody attention on his fingernails. "I wish you'd called me personally."

Jani shook her head. "Not after this afternoon."

John made as if to speak, but made do with a shaky exhale. The silence stretched. "Get some sleep," he finally said. "*Eat* first. Be careful, like your father said." He looked at Jani. His eyes were too dark for his sepulchre face, which seemed to glow in contrast. "Everybody's shooting at me tonight. I'm the right target he thinks you should hit, aren't I?"

Jani nodded. "I think so."

"That means I made a sterling impression on him, too. I'm . . . sorry, for what resulted." John groaned. "Val will speak up for me. They seem to like Val. But then, *everybody* likes Val. Hell, *Nema* likes Val."

"You need to get back to your singer. She likes you."

John shook his head. He had found a new scab to pick and refused to leave it alone. "She'd like Val if he'd have her."

"Don't underestimate yourself. You always did." Jani smiled as a few of the better memories resurfaced. "You have your moments."

"Oh yeah?" John perked. "I've got half a mind to press the accelerator to the floor. We could be in Seattle in two days." He sagged back in his seat. "Only problem is, the first time I slowed below forty, you'd bail out the window."

"I would—not—I—" Jani tried to formulate a lucid protest. But the fatigue and the emotional upheavals of the last few hours caved in on her, and she laughed instead. John gaped at her for a few moments, then joined in. They began quietly, then grew louder as various scenarios played through their minds.

The merriment fizzled. Jani wiped her eyes with care. She knew she had damaged her right film, and she no longer felt compelled to reveal herself to the world. "You don't want me, John. I'd make you as crazy as you'd make me. Go back to your singer. There's absolutely no reason for you to be alone."

John's grin died. "I've been alone since you left. The fact that another woman occasionally occupies your space doesn't make any difference." He unlatched Jani's gullwing, remaining silent as she disembarked, ignoring her good night and vanishing into the dark before she reached the building entry.

Jani stopped and stared at the place where the skimmer had parked, then to the dark into which it had disappeared. It had felt so warm inside. So quiet. So comforting. *If I just said the word, I could have that forever.* John would raise the walls and affix the locks, and nothing would ever reach her again.

Nothing.

Poor John. She yawned as she limped across the lobby. If she could beg any good luck from her Lord Ganesha, she would find Steve, Angevin, and Lucien asleep. Particularly Lucien. She wouldn't possess the energy to deal with him unless she slept through the night and into the following day.

Pondering Lucien deflected her attention from her surroundings. She didn't see the figure dart in from the sitting area until it intercepted her.

"Where the hell have you been!" Angevin grabbed her hand and pulled her toward the lift bank. "We have been calling everybody and everywhere! Lucien even woke up his CO trying to track you down."

Jani flashed on the possibility of taking John up on his Seattle offer. If he was on his way back to his singer, Val could forward him Jani's message. They could leave inside the hour. "Angevin, I know I left some things undone, but I'll get to them first thing tomorrow, I prom—"

"Oh, you think it's that simple!" Angevin's eyes gleamed green fire. *"You just wait."*

CHAPTER 22

"Angevin, what's going on? Angevin?" Jani hurried down the hall after the diminutive figure, who broke into a run as they neared the flat entry. *"Angevin!"*

"Did you know that the rear service entrance to this building isn't as well secured as it should be?" Angevin stopped in front of the door, then began to pace. Now that she'd made her goal, she couldn't follow through. "Did you? I sure as hell didn't. Heard the entry buzzer and assumed it was the front desk. Opened the door. *Guess what!"*

Jani looked from the door to Angevin's stricken face, then back again. "Who's in there? Are Steve and Lucien all right?"

"They're fine." Angevin took a step toward the door, then backed away again. "Maybe you should go in first."

"Oh, for—" Jani keyed in and gave a panel a good push to help it along. She strode through the entry, and saw Steve sitting at her desk, twisting an unlit 'stick between his fingers. "What's going on?"

Steve opened his mouth, then closed it. He held out his hand to Angevin, who had scuttled in behind Jani. Together, they pointed toward the sitting area.

Jani turned to find a robe-wrapped Lucien sitting in a chair that had been pushed in front of the couch. The couch itself was occupied by a formidably tall man, his head and shoulders towering above the seat back.

Man . . . Jani's senses gave her a swift kick, pointing out the dark gold tinge of the skin and the rigid posture. The jewel-rich green of the shirt, and the liquid-like way the material flowed over the broad back.

Then the head slowly turned, and she saw the eyes. Cracked gold glass, catching the light like gilt. "Ná Kièrshia." The Haárin tilemaster rose to his feet. "I am Dathim Naré. NìRau Tsecha trusts you are most as uninjured, and bids me offer you the glories of the evening." He spoke in English, flavored with the trilled R's and biting consonants of Vynshàrau Haárin.

Ná? Jani detected the shortened vowels and altered accent of the Haárin feminine title. Well, that made sense. Or at least as much sense as everything else had that evening. "Ní Dathim. I am uninjured, yes." She felt spun around, disoriented, like she'd just emerged from a pitch-dark Veedrome into the blaze of day. *What the hell time is it?* Too late at night to deal with an Haárin who sheared his head as humanish and felt no compunction about visiting his people's Toxin in her downtown Chicago flat, surely. "My home is not clean. Your soul is in danger." She had slipped from English into Vynshàrau Haárin without conscious thought, her straight back and anxious hand flicks defining her distress. "You should not be here."

"I go where my dominant bids me go, regardless of the threat to my soul. I have declared myself to him. Such is my duty." Dathim's arms hung at his sides as he continued his half of the conversation in English. "He has bid me come here to witness your condition, and to bring you something that you must take care of."

"Nema gave you something to give to me?" Jani groaned inwardly. Then again, judging by the odd looks she received from the assembled, maybe it wasn't so inward. She walked to the sitting area. She had a choice of perching on the arm of Lucien's chair or joining Dathim on the couch. Considering how she currently felt about Lucien and how her right knee and back felt about her, her choice proved no choice. She stepped past the chair without giving its occupant a look and sagged into a cross-legged slump on the couch, a respectful bodylength away from the Haárin.

Dathim sat as well. However, instead of pressing against the couch back, he shifted so that he nestled in the corner and faced Jani. That meant he couldn't plant his booted feet side by side on the floor in the knees-together seat of a typical idomeni. Instead, he lifted his left leg and crossed it over his right leg, ankle to knee. Then he placed his left hand on the bent knee and stretched his right arm atop the arm of the couch in the classic "this is my space" sprawl of a human male.

Jani glanced at Lucien, who stared at the Haárin, his lips parted ever so slightly. If she didn't know better, she'd have thought he had a crush on him. If she didn't know better—

John, take me to Seattle! No, the last thing she needed was John and Seattle in any combination. *I'm tired, hungry, and in pain. Someone tried to kill me and my lover may have arranged it. My mother called me mutant tonight. Now Nema has a job for me.* Maybe she should call him and tell him it was safe, so that he could leave the embassy grounds and do whatever the hell it was himself. *Except he's been locked down. He can't leave. He's in trouble. Wake up!* She buried her face in her hands on the off chance that augie had gone south and she hallucinated. *When I look up, the far end of the couch will be empty.* Lucien will be gone, too. *He'll have been transferred to Whalen's Planet.* Steve and Angevin will have moved out. *I'll be alone, and it will be quiet, and I can sleep.*

She looked up to find Dathim studying her full-face, auric eyes shining. When she'd lived in the colonies and dealt with Haárin merchants on a daily basis, she had grown used to their efforts to adopt humanish appearance and the habit of direct eye contact. *Make that "somewhat used."* Idomeni appearance could be startling—to that, Dathim Naré had added his own spin. His was the long, bony face of his Vyn-shàrau forebears—his shorn hair accentuated the hard lines even more. He wore no overrobe atop his open-necked shirt and belted trousers. He wore no earrings. Not even his *à lérine* scars, the elongated welts ragged and brown against his dark gold skin, hinted at his alien nature. They could have been caused by an accident. He could have been a human male suffering from genetic disorders of the bone and liver, an inhabitant of one of the colonial outposts that had slipped beneath Neoclona's detection limit.

"You are unwell, Kièrshia? You do not act as bold as I have seen you at the embassy." Dathim's appearance seemed to alter his voice, making it sound merely foreign rather than alien. Deep. Rich. Not quite the twin of John's inestimable bass, but definitely a sibling.

"I've had a very long day, ní Dathim." Jani broke contact with the probing stare. *And you're making it longer.* "You said you had something to give me, from Nema." She reverted to English, since sitting cross-legged on a couch didn't lend itself to proper Vynshàrau Haárin language postures. "Could you give it to me, please?"

"Yes." Dathim twisted around, reached over the side of the couch, and came up holding a large idomeni-style briefbag. "NìRau Tsecha said that you will know what to do with these." He dropped the bag in the empty expanse between him and Jani. "I know what to do with them as well, but nìRau Tsecha does not trust my judgment. This is most unfortunate—I must ponder ways to earn his trust, and truly."

Jani watched Dathim as he unclasped the bag's complicated fasteners. *Did I just hear an Haárin employ sarcasm?* He appeared perfectly serious, but Jani seldom met an idomeni who didn't. Nema bared his teeth more than most of his race and took pride in the fact that he had a sense of humor and knew how to use it, but he was an exception to every idomeni rule. *And now there's Dathim Naré.* The fact that he and Nema had found one another made her head ache. "Most as your dominant, ní Dathim, you possess a capacity to surprise."

"Surprise is a good thing, is it not, Kièrshia? A good thing for gaining humanish attention, and truly." Dathim undid the last fastener and pushed back the flap. "Surprise!"

Jani looked into the bag, and saw files and data wafers inserted in an array of upright pleated pockets. Files in burgundy folders. Files in white folders with burgundy trim. One file in a black folder. She tried to speak, but couldn't think of anything to say that Dathim would understand, even taking into account his expertise in sarcasm.

"Oh shit, Jan." Steve had wandered over to the couch. "Those are bloody Exterior Ministry Exec files."

The words "Exterior Ministry" brought Lucien out of his chair. He lifted one of the files out of its pocket, looked at the information tab that ran across the top, and shoved it back into place as though the paper stung to the touch. "I don't know about the rest of those files, but that one is classified 'For Ministers' Eyes Only.' At this moment, we're all facing at least twenty years in prison for violating the Commonwealth Secrets Act."

Jani looked at Dathim, who had resumed his cross-legged sprawl and looked extremely pleased with himself. "How did you steal these documents? More importantly, *why* did you steal these documents?"

"I took them out of Anais Ulanova's office. NìRau Tsecha wanted to learn more of your shooting, and believed that Anais Ulanova would possess information." He still watched Jani with interest, studying her reactions to his every revelation. "I was taken there to look at places to lay my tile. I examined the lobby, but the tilework that nìaRauta Ulanova wanted there was not suitable, so they took me to look at the conference room that was connected by a door to her office. She had many stacks of files on her desk. I took something from each stack."

Lucien slumped back into his chair. "I told her for years to seal that damned door."

Dathim finally used an Haárin gesture, a brush of his open right hand across his shirtfront that indicated relief. "I am most glad she did not listen to you, Lieutenant Pascal, and truly."

A glimmer of liveliness returned to Lucien's face. Oh yes, the fact that Dathim recognized him definitely pleased him. "You know me?"

"I have seen you at the embassy, with nìRau Tsecha. And alone. The lieutenant who remembers what he sees." Dathim regarded Lucien less intently than he did Jani. If he noticed Lucien's fascination with him, he gave no indication. But then, odds were overwhelming that he had no experience with human sexuality or any idea what that captivation implied.

"When Anais figures out that you rifled her office, and she will, Commonwealth–Shèrá relations are going to get interesting. I think the term 'major diplomatic incident' is applicable here." Jani fingered through the files. "And nìRau Nema expects me to do what with these? Return them?"

"Yes." Dathim gave a human-style shrug. "He said that

you would see to them. He called this an 'incident,' too. He said that he is quite good at them."

"Oh, yeah." Jani glanced up at Steve, who looked sick to his stomach.

"We could turn them over to someone in my department." Lucien spoke to Jani, but he looked at Dathim. "Certain people owe me favors. It would be a no-questions-asked return. The best way to go about this, in my opinion."

Jani pretended to consider Lucien's offer, then shook her head. "If Service Intelligence turns them in, Exterior is going to think they took them in the first place. Service and Exterior are just starting to get along again—I don't think we want to risk scuttling any tenuous truces over this." In truth, she didn't want Intelligence sticking their nose in. Not after the way they bobbled her parents' transfer. *This needs to be handled by someone I trust.* Someone she could . . . persuade. She knew where she needed to go—she just needed to get there without tipping off Lucien.

"One of the ministry Doc Controls?" Angevin had joined Steve, placing herself in such a way that she hid her from Dathim's view. "Stuff happens. 'So-and-so left her briefbag behind after a meeting' is the standard excuse. The Ministries exchange unauthorized acquisitions all the time."

But the Ministries won't let me analyze these files before I give them back. Jani closed the bag flap and dragged the strap over her shoulder. "I'll think of something." She stood, not quite as shakily as Lucien, and limped across the room toward the kitchen. "Steve, run interference for ní Dathim while he leaves." She pushed past the sliding door, then leaned against the counter until she could dredge up the strength to walk to the cooler. "I just need some juice." And one of John's meal bars. That would provide enough energy to get her through the next few hours. "Hours." She yawned as she cracked the seal of a dispo of lemon tonic.

Jani had leaned her head back to drink when she heard the kitchen door open. She didn't bother to turn around. If it was Angevin or Steve, the melodious howls of shock and dismay would soon fill the air, and if it was Lucien. . . . She felt her body tighten in anticipation of his touch, and gave herself a mental swift kick.

"You are not as you should be."

Jani's throat stopped in mid-swallow. Her head came down, luckily over the sink. She spewed, coughed, and sneezed tonic—the bubbly astringency filled her nostrils and burned her sinuses. Her eyes teared as though she wept—she felt the damaged right film split. *"Damn—!"* She grabbed for the sinkside dispenser, yanked napkin after napkin, blew her nose and wiped her face. Then she turned, taking care to cover her exposed eye.

Dathim stood just inside the doorway. The prospect of entering a humanish kitchen seemed to have tempered his boldness. He touched the edge of a counter, the handle of a cupboard door. "I surprised you again." Then he drew his hand back and examined his fingertips, as though he expected the contact to leave a mark. "You surprise easily, and truly."

Jani watched in amazement as Dathim opened a drawer and removed a serving fork. "Is there nothing you fear, ní Dathim?" She spoke in Vynshàrau Haárin, so that her words would better express her shock at his actions.

"I am already damned, according to the Oligarch. What difference?" Dathim turned the fork over, then returned it to its holder and slid the drawer closed. "This kitchen is cleaner than I expected. We are told that humanish leave their food on the counter for the insects and the parasites to season."

"We sometimes leave out food, but it's covered. The production is tightly controlled and the food itself is treated, so there are no parasites." Jani gestured around her. "Do you see any insects?"

Dathim shrugged. "The Oligarch would say that the insects come out later. For each question, he has a ready answer." He looked at Jani. "You limp. You were hurt in the shooting?"

"I fell on my knee. It is as nothing."

"Lieutenant Pascal was hurt."

"Yes. He was shot in the lower abdomen. As you saw, he is weak, but he will recover."

"He stares at me."

Jani racked her brain for the right words. "He has never seen an Haárin with short hair."

"Ah." Dathim brushed his hand over his stubble. "You have damaged your eye?"

"Yes." Jani probed behind the dispo to wipe away a film fragment that had slithered down her cheek.

"Then you must be in pain."

"No."

"Eyes hurt when they are damaged."

"I'm all right."

Dathim's lips curved in a disturbingly human-like smile. "You have eyes like mine, but you do not want me to see them. You are my dominant according to nìRau Tsecha, but it shames you to look as I do. Just like nìRau Tsecha. He takes an Haárin name, but he lives as born-sect, because to live as I do would shame him."

Jani shifted her footing to take the weight off her aching knee. "Shame has nothing to do with it, ní Dathim." She waited for her knee to stop throbbing before she risked speaking again—the pain made her voice shake. "I am not your dominant. I am a humanish female who had an accident. The way my doctor chose to repair me resulted in genetic changes that have led to my looking a little like you. That's all."

"NìRau Tsecha chose you before you had your accident. He believed you could lead us through difficult times. Those are his words. I have never led, so I must submit to his experience in such things." Dathim took one step farther into the kitchen, then another. He opened the cooler, removed a dispo of grapefruit juice, and studied the label.

Sarcasm. Jani hoisted her lemon tonic to brave another sip—

"You look most odd standing there with one hand over your eye."

—and brought it back down just as quickly. *"Ní Dathim—"*

Before Jani could finish, Dathim strode across the narrow kitchen, grabbed her wrist, and yanked down.

"You—!" Jani threw the dispo into the sink and let the bag slide to the floor, then used her freed hand to try to loosen the Haárin's brutal grip. She wanted to use her legs and teeth as well, but she didn't want the sounds of a fight to reach the sitting room.

Then she looked up into Dathim's face, saw his bared teeth, and stopped struggling. "Let. Me. Go."

"Green. Not a common color for Vynshàrau, except near the north where our lands border those of the Oà. Many Oà have green eyes." Dathim pushed up Jani's sleeve, revealing her healed *à lérine* scars. Then he released her and took a step back. His air of self-satisfaction dissipated. *"Which eye is the fake, Kièrshia?"* He lapsed into his language. The pitch of his voice turned guttural. His shoulders rounded. *"Decide, or leave the Haárin be. Leave nìRau Tsecha be. He fights his suborn because of you. He fights everyone because of you."*

"Sànalàn? He's fighting Sànalàn?" Jani massaged her right wrist, which bore the imprint of Dathim's fingers. "It's because of what he said at the meeting, isn't it? I knew she'd be angry, but I didn't think she'd challenge him."

"It is another incident." Dathim resumed both his English and his examination of the kitchen appliances, opening the door to the oven and looking inside. "In truth, Shai will not approve this fight, but nìRau Tsecha will not retract his acceptance." He ran a finger along the inside of the oven, like a chef performing inspection. "He does this for you. What do you do for him?"

"I never asked him to do this for me. I never asked him to do anything. He never asked me, either. He just told me, 'This is what you will be!' " Jani heard her voice fill the small room, knew it carried to three pairs of ears beyond, and didn't care. "I am unfit to lead. I have no skill in government. I have a past that makes me dangerous to know. I want to be left alone."

"You want to be left alone." Dathim opened another cupboard and removed a prepack dinner from the shelf. "Yet when nìRau Tsecha gives you documents and says, 'Dispose of them,' I do not hear you say no. Such causes me to think that you do not wish to be so alone, no matter what you say. Such humanish confusion—it is not sound. You need to decide, Kièrshia." He stood quietly and read the back of the package, as if he had no interest in Jani's reply.

Jani watched him study the container, return it to its place, and remove another. "What do you want, ní Dathim?" Her fatigued brain traveled in loops and whorls, driven by anger and confusion. "Why are you doing this?"

Dathim closed the cupboard and turned to face her. Over the past minutes, he had performed acts that would have earned him expulsion from his enclave, yet he seemed as relaxed as if he had just arranged his tools or worked some tile. "I tire of sneaking off the embassy grounds in the night. I want to visit this damned cold place in the day. I want to sell my tilemastery here. I want to live here. Many of us wish the same."

"You want to leave the embassy grounds?" Jani watched as Dathim nodded. "Cèel will never allow you to establish an enclave in Chicago, and neither will my government."

"What Cèel wants is of no consequence. And if the things we offer please humanish enough, they will let us come, because they want what pleases them. But if they hesitate, you will persuade them, Kièrshia, that such is the proper thing to do. They will listen to you, because your past makes you dangerous to know, and because they smell the blood of Knevçet Shèràa when you speak." Dathim offered another close-lipped smile. "It is past our time to establish an enclave here. Even when humanish lived outside Rauta Shèràa before the war, they did not extend us an invitation to live here. And many of us wanted to come." He looked around the kitchen as though it were land he wished to purchase, then at Jani, his smug attitude returned. "Surprise, ná Kièrshia. You will soon not be alone."

CHAPTER 23

Dathim left quietly, a reluctant Steve at his back. Angevin, rattled unto silence, adjourned to Jani's desk and poked through the dwindling stacks. Lucien remained in his chair, gaze moving briefly to Jani before settling with eerie concentration toward the door.

Jani sought refuge in her bedroom. She refilmed her eye, then focused on the mechanical task of transferring the Exterior documents from the idomeni briefbag to her duffel. When Dathim's parting words threatened to punch through her thought barrier, she dropped a file or fussed with a clasp to ward them off. The ploy even worked the first few times she tried it—

You will soon not be alone.

—but it couldn't work forever.

She sat on the edge of the bed and pushed up her right sleeve. Her scars caught the light like silken threads. She could imagine the skin reddened where Dathim had grabbed her, even though the impress of his fingers had long since faded.

Which eye is the fake, Kièrshia?

Jani blinked slowly, mindful of the fresh filming. "They both are, strictly speaking." She tugged the sleeve back into place, then dragged her duffel onto her lap and closed the fasteners. "That's what happens when your doctor builds you from whatever he finds in his basement." She tried to smile, but Dathim's words persisted in her head.

They will listen to you . . . because they smell the blood of Knevçet Shèràa when you speak.

Jani sat quietly. Then she pushed her duffel back onto the bed, rose, and walked to her closet.

Her knee griped as she stood on her toes to reach the toiletry case, which taunted her from its resting place in the rear of the shelf. She tested the hanger bar for strength, then braced her left foot against the wall and pulled herself up, a move to which both her lower back and sore shoulder took vigorous exception.

She opened the bag slowly, as though she expected the contents to leap out at her. She put on the redstone ring—it slid easily on the third finger of her right hand, as it had for months. The soulcloth, she looped around her left wrist like a bracelet in the manner of a Vynshàrau soldier reclaiming his soul after a battle. Her long-dried blood had stiffened the fabric, making the tying difficult. She finally settled for winding the loose ends around the length and tucking them.

She stood and regarded her changed hands. John had switched out her left arm several times that summer, for reasons he had refused to make clear at the time. But now she could see—he had needed to play catch-up with the rapid changes her real arm had undergone. The longer, thinner fingers. The narrowed palms. The brown skin tinged with gold, as though she suffered from liver disease.

Jani held her left wrist up to her nose and sniffed the bracelet. The cloth smelled old, musty. Cold, if an odor could be classified that way. "The blood lost its smell long ago." She pulled the cloth from her wrist and the ring from her finger and thrust them back in the bag. Then she shoved the bag as far as she could into a dark corner of the shelf.

The night had grown cold and crisp; the dry air pulled the moisture from her eyefilms. Jani tugged up the field jacket collar, wishing she'd thought to stuff a pair of gloves in the pockets. Her stomach grumbled, and she rummaged through her duffel for one of John's meal bars. The fact that she had crammed the Exterior files into the bag complicated the search, already made difficult by the dark and her fatigue-dulled attention span. She pulled up beside a chrysanthemum-filled planter to search more easily.

She didn't catch the movement at first. A passing skimmer

obscured matters, followed by the rowdy procession of some Family progeny out on a prowl. But as Jani returned her attention to her duffel, she caught the shadow flicker in the doorway across the street. The fidget of someone who thought themselves better hidden than they actually were.

Jani freed a meal bar from the morass with a flourish and removed the wrapper. Bit into it with apparent relish and continued her saunter down the street. She had traveled two blocks south of Armour Place. Her original destination had been a people-mover stop that she didn't often use. Now, however, she veered west toward an area of commercial buildings.

The quality of the safety lighting deteriorated quickly. Soon Jani could only track her stalker by the occasional distant footfall. Whoever it was remained on the other side of the street, well back and out of sight. During daylight, Jani conceded, they could have tracked her for blocks without her knowledge, since they seemed to possess a decent grasp of basic shadowing. But night had proved their enemy rather than friend, as their step echoed along the deserted street.

Jani continued to wend deeper into the commercial pocket until follower and followed were the only two people to be seen. When she encountered a narrow alley between two shuttered buildings, she slipped down it. Once she reached the end, she nestled into the shadows, and waited.

For a time, all was silence but for her breathing and the beat of her heart. Then Jani heard the staccato scrape of leather sole on scancrete; the sound stopped at the mouth of the alley, then began again, drawing closer and growing louder as her follower approached. She reached into her duffel for her parchment opener, then let the bag slide to the ground. Her hand tightened around the blade's handle. She waited.

The steps quickened as they approached the end of the alley. Stopped as the stalker surveyed the darkness. Then they resumed, slowly, one long, low crunch after another, drawing nearer.

Jani waited until the sounds drew alongside. Slightly ahead. She tensed to spring—

"Jani? Are you back here?"

—and pulled the knife back just in time as she barreled into Roni and they tumbled onto the hard, cold scancrete. "You *jackass*!" She rolled away from her and swore again as she banged her right knee against the sharp corner of the building. "Why the hell didn't you announce yourself!"

Roni lay flat on her back. "I trusted you." She tried to lift her head and shoulders, groaned, and sagged back down. "I let you have a look at the idomeni ambassador's letter, and you fed me back a fake. I want the real letter back."

"I don't know what you're talking about."

"Bull." Roni struggled to a semi-sitting position and pressed a hand to the back of her head. "To add to my joy— I've spent most of the day in an emergency meeting—concerning some missing documents."

Jani braced against the building and worked to her feet. "Are you all right?"

"Don't change the subject." Roni looked dazed; her hair stuck straight up in places. "I waited for you by the bookstore for over three hours. When you didn't show, I hung around. I saw the Haárin tilemaster enter your building carrying a bag. I saw him leave without it. I know you have those documents. Where are you taking them? I'm not too thrilled with you right now, so I suggest you give a straight answer."

Jani freed her duffel from its hiding place and hoisted it to her shoulder. The blade, she slipped into her jacket pocket for easier access—she had never seen the glittery look in Roni's eyes before, and she didn't want any surprises. "Like I said before, I don't know what you're—"

"Jani." Roni produced the female vocal version of Declan Kilian when he had had enough. "You and Tsecha are being set up. Now do you want to get to the bottom of this, or don't you?" She handcombed her hair, to little effect. "Look, you show me what you have, and I won't flag down the first green-and-white I see and have you arrested for possessing stolen property. Favor for favor—what do you say?"

"I just want to find out what the hell is going on." Roni lurched in her seat as the people-mover pulled away from the curb. "The Exterior Exec Wing has shut me out for weeks. I can't raise Ulanova on the 'port. And forget Beddy-Boy Lescaux. He's much too important to deal with the likes of me."

Jani looked up from her examination of her duffel. Her self-appointed partner had suffered a good scuffing from her tumble in the alley—cheek scratched and reddened, chin coated with a smear of blood. She'd cracked the back of her head against the scancrete, as well—a tuft of blood-matted hair marked the site of a scalp injury. "I still think you should stop by Neoclona to get your head checked out."

"Will you stop changing the subject?"

"Are you seeing double?"

"I can see you as clear as day." Roni glared at her sidelong. "Why did you duplicate that letter?"

Jani looked out her window in time to see a ComPol skimmer pull alongside. "I wanted to flush out whoever wrote it."

"Well, you sure flushed something, didn't you?" Roni probed the back of her head, and winced. "You know what was the main comment I heard around the offices today? That it was a shame that the wrong person got shot."

"I didn't realize Lucien was that well liked."

"He isn't."

The ComPol skimmer dogged the people-mover for half a block before speeding up. Jani watched it flit ahead of the lumbering vehicle and accelerate, warning lights flashing. "Like you said, someone is trying to set up Nema. I wanted to take the heat off him—whether people thought he'd actually composed the precis or not, they'd still use it as they saw fit. I thought the faked Brandenburg Progression would work, at least for a week or so, until I could figure out who was going after him." The ComPol lights disappeared into the distance, and she relaxed. "I took the chance that you wouldn't scan it as soon as you got your hands on it again."

"I scan that damned thing daily. It's become a hobby." Roni yawned. She wore a burgundy band-collared shirt beneath her charcoal trouser suit—the vivid colors accentuated her wounds. "I mean, it was a great idea. Take a Commonwealth document and twist it just enough to make it look as though an idomeni tried to fake it. Folks get so excited about catching an idomeni forgery that they don't stop to think whether the information in the document is worth a damn." She glanced at Jani a little less angrily. "What tipped you off?"

"I don't believe Nema would bother to sneak that sort of information. He'd tell us outright, and blow the consequences." Jani twitched a shoulder. "You?"

"I think he'd have done a better job. Any idomeni would have—they sure as hell wouldn't have tripped up on the damned initiator chip." Roni lifted one of her feet so she could study her shoes. "You even scanned the soles. You really are paranoid, aren't you?"

The Registry tower loomed ahead. Jani gathered her duffel and stood carefully. She had sustained less obvious injuries than Roni—a battering to her sore knee and a bruised elbow—but they combined to make her every movement a pleasure. "We're getting off at this stop."

Roni caught the view out the window, and shot Jani another hard look.

Jani shouldered her duffel as defiantly as she could with an elbow that delivered sparks along the length of her arm every time she moved. "I'm completely within my rights as an investigator-at-large."

"Oh, I'm sure you have an explanation for everything." Roni stood, and dabbed at her chin. "How do I look?"

"Like you just got rolled in a darkened alley."

"Gosh, I wonder why."

"Do you have an appointment?"

Jani looked around the waiting area that served the private side of Registry, which was empty but for her, Roni, and the bright young face that asked the question. "No." She forced a smile, and gazed down at the receptionist with as much benevolence as she could muster, considering. "But as a member of Registry, I am entitled to use the labs whenever I wish."

"Oh, I'm not questioning that, Ms. Kilian!" The young woman offered more of the wide-eyed Registry homage that Jani had not yet gotten used to. "But you've been through so much with the shooting and all and our lab staff is on meal break now and I'm sure one of the supervisors would be happy—"

"Jani?"

Jani restrained the urge to lay her head down on the desk as the familiar drawl wafted through the air. Instead, she turned and did her best to look wide-awake. "Dolly."

"We've heard all kinds of awful things. Glad to see none of them are true." Dolly walked toward them from the direction of the lift bank. "That being said, what *are* you doin' here?"

Jani glanced at the wall clock. "I could ask you the same question."

"I'm on-call this week. Resident expert to all and sundry at any time of the day or night." Dolly looked a little rousted herself. She wore another flowing outfit, crystal blue silk that matched her eyes. Not what Jani would classify as stay-at-home clothes—somewhere in Chicago, an expensive dinner grew cold on its plate. "I saw your names come up on the entry board and realized you're just the people to help me with my own little dilemma." She held her hand out to Roni, her gaze flicking over her roughed-up visage and disheveled clothes. "Hello, Ms. McGaw. You're the Exterior Chief."

"Yes, ma'am," Roni bubbled. "It's a pleasure to meet you at last." She grinned in starstruck rapture, then winced as her damaged face complained.

"Well, Doll, you tell us your dilemma and we'll tell you ours." Jani laughed, a single short hack. "Dolly's Dilemma. Dolly's Dreadful Dilemma. Dolly's Dastardly Dreadful Dilemma."

If Dolly felt any trace of good humor, she kept it to herself. "I remember a few times in Rauta Shèràa when you pushed yourself until the exhaustion made you silly. That never boded well for anybody." She turned and headed for the lift. "Let's adjourn to my office, shall we?"

"I was in the middle of a lovely supper when I received a call from Registry Security. The bottom has apparently dropped out at Exterior. They're missing some paper." Dolly walked to her sideboard and took a decanter from the liquor service. "The most interesting thing they had to say was that you were involved." She turned to look at Jani. "You and a staffer at the idomeni embassy." She poured a generous serving of gin, then dropped in a slice of lime and a few cubes of ice. "Does this have anything to do with that other matter you came to see me about?"

"Madame Aryton, I am also involved in that *other* matter." Roni glared at Jani, but turned professionally serious by the time Dolly returned to her desk. "Independent of Ms. Kilian, I have been trying to determine whether the alleged idomeni letter has any relation to certain other Exterior documents. Unfortunately, my experience with idomeni documents protocols isn't as extensive as it should be."

Madame? Jani stared at the scratched side of Roni's face, but was pointedly ignored. Therefore, she concentrated on picking up the thread Roni held out to her and weaving her part of the tale. "Ms. McGaw is consulting with me concerning these protocols. I'm comparing them to a wide range of humanish documents as a means of instruction."

Dolly sipped her drink, then set it down on the desk. She crossed her hands in her lap, every centimeter the dignified Family Lady. But her mind worked in circles—her acceptance into the Academy had depended on that ability, as had her survival in Chicago. "In other words, these documents that Exterior Security believes were taken by the idomeni—"

"—are right here in my possession." Roni hoisted Jani's duffel and patted it proprietarily.

Roni's revelation would have stopped a less-nimble mind, but it didn't even cause Dolly to tap the decelerator. "But why didn't you sign them out, Ms. McGaw? Exterior Security has no record of you doing so."

"According to Exterior policy, I'm exempt from that requirement. I have to remind Security of this on a regular basis, since it's not a policy of which they approve." Roni grimaced as she lowered the duffel back to the floor—apparently, not all her injuries were cosmetic, after all. "The built-in assumption is that I am cleared to see any piece of paper in the place."

"But is Jani cleared as well?" Dolly shot Jani a skeptical look. "My understanding from Exterior Security was that she would have to make several jumps in esteem to qualify as *persona non grata*."

"Roni only shows me what I'm cleared to see." Jani watched Dolly's posture, the way she held her hands. *All directions at once.* She knew the barrage was coming, she just wished she knew Dolly's mind well enough to know where she'd strike first. "I have Yellow clearance at Treasury and Orange at Commerce, so I'm not completely off-the-street."

Dolly paused to take another sip of her drink. "Roni? May I call you Roni?" She swirled her glass and smiled as Roni nodded and sat up expectantly. "What happened to your face?"

Jani sat back as easily as she could and watched Roni's jaw and neck tense.

"I'm not the most graceful thing on two feet, Madame." Roni grinned sheepishly and brushed a smudge of dirt from her sleeve. "I missed a step leaving a restaurant this evening, the results of which you can see."

Dolly's clear eyes never left Roni's face. "Did you fall on top of Jani? She appears a little bedraggled herself."

Jani shrugged. "I always look bedraggled, Dolly."

"No, you do not. You're a single word in a Commonwealth of paragraphs and one thing you have never been, Jani Kilian, is sloppy." Dolly set her glass down so that the ice clinked and liquor splashed. "I'm only going to say this once. You're dexxies who suspect documents fraud, and you're acting accordingly. A ticklish situation all around, but based on my experiences with my old school tie"—she nodded toward Jani—"I'm inclined to stand back and let you proceed. But you must let me know what is goin' on because one thing I most assuredly do *not* like—apart from having to excuse myself from an anniversary dinner with my spouse—is being surprised."

Jani knocked her fist against her forehead. Her timing with regards to other peoples' evenings just kept getting better and better. "You and Cairn."

"Twenty-six years today. We count from the day in prep school when she gave me her late great-grandmother's wedding ring and told me I was the one." Dolly offered the barest hint of a smile before the veil fell. "But enough about me and mine. I want to hear about you and yours, and I want to hear it fast, and I want to hear it now."

Jani looked at Roni. She eventually looked back. They communicated in the same way they worked, via mindreading supplemented by the occasional eyebrow twitch.

Jani opened the negotiations. "Can we talk while we work? Time may be getting short."

CHAPTER 24

They adjourned to another laboratory in a different part of the building. This time, Dolly assembled the equipment herself, eliminating the need for documents technicians with prying eyes.

The three of them worked to activate and calibrate the readers and interpreters, hands flicking over touchpads, speech reduced to the occasional short question or comment. Soon, all the start-up beeps and clicks silenced and indicator lights showed green.

Roni hauled Jani's duffel up on a desk in the middle of the room and cracked the closures, only to have Dolly encircle her wrist in a racing-hardened grip. "I'm waiting for that explanation."

Jani dug into one of the duffel's side pockets and snatched another meal bar. "A colonial business consortium called *L'araignée* may be the driving force behind this idomeni forgery. They may have also helped Service Intelligence compile information about my past for a white paper that's been coursing up and down Cabinet Row for the past few weeks." She pulled the wrapper from the bar and bit grudgingly. She'd grown sick of chocolate and caramel, but the sensation of a hollow pit where her stomach used to be convinced her that what she wanted had very little to do with what her body needed.

"I heard about that." Dolly released Roni's wrist with a small smile and left her to examine it, which Roni did with a pained frown. "Well, more than that, actually. I read it. So did Carson." She leaned against a counter and folded her arms. "After the news of the shooting made the rounds, he called to tell me that he'd double the salary-benefits package if you came to work for him. But then, Carson always did have a wild side." She looked at Jani. "You feel that the white paper and this idomeni letter are connected."

Jani bit, chewed, nodded. "I think some commercial factions are combining in an effort to destabilize human-idomeni relations in order to force the Haárin to end their business dealings with the colonies. The financial losses that humanish businesses are sustaining because of the Haárin influx are starting to mount. *L'araignée* is the name adopted by a Channel World business consortium that formed to fight the influx. It contains, unfortunately, both legitimate and criminal members, and the legit factions don't yet realize that they've made a deal with the devil. By the time they do, several colonial governments will be bankrupted and their business structures irreversibly damaged."

Roni had wandered from desk to counter. "*L'araignée*? Sounds like some of the outfits I had to deal with during my colonial stint." She examined her face in a cabinet's reflective surface, then stepped to the sink. "They'd be more than happy to help panicky Earthbound bureaucrats force out Haárin merchants, while they skim the cream off every transport payload that leaves a colonial dock." She ran the water and tried to scrub the dried blood off her chin. "That way, they can destabilize the Commonwealth system and make money off of it at the same time, which to them is the best of both worlds." She mouthed an "ouch" as her overzealous washing reopened the wound, and held a lab wipe over it to staunch the blood flow.

Dolly walked across the lab and plucked her glass from atop a reader case. She had exhausted the gin, and contented herself with crunching ice. "This all seems to boil down to money, and that conflicts with what I know of the idomeni. I lived in Rauta Shèràa for seven years. I schooled with them. Worked alongside them. Human business models do not apply. Their status has nothing to do with what they possess, but with what they are."

"You know born-sect, Dolly. The Haárin are different. They've developed a regard for the respect and freedom that doing sound business can earn them." Jani finished her meal bar and immediately sought another. "In the vast rambling construct of humanish commercialism, they have found a haven. A place where they can live and ply their trades without the interference from born-sect dominants. A place where the threats of born-sect unrest no longer touch them. They don't want to uproot their lives because two propitiators can't decide which spice should be used to flavor meats in the morning and which at night. They don't care about that anymore. Some of them are so far removed from their native culture that they've adopted humanish mannerisms and habits." Visions of Dathim Naré danced in her head. "I met an Haárin recently who wouldn't return to the worldskein if Cèel shoved a long shooter up his backside and threatened to press the charge-through." She comprehended the silence, and looked up to see both Dolly and Roni regarding her with their hands over their mouths.

Dolly spoke first. "Jani. What an image."

Jani pulled the black-covered file out of her duffel and walked to the reader. "You know what I mean."

"Yes." Dolly's eyes widened when she saw what Jani held. "Now that we've gotten the xenopolitical discussion out of the way, perhaps you could tell me what point of human documents protocol you needed to illustrate using a 'Ministers' Eyes Only' file?"

"I'll take that." Roni rushed to Jani's side. A subdued tug-of-war ensued until Dolly's intervention-with-arched-eyebrows gave the advantage to Roni, who plucked the top sheet from the file with an air of triumph and inserted the page in the reader slot.

Dolly cracked a cube between her teeth as she inserted herself between Jani and the reader, blocking Jani's view of the display. She removed the sheet from the reader slot and read it. "Roni, is this really germane to the discussion?"

Roni looked over her shoulder. Her eyes goggled. She took the paper from Dolly and tucked it back in the file.

Jani walked to the sink to wash her hands, and tried to catch a glimpse of the file along the way. "What is it?"

"Details of a Minister's personal life, which will no doubt be used to sway a vote or two in some future Council session."

Dolly's voice had taken on a roughened velvet quality that, like Jamira Shah's questioning lilt, Jani remembered all too well. "Just how did you go about choosing these files, Roni?"

"We were in a hurry, Dolly. Roni became confused." Jani returned to the desk and pulled all the files out of the duffel. "OK, we're looking for Channel World references. Guernsey. Man. Jersey. Acadia. We're looking for my name. Service C-numbers. Haárin or idomeni references. For damned near anything we can find."

Dolly walked up to the desk and braced her hands on the edge. "Jani, what did I tell you in my office? Do you remember that far back?"

Jani held a sheaf of files out to her. "And what did I ask you two days ago? Do you remember that far back?"

"Jani—"

"Do I need to repeat it?"

"Wait a damned minute—"

"Do you think I'm wasting your time? If you say yes, we'll turn these documents over to you right now. You can return them to Exterior, and tell them they magically appeared on the Registry front step. Tell them anything you like." Jani pushed the files into Dolly's hands. "But here's something to keep in mind as you cover your Registry backside. Someone tried to kill me. They tried to kidnap my parents. They're trying to destroy Nema. I'm trying to find out who they are. At this particular moment, I don't have much patience with proper form or peoples' feelings. At this particular moment, you're either with me or against me, and either way, I'll remember till the day I die."

"Ja—?" Dolly looked from Jani, to the files in her hand, then back to Jani. Started to speak. Stopped. Then she turned and walked to an open stretch of counter top, spread out the files, opened one, and began to read.

"And my assignment is?" Roni stepped up to the desk and held out her hand.

Whether the strong emotion that flushed Roni's face and tightened her voice was anger or embarrassment, Jani didn't know or care. She handed Roni her share of the paper, then watched her pull a lab chair up to a bench, sit down, and open a file. Only then did she sit down herself and open the topmost of those that remained.

"I think I found something."

Jani looked up to find Roni hurrying across the lab toward the reader, and rose to join her. "What is it?"

"Meeting notes. Stuck off by themselves in a file. Guernsey watermark. They're encoded, but the reader should be able to decrypt." She pounded a beat on the reader to shake it out of standby. "Why do people take notes? Don't they know that once they write it down, they're mine for life?" Roni inserted the sheet of parchment in the reader, then stood back, rocking from one foot to the other as the paper disappeared into the slot. "On the other hand, this could be another false alarm."

Jani flexed her stiff back, her eyes on the instrument display. "Let's see what it says before we write it off."

"Write what off?" Dolly entered the lab juggling three dispos of vend alcove coffee.

"Roni's found meeting notes." Jani took one of the cups from Dolly and sniffed the steam. It held a sharp, burning odor, which meant the brew was old, which in turn meant that it would taste like fuel to her hybrid tastebuds. She didn't want to ask Dolly if the Hands of Might could lay hold of some pepper to kill the taste, however—judging from the look on Dolly's face, those Hands wouldn't be averse to boxing an Ear. Instead, Jani drank, swallowed, and kept her grimace to herself.

Roni took her own cup with the look of a drowning woman who had just been thrown a float. "The whole damned thing's encrypted," she said between sips. "Why would someone encrypt meeting notes? If the topic was so touchy, why write it down in the first place?"

"Sounds as through someone wanted to cover themselves." Dolly tossed a couple of tablets in her mouth, then washed them down. "But that doesn't mean the matter has anything to do with what we're investigating here. Nothing in this melange has even come close to whatever it is Jani's looking for—we've found everything from personnel profiles to construction plans for colonial buildings." She pressed her fingers to the bridge of her nose. "This will turn out to be someone's shopping list."

Behind them, the reader beeped. The original document emerged from the slot, followed a few seconds later by a decrypted fiche.

Roni grabbed them both, then handed off the original to Jani as she plundered the copy. "It's a note to Anais Ulanova," she muttered after a few seconds. "Bet that's why they wrote it down. Probably kept copies in lockboxes, too. What the hell does this mean? 'Met with Le Blond—' "

"Let me see it." Jani plucked the fiche from her hands and read it. "Met with Le Blond today. He will be at Exterior Main in three weeks. He says there are no problems. Service is set." She glanced up. "I don't know whether that's service as in served or *the* Service." She continued to read. "Contracts are set. Are—?" She cleared her throat. "Are you sure we must use him? He kills with his eyes. He is so cold—I do not trust him."

"Jani?" Dolly leaned toward her, headache-narrowed eyes lit with question. "What's wrong? You look like you've seen a ghost."

"No. I've seen those before." Jani beckoned to Roni. "Can you recall whether Anais would have been at Exterior Main in time to meet with Le Blond?"

Roni glanced at the date. "I'd have to check her calendar history."

Dolly gestured toward the lab comport. "You can do that from here."

Roni shook her head. "Not tonight, Madame. Exterior Security disconnected the Annex from CabNet when they filed the missing doc report. We're in lockdown until further notice—I'd have to go back to my office to check this."

"I don't know how the hell you talked us out of there." Roni fell into the people-mover seat, then leaned forward and rested her forehead against the seat in front of her. "Dolly wanted to kill you. She wanted to string you up by your heels over boiling oil. She wanted—"

"She wants to find out what's going on more." Jani

watched the dead-of-night city drift past the 'mover window. "If Dathim could recall in which pile he found those notes, I'd send him back to steal the whole stack. It would all be there. The meetings. The payoffs. The plans. Everything pertaining to *L'araignée*'s birth. I bet the trail would lead right to whoever composed The Nema Letter and spearheaded the white paper."

"Let's not give Dathim Naré any more espionage practice, OK?" Roni sat back slowly. "Like I said back there, I'd dealt with outfits like them before. If you'd leveled with me from the beginning, *I* could have searched Anais's desk and uncovered the whole damned story."

"No." Jani shook her head, stopping when the rocking seemed to intensify. "*L'araignée*'s been leaving a trail of bodies. Ignorance is survival."

"Is it?" Roni rocked her head from shoulder to shoulder until the bones in her neck cracked. "That little bit Dathim stumbled upon is all we're going to get, unfortunately. My guess is that everything on Anais's desk has been locked up by Security, to be released into her hands only." She poked the plastic sack in her lap, into which Jani had transferred all the Exterior files except for The Nema Letter. Dolly had insisted on holding on to that "for safety's sake." Whether she meant the document's safety or their collective security, she didn't make clear. Considering her tense mood, Roni and Jani thought it wiser not to push for clarification.

"You're going to have a hell of a time burying those." Jani unbent her knee as far as she could without hitting the seat in front of her. The sharp pain had damped to a dull ache, but every step between the 'mover stop and her flat still promised agony. "What will you tell Lescaux?"

"I don't know. I'll think of something." Roni yawned and sagged further into her seat. " 'Le Blond.' You paled when you read that fiche." Her breathing slowed, as though she neared sleep. "You think it's Lucien, don't you?"

Jani yawned in response, wide enough for her jaw to crack. "I don't know."

"Don't give me that, all right—I've had a bad night." Roni scowled and touched her sore cheek. "I've been roughed up in an alley, I've made the Registry Inspector General's 'watch this one' list, and I've probably done myself out of a job." She pressed her hand to her face, bleary eyes locked in the middle distance. "When Lucien still worked at Exterior, I used to study him. Much as I hated him, I had to admire the way he just cut through the place. Peter looks like him—the hair, the eyes, but he really can't hold a candle. Lucien maneuvered people like pieces on a gameboard. Even Anais, although she didn't realize it until it was too late." She looked at Jani. "He threw her over for you. Did you ever wonder why?"

"Access to the idomeni, like I told you in your office." Jani thought back to Lucien's rapt studying of Dathim. "He finds them fascinating."

"Well, folks say you're part idomeni. Perhaps he thinks you're fascinating, too." Roni yawned again. "So, speaking of close but not quite, who was this person I remind you of?"

Jani turned her attention to the darkened buildings. "Yolan Cray. She was a corporal with the Twelfth Rover Corps. She died during the first bombing raid at Knevçet Shèràa."

"She was your friend?"

"Inasmuch as we could be, considering she was enlisted and I was an officer in the same outfit. We reported to an asshole—that promoted the sense of solidarity."

"Yeah, that'll do it." Roni nodded in the loose-necked way of the terminally punchy, then looked at Jani with bloodshot eyes. "You blame yourself for her death."

Jani started. "No, I don't—"

"Yes, you do. You think you're responsible for everybody. Nema, Tsecha, whatever you call him. Everybody, and everything." She fell silent. Her chin sagged to her chest. Jani had to nudge her awake when they arrived at their stop.

Roni hailed a 'taxi to take her to Exterior; Jani didn't hire one to take her to her building, out of habit. By the time she arrived, she had slipped into the auto-drive of the truly exhausted, barely lifting her feet above the ground, taking care not to stop for fear of never getting started again.

She entered her flat to find it darkened and quiet. As she passed her desk, she spotted a note attached to the back of her workstation so that she could see it on the way in.

Angevin's handwriting. *You have some explaining to do.*

Jani crumpled the note and tossed it in the trashzap. Trudged into her bedroom, tossed her duffel bedside, and fell onto her stomach into bed, fully clothed.

She had just drifted off when the sound of footfalls jarred her awake. The heavy breathing unique to a body in discomfort. The sag of the mattress as Lucien got into bed beside her.

Silence. Then the voice that touched her where none ever had. "I've been waiting for you. Steve and Angevin gave up hours ago, but I waited. I was on the couch—I heard you come in. You walked right past me." Silence again, as though he waited for her to speak. "Thinking about Dathim Naré helped keep me awake. I've never seen an Haárin like him before."

Jani recalled his rapt look as he drank in Dathim's every move. "I noticed."

"Jealous?" A short expulsion of breath, as though he laughed. "Why do you think he cut his hair? Do you think the braids got in his way, or what?"

"I don't know. Why don't you ask him?"

"Maybe I will." Silence again, flavored with peevishness. Then Lucien cleared his throat. "Angevin said you went to Sheridan this morning. Make that yesterday morning."

Morning. It seemed like a year ago. "Yes. I needed to talk to Frances." Jani edged her hand in her pocket and felt for the antistat containing the broken marker.

"If I'd known, I'd have asked you to stop by my room and pick up a few things." The mattress flexed as Lucien shifted position. "I keyed it to you. Months ago. You were still on-base at the time. I waited for you to visit, but you never did."

Jani closed her fingers around the hard, sharp plastic of the broken marker half, and massaged the rough edge.

"Your parents are here. I found that out tonight, when I called I-Com to try and track you down." Another sigh. "Everything I know about you, I have to find out from other people."

Jani turned her head. "There wasn't time to tell you."

The dark form beside her reached out and touched her

hair. "If you gave a damn about me, you'd make time." The hand moved lower, caressing her cheek. "But you don't, do you?" Lower, moving down her neck. "Where did you take the docs?"

Jani shifted her arm to block Lucien's hand so he couldn't work it lower. She wanted him to, in spite of everything, which was why she made sure to stop him. "I'm tired. We'll talk later."

Lucien pulled his hand away. "There's later, and then there's too late. Did you ever think of that?"

Jani didn't answer. She forced herself to remain awake until she heard Lucien's breathing slow and deepen in sleep. Then she struggled out of bed, her back aching, her knee popping with every step.

Her footsteps barely sounded as she walked across the sitting room, muffled as they were by Angevin's rented rugs. She opened the door to the entryway closet and hunted through the bags and boxes that had been delivered from the stores. She barely glanced at her beautiful sari, digging until she uncovered her Ganesha with its pedestal.

She set up the shrine in the corner of the room nearest her desk. After she set the figurine on its base and placed the brass bowl before it, she knelt, leaning forward and touching her forehead to the floor three times in rapid succession. *Help me, Lord,* she prayed to the embodiment of wisdom before her, to the remover of obstacles. *Help me find the answers I seek, even if they pain me.* She leaned forward again, this time keeping her forehead pressed to the floor.

I told Niall that there's no such thing as coincidence, that it's hardest to see that which is closest to you. Have I failed to heed my own warnings, Lord? Her knee throbbed from the press of her weight. *I have never obeyed my body instead of my brain—is this what I'm doing now?*

She remained on her knees on the hardwood floor and offered her pain as sacrifice, imagining it as gold coins that she tossed into the bowl. Only when her eyes teared and she bit her lip to suppress a cry did she struggle to her feet, store the empty boxes in the closet, and return to bed.

CHAPTER 25

Tsecha sat on the veranda of Dathim Naré's house and watched the lights of a Vynshàrau patrol skimmer flicker off the water. The activity had lessened considerably compared to earlier in the night. Then, the lake skimmers had traversed in pairs and triples, while demis swooped and glided above as seabirds chivying watercraft.

What do you look for, Shai? Tsecha watched the skimmer until it turned along the invisible border dividing idomeni waters from those of the Interior Ministry, then flitted toward the dim horizon. *What is out on the lake that you find so interesting? Do you search for documents, too?* He bared his teeth at the thought, but his humor quickly dissipated. He wished he had brought the timeform from his work table—the mental exercise of converting idomeni time to humanish would have occupied him, prevented his thoughts from wandering as the skimmers did over the water.

Where are you, ní Dathim? He focused his hearing in the still dark, straining for the distant wail of ComPol sirens. He had heard them now and again since the start of his vigil, their cry like the keen of the Rauta Shèràa alarms that had declaimed the arrival of the Laumrau bombs.

Ní Dathim?

Tsecha shifted in his strangely comfortable Haárin chair. Nowhere did the framing stab him. Not once did the angle of the seat threaten to tumble him onto the stones. He looked at the other dwellings—the enclave seemed as deserted in the darkness. No lights showed through windows. No Haárin sat outside and contemplated the water, or walked

277

the stone-paved lane. So different than the born-sect who lived in the embassy, who discussed points of philosophy upon the veranda throughout the night, or sat in the archives and studied . . .

. . . or waited in the Haárin sequestration for their sub-orn to return. Tsecha fussed with the cuffs of his overrobe, tugging them low over the sleeves of the coldsuit that he wore beneath. Blessedly warm though he felt, he shivered as a breeze wafted off the lake, bringing with it the promise of the hellish winter to come, and the chill of more immediate concerns.

Ní Dathim . . . where are you?

He heard the distant crunch of footsteps upon the lane, and felt the clench in his soul. *I will not call out.* What if it was a guard, who had followed him from the embassy? Or Sànalàn, who seemed to beg his forgiveness each time she saw him, even as she challenged his every thought and action. Or Shai, come in person to demand an explanation for his visits to the sequestration.

This is my place, Shai—am I not Haárin, as declared by Temple and Council? Is not my name of Sìah Haárin? Tsecha. "Fool." Have I not been as outcast since the war? Even more so since you removed me from my station and ordered me to remain on the grounds of this waterbound place?

The footfalls grew nearer. Stopped before the door of the house. Then, slowly, turned and circled toward the veranda.

Tsecha rose to his feet as the footsteps rounded the corner, heart tripping as the figure darkened the veranda entry, then slowing as he recognized the strange, sheared head. "Ní Dathim. You could announce yourself."

"That would sound foolish, nìRau. Why would I announce myself to an empty house?" Dathim picked up a weighty metalframe seat and placed it beside Tsecha's. He sat heavily, in the humanish sprawl that he preferred, and rubbed a hand over his face. His chair matched Tsecha's in the height of its seat, so that he sat at the same level instead of a higher, more respectful one.

But such are Haárin—all the same within themselves. Such chairs as these had not been designed with the idea that Chief Propitiators would sit in them. "So, ní Dathim?"

Tsecha sat down as well, then leaned forward so he could see the Haárin's eyes. For such purposes, sitting at the same level proved an advantage. "Where were you so long? Did you have trouble in the city?"

"No, nìRau, I had no trouble. I have been back for some time. I sat in the skimmer and thought . . . about many things." Dathim stared at the ground at his feet. "Humanish are strange."

"I know you think that, ní Dathim. You have said it before." Tsecha waited for Dathim to say more, but the Haárin's face held the grim cast of one not inclined to speak. He thought to wave his hand in front of him, as he had once seen Lucien do to Jani when he had asked her a question and she did not answer. But before he could make his attempt, Dathim raised his head and looked at him.

"So. I saw her. Your Kilian."

"My Jani! She is unhurt?"

"She limps. She said that she fell during the shooting, and hurt her knee. It is not serious." Dathim looked out over the water. "The lieutenant is with her. Pascal."

"And he is well?"

"He was shot here. A grave wound, he told me, and truly." Dathim placed a hand beneath his soul, near his right hip. "He walks. Slowly, but he walks. He is pale, and tired. But still he watches, as he did here. Nothing escapes him." Dathim shifted in his seat. "He watched me, every move I made."

"My Lucien watches, Dathim, as you said. Such is his way."

"Kilian said it was because he had never before seen an Haárin with short hair." Dathim sat forward and let his hands dangle between his knees. "You would say Pascal is her suborn?"

Tsecha gestured in strong affirmation. "Yes, ní Dathim, I would, and truly. In the way that humanish can be true dominant and suborn, they are. My Lucien provides my Jani protection. She provides him status. It is a most reasonable arrangement, as far as I can see."

"Then she must know him well, and I must defer to that knowledge." Dathim turned his attention to his hands, and picked at his nails. "I gave the documents to her."

"Did she seem as angry?"

"I could not tell, nìRau. She is most as a wall. Even now."

"Now, ní Dathim?"

"Now that she is as Haárin." Dathim turned his head—the incident light reflected off his broad, bare brow. "She is as Haárin, nìRau, and truly. She does not move as humanish. Her gestures are too smooth. Her hands and wrists—too long and thin. She walks as idomeni, as well. Even though she limps, her stride is long and smooth." He looked back at his hands. "I saw one of her true eyes."

Tsecha felt the shocks of the past days redoubled. "How did you do such?"

Dathim gestured in the humanish manner, as though such startling details held little import. "It is not yet as mine. The center is still too small, the sclera too pale." He gestured in disappointment. "And they are *green*, like Oà. Why did her doctors make them green, instead of gold as Vynshàrau?"

"That was their color before, Dathim." Tsecha tried to imagine Jani's eyes, tried to extrapolate the hints and shadings he had seen revealed in the bright sunlight days earlier. "John Shroud had tried to leave her a little of what she was before. He thought it important."

"Hmph." Dathim did not sound impressed by that which John Shroud thought important. He turned back to the water, his great head stilling like an animal's on alert as the patrol skimmer made another traverse. "She denies she is your heir."

Tsecha gestured reluctant acceptance. "Humanish deny, ní Dathim, until that which they deny buries them. Such is their way, and truly."

"She does not want to be as Haárin. She is ashamed." Dathim's tense posture eased as the patrol skimmer darted away from them. "Her eyefilm broke. When it broke, she sought to hide her eye with her hand. When I forced her to show it to me, she grew so angry. She would have struck me, nìRau, but she restrained herself. Even though she is smaller than me, she would have injured me, and truly."

Tsecha slipped into Low Vynshàrau to convey the bluntness of his feeling. "My nìa does not like to be coerced, ní Dathim."

Dathim sat back with such force that his chair legs scraped along the stone. "And as we shelter your *nìa* who does not like to be coerced, who speaks to the Elyan Haárin and their broken contracts?" He spoke in English, blunter and more forceful still, a barrage of hard and sharp sounds that hammered the ears as bombs. "Who promotes the final order you so desire, nìRau? The harmony of Shiou that follows the upheaval of Caith? Is it nìaRauta Shai, who speaks for the Oligarch without thought as to what the words mean? Who wishes us back to the worldskein, to serve only our dominants as we did before the war? Is it the humanish ministers, who think only of the money they lose if they allow Haárin to live among them? Who speaks? You cannot—you have been silenced. I cannot—I am as nothing. But your nìaRauta Haárin knows Haárin and humanish, life as it is and as it must become. But where is she now, as the Haárin converge upon this cold city and Shai prepares to hammer them with Cèel's words? In her rooms, asleep, with her strange lieutenant who watches and the humanish tricks that cover that which she is!" Dathim fell silent, his breathing labored as though he ran a great distance.

As Dathim's words echoed in his mind, Tsecha again felt the wind brush in from off the water. This breeze, however, he did not find as chilling, but as a warm gust that riffled the flowing sleeves of his overrobe, pushing them up his arms.

He brushed down the soft material, then fingered the red banding that edged the sleeves. So long had he served as ambassador, as teacher, as irritant to his enemies, that he at times forgot his place as priest. But he still understood signs, the hints of order and disorder by which the gods informed him of their will. Thus did he know that he felt Caith in the strange warm wind, as he had felt her many times over the past days. Her ever-present whispers, in the hallways of the embassy, in the wind itself, unveiled his old disorder and reminded him of that which he once had been. Warrior. Killer. Walker in the Night. "My Jani. You would have her here to meet the Haárin, ní Dathim?"

Dathim gave a humanish nod. "If she came here, the bornsects would not dare to keep her out. Shai would admit to your power if she did so, a power she claims you no longer possess."

"The humanish Ministers would fight her presence. Anais Ulanova would lead them."

"The humanish Ministers, I have learned, have to answer to their *reporters,* who batter them as ax-hammers and carry news of their actions to all. These reporters would ask them why they do not permit your Jani to see the Elyan Haárin, and how would Anais answer? Would she speak the truth, that the Haárin are better at humanish business than humanish, and she must therefore work to keep them away from her poor merchants because they cannot compete? Away from the many other humanish who would buy from Haárin if they could?"

"No, ní Dathim—my Anais is more intelligent than that." Tsecha stood just as another gust of rebellious wind whipped at his sleeves. He walked to the veranda entry, clasping his hands behind his back as he did so to keep his cuffs fixed in place, and hidden from Caith's laughter. "She would say mý nìa is unfit because of the crimes she has committed. She will talk of Knevçet Shèràa, and the death of Rikart Neumann. She will make my nìa appear most unseemly, and truly."

Dathim rose and stepped to Tsecha's side. He made no attempt to edge even a small step to the front of his propitiator, as would have been seemly. "Then let your Jani answer. She has met challenge before, nìRau—she wears the scars. She knows how to fight, and will continue to fight even as she bleeds." He held out his own arms and rolled back the sleeves, first one, then the other. Even in the darkness his scars showed, the ragged fissuring dark as ebon ink. "If I brought her here, she would see how it is for us, and she would fight for us. You say she fights for her own, nìRau. Who are more her own than we?"

Tsecha stepped off of the veranda and onto the lane. Past the dark, silent houses, then over the short stretch of dune toward the beach. He struggled to maintain his footing as his boot soles slid on the loose sand.

"You forced her yourself, nìRau." Dathim's voice sounded from behind, like the call of a tracking beast. "In the summer, you forced her to accept her first challenge, to fight nìaRauta Hantìa in her first *à lérine*. You did not think it such a bad thing then, when you used her *against* Cèel. But now I say we should use her *for* Haárin, and you hesitate. Why, nìRau? Is the chance to anger Cèel not great enough? Is the shock to the humanish when they see your Jani as she really is not great enough? Or are the Haárin not important enough?"

Tsecha wheeled, the sand dragging at his feet like undercurrent. "I warn you, Dathim! You vex—!" His words stopped as he watched Dathim mount the dune and stand astride it as a humanish statue—

—and as another Haárin mounted the dune and took her place beside him—

—and as the other Haárin scaled the short summit and took their places on either side, until the entire ridge filled. Shoulder to shoulder they stood, thirty or more, in their trousers and shirts and boots. Their overrobes, they had left behind. Their looping braids and nape knots, the males had sheared as Dathim had, while the females had undone theirs, or bound them in long tails in the manner of humanish females.

"Are we not important enough, nìRau!" Dathim stood with his arms hanging low, his hands curled in front of him, palms facing up. Not a gesture of idomeni, but of humanish question. "We who go out into this damned cold city so you can be as you are!"

Tsecha took a step back. Another. The Haárin made no move toward him, yet still he felt them push him back. "The battles will be fought in the embassy, ní Dathim! Against those who refuse to accept the truth as I know it will be!" Behind him, he heard the rumble of the lake, the dash of the low waves. The Haárin beach was not smooth sand as was the embassy's, but rock-strewn and rutted. He felt the water-slick rocks beneath his boots, and battled for balance on the uneven ground.

"Your truth, born-sect! The truth as you see it!" Dathim advanced a single stride down the dune, arms held out to his sides for balance. "But we have our truth, as well. Our truth is that we want to live here, in this damned cold place. As the Elyan Haárin do on Elyas. As the NorthPort Haárin do on Whalen's Planet. And the Phillipan, and the

Serran. This is our colony, *here*! We will choose an enclave, *here*!"

"The humanish will not let you. Not *here*!" Tsecha tried
to take an advancing step, but the strange warm wind
swirled from his back to his front, stopping him in his
tracks. He felt it rush up his sleeves, and damned Caith for
her disorder. "They are not as us. They cannot leave alone.
They will not allow you to live as you wish—you scare
them!"

"Then they will scare. And your Jani will show them how
not to fear."

"But they will fear her most of all!" Tsecha raised his
arms above his head—a pleading stance. "It must be done
my way, Dathim. First the embassy, and the meeting rooms.
First, the Ministers, and the generals. *Then* the city. The city
cannot come before. Humanish will not understand!"

Dathim had grown still upon the slope. He maintained his
balance without laboring, as though he had always stood in
such a way and could do so forever. The Haárin on either
side of him remained in their places, silent, watching as he
spoke their words, said that which they wished to be said.

"We are here," Dathim said from his slope. "We will stay.
I have asked your Jani to help us in this, and I will ask again.
It is your decision, nìRau, if you join us or not. You of the
Haárin name and the priestly life. Your decision." He backed
up the incline and disappeared over the other side. The other
Haárin followed him, in ones and twos, until the ridge
showed clear.

Tsecha listened to the rustle of the grasses, the rumble of
the lake. He pulled down one skewed sleeve, then let his
hand drop away, and heard Caith's laughter in the wind.

CHAPTER 26

Tsecha walked back to the embassy the same way he had come. Through the trees, across the lawns, toward the veranda.

He entered the sheltered haven with the timorous step of someone who now felt unsure whether he belonged, and looked around. Since her challenge, Sànalàn had taken to spending great stretches of the day and night in meditation, or in conversation with nìaRauta Inèa. Her accidental meetings with him had been frequent; Tsecha did not esteem these encounters, but now he anticipated them even less. With Caith's presence infused in the very air, who knew what disorder could ensue?

But the air felt cooler on the veranda than it had outside. He hoped it meant that Caith had been warned off, that Shiou and the other six gods had forced her back to her domain, a distant land of storm and upheaval. *Much as this place.* Tsecha turned, and looked out the entry toward the lake. *Storm and upheaval and shifting rocks beneath my feet.*

Tsecha looked around the veranda's main enclosure, and found it emptier than usual. He chose to take that as a favorable sign as well, and tucked into a darkened corner furnished with a pillow-seat and a low reading table. From there, he could observe the rest of the area as well as the entry from the embassy. If Shai or Sànalàn appeared, he could contract into his space like a cava into its shell and remain unobserved.

He lowered carefully. His hip no longer complained, but he must have twisted his right knee during his flight down the beach away from Dathim. The joint ached when he walked, and burned when he bent it. He took some time finding a comfortable position, and finally sat with his leg straightened before him. The mind-focusing ability of pain held no power for him now. He felt old and tired and discomfited, out of place in this most odd city that he had come to think of as his own.

You would live in Chicago, Dathim? Somewhere out in the storm and upheaval, amid the sirens and the shootings and Caith's strange winds. *The humanish are different here—this is their homeworld.* Tsecha rested his head against the stone wall that enclosed him, damning himself for his caution but unable to quell his apprehension. He who had gone out into the city so many times, in disguise and as himself, felt the raw stab of fear at the thought of Dathim Naré doing the same.

Dathim does not hide. The tilemaster displayed his work freely, and went about his business as though he lived in a worldskein colony. *He showed his cava shell tilework to Anais Ulanova, then walked into her office and stole documents.* Then he took them into the city as though such was something he did each day. Granted, his visit to Jani's home had upset him, but his was not the discomfort of an idomeni exposed to the ungodliness of a humanish house. He did not ask for absolution, or worry after his soul. *He wanted to convince her, persuade her.* Or, most likely, *order* her to assist him in his plans for the enclave. *And my Jani does not take orders.* Both idomeni and humanish had been forced to that conclusion long ago.

Tsecha felt his eyes grow heavy. It had become most late, and now that Dathim had returned safely from the city, he felt tired. He lay back in a half-recline, his head abutting cold stone, his sore leg braced against the hard edge of the table, suffering just enough discomfort to keep awake. *Dathim's chairs felt most comfortable.* Short hair, easeful furniture, no fear of humanish rooms—how readily Dathim Naré had adjusted to change. *More quickly even than I.* Tsecha felt a twinge in his soul, as though the pain in his knee had altered in location. *More quickly . . .*

He longed for the seclusion of his rooms, the quiet, the

warmth that emerged from the output of a facilities array, not the laughing breath of a mocking goddess.

I am Haárin.

But who considered him such? Cèel and Shai, most certainly. They felt him most disordered, a traitor to his skein and sect. The only thing that saved him from the full vent of their wrath was the security of his station. He was their Chief Propitiator. In secular matters, he owed them obedience. In religious matters, which held greater import for any born-sect, they owed him their souls.

I am Haárin . . . by name.

He had earned the name Égri nìRau Tsecha, and truly. Over twenty-five humanish years ago, he had fought in Council and in Temple to allow humanish to form an enclave outside Rauta Shèràa. Then, he fought even more to allow them to study at the Academy. He had engaged and attacked both with words and with blades. There had been days when his enemies stood in line to declare themselves, when he fought *à lérine* with a weapon still bloody from the previous bout, when he could barely raise his arms for the number and pain of his wounds.

The hum of conversation snapped Tsecha out of his grim remembrance. He tensed as he waited for the speakers to walk into view, relaxing when he saw them to be Communications dominants whom he did not know well. He watched them disappear into another of the enclosures, gesturing in animated discussion. Then he tugged in irritation at the tight sleeves of the coldsuit. He felt hot here in the enclosure. Constricted. He had donned the suit in anticipation of the chill of the Haárin enclave—he did not need such protection in the shelter of the embassy.

Shelter . . .

Dathim believes me sheltered. Unaware of the desires of Haárin. *But I know them now.* As his Jani must, as well. Such would explain her stubborn denials of her hybridization, and her anger as she did so. She did not like to be tricked, and Dathim Naré the Tilemaster had tricked them all. He had not journeyed into the godless humanish city to deliver stolen papers into the safety of one who could dispose of them. He had done so to confront his leader, to tell her the time had come for her to lead them to their place in this damned cold city.

But she had denied him.

And now he met with his enclave, in a crowded room in one of the tiny houses beyond the trees, to discuss what to do next.

Tsecha imagined the Suborn Oligarch standing before him now, glaring down at him from her imposing height, shoulders rounded and hands twitching in displeasure. He imagined telling her words that she had no desire to hear.

The embassy Haárin no longer wish to serve us, Shai. Their wish now is to serve themselves. The machinations of the meeting room meant nothing to them anymore, now that they knew the freedom of the humanish colonial enclave. The complexities and formalities of born-sect challenge, upon which their futures once depended, now angered rather than distressed them. *They no longer care what we do, Shai. We bother them. We interfere with them.* Even he, who chose the name Égri nìRau Tsecha to symbolize his expulsion from Vynshàrau, mean nothing to Dathim and the others who populated the embassy sequestration. *They needed me to bring them Jani, and I could not do so. To them, I am worthless, Haárin by name and name only.*

"*Name only.*" Tsecha spoke aloud in French, so that any who overheard him would not understand. "*I, who shed the blood of my enemies on the Temple floor.*" He tried to move his right leg to a more easeful position, but his knee griped and the top of his head ached from pressing against the stone. *I, Avrèl nìRau Nema, have become as nothing.* Passed over by those he had once led. Cast aside by those who had once served him. Denied participation in reaching the goal toward which he had strove for half his life.

Do you think to deny me, Dathim? Is this what you wish, and truly?

He stared out at the empty veranda, filled only by the occasional murmur of voices or passing footfall.

As my Hansen used to say, "Think again."

He rose slowly. He walked until the needling in his right leg forced him to stop, then leaned against a pillar until the pain and numbness left him. Then he stepped off the veranda and headed for the trees, his stride growing longer and surer with every slow, strong beat of his heart.

Tsecha pressed the entry buzzer of the first house on the stone-paved path. The second. The third. He did so for a sense of completeness, of orderly progression, and to allow himself time to prepare. He also did it as a warning—the alarms echoed within the empty houses, sounding through the walls and along the deserted lane. A barely detectable alert, like the distant wail of the ComPol sirens.

When he finally reached Dathim Naré's house, he stood in front of the door for some time before daring to touch the entry pad. He sensed an ending here, as well as a beginning. As his walk down the lane had consisted of the conclusion of one step and the initiation of the following, so did his action here presage the end of one stage in his life and the start of the next. Not as one to be left behind, no, nor as one to be shunted aside. Such a fate was not meant for him, this he knew, and truly. Chief Propitiator of the Vynshàrau he was and would be until his death. Haárin he had been made, and would be until his death, as well.

Intercessor between his Jani and her people, he would become, even if the steps he took this night hastened that death.

He offered a whispered prayer as homage to Caith, then touched the pad. This buzzer seemed to sound more loudly than had the others. But then, such was to be expected. He heard no footsteps or voices just prior to the door opening, which meant someone had stood there and waited for him to request entry. Again, to be expected.

That the someone turned out to be Dathim Naré was the most expected thing of all.

"Ní Tsecha Égri." Dathim offered his odd humanish smile and stood aside to allow Tsecha entry.

Tsecha stepped inside, making sure to touch Caith's reliquary along the way. Behind him, he heard a harsh expulsion of breath, but whether that breath resulted from Dathim's surprise or his laughter, he did not bother to confirm.

Dathim's followers sat crowded in the center of the main

room floor; they had arranged themselves in a tight circle as though to shelter themselves from nonexistent wind and cold. Not all the Haárin who had stood atop the ridge had gathered here. Tsecha recognized the female who had taken the place beside Dathim on the ridge, and several of the others who had stood closest to him. Eleven, he counted—the most wary, the most humanish-appearing, and thus the most outcast of all.

Dathim stepped around in front of him, gesturing to the others as he did so. "We have been waiting for you, ní Tsecha." He smiled again, as though saying the true Haárin version of Tsecha's name gave him pleasure.

"We have, and truly," Dathim's female said. She wore her brown hair unbraided and gathered in a loose stream that hung halfway down her back. From such, she gave no sign whether she was bred or unbred, whether any of the youngish who had stood watching Tsecha during his daylight visit had been birthed by her or not. "I am Beyva Kelohim, ní Tsecha. I speak for those who have awaited you but cannot be here to witness your arrival—glories of the day to come."

"Glories of the day to come," intoned the rest of the Haárin in one voice, a voice that held a wide range of accents, from crisp and clear to rolling and smooth.

"Glor-ries of the day to come." Dathim ended the round of greetings, his voice like the cold stone against which Tsecha had rested his head. He then joined his followers in the circle; Beyva edged aside, leaving a space for him beside her on the floor.

"How will we know if ná Kièrshia has succeeded in returning the documents, ní Tsecha?" Her voice sounded as Jani's, low for a female, and quiet.

And for my Jani, I know the voice means as opposite of that which she is. Tsecha drew close to the circle, and regarded Beyva most openly. She did the same, looking him in the face with no evidence of hesitation. She possessed the gold eyes of Vynshàrau; her particular variation darkened by brown flecks. Like Dathim, she wore trousers and a shirt of Pathen coloring. Bright orange topped with sea blue, a most startling combination, and truly.

"I have heard nothing. At times such as this, to hear nothing from humanish is a good thing." As Tsecha stepped up to the circle, two of the Haárin slid apart to make room for him. He lowered gently to the floor, his knee complaining with every incremental movement. "If Anais Ulanova had complained to us concerning these documents, I would have heard news of such from Suborn Oligarch Shai. The importance of the documents was such that she would most certainly have contacted us. Since she has not, I must assume that my Kièrshia has indeed managed to return them." He looked at the faces surrounding him—even Dathim regarded him with an air of solemn acceptance. All understood him to be the absolute authority in any matter regarding his Toxin. If he said something was so, than it was so. Knowing his Jani as he did, this unquestioning faith caused a clench in Tsecha's soul. Not that she would ever disgrace or betray him—of that he felt most sure. *But they expect that I know her mind. What she will do and when she will do it.* They expected him to know that which no *humanish* had ever divined. That terrified him.

"Ní Tsecha?"

Tsecha looked up to find Dathim's smile had returned.

"Should we remain here on the embassy grounds, or choose an enclave outside this city?" Dathim gestured toward the bare tile in the center of the circle, as though it contained a two-dimensional map or a three-dimensional relief. "Up to the north, in one of the lakeside preserves? Or out to the west, in the midst of Chicago's garden domes and kettle factories?" He watched the reactions of his followers. "In the midst of humanish food."

"Even the humanish would not subject us to such. Of this, I feel most sure." An Haárin who Tsecha recognized as one of the garden workers spoke with hesitance, his English an odd swirl. "They would send us further north, in the hope that the cold would freeze us into leaving."

"And they would not put us amid their food for fear of sabotage," Tsecha added. "Remember how they think. You cannot hope to live among them if you do not know how they think." He pointed to a nonexistent place on the imaginary map. "As I said before, this is the capital, home to the

Earthbound humanish. The colony humanish tolerate us because we provide them with supplies that they cannot obtain
from their own merchants, but in this city, all can get what
they wish. They do not need us here, and humanish dispose
of that which they do not need."

"You try to scare us, Tsecha?" Dathim's voice sounded
again as the stone.

"I speak only truth, Dathim. Because you do not agree
with it, you will not hear it. Allow me to honor you—you
have become most as humanish already." Tsecha waved a
dismissive hand as the Haárin's shoulders rounded. "And
this will proceed how? Will you visit Shai in her rooms and
demand the right to petition the humanish for permission to
live here? Can you imagine what her reply will be, she who
would send you back into the worldskein with the next sunrise? Or perhaps you will go to the humanish directly? I can
tell you what they will answer, Dathim, and you will not like
that, as well. Your shoulders will round and you will argue
and dispute, but they will not hear you anymore. They will
know what you wish, and they will refuse it. To confront directly as with idomeni is not the way to deal with humanish!" Tsecha waited for the sound of his words to die in his
ears before flexing his back, first one way, then the other.
Even the painful support of one of Shai's chairs would have
been preferable to this free-sitting agony. But even with that
being the case, he knew that he dared not leave. Intercession
had become his duty, as it had with his late Hansen. *My
Hansen, who died in the explosion of an Haárin bomb.*
Tsecha imagined the smoke and rubble of the long-forgotten
scene, and felt the frigid air once more through his coldsuit.

"Then what do we do, ní Tsecha?" Beyva tilted her head
and lifted a cupped hand in a most Vynshàrau display of
question.

"If I could speak with my Kièrshia, we could together determine something. If I could speak—"

Dathim again expelled breath. "If? Is not the question
when? Where? How? You are bound to this land, Tsecha.
You are under arrest."

Tsecha gestured agreement with a truncated Low Vynshàrau hand flick. "But you leave this land quite easily,

Dathim. Any time you wish, so it appears, and truly." He stared at the blank center of their circle, and considered his next words. So easily had they formed in his mind that he knew they had been put there by a god. Whether that god be Shiou or Caith did not matter. He felt their divinity. Therefore, he was fated to speak them, and take the consequences as they came. "You will take me to her."

Dathim stared him in the face as the rest of the Haárin grew most still. "You are bound to this land, Tsecha, by Shai's decree."

"Yes." Tsecha again gestured strong affirmation, adding a humanish head nod for emphasis. "I am ambassador to this damned cold city. I am charged with representing my people to the humanish. Tell me, ní Dathim, if I am not to act as ambassador at this time, when am I? If not to prevent you from enraging the humanish so that they expel us all, when should I?"

"If not to prevent them from killing us all." The garden Haárin spoke once more, his voice as dead. "If not to prevent another Knevçet Shèràa."

Tsecha flicked his left hand in strongest disagreement. "Only my Kièrshia could enact another Knevçet Shèràa, and she would not do so in this case. She might yell, and question most loudly, but that is not the same as killing us all, and you are most stupid to say so!" He slumped with fatigue as his aged back surrendered its efforts to maintain its straightness. "If we persuade her of the worth of our argument, she will help us. She helps when she can. Such is her way, just as it is Shai's to press the old customs upon us all and Dathim's to trick and enrage." His knee ached again. He shivered, and longed for the soft and warmth of his bed.

Dathim smiled once more. "You are so sure of her, ní Tsecha. You are so sure of us all. I must indeed take you to this meeting." He looked to the timeform that sat within a niche on the other side of the room. "It is too late to go now— the darkness will soon be gone, and we still need darkness to travel in this city. But this next night we will go, and I will learn much of the ways of humanish from your discussions."

Beyva gestured in strong affirmation. "I will go, as well, to witness this discussion."

"And I will go," said the gardener. "I have never seen ná Kièrshia."

"And I will go—"

"And I—"

"I, as well."

"We will all go, and truly."

Tsecha looked at the faces around him. Some appeared cool and questioning as Dathim's. Others, as Beyva's, held youngish enthusiasm. None held confusion. Such had been left for him, so it seemed, to hold in his soul. *I will disobey Shai.* Such, she would not forgive. *Perhaps she will challenge me.* After fighting her, he would be most as outcast, and truly. He worked his hand beneath the short braids that fringed his forehead, and massaged the tightening bands that encircled his skull.

"If you go out in this city looking as you do, Tsecha, all who see you will know you as idomeni."

Tsecha looked up to see Dathim brush his hand over his own sheared head. "I have gone out into this city before, Dathim. My hair fits under a tight wig most well."

"A wig is trickery, is it not, Tsecha? But I am the trickster, and I see no need for such." Dathim lowered his chin in challenge. "You are our ambassador to humanish ways. So you said. So you said." He rose to his feet and walked across the room, disappearing through the front entry and into the night. One by one, the others followed him, the gardener and the rest, until Tsecha sat alone with Beyva.

He watched the door close. "Ní Dathim is most vexing." Once more, he pushed his forehead fringe aside to rub his scalp.

"Such is his way." Beyva lifted her right hand, open palm facing down. A gesture of acceptance. "He wishes to live as he will, where he will. Such is what we all wish."

Tsecha nodded in such a humanish manner that even he did not understand what he meant. He tugged at one of his braids, felt something give, then pulled back his hand to look at the short length of unfurled silver cord that he held between his fingers.

"You must retie it before you leave, ní Tsecha." Beyva rose. "The loose hair hangs before your eyes."

"Yes." Tsecha rolled the lock between his thumb and forefinger, then released it and instead tied the hair cord into a knot. He heard Beyva's footsteps, but did not look up to see where she walked or what she did. When he heard her approach from behind, he did not turn back to look at her.

He flinched when he felt her hands work through his braids. Then he felt the steady pull as she gathered the twirled lengths of hair in one hand, followed by the gradual loosening as she applied the cutter to the root of each one in turn and snipped it through.

"You will have to wear a covering out of doors, ní Tsecha," Beyva said as she cut. "You are not used to the cold."

Tsecha listened to the soft grassy sighs as his hair fell to the tile. Felt the slackening over his scalp as Beyva hacked away the tight braiding, and the pain in his head ease. It took so little time, to turn away from that which he had been. It took such simple acts, to become as outcast.

He sensed Beyva step back from him, and knew that she had finished. He rose, his knee cracking as it unbent. She held out the cloth to protect his head; he gave his answer by walking out the door and into the chill night, uncovered.

None saw him as he crossed through the trees, the lawns, the veranda. He entered the embassy and walked to the residence wing, up and down the halls to his rooms, seeing no one until the last corner when he turned and found himself face-to-face with Shai.

"Tsecha." The Suborn Oligarch stared at the top of his head, then turned from him, her shoulders hunched and rounding.

Tsecha said nothing in reply; Shai said no more. Humanish often said that there were times when no words were necessary. This was one of those times.

CHAPTER 27

She stood in a hallway, or an alley. Dim light seemed to come not from a single point but from all about her, as though the surfaces themselves served as the source of illumination. But even though she could see, she couldn't tell exactly where she was. The light wasn't bright enough to define any doors or openings that could identify the space. She could only sense that she stood in a walled place, long and narrow.

Her breathing came quick and hard. She could feel her heart pound, the pulse in her throat. Her right knee ached. She knew she had been running, but she couldn't remember why.

She touched the nearest wall. Green, it seemed to be—she couldn't see the color, but green made sense for some reason. The wall felt smooth as glass. Cold. The surface possessed a strange translucence, like a leaf coated with ice.

"Jani!"

She wheeled toward the shout. She recognized the voice, knew the name it called was hers. Strange name. She hadn't used it in a long time.

"Where the hell are you!"

A man's voice. Young. Angry.

I'm running from him. She remembered now.

"They're waiting for us at Gaetan's." Lucien appeared in the distance. He wore drop-dead whites, the formal Service uniform; he looked like the officer in his painting. "Your parents are there. They're worried about you. Your mother asked me why you ran away. I told her they needed you at the embassy—I didn't know what the hell else to say."

Jani remained silent, watching him. He looked far away, but she knew that was illusion. He had always been closer than she thought.

"Jani?" Lucien stepped down the narrow space toward her. What little light there was reflected off the white cloth, the badges and the gold braid on his shoulders. His silver-blond hair. How he glowed, like a platinum column. "They're waiting. Niall. Nema. John. Everyone." He removed his brimmed lid, the same gold-trimmed white as his uniform, and tucked it under his arm. "We can take the long way back, if that would make you feel better." He smiled as he held his hand out to her. His face seemed as translucent as the walls, as though it possessed layers, as well. "Let's go."

She backed away. One step. Another. Then turned and ran—

"Jani!"

—and collided with Sasha. Blood streamed down the side of his face. Jani reached out to touch the blood—just as she did, the light exploded through the coated walls. The force of the blast drove shards of ice into her body. She collapsed, heard Lucien close in from behind as her blood poured from gaping wounds and spread across the floor—

"Jani! Damn it, come on!"

She felt a hand close over her sore left shoulder, and struck out with all her remaining strength—

"Shit!"

The voice jarred Jani awake. Her heart stumbled and her chest tightened as she pushed herself into a sitting position, her hands scrabbling for purchase on the soft pillows. She comprehended the familiar around her—the armoire, the dresser, the windows, and walls.

"Jesus, gel! Steady on." Steve backed away from the bed, his arm crossed over his stomach. "Tryin' ta knock the wind outta me, or what?"

"I told you to just keep calling from a safe distance until she opened her eyes." Angevin stood at the foot of the bed, arms folded. "The last time I tried to wake her up by shaking her, she almost broke my wrist."

"No I dint—" Jani coughed the dryness from her throat. Then she licked her teeth, which felt unpleasantly coated.

She looked down at herself. She recalled falling into bed fully clothed; sometime during the night, someone had removed her trouser suit and replaced it with a T-shirt and shorts. She hoped it was Angevin, but given the young woman's reluctance to approach her as she slept . . .

"We just wanted to see if you planned to wake up before the end of the year." Angevin remained by the footboard. "You've been sleeping for almost fifteen hours. Even Lucien's starting to worry."

"How is he?" Jani looked toward the door to make sure that *he* wasn't standing there, listening.

"He's fine." Steve's lips barely moved, as though two words concerning Lucien took more effort than he wanted to expend.

"You've had calls." Angevin frowned. "We wouldn't bother you otherwise."

Jani dropped her legs over the side, and let the momentum pull her to her feet. "What calls?"

"—and something stinks!" Derringer's reddened face filled the comport display. "Nobody questions this letter for weeks. Then you get involved and two days later, every dexxie in the city is backpedaling!" His eyes looked dull despite his anger, the skin beneath smudged with fatigue. Jani could imagine the late night meetings with Callum Burkett that led to his current exhausted state.

"I don't know what you did, you meddling pain in the ass bitch." Derringer paused to yawn, striking his desktop with his fist as it went on and on. "But I will find out and when I do, you can kiss any reversal of your bioemotional restriction good-bye."

Jani watched his face still, then shard like the ice walls in her nightmare. "What was the time stamp on this?"

"Oh-five twelve this morning. Judging from the look of him, he'd had a long day and a damned short night." Steve tipped back in his chair, his feet braced against the edge of Jani's desk. "I don't believe he let himself be recorded making a threat."

"He's panicked. He sees his quest for a star going down in flames, and every time he makes a move to cover himself, there's Callum Burkett asking him for a full and complete report." Jani stifled her own yawn. She still felt tired, even after her more than full night's sleep. "I'm not too worried. I think that by this point, he's screwed himself enough that Cal might be willing to listen to my side of the story."

Steve nodded, his fingers drumming a beat on his knees. "Not going to tell us what letter he's talking about, are you?"

"It's better if you don't know."

"You know, working with you is like punching through a GateWay without knowing if you'll make it out the other side. You just says yer prayers and takes yer chances."

"Sorry," Jani said, without feeling very sorry at all. The less you said, the less you needed to lie. The less you lied, the less you needed to remember.

"Well," Steve finally said, when it became obvious Jani wasn't going to say any more. "Then there's this cryptic masterpiece." He leaned forward and hit the comport pad.

Roni McGaw looked as though she'd gotten even less sleep than Derringer. "I left my stuff in your skimmer. Eight files, next to a big, empty box." The hollow-eyed face stilled, then fragmented.

"See what I mean?" Steve turned to Jani before Roni's image had dissolved completely. "You don't have a skimmer."

Jani suppressed a sigh as she watched the display dim. What had Roni found out? Had she been able to check Ulanova's calendar in Exterior systems? Had Security taken the next step and shut down the ministry entirely?

Steve crumpled a piece of notepaper and tossed it at the display. "She didn't even tell you what time she were bloody stopping by."

Yes, she did—oh-eight tonight. But she wanted to meet Jani in the garage instead of their favorite bookstore.

"Roni's good. She's been Exterior Doc Chief for three years." Angevin had dragged one of the dining room chairs beside the desk, and sat heavily. "At least she lends an air of legitimacy to all this muck."

"And what is *that* supposed to mean?" Jani started to rise, but Steve's hand on her arm compelled her to stay seated.

"There's one more." He picked up his nicstick case from its resting place atop a stack of files, and shook out a gold-

and-white striped cylinder. "This was the kicker. Took us both aback, me and Ange." He hit the pad and sat back, smoking 'stick fixed between his teeth.

Jani groaned as this face formed.

"Janila?" Her mother looked back and forth, then up and down, as if she could look into Jani's flat if she tried hard enough. "Are you all right? Dr. Parini says that you are, but he has not seen you, so how would he know?" She leaned forward and dropped her voice. "He said I should not call you, but why not? His comport is secure, is it not? And yours, surely—" Her eyes widened as something off-screen captured her attention.

"Mère Kilian? Who are you talking to?" John's bass resounded in sharp question. "Val asked you not to contact anyone."

"I am just playing, Dr. Shroud. I am bored and I am playing." Jamira's hands moved toward the disconnect, but not quickly enough. A white hand shot in from the side and caught her wrist. A white face followed.

"Damn." John's cheeks pinked as he comprehended the code on Val's display. He wore a jacket in Neoclona lilac, and had filmed his eyes the same startling shade. The purple accents heightened his flush so that he looked enraged. "You shouldn't have done this, Mère Kilian."

"No! No! Do not touch me, you—!" Jamira pulled back from John, but not in time—he caught her two thin wrists in one hand with a grip Jani prayed was more gentle then it looked. "Let me go!" Jamira tried to twist away, but John held on to her with brutal ease as he reached for the comport pad. "Janila, I am so sorry! I love you! Please come—"

Jani watched as the scene of her mother struggling in John's grasp faded. She hit the comport pad's reply button to try to reconnect to Val's flat, and felt only a little reassured to find the code had been blocked to all calls. Then she sat forward and buried her head in her hands.

"Jan?" Steve spoke. "Is that yer mum?"

Jani nodded. "My father's with her. They're"—she couldn't force herself to say the words—"at Val's flat," even though it didn't matter, even though every security force in the city knew where her parents were by now. "They're in a safe place." What had been a safe place. She wondered if John felt spooked enough to move them to one of the numerous Neoclona buildings located throughout the city. "Someone tried to set them up to be kidnapped, but we found out in time."

"You're sure about that?"

Jani's head shot up. Beside her, Steve muttered a not-so-soft "Shit."

Lucien sat on the edge of the couch back. He had exchanged his pajamas and robe for winter base casuals. Thanks to a combination of augmentation and a twenty-six-year-old body, he had lost the haze of pain and weakness; he looked merely tired now, rather than debilitated. "Neoclona's security force has always been overrated, in my opinion."

"Has it?" Jani rose, waving off Angevin's murmur of concern. "I disagree. Considering some of the things that had to be done, we didn't need an Office of Professional Standards getting in the way."

"Any security officer who answers to an OPS would have made sure the comports were blocked for outgoing. Failing that, they sure as hell would have canceled the transmission of that call." Lucien stood. "That's the problem when you use an actual home for a safe house—the people who live there tend to still treat it like a home." He waited for her to circle the desk, then walked to her. His step was still slow, but steady, unhampered by his injury. "I would have thought your good friend Niall would be involved in this, but no Service safe house that I know of lets their guests call out. Where are they, with John or Val?"

Jani brushed past him, her pace quickening as she neared her room. In the opening to the hallway, however, she stopped and turned back. Steve and Angevin regarded her as she expected them to, with a mixture of anger and hurt. She'd seen the look before, had accepted it as an inevitable and necessary part of her life. She would have worried if the faces around her looked too happy all the time. "I consider you my friends." She took care not to look at Lucien as she spoke. "But I've known people to die because they told their friends too much. I've known the friends to die, as well. The people Steve talked about at dinner, the ones who kill over a crateful of chips, those are the people we're dealing with here."

"We understand that," Angevin piped. "But—"

"But what?" Jani took a step back into the room. "But you wouldn't have said anything? But you'd have promised not to talk? How long would that promise last if someone held a shooter to your head? To Steve's head? How long would it last against an injector full of Sera? That was *my* mother's face on the display, not yours. If anything happened, you'd lose a few nights' sleep. But you'd get over it, because you'd have saved what meant most to you. Well, looking after what means most to me is how I've lived for the last twenty years, and I'm too goddamned old to change. You're both sweet kids, but if absolute push came to bottom line shove and you had to choose between each other and my mother, who would you pick?" She turned and headed for her room before they felt compelled to answer. Some things could never be spoken of between people who called themselves friends, or they wouldn't remain friends for long.

The memory of her mother struggling in John's grasp replayed in Jani's mind, and she struck the doorway with the flat of her hand on the way through. She already had her T-shirt up over her head when she heard the door open again. She pulled it off anyway, because she had slept the day away and had only a few hours before her meeting with Roni. Because she needed to shake off the last of her languor, shower and change clothes and brush the coating out of her mouth. Because she needed to contact John and find out if he had moved her parents, contact Niall and find out where the hell he was. "I don't have time for company."

"This isn't a social call." Lucien sat on the edge of the bed. His eyes fixed on her bare breasts, but only out of generalized interest. "Drives you crazy to be out of the loop, doesn't it? To not know what's going on. Well, triple it and you'll know how I feel."

"I didn't know that you felt at all." Jani sought the refuge of her closet, riffling through the hangers for her favorite Service surplus gear. She chose a muddy blue mechanic's coverall she'd swiped from a recycle bin, and added a black pullover to wear underneath in deference to the cold.

"Who are you meeting? John? McGaw? Going to go pound the last fastener in Derringer's career coffin?"

Jani turned to find Lucien standing in the closet entry. Even though he gripped the sides of the doorway, blocking her in, she didn't feel threatened. He wasn't yet back to full strength. If he did get out of hand, she'd just punch him in his burn. "Who said I'm meeting anybody?"

"Come on—I heard those messages!" Lucien's hair caught the light as it did in her nightmare. His show of anger weakened him—the way he sagged against the doorway implied that he needed the support. "You're going out there alone, with no idea who's waiting for you, unarmed, with no back-up. Is that what you call taking care of what means most to you?"

"Do you know something I don't?" Jani bundled her clothes in front of her bare chest and turned to Lucien. "That's nothing new, is it?" After a few seconds of warring stares he stepped aside with a huff and she retreated to the sanctuary of the bathroom.

CHAPTER 28

When Jani emerged from the bathroom, she found Lucien standing in front of the dresser, studying the painting of the lovers' triangle.

"This is about the shooting, isn't it? You think I set you up." His voice held the matter-of-fact tone he always used when discussing matters of life and death. "That's why you've shut me out. You don't trust me."

Jani tossed her clothes and towels in the cleaner. "I never trusted you."

"You did for some things. For things that mattered to both of us." He had managed something akin to a sad expression, which meant he felt as upset about someone else's feelings as he ever could. "I'll bet that's why you let me stay here. You wanted to keep an eye on me."

Jani turned her back on him and activated the cleaner. When the goal was to keep the lies to a minimum, you learned fast which things just weren't worth lying about.

"Do you think I'd have missed?" The injury in Lucien's voice had been replaced by chill pride. "If I had tried to kill you or had set you up to be killed, do you think I'd have failed?"

Jani walked to the dresser, working her fingers through her damp hair. "There's a first time for everything." She stepped around Lucien to collect her comb, and stopped in mid-grab when she saw the two halves of the casino marker lying atop the mirrored tray.

"Angevin tried to wake you to undress, but you'd turned to dead weight by that time. She didn't want to touch you—

you strike out in your sleep, it seems. So she asked me to help." Lucien leaned close, until he spoke directly in Jani's ear. "Did you go in through the front of the dresser, or the back?"

"The back." Jani looked at him. His eyes had gone brown stone, which meant that whatever anger he felt hadn't claimed him completely. What she needed to watch for was the truly dead light, when he looked at her the way he did at everyone else. That would signal the true point of no return, the end of the arm's length discussions and tense treaties. That would mean only one of them would emerge alive. "Drawers are too difficult to break into quickly. The back is always faster."

Lucien nodded. Knowing him, he'd filed the knowledge away for future reference, if he didn't know it already. "Did you leave a mess?"

"The rear panel is a little bent. Somebody with a protein scanner would know I was in the room, but they'd have expected that since you keyed your door to me." Jani picked up one of the marker halves. "You killed him. Etienne Palia."

"As if you didn't know." Lucien shrugged. He tried to insert his hands in his pockets, but the pull of the cloth over his wound made him wince, forcing him to settle for a one-handed lean against the dresser. "You were living in Majora at the time—I considered tracking you down."

"Don't change the subject!" Jani struggled to keep her voice level. "Who ordered Palia's death? I realize that neither the Service nor the government are above arranging the occasional convenient demise, but was Palia powerful enough to merit their attention? Or did you hire yourself out to *L'araignée*, help them rid themselves of an officer who had gotten out of line? Or was it a more private killing? An angry husband? A gambling debt?"

"You would have hated him if you'd met him." Lucien smiled with a distinct lack of humor. "His behavior definitely ran counter to your personal code of ethics."

"Which ethics are those, the ones you helped research for my white paper?" Jani watched Lucien's face, alert for any flicker or shadow, any sign that she'd struck what passed for his nerve. "You were the busy boy, weren't you? Between contract killings for whoever paid your freight and digging the dirt on me, it's a wonder you had time to file your official Intelligence Updates."

Lucien slowly raised his hand. "I'd like to bring up two points, if I could?" He extended his thumb. "One—you're not dead. I'm fifteen for fifteen, and you're not dead."

Jani shook her head. "First time for—"

"Two." Lucien extended his index finger, then pointed the mock weapon at her. "After you read that white paper, and I assume you did or Niall isn't half the ferret I think he is, did you stop to ponder the two interesting items that seemed to have been left out? The copying of the deed. The murder of that Family agent." He cocked his thumb back and forth, as though he activated a charge-through. "Of course, you had your reasons at the time. But they're the sorts of reasons that make sense to someone like me or Niall, not to people like Steve, or Angevin, or your good friends at Registry."

Jani felt her anger freeze into something more controllable, less human. "Are you threatening me?"

"No, I'd never threaten you. I know you too well." Lucien sighed. "A lot better, apparently, than you know me. I covered for you. I kept the really damning crap from getting into that white paper. No matter how much you try to deny it, you need me. I have always done you more good than harm. In every way." He took a step toward her, but stopped when she backed away. "You're unarmed. You're stupid to go out there."

"What good would you be? The ComPol turned your shooter over to your CO."

"You think that's the only one I've got! After all this, you think that's the only—" Lucien laughed, harder than Jani had ever seen him. He walked to the wall so he could brace against it as his shoulders shook, clasping his arms across his stomach and groaning as his wound complained. The pain calmed him—he wiped a hand over his face and looked at her, the animal ache dulling his eyes. "Do you really think that's the only one I've got?"

"No." Jani turned back to the mirror and focused on the periphery of her face. The part of her that she couldn't control worried after Lucien's pain and tried to think of a way to salve it, wondered why the implanted analgesic pump didn't do a better job. Yet again, she damned her weakness. "I don't need your help. Go to sleep. Go away. Go to hell." She pushed the comb through her hair and fought to keep from looking at herself too closely. So intent was she on avoiding her own gaze that she didn't sense Lucien's approach until she saw him in the mirror behind her.

He reached around her and picked up the two halves of the marker, one in each hand. "See these?" He held up one half to within a handspan of her nose. "This is you." Then he held up the other. "And this is me." He pressed the two halves together, broken edge to broken edge, until the plastic round looked whole again. "And this is us. Or it could be, only *you* won't admit it."

Jani bumped his stomach with the point of her elbow. The marker halves flew apart as he gasped and backpedaled; she barely kept from cringing, knowing his surprise and his pain. "Take that thing and get out."

"Why?" Lucien straightened slowly, his breathing irregular, the sweat beading on his forehead. "What are you afraid of? Is it that you need me? Or is it that you love me?"

"Don't flatter yourself." Jani resumed raking the comb through her hair. "I know what love is—you could never make that cut."

"Oh, I forgot. You love John." Lucien closed in again, this time grabbing her wrists so she couldn't elbow him. "Your creator." He wrapped his arms around her and rubbed his chin against the side of her neck. "Or maybe fellow freak is a better term these days."

Jani grew still. No, it was more than that. It was as though her blood ceased flowing and her heart stopped, as though her very cells suspended their function. She watched Lucien in the mirror as he nuzzled her neck, a neck that had lengthened over the past months. *My mother called me mutant . . .*

"I mean, compared to you, even *he* looks normal." Lucien rested his chin atop Jani's achy shoulder and regarded their reflection. "At least that's what I overheard at Neoclona. They talk about you constantly—you're their favorite pastime. It's the eyes that clinch it, according to the general opinion. Not that I have any basis for comparison. You've tied yourself in knots hiding them from me." He pressed close to her ear. "Here, kitty, kitty, kitty." He laughed as she struggled to break his grip. "Boy, they must be some sight. Creature from the GateWay. It Came from the Lost Colony. What did your parents say when they first saw you? 'Who are you and what did you do to our daughter?' Or did they just scream and run like hell?"

Jani stilled again, and watched Lucien's eyes in the mirror. His human eyes, which some would call beautiful, that obscured a hollow of a heart and a dried husk of a soul. *We are two halves of the same whole, aren't we? Both monsters, only you hide it so well.* She shook his hands from her wrists. Still captured by his arms, she turned to look him in the face. His smile brightened as their eyes met, like a bully who knew he'd hit his target.

Jani raised her hands to her eyes, slipped her thumbnails beneath the edges of the films, flicked out and down. The hydropolymer membranes came away with audible *pops*— they hung intact from her fingers, the green irises glittering, the white sclera milky and human and clean. She flipped them atop the dresser to desiccate.

Lucien's eyes widened. His smile faded. His mouth opened, but the words wouldn't emerge, even though his jaw worked, even though he tried to speak. His arms fell away. He stepped back, mouth agape.

"What's the matter, bully boy? Cat got your tongue?" Jani laughed in spite of her shame. Lucien stunned speechless was a sight to behold. An event to treasure, no matter the circumstances. *No matter . . .* If she told herself that long enough, maybe she'd believe it.

Then Lucien reached out. A tentative move, as though he feared rebuff. He brushed his fingers down her cheek, along the curve of her jaw. Then he gripped her by the shoulders and spun her so that she faced the mirror. *"Look."* When Jani tried to twist away, he flung one arm around her shoulders to hold her fast, then seized her jaw so she couldn't move her head. "I said *look,* damn it!"

Jani tried to look at the ceiling, the wall, the carved wood frame of the mirror. But Lucien held her so firmly that all she could move were her eyes—her head ached from the strain of trying not to look straight ahead. She surrendered, finally, and did as he demanded, bracing herself for his sly insults as she stared into the overlarge irises, the glass-green sclera.

"See." Lucien relaxed his grip on her jaw, until it became a caress. "They're beautiful. Like veined jade." He released her jaw and ran his hand over her breasts, down her stomach. "Gorgeous." He gripped her hip and pulled her closer, pressing himself against her.

Jani felt her nerves flare and her stomach tighten as Lucien's erection ground against her. She looked again at his reflection, and saw the same parted lips and focused dreaminess that he had displayed during Dathim Naré's visit. "Now who's the freak?" She heard the deepening catch in her voice, and hated herself just a little more.

"You're what we're all going to be someday, according to Nema. I'm just getting a head start." Lucien gripped her waist and turned her slowly, pressing against her as he did so their bodies never broke contact. It seemed to take forever. A single second. By the time she faced him, Jani's breathing had gone as raspy as his.

"This is ridiculous." She tried to squirm away, but her legs wouldn't listen. "You're in no condition."

"Never felt better." Lucien smiled lazily and reached for the top fastener of Jani's coverall.

"No!" She thrust her arms up and out, breaking his hold and driving him back. "You want to fuck the bizarre so damned bad, go cruise South Wabash and leave me the hell alone!"

Lucien blinked in unfocused confusion before shaking his head. "You're not bizarre. You're a beautiful woman."

"Damn you for a liar!" Jani's voice caught again. *Anormal . . . mutant.* Her throat ached and her warped eyes stung and passion had nothing whatsoever to do with it. "I'm not—a *woman* anymore."

Lucien hesitated. "I know." He held out his hand. "Please?" When she didn't answer, he stepped closer and reached once more for the neck of her coverall. He opened one fastener, the next, slid the coverall off her shoulders, then knelt in front of her.

Jani leaned against the dresser and closed her eyes.

"No!" Lucien grabbed the front of her pullover and

yanked, forcing her to look down. "Watch every move I make." He undid the rest of the fasteners, then pulled the coverall down. Off one leg, then the other. Tossed it aside. "Look at me." He peeled Jani's pullover over her head and flung it atop the coverall. Then he slid her bandbra and underwear down her body, leaving a line of kisses in their wake.

Jani braced her hands on the edge of the dresser as her knees sagged and her body ached and warmed. A human ache. Blessedly human warmth.

"The idomeni don't get as wrapped up in this as we do, do they?" Lucien's eyes shone.

"No." Jani reached down and pushed her hand through his hair. "They think we overcomplicate it."

"I guess they don't know everything." Lucien massaged her inner thighs, then looked up to make sure she still watched. "It's like gold. Warm gold." He kissed the softest, warmest place, then stood up and undressed. He pulled his shirt over his head, pausing when he saw Jani stare at his burn. "It doesn't hurt as long as I'm careful."

"It looks like hell." She stepped close and placed both her hands over the shiny pink expanse of flesh, then ran a finger over the whispery-thin grid lines of the grafting support. "And I know it hurts—you wince every time you move too fast. You can't—"

"Yes, I can." He pushed down his trousers, kicked off his trainers and socks and stood before her, naked and beautiful, but changed. Uncertain, faltering, as if he expected her to turn him down, even now.

Jani pressed close and kissed him, savoring his human taste, his human hands caressing her breasts and moving down her body. The sweet human agony that radiated from between her legs and the human moan that rose in her throat. She held him as he maneuvered her backward and braced her against the dresser. "This isn't going to work," she whispered into his hair. She felt his hands slip inside her and then she felt him inside her, slowly at first and then faster and faster, matched his every rhythm, and realized it worked just fine. She wrapped her legs around him to steady herself. Moved her hands over his back and chest, avoiding the burn.

Heard him call to her and answered back. Watched his every response as he watched hers. Accepted him to her strange home and felt him embrace—embrace—what she didn't want and beg for—what she hated—and ask—and ask—

"Look at me."

—and ask—

"Look at me."

—until his human eyes finally closed and his back arched and his body stiffened and he cried out as he had on the floor of the garage after she fell and the shot took him instead.

Lucien sagged against her, his breathing slowing, his hands easing their bruising grip, his head cradled against her neck. Jani held him because she had no choice, because her body had frozen and she didn't know what else to do. "Let me go."

"No, not yet—"

"Let me go."

"No, not yet. Why—?"

But she had pushed him away and gathered up her clothes and fled to the bathroom before he made her answer the question.

Jani showered quickly. Dressed slowly. Refilmed her eyes carefully. If she could have drilled a hole in the wall so she could leave without having to walk through her bedroom, she would have. But she couldn't, so she gathered her frayed wits and faced what needed to be faced.

She found Lucien dressed, sitting on the edge of the bed, socks in hand. He seemed to know her thoughts—he barely looked up when she walked in the room.

Jani leaned against the armoire; the carved scrollwork of the doors dug into her back. "As soon as people heard about the shooting, they assumed you had something to do with it."

"Yes, they did, didn't they?" He shrugged. "Lucky you fell when you did." He draped one sock across his knee, then worked his fingers through the other. "Lucky I was there."

"What are you telling me, that you shoved me out of the way?" Jani pushed off the armoire and paced. "You expect me to believe that you took my shot on purpose? *You?*"

Lucien didn't answer. He didn't look at her, but kept his human eyes fixed on his bundled sock.

Jani waited for him to argue, to try to charm her with a smile, to lie. When he didn't, she knew that he realized that it would do no good. That told her all she needed to know. "I want you to leave," she heard herself say, her voice hollow and distant. "Now. I'll have your gear sent to Sheridan tomorrow."

"This—" Lucien stopped. The cast of his face had turned tentative, as it had been such a short time before. As though he walked unfamiliar ground, and hated the sensation. "This *arrangement* of ours, as Nema calls it—it's not what I had in mind, either. I mean, it's just been one damned thing after another with you ever since we met!" He raised his thumb to his mouth and nipped at the nail. "What aggravates me the most is that you never stop to think about where you could go in this city if you could keep your mouth shut for five minutes at a stretch! You'll beat your head against the wall when there's a perfectly good door just around the corner." He yanked the sock straight, then bundled it again.

"I do not—love you. I have never—loved anybody. I can't, and I wouldn't want to if I could." Lucien's fingers slowed, stopped. "But according to all the testing I've had over the years, I am capable of remembering . . . what it may have been like once. If I try. Like when you catch a whiff of something, a flower, or something baking, and the memories come back." His uncertain expression combined with stray shadow to soften his face so he looked as he did in his teenaged portrait. "I've always been loyal to you. Always."

Jani watched the light play over Lucien's hair as once more, Val's words came back to her. *He's always shown me the face he knows I want to see. That's all he is—shadow and reflection. That's all he's ever been. Why can't I accept it?* "You don't know the meaning of the word."

"I beg to differ," Lucien replied. "When loyalty is your profession, you learn what it means and you do not dare forget."

"Don't you? I'd think after the first half-dozen deals, the lines would start to blur." Jani slumped against the armoire. She knew she sounded petulant, childish, but she didn't care. She knew he had betrayed her and tried to hate him. Knew she couldn't and that she probably never would, and hated herself instead. "Service. Exterior. *L'araignée*. The occasional freelance." She heard her voice scale upward, and struggled to bring it under control. "What term best describes you? Double agent? Triple agent? Dodecahedral agent?"

"You always knew what I was. What I am. Are you saying you only realized it now—who are you kidding?" Lucien pulled on the bundled sock, then the other. "If anyone ever compiled a white paper on me, I daresay it would hold your attention. I have a talent for deceit, and I've made it pay. But I also have a talent for picking the winning horse, and I've made that pay, too." He pushed his feet into his trainers and adjusted the fasteners. "Along the way I've had many masters, and I've served them all very well." He stood slowly, one hand resting over the shooter burn. "But I served you best." He walked to the door without looking at her, his step silent, the only sound that of the panel opening, then closing.

Jani waited before walking out to the main room. She didn't want to see Lucien leave, in case the sight of him compelled her to change her mind and ask him to stay. She concentrated instead on what she'd tell Val when he asked the whereabouts of his patient, and on how she'd remove the outpatient gear from the spare bedroom. She thought of everything but Lucien. Everything but . . .

. . . and found that that ploy didn't work for long either.

She found Steve and Angevin sprawled on the couch. "Right ho, Jan!" Steve said as he stuck a celebratory 'stick in his mouth.

Before he could ignite it, Jani pulled him to his feet and dragged him after her to the door. "We'll be right back," she called to Angevin, who stared after them in bewilderment.

"Where we goin'?" Steve tried to squirm out of her grip as they hustled toward the lift.

Jani pushed him into the car and thumped her fist against the pad until the doors closed. "I want you to help me with something."

Hodge called to them as they crossed the lobby. Jani offered a quick wave, but kept moving. Out the door. Across the street to the garage.

"Jan?" Steve sounded edgy now. "What we doin'?"

"A demonstration, to ease both our troubled minds." Jani pushed Steve ahead of her down the entry ramp, then pulled him to a stop when they reached the place where Lucien had fallen. "Stand behind me."

" 'K."

"Closer."

"Right."

"Off to the left, half a meter, *stop*."

" 'K."

Jani pointed to the left and down. "The shot is going to come from there. I'm in position for it now, but I'm falling." She bent over and to the right, a slow-motion version of her head-first tumble. "You want me to get hit—what do you do?"

"I—" Steve reached out and grabbed her around the upper arm. "Hard to get a bloody grip. Nothing else to hold on to if I want to pull—" His hand fell away. "Jan, what the hell—?"

Jani turned on him. "If Lucien wanted to drag me back into the line of fire, he'd have grabbed my arm and pulled, like you did. But he pushed, down and away. Hard. He almost dislocated my shoulder—it still hurts."

"So?" Steve took a step back. Another. "He pushed you down on the ground so you'd be a sitting duck for the shooter. So you couldn't run."

"The pulse was aimed *here*, Steve." Jani held her arm straight out, her fist marking the spot where the shot impacted Lucien. "This was a quick 'n' dirty attempt. The shooter only had time to fire once. The set-up was supposed to do the work. Lucien botched the set-up." She turned, and saw Angevin standing at the top of the ramp, her hands over her mouth. "He found out about the hit on me. Not soon enough to stop it, but soon enough to screw it up." He couldn't afford to stop it. He owed a certain amount of loyalty to someone in *L'araignée*, and Lucien always took care to cultivate his loyalties. No one ever questioned you when you took care to appear unquestionable.

"You can't say you believe that!" Steve hurried after Jani as she mounted the ramp and fled the garage. "You can't say he's got you believin' that!" He picked up his pace as they burst onto the sidewalk, which was lit by late afternoon sun and clear of pedestrians. "He's a bloody damned liar, Jan—he's been one all his life!" He shouted after her as Angevin grabbed his arm and tried to drag him across the street and into the quiet, calm lobby. "Jan! *Jan!*"

But Jani didn't answer him. She walked down the street, toward an office building that contained a bank of public comports. She concentrated on the call she needed to make to John, on the wording she'd use, so that no one who happened to overhear would think she talked about her parents. So no one would think her questionable, or wonder at her loyalties. She didn't think about anything else. Or anyone. Or so she told herself. She'd had lots of practice in telling herself things, just as she'd had practice in avoiding them. Things she didn't want to hear, didn't want to know. Didn't believe, despite the evidence to the contrary. Of damning testimony that disappeared. Of a sore shoulder that wouldn't heal, and a shooter pulse that cracked half a meter up and to the side. Stood to reason. She could be a bloody damned liar herself when she needed to be. So she knew a lie when she heard it, and knew the truth when she heard it too.

CHAPTER 29

A harried-looking Neoclona staffer answered Jani's call. No, Dr. Shroud was not available. No, Ms. Kilian, he didn't leave a message for you. Yes, Ms. Kilian, I will tell him that you called.

Jani tried the code to Val's flat, and found it still blocked. That bothered her. Blocking was a viable method for silencing talkative mothers for the short term, but it lacked elegance when employed for too long. In other words, it blared to one and all the fact that something highly unusual had occurred at Chez Parini. *Maybe Val just forgot to lift it.* She hoped that didn't mean that her parents still remained with him. She hoped John had the presence of mind to move them, or that Niall had overstepped the boundaries she had imposed on him and stuck his nose where it needed to be stuck.

Jani sat forward, elbows on knees, and thumped her head against the wall of the comport booth. "John, you're not an idiot—couldn't you have left me *something?*" When this was all over, she'd have to ask Roni McGaw to give him lessons in veiled communication.

Roni McGaw. Jani checked her timepiece. She still had an hour to wait before she met with Roni. *Did you check Anais's calendar? What did you find?* Proof that she had met with Lucien on Amsun during the time *L'araignée* formed? That she had approved plans, authorized expenses, requested assassinations?

Jani called Niall's flat, received no answer, left no message. She struggled to slow her racing mind, to keep the crazy thoughts from leaping to the fore. That Niall had been waylaid on the way back to Sheridan, and now lay trussed and drugged in a shielded room in an anonymous house somewhere in Chicago. Or that he had taken her distrust of the Service and turned it into distrust of him, and instead lay in a bed in the Sheridan Main Hospital, turning ever more inward as the psychotherapeuticians labored yet again to bring him back.

Jani thumped her head against the wall again, as though she could pound the thoughts from her head via brute force. *An overactive imagination is a terrible thing.* The OCS instructor who had given voice to that gem had referred to excessive overstrategizing, but he could have been referring to the fix in which she found herself now. Out of the loop, dependent on others' skills to protect what meant most to her, with only her own questioning mind for company. *Drives you crazy, doesn't it . . . ?* If Lucien had appeared before her now, she would have struck him.

Her stomach interrupted with a grumble, and she debated returning to her flat to get something to eat. But she didn't want to face more of Steve's protests, his arguments delineating Lucien's guilt. Instead, she dug into her pockets and collected all the vend tokens she could find. Somewhere in the building there was a vend alcove, and somewhere in that alcove's coolers and hot boxes was something she could eat. Then she'd find a quiet corner, a place where she could close her eyes and clear her head. And wait.

The clip of Jani's bootheels on the scancrete echoed along the alleys she cut through, sounded more softly within the wider brick canyon of Armour Place. She passed few people on the way to the garage during this dividing time between day and night. She recognized some of the faces, and watched them just as warily as the ones she didn't. When she finally reached the garage, she kept walking, circling around the renovation and down the next street so that she could enter the garage from the rear.

Jani surveyed the space as she had on the night of the shooting, on the lookout this time not for returning assassins, but for Roni, or for her skimmer, if she had used one.

She paced, suddenly self-conscious and wary of being seen. She knew she could pass for an employee from a nearby shop waiting for her ride, for an impatient girlfriend waiting for her date. She wished Niall could have shadowed her. She wished augie would show up to calm her nerves. She—

A *thud* sounded as something heavy hit the floor above. Jani patted her coverall pocket for the shooter that wasn't there, and headed for the stairwell she and Niall had used to gain access to the garage's upper level. As she approached the door, she looked down and saw a metal wedge lying on the floor nearby. She picked it up, hefted it, then swung it by the narrow end. A doorstop, hollow-forged and badly dented. It was barely heavy enough to serve as a suitable weapon, but it would have to do.

She crept up the stairs, her eyes on the door above. She heard another sound as she neared the landing, the scrape of a sole against the smooth scancrete. Whoever it was, they made no effort to hide their presence. *It's probably just someone come to collect their skimmer. This* is *a garage.* Her hand tightened around the doorstop anyway.

She stopped in front of the door and debated how to go in. Slowly wouldn't work. The safety lighting in the stairwell couldn't be quenched—she'd be perfectly backlit as soon as she cracked open the door.

Jani crouched low. In one smooth motion, she pushed open the door and drop-rolled into the shadow of the same column she had hidden behind during her foray with Niall. She hugged the base and scanned the area, staying low so she could look beneath the skimmers. Row after row hovered silently in the half-light, the hum and click of the charge units the only sounds Jani heard but for her breathing. *Someone must be throwing a party tonight.* That would explain the number of skimmers. She felt like a child trying to see around a roomful of furniture.

She heard the running steps before she saw motion off to her right, partially hidden by broken rows of skimmers. She darted after the sound, because the innocent didn't run, because a chase gave her something on which to focus her twangy nerves. She kept her head low, gaze flicking above and below the vehicles, and caught the shadowy reflection of someone on the enameled surfaces.

There were three exits, not counting the do-it-yourself doorway that the construction crew had made—the door Jani had used, another door at the far end of the space, and the ramp used by the vehicles. The shape headed for the far door, but it had a great many skimmers to dodge around to get there. Jani heard the slide of shoes on scancrete, another *thud* as her quarry tripped and fell, a gasp of pained surprise. She rounded and cut in an intercept pattern, so she could head them off before they made the door.

As she drew closer, she heard the slide of cloth over smooth floor. One of the skimmers trembled, a four-door sedan that covered a lot of floor space.

She circled back behind the skimmer, in the hope that whoever had crawled beneath would still be looking toward the door, and that if they'd been armed, they'd have shot at her by now. When she reached the rear of the vehicle, she ducked down, tossed the doorstop aside, reached out, and grabbed. Her hands closed around two thin ankles. *Kids!* She dragged the squirming, struggling form into the light as she squelched the urge to howl. *Kids playing—!*

Then the garish clothes struck her—sapphire and glaring orange—the liquid flow of the cloth—long brown hair bound in a horsetail, but something wasn't right—*damn, this is a tall kid!*

Her quarry twisted around and goggled at her, cracked amber eyes catching the dim light and holding it fast.

Jani let loose the Haárin's ankles and stumbled backward, falling against a late-model sports skimmer. The vehicle's proximity alarm emitted a warning chirp—she fell to her hands and knees and scooted across the floor to get out of range before the tiny sound erupted into a blare. Something in her right knee shifted as it impacted the scancrete—she fell onto her side and clasped her hands around the throbbing joint.

The Haárin boosted herself into a crouch, ready to dart away. Then she eased back on her heels and looked Jani in the face, openly and boldly. "You are—ná Kièrshia?" Her

English sounded crisp, as though she'd spoken it for a long time.

"Yes." Jani tried to straighten her knee, stopping in mid-flex when she heard the near door open and a jumble of footsteps pad toward them. She looked up, and almost gave voice to her howl as eight more Haárin heads regarded her over the top of the sedan.

Then the door opened again. More footsteps. Two more heads, the sight of which stopped the howl in Jani's throat. Dathim Naré, and next to him, Nema. "NìRau?" She boosted to her feet and limped toward him. "What's going on?"

"Ní Tsecha," Dathim interrupted, giving the title the long "a" twist of the Haárin. "He is nìRau no more. He has joined us now, and truly."

"NìRau," Jani repeated with feeling as she ignored Dathim and confronted her silent teacher. "Why have you left the embassy? Did Shai lift your restriction?"

Dathim tossed a Low Vynshàrau hand twitch of dismissal. "He does not answer to nìaRauta Shai anym—"

Jani swung around to face him. "I am *not* talking to you!" Her knee complained at the rapid movement, and she turned back to Nema more slowly. "NìRau? Did Shai give you permission to leave the grounds?"

"No, nìa." Nema looked down at her, his expression so somber that she feared him ill. He didn't wear the marks of the sickbed, however, the black-trimmed overrobe or the single hoop earring in his right ear. In fact, he wore no overrobe at all, only his usual off-white shirt and trousers, topped by a brown knee-length coat made from the idomeni equivalent of wool. He wore no earrings, either—the multiple holes dotted his lobes, more glaring in their emptiness than the most complex goldwire helix. Strange that Jani could see his ears—he must have bound his braids in the brown scarf he had twisted about his head in imitation of Dathim—

Jani raised her hands to the sides of Nema's head and pushed back the scarf. The pale brown stubble that covered his scalp shone in the soft light of the garage. She brushed her hand over it as her breath caught. She felt the tears course down her cheeks, and made no effort to wipe them away. "Did you do this?" She spun toward Dathim, and used the pain in her knee to stoke her anger. "Did you!"

"Are you talking to me *now*, ná Kièrshia?" Dathim bent low to look her in the face. "No, I did not cut ní Tsecha's hair."

"I did it." The female whom Jani had pulled from beneath the skimmer stepped forward. "He bade me, and I did as he bade. He chose his own way, ná Kièrshia, and truly."

"Ná Beyva speaks the truth, nìa." Nema gripped Jani's chin between his thumb and forefinger. "I have chosen to declare myself as Haárin, to declare my faith in the future as I know it must be." He tilted her head to one side, then the other, his eyes searching hers. "We have come here to request that you do the same, that you appear at the conclave as a supporter of the Elyan Haárin, that you show your faith in the future as well."

Jani tried to pull back. "I begged you to wait. The problem I told you about—I took care of it. Another day or two, and all the fuss over the shooting would have dissipated. Shai would have had no choice but to release you to attend the conclave." She knew Nema attempted to discern her eyes through their filming. Dathim must have told him about the incident in the kitchen, and the glimpse he had managed to steal. *If he could see them for himself, he would be so happy.* But she had no film with her to cover them again. What if one of the partygoers chose that moment to return to their skimmer? But, but, but . . . She tried to concentrate on policy, to veer away from the personal. "NìRau, it is much more important that you participate in the conclave rather than me. You're the Haárin's religious dominant, as well as Cèel's." She touched the side of his shorn head. How old he looked, without his braids and his jewelry. "Have you stopped to think how the Elyan Haárin might react to this?"

"They will rejoice to see it. The Elyan now cut their hair as well." Dathim stepped to Nema's side, an action that made him look for one surreal moment like a Cabinet press aide intercepting an inappropriate question. His chill attempt at a humanish smile only served to reinforce the image. "Ah. My apologies, ná Kièrshia. You did not ask me."

"NìRau." Jani took Nema by the elbow and steered him away from the hovering Dathim. "Cèel and Shai have begun to act as humanish leaders. They have chosen to treat your attempts at open disputation as an affront, a threat to idomeni solidarity. The fact that your suborn had challenged you must have infuriated them. How do you think they will treat your adopting the appearance of their most rebellious Haárin?"

A lick of the old fire flared in Nema's eyes—he bared his teeth. "They will be most as outraged."

"They may recall you to Shèrá."

"Yes, nìa."

"They may execute you."

Nema paused. Then he pulled the scarf from its tenuous perch on his head and regarded it thoughtfully. "It occurred to me that when the gods informed me of the future, they did not also guarantee my presence in it." He turned the scarf over in his hands. "But you will live, I think, nìa. John Shroud would split the universe in half rather than allow you to die. And you will ensure that the future develops as it must."

Jani glanced at her timepiece, and swallowed a curse. "I must meet with someone. It is important that I see her. What we discuss will affect what happens at the conclave." She looked up at Nema's face, and blinked as her eyes filled. "I wish you would have discussed this with me. I wish you would have waited."

"The time for waiting is past, nìa." Nema unknotted his scarf and wrapped it around his head. "You must attend the conclave."

"Yes, you must." Dathim again stepped up to Nema's side. "Even though you are not talking to me, I am bound to question you on this matter." He had allowed the barest hint of supplication into his voice, which up until then had emerged a most idomeni low-pitched growl. "Will you speak for us?"

Jani sneaked another look at her timepiece. Roni must be awaiting her in the garage's lower level, pacing and muttering to herself. It struck Jani that she might be the searching type, and that if she was, she could burst through one of the doors at any moment. *And wouldn't she get an eyeful.* She had to get Nema and his band out of sight and out of reach. Now. "If I do, will you take nìRau Nema back to the embassy?"

"No. I will not return nìRau Nema." Dathim stood with his hands behind his back and his head cocked to the side. He hadn't learned to match the humanish gestures and postures he had learned with his attitudes—his pose of innocent question warred with the challenge in his voice. "But I will take back ní Tsecha."

Nema watched the interplay with an expression of contentment. "He is most vexing, is he not, nìa?"

"Most." Jani took Nema by the arm and steered him toward the same door through which he had entered, herding the rest of the Haárin ahead of them as she did.

"I assume you came here in one of the embassy vehicles?" An image flashed of eleven idomeni crammed into a sedan, arms and legs jutting through open windows, like teenagers on a spree. "Where did you hide it?" she asked as she pressed her fingertips against her tightening brow.

"In plain sight," Nema replied, "something I have learned during my time in Chicago."

"Define 'plain sight.' "

"On the street next to this one, with some other skimmers." Nema looked at Jani, head tilted in question. "Are you unwell, nìa?"

"I'm just fine, nìRau." *And I'll feel even better when I know you're on your way back to the embassy.* She felt the pressure of the other Haárin's stares. Ná Beyva, she noticed, watched her particularly, her horsetail whipping back and forth as she tried to keep from trodding on the heels of the Haárin ahead of her.

"You are short," she finally said, hesitating in the doorway.

"Most humanish are short compared to Vynshàrau, ná Beyva." Jani raised her right hand in a gesture of submission, an acceptance of fate.

"But as you change, you will grow taller?"

Jani's gesture altered to something less submissive. "I have grown already."

Beyva bared her teeth. "Such is a great thing, ná Kièrshia, and truly!"

Jani watched as Beyva brushed a large smudge of dirt from the front of her shirt. "Did you hurt yourself?"

Beyva looked at her. "Hurt? You did not hurt me, Kièrshia. You only pulled me."

"Not then. Before, when you fell."

"I did not fall, Kièrshia. I heard someone fall, but it was not me!" Beyva bounded down the stairs two at a time, hair flouncing, and disappeared around the bend before Jani could question her further.

"I can no longer step down stairs in such a way." Nema disengaged himself from Jani's grasp and walked out onto the landing. "My poor bones would shatter, and truly." He pulled his coat more tightly about him. "It would not be so sad a thing, to leave this damned cold place."

"I thought you liked Chicago." Jani's voice shook, although she tried to stop it.

"In the summer." He started down the steps. "But this cold makes my bones ache, and gives me strange dreams." He maintained his measured pace, his eyes focused on the downward trek. "Glories of the night to you, nìa." He didn't look back at her. His steady plod echoed within the stairwell as he descended out of sight.

"He is afraid."

Jani spun around, her breath hissing through her teeth as her knee twisted. "What the hell are you still doing here!"

"I want to see what you look for. What makes you fear, as ní Tsecha fears." Dathim leaned against the stairwell doorway in a slump-shouldered pose that would have made Lucien groan in his sleep. "Although his fears are as different, I believe. He fears that Cèel may indeed kill him. Cèel has his own fears. He fears the Oà, who have never ruled over idomeni. But now the Oà grow strong on Shèrá as the Vynshàrau spread themselves throughout the worldskein. He also fears Anais Ulanova, who lies." He pushed off the entry and walked toward her. "But mostly he fears you, because he knows that if he kills Tsecha, you will do to him what you did to the Laumrau."

Jani started down the stairs. "You should catch up with the others, or they will leave you behind." If she had met

Dathim on a colony, she would have admired his rebellious attitude, but this was Earth and his defiance threatened someone she cared for and at this moment she despised him.

"I can find my way back without them. I have walked the night city before." Dathim quickened his step so he edged up beside her. "You have covered your eyes again."

"Yes."

"You are still ashamed."

"Humanish do not like those who look too different. If I am to work in this city, if I am to help you, I must blend in as well as possible."

"That is what ní Tsecha gave as his reasons for living in the embassy, for calling himself Haárin in name only. Work. Blending. Fear of upsetting. All excuses, to deny that which he was." Dathim looked at her. "You do not like these words, ná Kièrshia. And because I speak them, you do not like me." His voice sounded full and strong, as though he enjoyed the prospect.

"You have risked my teacher's life," Jani replied in High Vynshàrau, because she knew Dathim would understand both the words and the formality behind them, and that the decorum would irritate him. *"Such is a concern to me, and truly."* She blew through the stairwell door and down the walkway behind the garage, looking for a skimmer that hadn't been there when she had walked the place before, and not finding one. "Damn it!"

"You wait for your lieutenant?" Exhibitionist though he was, Dathim had sense enough to duck into a shadowed doorway.

"No." Jani walked to the corner and looked around. No agitated Exterior Ministry Documents Chiefs to be seen, unfortunately. *Someone fell and fell hard, and Beyva saw nothing.* She rejoined Dathim, who still stood in the doorway. "I'm worried. The one I wait for is never late, and I don't see her." She eyed the doorways across the street and waited for Roni to stride out of one of them and berate her for being late. And waited. . . .

Someone fell . . .

Jani backed away from the skimmer and rejoined Dathim

on the sidewalk. He had taken a seat on a bench in front of a shuttered shop. Wise move on his part, whether he realized it or not. He looked much less distinctive sitting down.

"You have found nothing?" His voice held the barest hint of uncertainty.

Jani sat down beside him. "Nothing."

Dathim leaned back and crossed his legs. "You will return to your home."

"No." *Someone fell . . . on the second level, damn it!* Jani bounded to her feet. "I need to go into the construction next door."

Dathim made as though to rise. "I will go with you—"

"*No.*" Jani watched a couple walking hand-in-hand down the opposite sidewalk. They looked in her and Dathim's direction, then turned to one another and fell into whispered argument. Jani could fill in the words without hearing them. *Did you see—! Yes, I saw—! Do you think—? No, it can't be. Yes, it can. No, it can't!*

Jani watched them disappear around the corner, still arguing and looking over their shoulders. "You've been spotted. You need to get out of here." She stood. "How will you get back to the embassy?"

"There is a plumber near this place—the embassy purchases from her. She will take me."

"Ask her to make a call for you." Jani scrabbled through her pockets for a stylus and a scrap of paper, and wrote down Niall's code. "She should say, 'Come to the shooting gallery.' "

"Come. To. The. Shooting. Gallery." Dathim nodded after each word. "And this humanish will come?" He studied Niall's code before stashing it in his trouser pocket.

"I hope so." Jani walked to the garage entry and searched the dark corners near the walls. "Ah-ha." She bent and picked up another metal wedge. This one was larger, heavier, like a chock used to brace a wheeled vehicle. She hefted it, trying to gauge its balance. So intent was she on it that she didn't notice Dathim had rejoined her until he took it from her hands.

"What is this?" he asked as he examined it.

Jani reached for the stop, but Dathim held it just beyond her grasp. "Damn it, give it to me!"

"Is it a charm?"

"No. It's a weapon." Jani tried once more to grab it, but Dathim backed away from her.

"This is not a weapon." He wrinkled his nose. "A shooter is a weapon."

"I can't carry a shooter!"

"Why not?"

"Because I'm crazy, now give me back my chock!"

Dathim's hand lowered slowly. "Crazy?"

Jani tapped the side of her head. "Most ill. In the head. If I'm caught carrying a weapon, I will have to live in a hospital until someone decides to let me out."

"House arrest, like ní Tsecha." Dathim looked at the chock again, then reached beneath his coat and unlatched something from his belt. "Here." He pulled out an ax-hammer, and held it out to her handle-first. "This is not a weapon either, so even a crazy humanish can carry it."

Jani hesitated, then gripped the ruthlessly elegant tool. So perfectly balanced was it that it felt weightless, even though it weighed several kilos. She swung it, and watched the hammerhead catch the light. "You carry this everywhere you go?"

Dathim nodded. "As I did during the war, when things that were not weapons were the only weapons to be had." He looked up the quiet street, then down. "May you find she who you are meeting. May there not be blood. If there is, may it not be yours." He trotted across the street, disappearing down an alley just as the curious couple reappeared around the corner, a friend in tow.

Jani backed into the darkness of the garage entry and watched the trio point down the now-deserted street and argue. Then she slipped the ax-hammer through a belt loop and reentered the garage.

CHAPTER 30

A cluster of couples entered the garage as Jani crossed the floor, their laughter as rich as their clothing. They paid her no mind. She looked like staff in her coverall and boots, and their sort never paid attention to staff.

Jani slipped into the stairwell as the cluster stopped before the lift that would take them to the second floor. She ran up the stairs, her knee singing, and hurried along the wall toward the foamfill. She pushed against the foam as the chime from the ascending lift sounded from the adjacent wall. Enough spraylube remained to quench the surface-surface rubbing to a mouse-like squeak. She slipped behind the barrier and pushed it back into place just as she heard the lift doors open and the laughing voices sound.

She turned slowly, giving her eyes time to adjust to the dark. She exhaled through her mouth and watched her breath puff. The cold, half-lit garage was a haven compared to this clammy, dim place.

—goddamned shooting gallery—

Jani crept toward the vast interior. As she approached the entry, she looked up at the tier upon tier of scaffolds strung with safety illumins, like the balconies in a skeletal theater. She looked down at the floor, checking the dust for the ribbon trails that two heels would leave if the body they belonged to had been dragged. She stilled, straining for any sound.

I can stand right here until Niall shows up. Assuming he showed up at all. Even if he did, it wouldn't change whatever had already happened to Roni, and it sure as hell wouldn't prevent what could still happen in the next few minutes.

Jani removed the ax-hammer from her belt and held it against her leg so the safety illumins wouldn't reflect off the metal and highlight her position. Then she stepped out into the dim, trying as best she could to hide behind the tool trolley.

"Jani."

A voice Jani knew. A voice she hadn't expected until she heard it. She wondered if Roni had felt the same. "Is that you, Peter?"

"Step out to the middle of the floor. I can't see you very well."

Jani slipped the ax-hammer behind her back to her left hand and plucked a short length of pipe from the top of the trolley with her right. "I'm coming." She paced carefully, one foot in front of the other, a stride she knew made her look unsteady, tentative. "What are you doing here?"

"I could ask you the same question." Peter Lescaux looked down on her from the second floor scaffold. He rested only his left hand on the rail, which meant he held a shooter in the right. Construction dust lightened his black evening suit to grey.

"I had a surprise encounter with some idomeni." Jani smiled. Odds were good that he had seen Beyva when he subdued Roni and dragged her through the opening, so it would do no good to lie about it. "I've become a tourist attraction, someone they want to meet. I just saw a group of them off."

"I saw you with one of them, looking at skimmers." Lescaux pointed across the space, toward the tarpaulin-covered windows. "Through there. You looked worried, as if you waited for someone and they didn't show." He tugged at his jacket. "That was my problem. I should learn never to believe a lady when she says she'll be right along."

Jani kicked at the floor, raising a cloud of construction dust. "Messy place for an assignation, don't you think?"

"Oh, I've used worse." Lescaux shrugged. "Ani has informers staking out every mattress in the city. Pascal warned me she was the jealous type, but in the interest of career advancement, one does what one must."

Jani felt augie dig his heels into her sides to prod her.

Lescaux was trying to delay her, and augie whispered that she couldn't afford to be delayed. "This is ridiculous, us talking like this. Why don't you come down here?" She started across the floor. "Better yet, why don't I come up there?"

"No!" Lescaux shifted from one foot to the other, still taking care to hide his right hand behind him. "You'll get as dirty as I am."

"What's a little dirt?" Jani tossed the pipe aside so that it banged and rolled across the floor, so that Lescaux would think she was no longer armed. She scrambled up the ladder, taking advantage of the dark at the top to switch the ax-hammer back to her right hand. Her knee didn't hurt at all now.

She legged over the safety rail and onto the scaffold platform. She had only taken a couple of steps when she saw Roni's crumpled body laying near a smaller version of the main floor's massive tool trolley. She could see the back of her head, the drying blood that matted and blackened her hair.

"I told you you'd get dirty." Lescaux withdrew his right arm from behind his back. He indeed held a shooter.

Jani took a step toward Roni. "Is she still alive?"

"Not for much longer." Lescaux raised the shooter to eye-level and sighted down. "I knew it was a mistake to show you that letter. But Derringer was so damned hot to turn you into his agent and grind you under his heel. He laughed about it on the way to pick you up. But I knew. I knew."

Jani shifted her weight and edged another half-step forward. "You know a lot, Peter, I'm sure."

"Stick your flattery up your ass!"

Jani shifted her weight again. A quarter-step, this time. "Lucien visited Guernsey. Lucien visited Anais. Whenever we read the name Le Blond, we thought of him."

"Your mistake." Lescaux grinned. "The one time I didn't mind my predecessor getting the credit." His hand tightened around the shooter, but not enough. If Lucien had stood in his place, he'd have shot her by now. *"Stop."*

Jani halted in mid-step. "Roni must have made the leap, figured out that since you were on colonial assignment, you could have been Le Blond." She hesitated, then made a leap of her own. "Did you plan my parents' kidnapping?"

"Yes. Tried to. Damn that split-lipped bastard anyway." Lescaux's look chilled, but with his weak chin, it just made him look petulant.

Jani glanced at Roni, looking for any movement of the back or shoulder to indicate she breathed. As long as she breathed, however poorly, they had time. If she stopped, they had four minutes.

Roni lay still. So still.

Jani felt the head of the ax-hammer nudge her leg. She had to play this her way. Lescaux held a shooter, yes, but having the better weapon didn't always confer the advantage. Lescaux needed the experience to go with it, and judging from the wild look in his eye, he didn't have it. Niall, yes. Lucien, definitely. *Me . . . yes.* It took a certain brand of nerve to keep killing after the first blow had been struck, and Lescaux had already expended his initial burst on Roni. Now, he'd had time to think of all the complications, feel his mouth go dry as he watched them multiply beyond belief. How would he get rid of Roni's body? Jani's body? How would he clean up the trace evidence and could he do it before the morning construction crew arrived in a few hours and who could he use as an alibi and had anyone seen him enter the garage . . . ?

My way. My speed. My call. Force his hand. Make him act. He was a changeling, not the real thing, and changelings always gave themselves away.

She took another step forward.

"I told you to stop!" Lescaux sighted down again. His hand shook just enough.

Jani brought the ax-hammer around and hurtled forward. The shooter cracked—the pulse packet struck her left side and sent her spinning into the trolley. The edge of the up-ended lid caught her alongside the head. A corner of the case punched her square in her left ribs. She tumbled to the scaffold floor as tool trays flipped into the air, fell across her body, her head. Tools clattered and rolled, tumbling over the side to the main floor two stories below.

Jani lay atop a pile of fasteners and cutter blades. The edges and points razored through her coverall into the skin beneath. Her limbs twitched and her heart skipped beats as the energy from the shot dissipated throughout her body.

Then augie placed his hand over her heart. Her scattered thoughts collected. The pain in her ribs faded. She lay still, still as death. A cold metal tray had fallen across her head and pressed atop the side of her face. The ax-hammer remained looped to her right wrist—she tried to close her fingers around the handle, but they refused to obey. Once more she squeezed. One finger tightened. Another.

The footsteps approached, as Jani knew they would. Stopped at her feet. She lay twisted, her chest facing the floor, her head close to the wall, covered by metal. If Lescaux just wanted to make sure she was dead, he could administer the coup de grace to the heart. If he wanted to eliminate all hope of revival, he would have to shoot her in the head.

If he wants to shoot me in the heart, he'll have to turn me over. If he wants to shoot me in the head, he'll have to move the tray. If Lescaux decided on the heart shot, he'd have to touch her. *He won't. He can't.* She held her breath as he stepped closer to the wall to push away the tray and take the head shot. *Lucien would use a stick to move the tray. He wouldn't risk getting too close.* But Lescaux wasn't Lucien.

Just as Jani felt the pressure of the tray lessen, she pushed up and twisted around, swinging the ax-hammer in an upward arc. The blade end caught Lescaux in the jaw—blood sprayed as he stumbled back.

Jani struggled to her feet. Her ribs squeezed her left side with every breath. Her left leg shuddered, and she stumbled. She tried to raise her left arm for balance, but it seemed glued to her side.

Lescaux raised his shooter once more. Jani thought he smiled, at first, until she saw that her blow had hacked and torn his lower lip and chin so that the skin hung down, revealing his bottom teeth. His jaw looked skewed. Blood spattered his crooked face and soaked the front of his dinner jacket. He stood in front of the railing, placed his free hand on it to steady himself, and sighted.

Jani slipped the strap from her wrist and hurled the ax-hammer. It hit Lescaux high in the chest—his shooter arm jerked up, the momentum curving him backward. He cried out as he tumbled over the railing.

Jani sagged to one knee, then down on her side. The room tilted, spun, darkened around the edges. She could see the ax-hammer from where she lay. It had fallen near the edge of the scaffold, the handle and part of the head coated with Lescaux's blood. What bare metal remained reflected the light from a safety illumin. The shine drew Jani's tunneling stare, fading and flaring as a tremor shook her body and her eyes closed.

She heard. Hearing was the hardiest sense, and she heard. The squeak and flex of the ladder. Footsteps approaching, the scaffold floor shuddering beneath their weight. She tried to get up, to move away. It was Lescaux. Had to be. He had survived the fall and come to kill her—come to make sure—

She opened her eyes when she felt the hands. Gold-skinned and long-fingered, they ran along her body from her head down, probing shooter-burned tissue and dislocated joints and cracked bone with the sure touch of a medic.

Then the probing ceased. The hands disappeared from Jani's view, then returned to pick up the ax-hammer. The last thing she saw before she blacked out were the hands bundling the weapon in a length of patterned brown cloth.

"Look at the light."

Jani raised her grudging gaze. "Didn't we just go through this a couple of days ago?"

Calvin Montoya glared at her over the top of the lightbox. "Humor me."

Jani stared into the blackness that hid the rest of Montoya's body from view. She gripped the edge of the bed as the first red lights flickered, then weaved from side to side as the progression continued.

"Oh, you're tailing quite nicely on your own. No take-down for you." Montoya shut down the lightbox and rolled it to the far side of the examining room. "Although I really wish you would reconsider this takedown-avoidance method of yours. Being attacked twice in three days is a bit much, don't you think?" He wore casual trousers and a pullover instead of eveningwear. A quiet night at home with his girlfriend was all Jani had disrupted this time.

Jani stared down at her stockinged feet, flexing her toes and knocking her heels together. The orderly who had prepped her had confiscated her blood-spattered boots, but had let her keep her socks. He had also made her exchange her bloodstained coverall for a set of bright purple Neoclona work clothes. She looked like a walking bruise, and judging from the stabs and aches that radiated up and down her left side, she'd feel like one in a few hours. *But at least I can sit upright and bitch about the fact.* She glanced up at Montoya, who downloaded data from the lightbox into his recording board. "How's—Roni McGaw?"

Montoya didn't look up. "I don't know."

"So why don't you find out?"

"Because *you* are my concern right now. After I take care of you, I will visit Neuro and find out what I can about Ms. McGaw." Montoya looked up and sighed. "All right?"

Before Jani could respond that, no, it really wasn't all right, the door swept aside and Val blew in like a lake breeze. He wore dark blue trousers and a green and blue patterned sweater and looked like he had been somewhere spreading charm. " 'Lo." He sidestepped over to Montoya and peeked over his shoulder at Jani's chart. "How is she?"

Jani waved at him. "She's sitting right here and can answer for herself, thanks."

Val stuck out his tongue at her, then turned back to Montoya. "So?"

"She brained herself on the edge of that tool trolley. Scan's negative. I closed the gash with glue before anything important leaked out. I'd label that the least of her injuries." Montoya answered Jani's glower with one of his own. "Fractured clavicle—I injected bone sealer and reseated the arm. Minor burns in the same area caused by the shooter pulse. First degree—I applied that new salve the Pharma group developed, and it took the reddening and pain right out. Three cracked ribs, all on the left side. I taped them. We can leave the rest to augie. Had to refill the carrier in her left leg and close up forty-seven assorted hacks and gashes—according to Niall Pierce, she fell on a pile of building fasteners after she was shot."

Jani perked up. "Niall's here?"

"Oh yes." Montoya gazed up at the ceiling, begging respite. "They're lined up waiting to see you. Mainline colonels and attorneys and parents—"

"My folks are here!" Jani slid off the scanbed, but as soon as she tried to stand, the room tilted and wobbled. She grabbed the edge of the bed to keep from falling, swallowing hard as the acid bubbled up her throat.

"Yes! Now sit down before you fall down!" Montoya pushed Jani's chart into Val's hands and hurried to her side. "They're in the VIP suite in the penthouse, receiving the royal treatment." He helped her climb atop the scanbed and held her while she steadied. Only when he felt sure that she wouldn't tumble to the floor did he return to his chart entries.

"We had to flee to the North Bay compound after . . . you know." Val shuffled guiltily to her bedside. "But as soon as we got the call that you had been brought in, we piled into skimmers and made the trek back down, breaking all existing speed limits along the way." He eyed Jani sharply. "We made the assumption that the danger is probably passed at this point."

Jani shrugged, and regretted it immediately. "Probably."

"Good, because I don't think those poor people can take much more of this." Val leaned against the bed. The vivacity vanished—he yawned and rubbed his eyes. "Hell, *I* can't take much more of this." He boosted upright. "We stopped by your flat on the way in, just to check things. Steve and Angevin were there, going not-so-quietly mad. Lively pair, those two." His bleary gaze sharpened. "They told me you threw out Lucien."

Jani examined her hands. An abrasion encircled her right wrist, courtesy of the ax-hammer strap. "I did, but I think I made a mistake."

Val shook his head. "No, you didn't. Not even close."

Jani watched him grow still and dull. "Can you tell me how Roni McGaw is?"

Val looked back at Montoya, who nodded. By the time he turned back to Jani, his shiny air had tarnished completely.

"She was dying when the ambulance brought her in. We had to install a DeVries shunt to halt the brain damage caused by the prolonged reduction in blood flow. Right now she's in induced coma while we try to fix what broke. We won't know how she is until we drain the regen solutions and test functional levels."

Val's every word struck Jani, one blow after another. It never changed—she never changed. She was slow. Stupid. She didn't think. Delays, and more delays. Her past dictating her future, defining it, predicting it. Yolan died because of her slowness. Borgi. The other Rovers. And all she could do to honor their memories was steal them a place on someone else's monument. "I should have gone in there as soon as I felt something was wrong, but I waited too long. *Again.* I wait—"

Val's face flushed. "You stepped in front of a shooter to get her here. If that shot had been a little lower and to the left, you'd be lying in the room next to her and that's only if you'd been damned lucky. So I don't want to hear about how this is all your bloody fault, do you understand!"

Jani looked away from Val and stared at the blank wall until her eyes stopped swimming. "Can I see her?"

Val and Montoya shook their heads and answered as one. "No, your parents want to see you—Niall—calls from Registry—Dolly—John—Loiaza has some questions—"

Jani raised her hand, and the babble ceased. "I want to see her."

Montoya wouldn't let Jani attempt the long walk to the Neuro wing on her own, so Val volunteered to play skimchair navigator. He pushed her slowly, and made a few wrong turns along the way. Jani knew he wanted to tire her out in the hope that she'd change her mind and postpone her visit. One would think that after all they'd been through together, he'd have known better.

As they turned down Neuro's hushed main corridor, Jani eyed the nurses' stations and looked into every open door. "Who's guarding her?"

"Ours." Val looked cowed as Jani twisted around to stare

at him. "They've been briefed by Niall. You don't need to worry about them."

They pulled up in front of a door bracketed by a man and woman wearing street clothes and packed holsters. Jani took a deep breath, then nodded to Val. He edged the skimchair forward, and the door swept aside.

The room was lit with soft background illumination. Silent, but for the soft murmurs of the assorted instruments that surrounded the bed.

Roni McGaw didn't take up much space. Her bedclothes barely seemed to rise above the level of the mattress—Jani had to squint in the half-light to assure herself that a person really lay there.

Then she looked more carefully, and her breath caught. Roni looked mummy-like, her head swaddled in a white wrap that shielded her eyes and left only her nose and mouth visible. Her head and upper body lay slightly elevated on a wedge-shaped pillow. Her hands rested on her stomach. Tubes everywhere—nasogastric, catheter, IV. The apparatus for the DeVries shunt filled the wall behind the bed like a vast and complex headboard, a multicolored array of blinking indicators and scrolling displays.

"That was you last summer." Val pushed Jani close to the bed. "Eamon installed some improvements when he visited last month, as well. The shunt inlet and outlet are fixed inside the pillow assembly. Roni's head is immobilized within a light restraint cage that's attached to the pillow. The last thing we want is for any of that plumbing to shift."

Jani reached up and touched the back of her neck, just above the hairline. She could barely feel the thread-fine scars that marked the sites of her own shunt jacks. "Did you shave her head, too?"

"Yes. We have no choice, what with all the relays and monitors we attach. But hey, your hair grew back. Hers will, too." He grasped one of Jani's curls and gave it a tug. "I'm going to check in with John, give your folks an update. I'll stop back in, say, fifteen minutes?"

Jani nodded. She felt Val's hand on her good shoulder, the increase in pressure as he squeezed. Then it was gone. She heard the muffled tread of his shoes on the lyno, the hush and whisper of the door.

She sat, silent. She'd never possessed the gift for knowing the right words, but what could one say at a time like this? *I'm sorry I missed the cues . . . I'm sorry I lost sight of your back.* How many people over the years did she have reason to say that to? Yolan. Betha. Sasha. You'd think the words would come easily to her—she'd needed them often enough.

"I had the same thing you've got now." Jani paused to clear her throat. "A DeVries shunt. Eamon DeVries is a creep of the first press, but he designed a good shunt." She fingered the crease of her grape-colored trousers, feeling like an inkblot amid the light-colored surroundings. "You'll have a headache after they bring you out of coma. It lasts for a few days—you think your brain is going to burst out your ears every time you move your head. But you get over it." She looked to the wall opposite. No window, not even a nature holograph. It irked her that they would assume Roni wouldn't need any diversions. Jani recalled many details of her own hospital room, things she confirmed after she regained consciousness. She made a mental note to discuss the matter with John.

"Did it catch you by surprise when you realized Lescaux had spearheaded the letter? It did me; I never thought he had it in him. And he didn't, really, he only wished he did. That made him doubly dangerous." She recalled the Lescaux she had seen at the idomeni embassy, his barely suppressed rage when he caught Anais gazing longingly at Lucien. The jealousy had shown itself then—she should have known it would matter. "I'm sorry. I should have realized." She switched her attention from the still figure in the bed to the blinking illumins above, on the alert for any signs of trouble.

"After you get out of this. . . ." She dug a thumbnail into the arm of her chair and waited for her throat to loosen. "If you're going to continue in this line of work, you need to learn a few rules. Laws of survival. They're simple, but they're not always intuitive. One, remember that trust is earned, not bestowed. Two, travel light and travel armed. Three, don't write anything down—sheer hell telling a dexxie something like that, I know, but it's better for you in the long run. We wouldn't have had a thing on Lescaux if that idiot in Helier hadn't written down the details of that meeting. Up until then, all signs pointed to Lucien." Thoughts of Lucien intruded, and she quieted until they went away.

"Back to the commandments. Use public whenever possible. That applies to comports and transportation. Lescaux must have had a snoop on your office line—that's how he knew you were meeting me somewhere tonight. All he had to do was get into his skimmer and follow you. If you'd stuck to the L's and people-movers, you and I could be sitting right now in my flat setting up our case against him and he'd be stuck on a train to Minneapolis wondering what the hell happened." She smiled at the thought, but it faded quickly.

"I'm sorry I didn't get to you sooner. But Nema came out of nowhere and Cèel will execute him if he gets any sort of chance. I had to make sure he got back to the embassy. Then Dathim wouldn't leave me alone." She thought of long-fingered gold hands evaluating her wounds, reclaiming the ax-hammer, and wondered if she had hallucinated them. "But then, if he hadn't given me the ax-hammer, I wouldn't be sitting here jabbering at you now." She relaxed, a little, as the truth of the statement settled over her. "That chock wouldn't have had the same effect, no matter how hard I threw it. And I could only have thrown it once. I would have saved so much time if I had a shooter. This bioemotional restriction is a pain in the ass. They'll probably pin one on you, too, until you show them to their satisfaction that you haven't gone over the side." She slumped in her chair. Her entire body ached.

"You're too nice for this sort of work. You need to be a bit of the bastard. Like Niall. Like me. I'm not saying that you have to . . . stop caring—do that, and you become a monster. I think we both know a few names we could plug into that category." She thought of Lucien again, and paused for a time before speaking. "But caring too much freezes you, hangs you with targets that everyone one else can see. It makes you vulnerable, and you can't afford that. Not in this city. It's a delicate balance. Difficult to achieve. I can't quite seem to get the hang of it myself." Her voice dropped in volume, dwindled to nothing. She felt useless and stupid talking to the air.

"Get well, Roni, please." She fell silent, her eyes on the door, and listened to the soft clicks and hisses of the shunt pumps and the faint hum of the monitors.

CHAPTER 31

"And the worry, Janila. When we could not speak with you. When Dr. Parini told us we had to flee Chicago, but that we could not take you with us." Jamira Kilian broke off a piece of breakfast cake and dipped it in her side dish of maple syrup. "Then we get the call that you had been in a fight, that you had been hurt." She grimaced at the sodden tidbit and set it down on her plate. "Your Dr. Shroud drove us back. The speed! I wondered if we would make it back here alive."

Jani stirred the dregs of her soup. Chickpeas and rice in a tomato sauce spicy enough to make *her* eyes water—not her usual morning fare, but someone must have thought she needed an olfactory kick in the pants. "He's not *my* Dr. Shroud, Maman."

"Hmph." Declan Kilian eyed her over the rim of his coffee cup. "Remember that white tiger they kept at the park preserve when you were little? The one that spent all his time pacing the grounds and standing on the highest points, watching everyone? The one where you felt better knowing that a very wide moat separated the two of you? Shroud reminded me of him. I would not like to be the person who makes him angry."

Jani pushed her bowl aside, then tried to appreciate the view as she avoided her parents' probing looks. They sat in the dining room of the Neoclona VIP suite, seventy-five stories above Chicago. Tinted windows formed the exterior walls, allowing well-filtered views of the sunrise over Lake Michigan, the Commerce Ministry compound, and the sky-scraper jungle of the deepest downtown. *Tiger John's stalk-*

ing grounds. She looked at her mother. "I thought you didn't like him."

"I do not. Not really. He did not think things through where you were concerned. Now he spends all his time trying to play catch-up, and it is you who pay the price." Jamira held out her hand, her eyes shining. "*Ma petite fille,* it was not you that I yelled at that night."

Jani brushed her fingers with her own. "I know, Maman."

Jamira chuffed and fussed with the napkin on her lap. "No, you don't know. But you won't talk about it, either, so we are left where we were." She exhaled with a frustrated gust. "I want you to be happy, and healthy, and live without pain. Ridiculous things for a mother to ask for her child, I know." She sat back, a cup of jasmine tea cradled in her hands. "Two things I can say in Dr. Shroud's favor. He never left us alone, even when we wanted him to. He made sure we were safe. And he worried about you so—I could tell." She inhaled the fragrant steam that rose from her cup. "And as your father said, better a man like him as a friend than as an enemy. In this day, the way things are, it is good to have friends."

Jani pushed back her chair and walked to the window. The grandness of the dining room made her restless. So had the plush gold and white bedroom where she had spent what little had remained of the night, and the eerie way that the staff seemed to know what she wanted before she asked for it. *I was not born to the purple, royalty's or Neoclona's.* She longed for her flat, her piled desk. Her own bedroom. *I must be feeling better.* She could already raise her left arm level with her shoulder, and scarcely felt any twinges in her ribs when she breathed. *All the little factories must be running full-tilt.*

"What are we doing today, Janila?" Her mother had adjourned to a couch by the lake-facing window, tea and the day's *Tribune-Times* in hand. "Dr. Parini made lists for me of things to do in Chicago—sheets and sheets. Parks and museums and shops. If I stay here until I am one hundred, I will not be able to do all he suggested."

Declan joined his wife, plucking pages from the newssheet after she finished perusing them. "The Commerce

Ministry is giving a party next week in honor of the Commonwealth Cup Final Four. Dr. Shroud said that we are all invited." His eyes lit in anticipation. "All of the United will be there. Desjarlais, even. And Heinrich and Zaentz, from Gruppo."

Jani perched on the far end of the couch. Replace the posh surroundings with a crowded eating area that vied for space with the overflow from her father's workroom and her mother's collection of glass figurines, and it was a replay of her childhood mornings—breakfast, newssheets, plans for the day.

I have plans for the day. The Elyan Haárin had arrived with the dawn, and she had already received a formal request from Cal Burkett to attend the afternoon's conclave. After that, she received an identical invitation from the Commerce Ministry. Then one from the Treasury Ministry. No word from Nema, however. Not that she expected Shai to allow him to contact her.

Jani picked at her sleeves. She still wore the purple outfit the orderly had scrounged for her the night before. John had, of course, offered her access to every shop in Chicago, but she planned to use the need to change clothes as an excuse to return to her flat. She had not yet decided whether to attend the conclave. Even thinking about the need to think about it made her nervous. But when she made the decision, it would be on her own turf, and in her own good time. And in the meantime, she had time. *Free* time, the first she'd had in weeks.

"Hand me the Government page, please." She took the newssheet section from her father, then walked back to the table to get another cup of coffee.

Jani left her parents a few hours later with the pledge to return that night. She departed Neoclona with every intention of making the northward trek via her usual system of L's and people-movers. It didn't disappoint her, however, to find Niall waiting for her in the building entry circle, wearing dress blue-greys and a smug expression.

"I'm your new best friend, by special request of General Burkett." He led her to a dark blue Service-issue two-door, popped the gullwing for her, and shut her in, his eyes on the teeming morning traffic.

Unlike the sleek Lucien, Niall *looked* like a walking sidearm. Jani waited for him to close himself in and merge into traffic before speaking. He had a job to do, and her new job was to let him do it. "Who else is out there?" she asked, after a slight easing in Niall's level of alert let her know it was OK to talk.

"Five vehicles behind, five ahead, and checkpoints all along the way." Niall grinned. "Nowhere near the level of the PM. More a Deputy Minister."

"You trying to tell me my days of hopping the L are over?"

"You got it." He reached into his tunic and pulled out his nicstick case. "Burkett wants you to have it. Burkett called in all kinds of markers to get it. Pledged a few, too, from what I heard. That attack last night sure lit a fire under his brass." As if to illustrate his point, Niall shook out a 'stick and bit the bulb end. The tip flared orange; the smoke streamed.

Jani recalled Derringer's last message, his sleep-starved face. "When did you talk to Burkett?"

Niall nodded through the haze. "At about 0300. He looked pissed as hell. Not that he doesn't always look like that, but this held a special edge."

"You talk to him in person?"

"Yeah."

"Derringer with him?"

"Nah. Didn't see him."

Jani smiled. *Looks like your career plans hit a snag, Eugene.* She wondered how long it would be before he turned up again at the embassy, if ever.

Then the thought occurred that Derringer could face something more drastic than mere reassignment. *Lie down with dogs, get up with fleas.* That didn't bother her, either. She settled back in her seat and watched the city float past. "Montoya mentioned that you had been at the hospital. I looked for you later, but I couldn't find you."

"I rode point for your ambulance. Then I spent the rest of the night running from pillar to post trying to find out what the hell happened." Niall looked at her. "Care to compare notes?"

"Who else was at the scene?"

"No, none of this answering questions with questions. I've watched you tie other people in knots doing that, and I'm not going to let you do it with me." Niall blew smoke as he turned onto Armour Place a little more sharply than necessary. "I was on the way back from North Bay when I got your message."

Jani smiled at him. "You helped move my folks. Thanks."

"You're welcome and don't change the subject." Niall slowed to a stop in front of her building. "I wonder how long it's going to take these people to realize that you're the reason their nice, quiet neighborhood has hosted three attempted murders and one accidental death in the last three days."

"Lescaux wasn't an accident."

"Well, rumor has it." Niall tossed another, colder grin at her as he waved the doorman away and popped his own door. "I say we let rumor keep it."

Steve and Angevin reacted predictably to Jani's return, giving loud and persistent voice to the fact that while they were thrilled that she lived, they'd kill her themselves if she ever put them through "hell like this" again.

"Calls. Let's talk about calls." Angevin fell onto the couch next to Jani, recording board in hand. "*Trib-Times,* chief Cabinet correspondent. PM's office. Commerce office. Treasury. AgMin. Hodge, begging our pardon but asking if you were all right."

Jani looked across the room at Steve, who sat next to Niall on the window seat and smoked. "What did you tell him?"

"We lied. Said you were fine. Like we knew what the fook were goin' on." Steve punctuated his displeasure with a smoke ring.

"General Burkett," Angevin continued the litany of calls. "Frances Hals. Aunt Dolly."

Jani waggled her eyebrows. "*Aunt* Dolly?"

"Swank," Steve muttered.

"And the list repeats." Angevin dropped the recording

board on the seat and slumped dramatically. "There are a lot of deputy ministers mixed in here too, all asking whether you'll be attending the conclave at the embassy this afternoon."

"Can't be bothered with the names of mere deputies—just too fookin' many to count." Steve walked to the couch, planting himself in front of Jani. "Gel, I'm enraptured that you're all right, but I can't live like this. It's aging me prematurely."

Jani turned to Angevin. "I'm sorry. Really."

Angevin shrugged. "We lived. Kept busy. Your projects are caught up—I've learned a whole lot about many subjects of which I knew nothing two days ago." She yawned. "And a few of your clients asked that their stuff be put on hold until after the conclave. That saved us some grief." She blinked. Yawned again. Her eyes watered. "So, are you going to the conclave?"

Jani looked down at her clothes. The brilliant purple held a magenta cast in the morning light. She hated magenta.

"I need to get out of these clothes. I'll be back." She had darted into her room and locked the door behind her before anyone had a chance to stop her.

She perched on the windowsill overlooking the alley and watched the occasional lunchtime trespassers cut through on their way back to work. She wanted to stop them, ask them questions. About their lives. Their thoughts.

Did anyone ever hate you enough to try to kill you? Did anyone ever think you dangerous enough to kill? Did you wonder how the hell you got in that position in the first place? Was it something you did, or was it simply the fact that you were*?*

She tried to transmit her questions to a young woman who scurried down the alley, a sheaf of papers flapping in her hand.

Have you ever killed anyone? Did you ever put a friend in the hospital because of a mistake you made? Did a friend ever die because of a mistake you made?

She pulled her right knee up to her chin. It didn't hurt much now, and last night she could barely walk on it.

If someone asked you to be the point man for a new world

*order, would you say yes? If you knew saying yes would sep-
arate you from work you enjoyed, people you loved, would
you agree?*

*If you knew that saying yes meant never being able to call
yourself human again, would you still think it a good idea?*

She rolled her left shoulder, and felt the mildest of
twinges. *Four hours to go.* She shifted position so she
couldn't see the clock atop the armoire.

She tried to ignore the knock at her door. Neither Steve nor
Angevin were the most patient of souls—they'd give up and
leave, eventually.

But this knock went on, and on, and on.

"Wait a minute!" Jani struggled to her feet, shaking the
life back into her right leg as she limped to the door and deactivated the lock. "I just wanted a little bit of downtime—is
that too much to ask—?" Her complaint fizzled when she
found Niall standing in the hall, hand clenched in the mail
fist salute of someone who would knock as long as he had to.

"We the hapless bystanders wondered if you planned to
come out sometime this year." He lowered his arm and took
a step back, his manner suddenly tentative.

Jani stepped aside. When Niall still held back, she
grabbed his sleeve and pulled him into her room. "This isn't
the sanctum sanctorum—come on in."

"I didn't say it was." He hurried toward the window,
shooting his cuffs along the way. "You're going to need to
move to a higher floor—this won't do."

"It's cheap."

"And for good reason." Niall fiddled with the privacy setting on the windowside touchpad; the glass darkened to
black. "I'll talk to the building manager—what's his name—
Hodge—and find out what else is available. If I don't like
anything here, be prepared to move." He turned to her, the
hard-edged Spec Service officer once more. "Is this something I should plan to do this afternoon, or will you need me
to drive you someplace?"

"Is this your way of asking me if I'm going to the conclave?" Jani crossed one foot over the other and lowered to
the floor. "I've still got two hours to make up my mind."

"One, if you take preliminaries into account." Niall wandered over and sat on the floor across from her. Like John, he didn't relax well—he braced straight-backed against the bedframe, and even though he tugged at his tunic's banded collar, he made no move to loosen it. "So?"

Jani had no trouble defining the question contained in that single word. "I'm not political. I'm not the least bit skilled in that area."

Niall shrugged. "So much the better. Politicians got us into this mess in the first place."

"No. Greed got us into this mess. For money, power, career advancement. Simple, dull, boring greed." Jani tried to pull both knees to her chest, but her cracked ribs objected, forcing her to sit with her left leg straight in front of her. "And say what you will, but we are going to need politically skilled people to get us out of this mess. The ability to deal is necessary. To compromise. To not take everything personally. I don't possess that mind-set, and it's not something I can learn. I could butcher these negotiations and set back human-idomeni relations twenty years."

Niall rested his head against the footboard. His scar skewed his quizzical frown into a scowl. "What do you think should happen?"

Jani groaned. Her head had started to ache. "I think we should purchase the microbial filter from the Elyan Haárin until we can build a new Karistos treatment plant. We need to set up a timetable for the construction, and stick to it so that the unaligned Elyan merchants see that we mean it when we say that we won't tolerate any bullshit. Any businesses affiliated with *L'araignée* shouldn't be allowed to bid for the job, but I doubt that will happen. So, if any of them win, they'll need to be watched."

Niall nodded. "Accounts to be paid on a milestone basis. Have their work inspected every step of the way." He paused. His hand went to his tunic collar, as though it felt tighter.

Jani grinned humorlessly at his discomfort. "Yep. They'll scream, and the Elyan government will scream, and the Elyan Haárin will scream. We're probably going to have to drag the Service in to act as a silent threat, so someone from

Intelligence will scream that we're blowing their deals with *L'araignée*. It will be a mess however it's handled, but the important thing is that we're left with a working water treatment plant. Once the Elyans have one thing that works, they're going to want more things that work. If they know they'll have the government watching their back as they obtain those things, they can begin to rebuild their broken system. Something like *L'araignée* needs to be excised one tendril at a time. You do that by making their method of doing business uneconomical, and vigilance backed by a strong Service threat equals uneconomical. That's my solution, and if you think it will be as easy as I make it sound, your collar really is too tight."

Niall pulled his hand away from his neck, his face reddening. "I think what you've said sounds quite reasonable."

"Once I proposed it in open session, I'd give it five minutes before Ulanova's team tears it to shreds." Jani straightened her right leg and lay back. Everything hurt now—her shoulder, her ribs, her back. "Does what I want to do have any bearing on this? Does the fact that I do not want to spend the rest of my life grappling with the Anais Ulanovas of the Commonwealth come into play at all?"

"How often does what you want have anything to do with anything?" Niall regarded her with an odd admixture of impatience and kindness. "You and I came up from the same place. A hardscrabble colony youth leaves wounds that never heal." His honey eyes darkened. "One thing you learn is that what you *want* to do doesn't always matter. It's what you *can* do. What you have to do. What you must do."

"Duty?" Jani cocked an eyebrow. "I was never the best soldier in the Service, Niall, or didn't you notice?"

"Obedience isn't your strong suit, no." Niall's lip twitched, but the smile soon faded. "But I will say without reservation that you're one of the most dutiful people I've ever known." He fixed his gaze on the opposite wall. "I'd follow you into hell, because I know you'd bring me out, or stay behind and burn with me. What you'd never do is leave me behind to burn by myself. That's not a bad quality for a future Chief Propitiator to have, I should think." He boosted to his feet. "I can't tell you what to do. I wouldn't try—not with a decision like this. But I've never seen you give less than everything, no matter who you angered, and regardless of the cost to you. That has to count for something, even in this lousy city." He nodded sharply to her, his manner turned formal, distant, as though he felt he'd revealed too much and needed to shut down fast. "I'll be in the other room."

Jani listened to the door close, the fading echo of Niall's footsteps. "Dutiful." She stared at the ceiling. "I don't want to be dutiful. I want to be left alone." The armoire clock chimed the half-hour. "They'd eat me alive, Niall. I'm not political. I'm . . . what I am." Derringer's "meddling bitch." Frances's "lone operator."

She sat up by rolling onto her right side and pushing herself to her knees. Then she went to her closet and hunted down the lightest-color suit she owned, a tan tunic and trouser combination. She tossed it on the bed, then retired to the bathroom to shower. Her left side had indeed turned into a relief map of bruises and gashes. She stood sideways in the water stream, and counted down the minutes.

Dutiful. The suit fit her, even though she had bought it months before. Shoes had become as big a problem as clothes, since her feet had grown longer and narrower, but she managed to uncover a pair of brown boots that didn't feel too tight.

She studied herself in the mirror as she arranged her hair. The suit, spare and utilitarian, looked like a uniform of sorts. It lacked medals and badges because she hadn't yet earned any in this particular war, and it lacked rank designators because thus far, she didn't need any. *I belong to an army of one.* She laughed at her own pomposity; the sound died as she continued to stare in the mirror, and thought of sheared heads and horsetails, and gold hands closing around the handle of an ax-hammer.

Not alone. Not really. Not anymore. Others followed her, which meant she needed to lead.

She peeled off the eyefilms one at a time, then returned to the bathroom to wash them down the sink. As she walked back into the bedroom, she watched herself in the mirror to observe the effect.

Her eyes caught the light in strange ways, shades of green

from forest to lightest sea. *They're not . . . beautiful.* But they defined her somehow, as her filmed eyes never did. Not human anymore, but not idomeni, either. *In-between.* She tried to see what Lucien saw, even though she knew that she never would. *Not beautiful.* But what she was, now. Point man.

She headed for the door, then stopped and detoured to her closet. Given the state of her ribs, stretching proved impossible—she had to drag the clothes cleaner into the space to serve as a stepstool so she could reach the back of the shelf.

She slid on the redstone ring, then wrapped the soulcloth round her wrist. The single knot stayed tied and the ends remained tucked. She took that as a favorable omen.

The armoire clock chimed the hour as Jani walked out into the main room. Steve and Niall stood by the window smoking and talking while Angevin sat on the couch and leafed through a magazine.

Angevin saw her first—she tossed the magazine aside and bounded to her feet. "Hey, there she—!" She stopped. Stared. Squinted. Then she emitted a tiny yelp and slapped her hand over her mouth.

Steve and Niall had fallen silent. Steve took one step closer, then another. "Bloody hell, Jan." He stuck his half-spent 'stick in his mouth, and worked it from side to side.

Niall extinguished his own 'stick and brushed off his tunic. Then he stepped around Steve and walked to Jani's side. "Are you sure?"

Jani tried to smile, then shook her head. "No. But I doubt if I ever will be." She walked to the desk and gathered up her duffel. "Let's go."

CHAPTER 32

The ride down to the lobby proceeded without incident, if only because they didn't encounter anyone. The traverse of the lobby itself drew no notice until Hodge negotiated an intercept route from the front desk, meeting them just before they reached the entry.

"Mistress Kilian, I'm so glad to find—" Trained in the art of ignoring Family foibles, he cropped his start before it turned into a stare and barely missed a beat. "—that you are all right." He took a step closer, and dropped his voice. "I'm so sorry about that young lady. So lucky that you found her before that awful young man—" His lips pressed in a thin white line as he dealt with yet another blow to his gentle neighborhood. "Well. As I said. So glad. Mistress. Sir." He nodded, then returned to the refuge of his desk.

"Mistress? What year is this, anyway?" Niall waved off the doorman who stood beside the skimmer they had arrived in. At the same time, another sedan, a dark green four-door, lumbered curbside. The gullwing popped up and Lieutenant Pullman emerged, wearing dress blue-greys and an anxious smile.

"Check that one over"—Niall pointed to the dark blue two-door—"then rotate it out."

"Sir." Pullman saluted, then turned to Jani. "Ma'am, I hope"—his eyes widened, but he clamped down as quickly as Hodge—"hope that you and your folks are OK."

"Yes, we are." Jani lifted her chin and smiled broadly. The idea of an idomeni teeth-baring crossed her mind, but she liked Pull. Better to save that surprise for someone she didn't. "Thanks."

"My job. Ma'am." Pullman led her around to the passenger side and closed her in.

"A different skimmer for every trip?" Jani watched Pullman recede in her side mirror. "What did you do, requisition the entire Sheridan vehicle pool?"

Niall shrugged. "Just standard precautions."

"You're enjoying this, aren't you?"

"Frankly? No." He expression sombered. "The courtly Mr. Hodge isn't the only one disgusted by the actions of his fellow man."

"He seemed to have a good idea of what happened. What are they saying? I checked the *Trib-Times* from cover to cover. Couldn't find a thing."

"I hit the garage just as the clean-up was winding down. Family security everywhere, tidying up for the ComPol. The official story is that you stumbled upon Lescaux attacking Roni, and were injured trying to intervene. Lescaux fell to his death trying to get away." Niall steered onto the Boul access road that skirted the idomeni property. "I'm guessing that's close enough to what actually happened to pass ComPol muster?"

"I haven't talked to them yet. With Joaquin Loiaza around, I may never."

"I met him once, you know. He was van Reuter's attorney. Sold him out but good."

"Niall, that doesn't make me feel better."

"Oh, you've got nothing to worry about. You're the sort of client he likes—on your way *up* the food chain." Niall slowed through the first unstaffed idomeni checkpoint. "So, feel any different?"

Jani's stomach clenched as they passed beneath the silvery arch. "Except for assorted hospital stays, this is the longest I've ever gone without filming since Rauta Shèràa." She widened her eyes, closed them, then opened them. "I got used to them always feeling a little tight, and now that feeling's gone." She looked out her window and watched the landscape drift past. Blue-tinged grasses. Stunted yellow and green-leafed shrubs. "It's strange."

Niall slowed the skimmer. "If you want to go back—"

"*No.*" Jani held an image in her mind now, of a shorn

head and a look of quiet acceptance. *It occurred to me that when the gods informed me of the future, they did not also guarantee my presence in it.* "I owe someone this."

"What?" Niall looked alarmed. "Are you sure you don't—"

"I'm sure." Jani watched the first of the staffed checkpoints appeared in the distance. "I'm sure."

Vehicles filled the stone-paved courtyard. Jani recognized Callum Burkett's steel blue triple-length, along with the color-coded entries belonging to the various Ministries: green for Commerce, gold for Treasury, black for Interior. She recognized Anais Ulanova's triple-length, as well, its burgundy color damped by a spray-on filter to the color of coffee beans.

Niall steered them to an opening beside Burkett's vehicle, lowered the power to standby, and waited. "You've gone quiet," he said after a time.

Jani leaned back her head so she could check her eyes in the side mirror. "Be honest—what do I look like?"

Niall fingered the steering wheel. His mien altered from professional vigilance to the sort of introspection he saved for his off-hours. "I met a lady in the meads, full beautiful, a faery's child. Her hair was long, her foot was light, and her eyes were wild." He smiled softly. "Keats. *La belle dame sans merci.*"

"The beautiful woman without mercy." Kind of Niall to say. Not that Jani believed it. She tugged at one of her curls. "Not long. Rather short, in fact."

"Ah, well. So much for that." Niall popped his gullwing and exited the skimmer.

"So my eyes look wild, huh?" Jani asked as she followed suit. "That should go over big." She hoisted her duffel to her right shoulder and watched the faces that turned toward her, bracing for the reactions. The courtyard air was still and cool. She shivered, and blamed the temperature.

"Kilian!" Callum Burkett broke away from a Minister-cluster and crossed the courtyard toward her. Dressed in desertweights, his expression grim, he resembled Derringer enough to have fathered him. "We should talk before this thing sta—" He froze in mid-stride, his front foot in the air, looking as though he'd caught himself before he stepped in something embarrassing. Then the foot lowered. So did his voice. "Is this some kind of joke?"

"Not by any means, General." Jani felt the heat flood her cheeks. "This is what I really look like." She glanced past him in time to see more heads turn in their direction.

Burkett directed his stone-grey glare at Niall. "Did you know about this, Colonel?"

"Do you mean, sir, have I noticed that Ms. Kilian's eyes look different?" Niall regarded Jani with a look of studious examination, the duck-and-dodge in full force. "Yes, sir. Rather striking, I think—"

"I mean, did you help plan—"

"No! He did not. He did, in fact, ask me several times if I wished to reconsider." Jani wedged herself between Niall and an Article 13. "My eyes. My call. I have my reasons, which will reveal themselves presently."

Burkett's face reddened. His arms hung at his sides, hands slowly clenching.

Oh, Cal, you hate surprises, I know, and you've had a couple of zingers over the past few days, haven't you? Jani made a show of scanning the crowd. "Where's Eugene? I don't see him."

Burkett's eyes narrowed. "He's . . . been reassigned."

Jani nodded. "Thank you for the security."

"You're . . . welcome. I trust you're . . . all right?"

"Yes. Thanks. You're going to take care of my bioemotional restriction, aren't you?"

A pause. "Yes."

"I know what I'm doing."

"I hope so." Burkett dropped his gaze, then tensed. "That's a soulcloth."

Jani followed the angle of his stare and pulled down the red braid, which had been half-hidden by her tunic cuff. "Yes."

Burkett started to speak. Stopped. He looked at Jani, his expression altered to hangdog uncertainty. "Well." He nodded to her, then turned on his heel and clipped toward a concerned-looking major who had emerged from one of the groups.

"Poor Cal. Every time he thinks he's got you sussed, you

throw him another curve." Niall veered close. "Do you know what you're doing?"

Jani nodded. "The idomeni have an idea what I look like. So do most of the people I work with. It's . . . time."

"Well, I'll be out here with the rest of the chauffeurs if you need me." Niall tried to look encouraging, but he could only manage tense. He scanned the assorted faces one last time, then moved off to the far side of the yard.

Jani caught sight of the brown-clad diplomatic suborn emerging through the beaten bronze door, and made her way to the center of the courtyard to take her place in the rank line. As she walked, she grew conscious of an invisible barrier growing around her, formed from unease and the pressure of scrutiny. She would have expected it even if she hadn't chosen to reveal herself—word of Lescaux's death had had almost a day to percolate through the Ministries; the true story that the Family security officers had pieced together had no doubt whipped around, as well.

She heard a few gasps, followed by low muttering, as she took her place. Some stared openly, others, furtively. *Look at it this way—it could be worse.* For example, she'd yet to negotiate a Chicago city street.

Jani realized that the voices behind her had receded to nothing. She turned, and found herself looking into Anais Ulanova's red-rimmed eyes.

The woman wore black. No jewelry. She seemed oblivious to the change in Jani's appearance—the emotion in her pained brown stare originated in a deep place, slicing past the physical into Jani's own inner dwelling. For an uncounted time, no one moved. No one breathed.

Then the suborn broke the silence with her call. *"Time!"* People hurried to their places in line, jostling and muttering.

Jani turned to face front as the bronze doors swung wide, conscious with every forward step she took of the danger bearing down from behind.

They trooped the halls in single-file, like prep schoolers returning from recess. Jani looked down each bare-walled hallway they passed, through each open door, on the watch for the faces from the night before. Beyva's. Dathim's.

Nema's.

Her anxiety ramped as they entered the meeting room. Under normal conditions, Nema would have met the delegations by now, moving down the line shaking hands and commenting loudly about the weather.

But conditions aren't normal, are they? Jani wended through the banked rows toward her usual place behind Burkett, then remained standing as those of higher rank filed in.

Burkett fractured a few minor rules of protocol by dodging around assorted deputies to reach his seat ahead of them. His eyes still had that slitted look, which meant a headache had settled in for the duration. A thin film of sweat coated his brow, as well.

Jani touched her own forehead. *Still dry.* She felt quite comfortable now that she thought about it, which meant that the Vynshàrau had cranked up the temperature to the upper limit of humanish comfort.

"Someday we're going to have one of these get-togethers in my neck of the woods and so help me God, it will be payback time." Burkett tugged at his trousers as he sat.

Jani took her seat. This allowed her an unrestricted view of the back of Burkett's tan shirt, through which the first faint splotches of sweat had bloomed. "Lieutenant Ischi once suggested the Arctic test facility."

Burkett's stiff posture unwound ever so slightly. "The ATF?" A ghost of a smile had crossed his face by the time he turned to face front.

Most of the humanish had settled into their seats when the doors opened again and the lower-ranked born-sect idomeni filed in. Clothed in shades of sand and dun, hair bound in napeknots or arranged in fringed braids, earrings flashing in the chandelier light. Documents and communications suborns, charged with recording the minutes. Shai's clerks and researchers. Dominants from various departments. Religious Suborn Sànalàn, looking worn and subdued.

Then came a blue-clothed figure, like a fault in a pale stone. The lowest-ranking of the Elyan Haárin. Female, her waist-length light brown hair bound in a single braid. Then came a male, clad in orange and yellow, brown hair sheared so closely that the room light flashed off golden patches of exposed scalp. They seated themselves on the highseats at the far end of the V-shaped table and busied themselves pulling documents from the briefbags they wore slung across their shoulders.

Another shear-headed male followed. He wore black trousers and shirt, topped with a leopard-print jacket cut like a humanish male's daysuit coat. Around his neck, he had knotted a long strip of orange cloth that was without question the Elyan Haárin version of a humanish neckpiece. He carried his briefbag using a handstrap. Jani harbored the sense that he didn't want to rumple his jacket.

Burkett twisted around in his seat. "Did you know about this?"

Jani shook her head. "It doesn't surprise me, though."

"That makes one of us." He pressed his fingers to his temple as he turned back to the entry procession.

Two more Haárin had entered—a male and a female. The male wore more traditional garb, a pale green shirt and trousers topped with an overrobe the color of dried grass. He wore his brown hair in an odd hybrid style, a humanish pageboy that he had braided into a skull-defining cap. The female, the group's dominant, leaned toward a taut humanish look—grey tunic and trousers, her grey-streaked brown hair bound in a loose horsetail. She and the male took their seats on the same arm of the V, and leafed through files that had been laid out for them by their three suborns.

The room's atmosphere had altered with the successive appearance of each Haárin. Jani likened it to walking out on a sheet of ice and feeling that subtle shift beneath one's feet, hearing the faintest of squeals as the first cracks formed and radiated, then tensing for whatever came next.

After the Haárin dominant seated herself, the first wave of Vynshàrau diplomats entered. Speaker to Colonies Daès and his suborn, followed by Suborn Oligarch Shai's suborn, and finally, Shai herself. With them came the return to sartorial sanity, born-sect-style, sands and off-whites and hair arranged in fringed braids.

Anais Ulanova then entered, partnered with a young

woman who had the look of the hurriedly briefed about her.
Prime Minister Li Cao's chief aide, followed by the PM herself. Arrangements at table, murmured greetings in High
Vynshàrau and English, the scrape of seats. Only one seat
remained empty at the table now, the lowest seat at the head
of the V.

Jani looked to the door, and prayed. To Ganesha. To
whichever god cared to listen. She wondered if she could
dash to the door before Burkett could stop her, mount a
search through the winding halls of the embassy until she
found whom she sought. Until she made sure Nema still
lived.

Then Sànalàn rose, crossed her right arm over her chest
until she grasped her shoulder, and spoke, flowing syllables
uttered in a high keen. The official opening of the conclave,
a prayer to Shiou to instill order, that had once been Nema's
duty to perform.

Jani watched the figures seated at the table. All sat with
their heads high, their eyes closed, the standard idomeni position of invocation. Not a word had they said about Nema's absence. *How humanish of them.* Yet somehow, the determined
ignorance of the situation imbued the empty chair at the head
of the table with a strange power, like the gap in a demiskimmer formation left to commemorate a missing pilot.

Anais broke this particular formation only once, looking
out toward the crowd until she saw Jani. The cold light of triumph shimmered in her eyes as she turned back to the table.

It took some time for the sound to cut through Sànalàn's
pitched voice. By the time Jani heard it, she had the impression it had gone on for some time. The muffled sounds of argument, audible through the panel. Faces turned toward the
door.

Then the panel flew aside and Nema swept in, a guard at
his heels. Jani didn't recognize him at first—his sheared
head looked even more startling in the bright light of the
room. He wore his off-white shirt and trousers, his red-
cuffed overrobe and rings. His earrings glittered in garish array, fully exposed as they now were to the light. He looked
traditional in every way, but for the hair.

He scanned the rows of banked seats. Jani knew he searched for her—she raised a hand to gain his attention.

"Nìa." Nema's face seemed to split as he bared his teeth. "You are most well, in spite of your battle!"

"Inshah." Jani was dimly aware of Burkett leaning forward to cradle his head in his hands. "Yes, I am well."

"I had heard you had been *shot*."

"Grazed, inshah." Jani felt the tension suffuse the air around her. She watched Ulanova at the table, her face averted, her back straight.

"Grazed." Nema seemed to ponder the word. "My Anais's Lescaux tried to kill you."

"*Tsecha.*" Shai's shoulders rounded in threat. "You have been removed from these proceedings. You have received warnings to not interfere. You have disobeyed."

"You removed Égri nìRau Tsecha from the proceedings, Shai. The ambassador of the Shèrá worldskein. I am not here as such." He ignored the guard who stood at his shoulder, which seemed a safe thing to do—her reluctance to lay hands upon her Chief Propitiator was evident in her posture. Instead, he directed his attention toward the Elyan Haárin dominant. "I come here as Tsecha Égri, dominant of the Earth Haárin, sect-sharer with the Elyan Haárin. It is they I ask for the privilege to sit at this table. It is their right to extend or deny."

The Elyan Haárin dominant looked at her suborn, who responded with a truncated hand flip that Jani couldn't interpret. Then they leaned close to one another and took turns speaking in each other's ears, a profoundly humanish conduct that caused Shai to round her shoulders even more and set the human half of the room abuzz.

"Ná Feyó?" Shai barked after the conversation had gone on for some time. "Do you agree to ní Tsecha's request?" Her tone implied that any agreement would be looked on with disfavor. Murmurs filled the air again when the assembled realized that she had called Tsecha by his true Haárin title, not the dressed-up "Rau" version.

Feyó lifted her head. "I do with gratitude, and truly, nìa-Rauta." Her English rang mellow and slightly drawled. She reminded Jani of Dolly Aryton at her most formal, and like the Hands of Might, she radiated calm. "He should sit next to me." She indicated the space between her and her suborn.

The assembled grew restive as a guard was dispatched to find a chair of the proper height. Burkett took the opportunity to lean back. "What the hell is going on, Kilian?"

Jani grinned down at him. "I think it's the new order asserting itself, General."

"*New* order? I haven't gotten used to the old one yet." He dug into the briefbag that the major had handed off to him during the seating, and pulled out a recording board to take notes.

Nema, meanwhile, walked to his seat beside Feyó, letting his hand trail along the back of his former seat at the point of the V. "I have right of suborn, ná Feyó?" he asked as he sat.

"Yes, nìR—" Feyó stopped herself. The new order had apparently caught her by surprise, as well. "Yes, ní Tsecha."

"Nìa?" Nema held out his hand toward Jani. "Come."

Jani hesitated as every face in the room, humanish and idomeni, turned toward her. Then she rose and stepped out onto the floor. Nema bared his teeth when he spotted the ring; the look sombered when he caught sight of the braided soulcloth. "So the soldier has at last reclaimed her soul." He took her hand and squeezed it in most humanish reassurance.

Jani's aches had receded in the background, supplanted by a soft roaring that filled her head. *Welcome to the way it is.* She took her place at the meeting table, in a hastily acquired highseat next to Feyó's suborn. She looked across the V, and found herself the focus of distressed examination by PM Cao and her aide. Jani bared her teeth wide, which only seemed to alarm them more.

The blue-clad Elyan Haárin clerk set a folder before Nema, then walked downtable and handed one to Jani. Their eyes met. The Haárin's widened. Then she bared her teeth. "*Hah! Ná Kièrshia!* I rejoice that Lescaux did not kill you, so I could laugh at your eyes!" Her sharp laugh cut through the room, an open acknowledgment of everything the humanish avoided, passed over, or studied with sidelong glances.

The renewed conversational buzz settled eventually.

"Now." Shai lifted her right hand upward in supplication. *"Now,* we begin."

"—not possible." Ulanova's aide shook her head. "Our position has not changed from that of early this week. The Haárin components cannot be readily retrofitted to the existing plant, and the time it would take to develop the necessary adaptive technology would be better spent designing and building a new facility."

"Your Elyan governor signed a contract with us," Feyó said softly, "through his Department of Utilities suborn."

"Suborns make mistakes, Nìa Feyó." PM Cao closed her left hand into a fist and held it up to chest height, palm-side facing up. "Their dominants cannot always be held responsible for what they do." She smiled, but the expression soon froze when she heard Shai's suborn laugh and saw the increasing curvature of Shai's shoulders.

Jani bit her lip and avoided Nema's stare, which was at that moment burning a hole in the side of her face. *I will not laugh at my Prime Minister.* Not even when she calls a made-sect Haárin by a born-sect title and compounds the offense by gesturing in High Vynshàrau that said Haárin is acting like a brat, thus insulting the Suborn Oligarch in the process.

"I am not born-sect, Your Excellency." Feyó kept her voice level and her hands folded on the table. "And I do not believe that I am acting as foolish."

Cao's golden face darkened. "I meant no offense, nì—" The apology fizzled as she tried to figure out exactly what her offense had been.

"No, I know you did not, Your Excellency." Shai uncurved her shoulders, but only a little. "Humanish never do. They make mistakes, because their suborns do not instruct them properly, and they cannot be expected to know such, because they are not responsible."

Cao's eyes widened in surprise. She looked at Nema, who gestured in commiseration, but didn't speak.

Well, you wanted him out and you got your wish. Now you get to deal with Shai, who doesn't like you and won't cut you

any slack when you garble her languages. Jani flipped the
file folder open, then shut it. "We cannot allow insults, unin-
tentional or otherwise, to obscure the matter we are assembled here to discuss. Karistos city engineers have stated that
the soonest the new treatment plant can be constructed and
qualified for use is eighteen months from the day of ground-
breaking. This means a new plant is at least two years away.
The current facility is already functioning at maximum and
the feeling is that service cut-offs will need to be instituted
in order to meet demand for the coming summer. These
same engineers have also stated, in writing, that the Haárin
microbial filter array being offered for retrofit can be in-line
within sixty Common days and if put in place will alleviate
the need for any type of service slowdown." She looked
across the table to find a bank of humanish faces regarding
her as the enemy. "Will someone tell me what the problem is!"

Ulanova spoke slowly, grudgingly, as if any word spoken
to Jani was one word too many. "My engineers disagree."

And so it went. Two hours passed before Cao requested a
recess, which Shai reluctantly granted.

"She'll just keep pitting her experts against Elyas's experts,
and she'll win because she's here and they're there." Kern
Standish kicked at the ground and shoved his hands in his
pockets.

"Why aren't the Elyan engineers here?" Jani leaned
against a tree to straighten her back. She had left Nema to
the Elyan Haárin and Burkett to his major, and had adjourned to the allowed gardens with Kern and the other Cabinet aides she had worked with over the months. She had
steeled herself against their reactions to her appearance, but
thus far had fielded no more than a few pointed stares. "If
they'd left Elyas the same time as the Haárin, they'd have
been here."

"They were supposed to be," a young woman from Ag-
Min piped. "All hell broke loose just before they were
scheduled to leave. A shuttleport nav rig blitzed out—nothing could leave the ground for four days."

Jani looked at the averted faces around her. "Sabotage?"

She received a mime's chorus of shrugs and headshakes in reply. "Did anyone see where Ulanova went after we adjourned?"

"The public veranda, like usual," replied the AgMin aide.

"I'll see you inside." Jani set off in that direction.

"Gonna give her the evil eye?" One of the Treasury aides, who had been silent up until then, shot Jani a guilty glance, then turned his back.

Kern bristled. "Damn it, Maurier, you really are as stupid as you look, aren't you?"

"Well, it's one more idea than we have at the moment." Jani forced a smile and received a few in return, which under the circumstances was probably the best she could hope for.

She cut around the outer perimeter wall of the public veranda. As she neared the entry that led out to the gardens, she heard voices, Cao's and Ulanova's.

"—smoothing things with Shai will be difficult, Ani."

"We'll think of something."

"I suppose we'll have to pay attention during our language lessons from now on." Cao's voice held a bite she never let her public hear. "Do you think they'll send Tsecha home?"

There was a weighty pause before Ulanova replied. "It is to be hoped."

"Do you think so?" Cao sounded doubtful. "I would miss him. Even when he aggravated the hell out of me, I felt no malice in him."

"He only hides it better than the rest."

"Hmm." Now it was Cao's turn to ponder. "I think this revelation puts a new spin on things, no matter what you say."

"We all knew she was a medical freak, Li. Shroud's pet experiment. If she thinks this qualifies her as some sort of emissary, it is up to us to let her know that she is mistaken. We will have to wait until after Tsecha is recalled, of course—she is his favorite. But we shouldn't have to put up with either of them for much longer."

"As you say." The high-pitched click of heels on tile sounded. "I have to talk to the moderates before we reconvene, make sure they understand our point of view." The steps silenced. "Will you be all right, Ani?"

"Of course." Ulanova's voice sounded smooth and strong. "I'll meet you inside."

Jani waited until she heard the door to the embassy close. Then she stepped through the opening and onto the veranda.

Ulanova stood before a column-like fountain. She held one hand under the gentle stream and let it trickle over her fingers. She appeared thoughtful, calmer than she had in the courtyard, but still not relaxed.

Jani took another step, making sure that her shoes scraped against the tile. "Have you visited your Doc Chief in hospital, Your Excellency?"

Ulanova spun around. Water sprayed from her fingers, splashing over her tunic and arcing through the air.

"She was dying when they brought her in." Jani tried to clasp her hands behind her back, but her cracked collarbone balked and she had to settle for sliding them in her pockets. "They've jacked a DeVries shunt into her brain. It will be some time before they know if she'll recover, and to what extent." As Jani circled, Ulanova kept turning ever so slowly so that she faced her at all times.

Jani kept talking. Idomeni meeting breaks were short, and she knew she didn't have much time. "She and I found paper linking Peter to the Helier meetings during which *L'araignée* was formed. That paper also shows that he met with you during your trips to Exterior Main on Amsun. His meetings with you followed his trips to Helier. Coincidence, I'm sure you'll say."

"I have *nothing* to say to you." Ulanova's voice emerged as a hiss; she turned and walked toward the door.

"Then you brought Peter home with you," Jani called after her. "He lacked the skill and experience to act as a Cabinet-level Chief of Staff and it showed, but people laughed it off. Just a case of Anais's glands getting the better of her, silly woman. But that wasn't his purpose for being here. As *L'araignée*'s point man, he needed access to the people the Chief of Staff job would bring him in contact with. He needed to feel out the Merchants' Associations, the other

Ministries. Mark the dangers with red flags and arrange their removal." Jani watched Ulanova slow to stillness as she spoke. She knew she was right, but she appreciated the reassurance. "Nema was one of the dangers—he promoted Haárin business interests, and some of our trade groups were listening. So Peter tried to set him up as a traitor to his people."

Ulanova laughed, a dry, old sound. "My poor Peter did that, did he?" She turned to face Jani, dark eyes shiny with hate. "My poor Peter, whom you killed."

"Have you visited your Doc Chief in hospital, Your Excellency? Your poor Peter stove in the back of her head." Jani pressed a hand to her aching ribs. "When he had a chance to plan, he did all right. With a few tweaks, The Nema Letter would have worked a charm. But when he had to think on his feet he fell back on the tried and true methods of his kind, and that's where he stumbled. When he realized that I had figured out that The Nema Letter was a fake, he abandoned his attempts to ruin my reputation with the white paper and just tried to have me killed outright."

"Your *reputation*!" Ulanova paused to gain control of herself—her face had reddened alarmingly. "You stole documents, you and my Documents Chief. You forged, you deceived—"

"With Registry support. We were dealing with suspected fraud, and Dolly Aryton and I do go back a ways." Jani checked her timepiece. She didn't have more than a few minutes left. "Funny thing—throughout all this, I found allies I didn't know I had. After the white paper came out, after the shooting, even after last night, the calls never stopped. Family members asked me to attend this meeting. They've asked my advice for months: how to work with the Haárin, how to deal with Cèel, how to function in a Commonwealth that's starting to blur around the edges. It's as if I've become the ad hoc Exterior Minister. They're coming to me for this information because they either know they won't get it from you, or they know they can't believe what they get. Your old friends don't trust you anymore."

The first quiet ripple broke Ulanova's still surface. A

barely perceptible twitch around the eyes. "No, but they fear me, and fear is much the stronger."

"Is it?" Jani leaned against the wall as her back tightened. "If I advise them that your actions pose a threat to the Commonwealth and that they need to shut you down, they may balk at first, but in time the idea will appeal to them. They're afraid of you, yes, but they fear for themselves more. The pie is shrinking, and it will occur to them that if they cut you out, there will be more for them. So if you keep to your present course, you won't be fighting me. You'll be fighting Li and Jorge and Yvette and Gisela and all those other old friends. All I'll have to do is show them where to slip the knife. What happened to Evan van Reuter could happen to you. Death by gutted home and confiscated fortune and no one answering your calls. And what will *L'araignée* do when they realize you're no longer the power they thought you were?"

The door leading into the embassy flung open. A diplomatic suborn stuck out his head, called *"Time,"* and slipped back inside, leaving Ulanova standing with her hand to her throat.

"It won't be simple, slipping out of the arrangements you've made. This water treatment plant fiasco, for example—awarding the short-term contract to the Elyan Haárin will cause you problems. You may have to up your security—I know someone who can advise you in that regard." Jani walked to the veranda's garden exit, then paused and turned back. "I'd suggest mending fences with Nema, too. If he takes his place as full Haárin, the colonial Haárin will look to him for guidance. If he broaches the subject of an Haárin enclave, I'd listen to him." She looked at her right hand—her ring flashed in the sunlight. "You might also let Dathim Naré follow through on that tile project at your Annex."

Anais's face flared anew. "That—he *stole* from my office!"

"Did he?" Jani stared at Anais until the woman broke contact. "I'll see you back at table, Your Excellency."

CHAPTER 33

Tsecha followed ná Feyó back into the meeting room. He could sense many sorts of emotions in the humanish he passed in the hallways. Discomfort. Surprise. Confusion. He understood their reactions. *They believe I have shown disloyalty to Shai and through her, to Cèel.* Some, such as Li Cao and Anais, rejoiced in this since they believed his behavior would lead to his recall to Shèrá. Others such as his Jani despaired, for the same reason.

And so it may be. Shai, now grown so mindful of humanish opinion, would retaliate, of that he felt most sure. *In the name of the worldskein,* she would entone as she condemned him. *In defense of order.* And so would Cèel support her in her decision, because he hated him so.

Tsecha lowered into his chair and looked about the room. Odd, to sit in this higher seat—he could see the tops of heads for the first time since his youth, before his ascension to Chief Propitiator. *Daès has a bald spot.* He bared his teeth at the discovery, but his enjoyment soon abated as less amusing thoughts intruded.

I should have challenged you before the war, Cèel. At least their animosity would have been well and truly declared. As it was now it felt an unfinished thing, like Dathim's half-formed shell. And so it would remain, if the fate his Jani feared came to pass. *Will Cèel kill me outright?* Or would he let Tsecha live in a death of his own devising, a sequestered existence spent knowing that the future that the gods had foretold would never come to pass?

"I looked for you, nìRau. I thought we should at least confer before this starts up again, seeing as I am your suborn."

Tsecha turned to find his Jani standing beside him. He looked into her eyes and joy filled his soul, expelling the despair. "Green as Oà—just as Dathim said!"

"Not dark enough yet. I have seen Oà, you know." She looked about the room, her posture tense, as though she watched for something. "I thought ní Dathim might attempt to attend this."

"He would not be allowed, nìa. He is not government Haárin." Tsecha gripped Jani's chin, turning her head so that he could again look into her eyes. Even the fact that they were colored the same as Cèel's could not diminish his delight. "You should not have hidden them for as long as you did."

"I may be sorry I didn't hide them longer." She winced and pulled his hand away. "Ouch."

"Ouch?" Tsecha slumped more formally. "Ah. Your graze gives you pain. Your inconsequential injury, which is as nothing and may thus be ignored."

"I never said it didn't hurt." Jani turned her neck one way, then the other, until bones cracked.

"Young Lescaux died trying to kill you. That is what ní Dathim told me." Tsecha looked toward Anais's still-empty chair. The call to return had been given some time ago— why had she not yet come? "If she did not hate you before, she most assuredly hates you now."

"Such is of no consequence."

Tsecha again regarded his Jani. Her voice sounded odd, as it had during their talk in the garden, days before. Devoid of inflection. Stripped of emotion. The sound of words struck on stone. "Nìa, what have you done?"

"No more than was necessary." She looked down at him. "And no less." She had bent over the table, her hands braced on the edge as though she needed the support. The posture caused the sleeves of her jacket to ride up her arms.

Tsecha touched the soulcloth encircling Jani's left wrist. The material felt stiff. "No more. And no less."

Jani lifted her hands from the table so that her sleeves slipped down. "Did you and the Elyan Haárin discuss any strategies to try to sway Shai's opinion away from isolationism?"

"How you change the subject, nìa, whenever you do not want to answer the question."

"At the moment, the answer to *my* question is more important."

Tsecha swept his right hand across the table. Not strictly a negative gesture, but not one that allowed for much hope either. "Shai does not wish the Haárin to trade with humanish, especially materials as sensitive as those that treat water. It is more blending than she can bear, and truly."

"It is a vast step." Feyó leaned forward so she could speak to them both. "Since we ourselves will not be drinking this water or attempting to reclaim the filter assemblies, we do not feel there is a violation of our dietary protocols. But nìa-Rauta Shai is born-sect, and as such is conservative in the extreme. We are at a loss, and truly, as to how to convince her to reconsider." She looked up at Jani and held out her hand. "Ná Kièrshia. It is a pleasure to meet you at last."

Jani hesitated before shaking hands. "Glories of the day to you, ná Feyó." She seemed to be trying not to smile, but since Feyó smiled at her, what difference could it make? "May your gods and mine allow for a seemly outcome to this muddle."

Then Anais Ulanova reentered the room, followed closely by Li Cao, and brought an end to all smiles. Cao held her hands in front of her, as would a youngish who reached for her parent. She appeared as surprised, even angry. Tsecha had seen her look as such before, but never had her good friend Anais been the cause for her alarm.

Tsecha watched the women take their seats, then he looked up the table at his Jani. She had already sat down, her balance easy and sure. *Angel on a pin.* She watched the women, as well, her face as stripped of feeling as her voice had been when she told Tsecha what she had done. *No more than was necessary.* Whatever that was.

Then Anais lifted her gaze. She and Jani looked at one another in that intense humanish way that said something had occurred between them. Tsecha tried to analyze the look, define it as his handheld defined words, but the challenge of spoken humanish language was as nothing compared to this, their language between the lines.

His pondering was interrupted when Daès returned, followed by Shai. The Suborn Oligarch offered him her own intensity, a subtle rounding of her shoulders that foretold the tone of their next encounter.

Papers shuffled. Shai's suborn raised her head to speak, a sign that decisions had been made and this meeting neared its end. "It is considered that the contract signed between the representatives of the Elyan Haárin enclave and they of the Commonwealth colony should be set—should be—" The suborn's voice faltered. The murmurs from the banked seats rose once more as Anais Ulanova raised her hand.

She did not sit straight and tall as she spoke, as she had before. Her words did not emerge strong, but came softly, almost as a whisper. Several times, the swell of sound from the other humanish overwhelmed her, compelling her to repeat herself. ". . . reconsidered the Exterior position," she said as Cao watched her, her own confusion displaying itself in the constant working of her fingers. ". . . safety of the Karistos water supply is of paramount importance . . . needs of the citizenry. . . ."

Tsecha looked out at Burkett, who sat with his hand to his face, finger curled over his upper lip, his eyes on Jani. The other Cabinet suborns watched her as well, Standish from Treasury and all the others who found her during every recess or questioned her in the hallways. They did not appear triumphant, though. They did not seem pleased. Surprised, yes, as Shai appeared surprised, shoulders straightening in puzzlement as her suborn took notes, flowing script coursing across the surface of her recording board. For while it was Anais Ulanova who spoke as herself, it was Jani Kilian's words that she uttered, the same words heard in this room only a few days before. Words that Anais herself had denied as foolish and without merit.

Anais completed her mouthing of Jani's words. Then came the scratch of styli, the rustle of documents, the occasional swallowed cough.

The waiting.

Tsecha watched Shai. He had known her since their youngish days, when he lived at Temple and she schooled there. They had despised one another from their first meeting. But it had been a dull, simple dislike, not the pitched battle of wills and ideologies that would have led to an offer of challenge. Until now. *If you challenge my Jani, I will challenge you.* He watched her page through her documents using only her thumb and forefinger, as though she picked petals from a thorny bloom. *You even fear paper, Shai. How do you think to govern Haárin?*

"I am surprised, Your Excellency, at your most sudden change of mind," Shai finally said, after she had plucked the last of her pages. "I have known since my arrival of your distrust of idomeni, and I felt most sure of your decision in this."

Tsecha felt the clench in his soul as his shoulders rounded. "You hoped for her to take action so you would not have to take it yourself. You wished her distrust of idomeni to obscure your distrust of humanish and of your own Haárin. You are dishonest, Shai."

No murmurs followed Tsecha's words. No sound of any type, or movement, either. He could sense Jani's stare from downtable. But he knew that if he turned to her, she would try to compel him to silence, and now was not the time for such. She had already done what she felt was necessary, and bent Anais to her will. Now, it was his turn to bend Shai to his.

Shai's fingers shook as she reached for a piece of paper that she did not need. Such had been her way at Temple school, when she nursed her angers until they caused her stylus to shake and blot her writing. "Your opinion has no place here, Tsecha." Her voice shook as well, as it had always done. "Your right to speak for Vynshàrau is no more."

Tsecha gestured insignificance. Next to him, he could sense Feyó's surprise, the sudden spark of tension. "I have said already that I do not speak as ambassador."

"Then you will speak not."

"As Tsecha Égri, I will speak as Haárin. The Elyan Haárin traveled here to speak for themselves, therefore Haárin are allowed to speak!"

Shai's shoulders curved in extreme upset—if she had been humanish, one would think her violently ill. "You cannot speak as one, then the other, Tsecha—such is as ridiculous!"

Thank you, Shai—in your clumsiness, you provide me the

opening I require. "But Vynshàrau and Haárin have always worked together, Shai. Haárin served us most well during the war of our ascendancy. Many of our military strategists have stated that without their assistance, we would not have won. That without their actions during the Night of the Blade, we would not have maintained that victory."

"Vynshàrau have always acknowledged the acts of Haárin, Tsecha. You are not the only one in this room who remembers the war. Godly though it was, it changed us all." Shai looked in Jani's direction, but so far had she come down the damned path of discretion that she did not mention Knevçet Shèràa. "We who honor our traditions wish to mend all that fractured during that time, and to reaffirm the pact between Vynshàrau and Haárin."

"Tradition." Tsecha tugged at his red-trimmed sleeves, as he had at every meeting. His own tradition—he took comfort in it now. "In our born-sect tradition of dominant and suborn, we offer respect for respect, protection for honor. Even as a dominant compels obedience, so must their domination be as godly, as seemly. We do not misuse our suborns as humanish have at times misused those who served them." That comment drew a rise of discontent from the banked seats, but such did not bother Tsecha. He liked humanish a great deal, but he had read their histories and he knew their faults. "We reserve that misuse for our Haárin. We send them to fight when it suits us. To kill. To die. We send them into this city, demand that they forfeit their souls so that our utilities function and our gardens remain alive. And then when they take one action to help themselves maintain the life they have, we demand that they cease, because we suddenly fear them when they do what they do."

"To live with humanish!" Shai's humanish restraint shattered. She bowed her back and twisted her neck in an extreme exclamation of outrage as Tsecha had not seen since Temple. "To sell them the mechanisms of our food and water!" She flicked her hand in disgust at the Elyan Haárin. "To dress as they do, talk and act as they do! To behave in godless ways and then come here and demand our benediction as they do so!"

As one, Feyó and the other Elyan Haárin slumped into

postures of extreme defense. "Such have we always done!" cried the male in black and orange.

Tsecha raised a hand, gesturing for the male to restrain himself. "Indeed. Such have they always done. The Haárin serve as our blade, and a blade does no good in its sheath. It only serves when it cuts, even when it cuts the one who wields it. Such is as it is—it knows no other way!" He sagged back in his chair—the act of blessed disputation drained so. "To live as idomeni is to live in balance. Within our skeins, our sects, our worldskein, all must be as symmetrical. Cooperation occurs, even between the most opposite. Differences are acknowledged, but they do not eliminate collaboration. Or as the humanish say, give and take." He bared his teeth at the phrase, since it reminded him of Hansen.

"Our gods do so," he continued. "Give and take. Shiou and Caith have walked together on the Way since the birth of the First Star. They battle, yes. Such is their way. But for one to live without the other? Such desolation! How could one define themselves if the other did not exist?" He held his hands out to Shai in entreaty. *Think! As you have not done since Temple, think!* "How does the order of Vynshàrau define itself if the chaos of Haárin does not exist? And if you compel Haárin to draw back into the worldskein, to cease to function as our blade, where is our balance?" His hands dropped. So quickly he had lost the will to argue, but how long could he posit that air was to be inhaled with one who insisted upon holding her breath? "So speaks the priest, which I will be for not much longer, if Cèel has his way. Yet so I speak, regardless. Order must be maintained, and if the Haárin are not allowed to do as they must, then so ends order. Will you end order here, Shai? In this room, now, will you cause it to cease to be?"

Shai had gradually straightened as Tsecha spoke. Not, he knew, because his words did not anger her, but because her bones were old and she could not maintain the true posture of rage. "You have had your life to practice twisting words as rope around your adversary's neck, Tsecha. One who has not studied as you have suffers a disadvantage." She fingered the edge of a document, tapped the end of her stylus on the table, delayed as humanish delayed when the last thing they wanted to do was decide. "If these filters are provided to the Karistos humanish, they will be gone from us. It will be as though they never existed."

Feyó's back unbent gradually. "Indeed, nìaRauta, such is so. The assemblies will be turned over to the humanish engineers to reconstruct as they will—we will never see them again."

Shai sat in silence, until humanish fidgeted and sneaked glances at their timepieces. But in the end, she acceded to the will of the gods, because she was a most orderly Vynshàrau, and as such, it was the only thing she could do.

They stood outside the meeting room afterward, in the huddled groups that humanish always formed after such occasions. Tsecha watched them gather, break apart, then gather once more. *Like mist into droplets,* Hansen had used to say. *Just watch out for the flood.*

"I still don't believe they gave the OK. Shai was one baby-step away from adjourning the meeting." Standish pushed a hand through his hair, which had grown more curly and unruly in the heat of the embassy.

"She really didn't have a choice. Neither of them did." Jani leaned against the wall. Her eyes had dulled. She looked as tired, as pained. "The citizens of one of the largest colonial capitals go without potable water because a Family sweetheart deal prevents them from implementing the quick-fix? That's a kick in the head to every pro-colonial claim the government has made since the spring, and they can't afford to act that way anymore."

"They saw the light?" Burkett wiped a cloth over his face, which shone with sweat. His hair looked as though he had walked in rain. "*Somebody* saw *something*, and it sure as hell wasn't the light. I can't carry tales of smoke-filled rooms back to Mako, Kilian—I need to know what the hell is going on."

Jani's wearied manner did not alter as she regarded the angry general. She had seen him enraged so many times— perhaps she had grown used to such. "What would any intelligent being consider to be the desired outcome of this?" She waited for Burkett to respond, even though she must have known that he would not. "A working water treatment facility for Karistos, right? Well, we'll have it if we keep on top of it, and I gave nothing away. That's goal in this game, by any measure." She pushed off the wall and walked to Tsecha, her step slow. "If you'll excuse us." She took his arm and pulled him down the hall. "Let's see—how much trouble are you in now?" she asked when they had walked far enough away to not be overheard.

Tsecha looked back at their group, which had already re-coalesced. Other droplets formed nearby, with members moving from one to another quite freely. *The flood begins . . .* "My theology is quite sound, nìa."

"Yes, I'm sure it is. Shai has probably already Misty'd a recording to the Temple scholars with an order to come up with a rebuttal immediately." She turned to watch Anais and PM Cao leave the meeting room; neither looked back at her. "The Elyan Haárin seemed quite pleased."

Tsecha bared his teeth. "We are to meet after early evening sacrament to discuss their situation."

"Their situation?" Jani smiled. "Congratulations, nìRau, you've become a lobbyist." She looked at him. Her true eyes had shown for but a short time, yet it seemed as if they had always been such. "You're lucky that Cèel can't afford trouble with the Haárin—their support may save your life. That life, however, may be very different from the one you have now."

Tsecha hesitated, then hunched his shoulders in a human-ish shrug. "It is the life I am to have. The life on the edge of the blade." His soul ached as he pondered the quiet of the embassy, a quiet in which he took comfort, but that he had most assuredly sacrificed. "I will not be alone, nìa, of that I am most sure. You will be there, I believe, if only to anger General Burkett."

"That's a full-time job." Jani looked down at the floor. Some time passed before she spoke. "You still call me nìa. That's wrong—you should call me ná, in proper Haárin fashion."

"I shall call you as I wish, *nìa.*"

Her eyes brightened. Her idomeni eyes. "Does that mean I can still call you Nema?"

Tsecha gripped her chin and tilted her head upward. Gently this time, in deference to her pain. "That is not my name."

Jani's eyes filled, mist into droplets. "You know how to reach me, just in case." She lifted his hand away, squeezing it just before she let it go. "Be careful, ní Tsecha."

Tsecha watched her walk away. Her strange colonel waited in the entry for her. Pierce, who seemed so much as Dathim. *We each have our blade, and truly.* He wondered whether he would soon have need of his.

Tsecha met with the Elyan Haárin several times over the next days. He greatly esteemed ná Feyó. She was first-generation Haárin, an agronomist who had been expelled from the Academy before the war. They discussed her theories from sunrise to sunset and beyond. How the idomeni insistence on grown food played a major role in holding back their colonial expansion, how synthesized foods as those humanish used offered the best solution to this problem. Such discourse thrilled him, terrified him, and told him how much he needed to learn to consider himself true Haárin.

The morning the Elyan Haárin departed, Tsecha rose to bid them well. He stood out on the beach in the cold damp as their demiskimmer took to the air and veered toward HollandPort, watching it until it vanished in the glare of the rising sun. When he turned back to the embassy, he did not feel surprise to see Shai's suborn waiting for him atop the grassy rise. He only wondered why Shai delayed as long as she had.

"Seat yourself, Tsecha." Shai sat at her work table, the latest delivery of Council documents stacked in piles around her. "So, your Haárin have departed."

"They are not my Haárin, Shai."

"Are they not?" She looked at him, her posture still as clenched as it had been days before. "Whose are they, then? Not mine. That I know, and truly." She paged through one file, then another, as though what she sought was so unimportant that she had lost it. Tsecha had often seen Anais Ulanova do the same—he wondered if Shai had stolen the strategy from her.

Shai finally found what she searched for at the bottom of a high stack of files. She must have worked quite hard, to lose the fate of her Chief Propitiator so completely. "Cèel is most angry with you."

Tsecha squirmed against the seat back. The discomfort of Shai's seat aggravated him, for he had grown used to the comfort of Haárin chairs over the past days. "Such does not surprise me."

"So angry is he that he did not record his own pronouncement of your fate. He had his documents suborn write it out, and sent it to me to read."

Tsecha laughed. "He thinks he can mislead the gods by obscuring his trail! How humanish he becomes!" His laughter grew even more as Shai's back hunched. "Pronounce my fate, Shai. In Cèel's words, which he denies before they are even uttered."

Shai hesitated before she spoke. When the words sounded at last, they came quickly, as Vynshàrau, showing that Cèel had not yet lost himself completely. "Haárin you say you are. Therefore Haárin you will be, from this time forth." She closed the file, and pushed it away as though the contents repelled her. "You bring disorder upon us, Tsecha. Chaos. Never has a Chief Propitiator been expelled from office. The humanish will believe us mad."

"The humanish can match us, madness for madness. Some may even wonder why Cèel waited so long." Tsecha regarded his red-trimmed cuffs for the last time. "NìaRauta Sànalàn is not ready."

"Lecturers from Temple will arrive as soon as their absences can be arranged. They will see to her instruction."

"And you will continue here as ambassador?"

"Until Cèel chooses a replacement, yes."

Tsecha took one breath, then another. Haárin breath, inhaled by an outcast. He stood, slipped off the overrobe of his office, and draped it across Shai's desk. "I look forward to sitting at table with you in many meetings to come, Shai. You will wish you had killed me, and truly." Then he left before she could pronounce more of Cèel's anger, and returned to his rooms to claim the few objects he wished to keep.

*   *   *

He crossed the veranda for the last time as the humanish sun ascended to prime. Walked across the lawns. Disappeared into the trees. He had packed his few possessions in a car-ryall that he wore slung across his shoulders, in imitation of Feyó's suborns. He had changed his clothes, trading his crisp off-white for dark and worn. Black shirt. Brown trousers. Black boots. He would obtain colors as soon as he could, dress in blues and greens and oranges. But for now, he walked as shadow.

They awaited him in the lane, Beyva and the rest, wel-coming him with smiles and greetings and laughter. They herded around him and pushed him onward, as the sea pushed the wave, toward the house in which they had gath-ered a seeming age of evenings ago. Dathim stood in the en-try, brightly clothed, ax-hammer gripped in his hand.

"We have been waiting for you, Tsecha. We, the em-bassy's blade!" Dathim stepped aside and gestured for him to step forward. "Your house has been waiting for you."

Tsecha stopped short. "*Your* house, ní Dathim."

"No, this is not my house, ní Tsecha. Mine is that one." Dathim pointed to a smaller dwelling at the far end of the lane, near the base of the grassy rise. "This house"—he pat-ted the side of the entry—"this house has been empty for some time. I have labored to prepare it for he who would live here."

Tsecha took a step forward. Another. He touched the en-try stonework, and pondered what he knew of this place. A place blessed by annihilation and adorned with the dunes of Knevçet Shèràa. A place of meeting, and rebellion, and change.

"It is a good house, and truly." He touched the reliquary, muttered a prayer, and walked inside.

CHAPTER 34

"Do you know who's going to be at this thing, besides the Commonwealth Cup semifinalists? Everybody. Absolutely *everybody*!" Angevin dug through the pile of gowns on Jani's bed, flinging about expensive fabrics like used dispos.

"I already know what I'm going to wear. Bought it last week. Fits perfectly." Jani sat on the floor in front of the dresser, well out of range of flying dresses. "You've had a week to prep for this. I kept telling you, 'Go shopping.'"

"*When?* This place has been a zoo ever since the conclave." Angevin stretched out a gold column gown on the bed and eyed it skeptically. "First, the move." She gestured vaguely around the larger bedroom, with its tenth-floor cityscape view. "Security in and out all week, installing things. Then the workload. You get any more two-hundred-page Cabinet contracts, you're going to have to charter someone to close out your books at the end of the year."

"I planned on doing that anyway." Jani walked to her closet and took out her own choice for the evening. "Dolly recommended a firm that Registry uses. They cost a mint, and they're reputed to be real pains in the ass. Chances are good that they're as honest as you'll get in Chicago and no one could persuade them to set me up on an embezzlement charge."

"You're worried about that?" Angevin dragged her gown to one side so Jani would have room to set out her own outfit.

"Worried, no. Ever mindful, yes." Jani took her clothes from their wrappings and laid them out. "The old-fashioned frame-up seems to be the standard way of doing business in this city, and I'll be damned if I'm going to make it easy for somebody." She swept the sea-blue sari across the silvery pants and top. "What do you think?"

"I could cry." Angevin whimpered as she stroked the turquoise silk. "How are you going to wear your eyes?"

Jani grinned. The question had become a point of fun between them, as well as a way to help everyone, herself included, adjust to the change. "Clothed, I think. It's not an official government function and I don't feel like being gawped at. Not that I may not be anyway, but why ask for it?" She walked to the dresser and picked through the multitude of packages her mother had brought her from Acadia. "I need to decide on jewelry," she said as she liberated a huge padded bag from the collection.

Angevin gasped as Jani unfastened the bag's flaps and opened it like a book, revealing row after row of gems and metal. Platinum earrings and rings. Gold bracelets. "My God!" She held up a necklace of hammered gold discs. "When are you supposed to wear all this?"

"My wedding day. All in one shot." Jani chuckled at Angevin's shocked look. "You never heard the term 'more metal than an Acadian wedding'? A bride was supposed to wear her dowry on her back. You should see the daughters from wealthy families—they can barely move for the gold. I remember when I was little, seeing holos of a bride who had to be floated up to the altar on a skimdolly." She examined a pair of aquamarine teardrop earrings. "Course, this stuff isn't worth near as much now as it was when the tradition began. But it's bright and shiny and custom dictates that it matters."

They both started as the comport buzzer blatted; Angevin glowered at the extension unit on Jani's end table. "Let Steve get it. If I never again see another begging, pleading face on a display, I'll survive quite happily." She hefted a gold-link bracelet and mouthed a *wow*. "Isn't it bad luck to wear this stuff before your wedding or something?"

"Oh, I think all bets are off where that's concerned. When your folks turn it over to you, it becomes yours to do with as you please." Jani perused her nuptial stockpile with a hand pressed to her forehead. "I think I'm going to make do with about five percent of this, so Maman can ask me why I'm not wearing anything." She set aside the aquamarine earrings, the huge stones set in platinum, and the matching collar-like necklace. Then she added an array of gold and platinum bracelets because she liked how the wide bands covered the *à lérine* scars on her forearms.

"You're going to look *so* exotic, and I'm going to look like I should be parking skimmers." Angevin glared at the door as a knock sounded. She bundled her dress over her arm and hurried to answer it.

"Hey, don't leave this stuff—!" Jani stopped in mid-sentence when she saw Steve standing in the doorway, an anxious-looking Lt. Pullman at his back.

"That was Val on the com." Steve grinned. "You need to get to Neoclona right away."

"We started picking up the increased neuronal activity as soon as we flushed out the regen solutions and unjacked the shunt." Dr. Wismuth, one of the many neurologists Jani had come to know, was short and round and bobbed like a happy balloon down the hall ahead of her. "Then we began what we call our systems checks—somatic, visual, auditory, etc. . . ." She pushed the door to the room aside before it had a chance to open completely, ignoring the warning buzzer. "We've noted some issues with visual acuity that may or may not repair themselves. Her speech is slurred. She remembers nothing that happened the day of the assault"— Wismuth's bubbling ebbed—"which isn't entirely bad." She beckoned for Jani to follow her into the darkened room. "Her head is still restrained, and will be for a few more days. She's still swaddled. We don't normally allow visitors other than immediate family at this stage, but I know you've been here every day since she arrived, and Val insisted that you had a right to know." She stepped aside, allowing Jani a clear path to the bed.

The headboard blinked and fluttered less now that the shunt had been removed and Roni had regained some level of consciousness. Her hands moved constantly, fingers first flexing, then bending, then straightening as though she pointed. The part of her face that was visible held a tense, knitted expression, as though she suffered a severe headache. Considering what Jani recalled of her own post-shunt return to consciousness, she probably did.

Then Roni's eyes, mere slits due to the swelling caused by the shunt, opened. She moved her mouth like an infant trying to vocalize. The rate of her hand movements increased. The psychotropic headboard blinked and fluttered more rapidly. Jani hung back, her heart in her throat and her hands clenched in her pockets, until Dr. Wismuth pushed her forward. "You need to move up—all you are is a blur from this distance."

"Sorry." Jani stepped closer to the bed, and hoped Wismuth couldn't see the tears running down her cheeks. *Sorry. Sorry. Sorry.*

"Jah—" Roni's agitated movements slowed. A corner of her mouth twitched. " 'lo."

"Hello." Jani coughed to loosen her tightening chest. "I won't ask how you feel. I know how you feel."

Roni blew out a very weak snort. "Yah. Head hur'. Stup' shunt." Her mouth curved a little more. "Mom here. Da. Helluva way to ge' a vis-it." Her hand movements increased again. "Thinkin'. Some'en wron'. Luu-sheen. Peeth-aah. Bot' blon.' Col' eyes." Then the motion slowed again. Her face relaxed as though she slept.

Wismuth tugged on Jani's sleeve. "Does that mean something? She's been repeating it for hours."

Jani nodded. "It concerns the matter we were working on the day of the assault. We were trying to determine an identity with a very sparse physical description."

"Oh, this is good, yes!" Wismuth bustled toward the door, barely avoiding a collision with Val in the entry.

"Wiz is wearing her note-taking face." Val sauntered up to Jani and wrapped his arms around her. He wore a green plaid shirt—he pressed her face to his shoulder and patted the back of her head. "It's absorbent—go ahead."

Jani hugged him back. "If I had—"

"I don't want to hear any ifs out of you, remember?" Val pushed her back so he could look her in the face. "She can hear us. If you're going to beat yourself up, we need to go someplace else." He glanced at the bed. "We should leave anyway—that woman needs her rest."

They walked into the hall, arms around each other's waists. Jani blinked as the bright lights struck her and she felt the old familiar tightening of her eyefilms. "What's the prognosis?"

"At this stage, a hell of a lot better than average." Val hugged her again. "I won't go into gory details, but judging from the severity of that blow she suffered, she's lucky she stayed alive long enough to get here."

"Lucky I finally found her, you mean."

"Jan, we still know very little about what happened that night, and until we do, I wish you'd stick the guilt back in the box." Val slowed to a stop, gripped Jani by the shoulders, and turned her to face him. "She's alive. She's lucid. The vast majority of her responses to stimuli fall within normal variation. She suffered less serious cerebral damage than you did. You were out for almost five weeks, not five days, and look how you turned out. Given time, she stands a great chance of making a full and complete recovery."

Jani exhaled with a shudder. "Her personality—"

"Initial signs look good, but we won't know the fine detail for weeks." Val shook her gently, in deference to her mending collarbone. "Let's discuss some items that we do know. You saved her life. You could have died in the process. The two things that saved you both are that she's a very lucky young woman and you're a medical wonder." His green-brown eyes shone with a hard light. "Give yourself a break, for once in your damned life. Not everything that happens to everyone you know is your fault." He hugged her again, and they continued walking. "You going to the party tonight?"

Jani shrugged. "I guess."

Val nodded with medical finality. "You better. You should have a great time, a wonderful time." He led her to the lift that would take her down to the garages. "Then tomorrow morning, you should come back here and tell Roni all about it. It'll do you both good." He shoved her gently into the open cabin, in which Pullman already stood waiting. "Now go."

Pullman escorted her to the VIP level. He looked the gentle giant in his dress blue-greys; it was hard to believe he carried enough firepower on his person to flatten a fair-sized building. "Good news, ma'am?" He popped the rear gull-wing of Jani's latest conveyance, a dark red four-door.

"Yes. Good news." Jani slipped into the backseat, and smiled up at Pullman as he closed her in. *She's alive . . . she's lucid . . . we talked a little. I'll tell her all about the party in the morning.* Yes, she would. Oh yes, she would.

"Janila, look at all this food!" Jamira held her plate in front of her like a barrier. Then she edged closer to Jani and dropped her voice. "Can you eat any of it?"

"Some of it, Maman." Jani looked over the banked tables, a stationary feast moored by goldware and crystal and candlesticks the size of Pullman's forearms. "I just don't know where to start."

"Allow me." John Shroud took the plate from Jani's hands and filled it. He wore a smart evening suit in pearl grey and had filmed his eyes to match; the tempered light of the ballroom softened his spectral edge. "Good evening, Mère Kilian," he rumbled with a host's smile. "Are you having a good time?"

"Yes, Dr. Shroud." Jamira's smile stayed true, her truce with John still in place. "How Declan and I danced. Such wonderful music, waltzes and à deux. Now he is in the other room, watching football holos and stuttering like a young boy in the presence of Le Vieux Rouge."

John looked back at Jani, near-invisible eyebrows arched in question.

"The Old Red. Acadia Central United's nickname." Jani took the plate from him and stared at the numerous tiny servings of meats, breads, and hors d'oeuvres. "You expect me to eat this tonight?"

"It's just a little of everything."

"I think *everything* is the key word." Jani used a two-pronged fork to skewer a shrimp the size of her finger as she surveyed the huge ballroom. "I saw the PM a little while ago."

"She made one pass through the room and left. Anais sent her regrets this morning. The people I spoke with who asked about you seemed eager to talk to you. The usual Ministers, along with business leaders anxious about the Haárin influx. So in answer to your unasked question, no, I don't believe there's anyone here you need to avoid." John looked down at her and smiled. "See, I can be useful."

"I never said you couldn't." Jani stuffed the shrimp in her mouth to forestall further conversation, then turned as a familiar babble of voices sounded from behind.

"My dear, you look lovely!" Jamira handed Steve her plate so she could offer silent applause for Angevin's golden gown.

"Oh, so do you!" Angevin touched the gold-trimmed edge of Jamira's fuchsia sari, which flowed over trousers and top of muted gold. Behind her, Steve stood in his basic black evening suit and juggled his and Jamira's plates. He glanced at Jani and rolled his eyes as Angevin and Jamira fell into animated conversation.

Jani felt a hand touch her shoulder, and turned to find John beckoning for her to follow him. They walked to a small pedestal table near the dividing line between the dining and the dancing. Couples in rainbow eveningwear swirled past as the music swelled, forcing them to bend close together so they could hear one another.

John had gotten a drink, something caramel-colored and potent-looking, like the bourbon Evan van Reuter used to imbibe incessantly. "I assume your folks are staying?"

"Do they have a choice?" Jani looked out over the Commerce Ministry ballroom, an immense space with high tiered ceilings, chandeliers, and walls of french doors leading out to terraces and gardens. "They can't go back to Acadia. I think they realized that the day they bugged out. Maman brought my dowry jewelry and all her family holos and mementoes. Papa brought most of his tools and handheld instruments. Niall has them in his sights—they've got round-the-clock protection although I don't think they realize what that means." She studied the milling diners and dancers, on the lookout for the waiter who strayed near, the gowned woman who asked for the time. Watchers all, guardians all, shadows all, courtesy of Niall Pierce, who currently resided in a command center in a nether part of the building and rode herd over a score of Cabinet and Family security forces. "I never thanked you for taking care of them."

"No need." John bent closer, until their arms touched. "You ask—I comply. Or haven't you figured that out yet?" His voice seemed to emerge from the very air surrounding them. "That's all you have to do. Just ask. It's very simple."

"No, it isn't."

"Of course it is. All it takes is practice. 'John, do this. John, attend.' "

John, take over my life. Jani kept that thought to herself. John was better at that sort of argument than she. The only sure way to fend him off would be to say something cutting, and she didn't want to spoil the evening that way. The music, the lights, and the color combined to make a storybook setting and she wanted to enjoy it, if only as a spectator.

She let her gaze drift over the heads of the dancers, to the view through the french doors. The night air chilled, but assorted weather barriers had made the terrace a haven for those in search of respite from the noise and glitter. At first, she ignored the distant glimmer of white as it drew near the windows, taking it for a guest returning from a wander among the trees. Then the figure walked into the full blaze of light that flooded the terrace, and her heart skipped.

Lucien stepped up to the doors and scanned the interior scene. He wore drop-dead whites, the gold shoulder boards and looped braids snagging the light and slicing it into metallic rainbows. He stiffened like a hunting dog on point when he spotted her, but instead of entering the ballroom immediately, he held back. One hand on the door catch, eyes on her, like the soldier in her painting, he stood still and straight and awaited his mistress's pleasure.

After a moment that seemed like nothing and like forever, Jani smiled. Only then did Lucien open the door. He strode the perimeter of the ballroom, chased by stares, the light of the chandeliers shimmering off his silvery head.

John's voice sounded like distant thunder. "What the hell is he doing here?"

"Good evening." Lucien set his brimmed lid atop the table, and immediately nabbed a glass of juice from a passing waiter. "My God, I haven't seen a scrum like this since Cao's granddaughter's wedding last year."

John didn't appear impressed with that social credential. "I don't recall your name on this invitation list, Pascal."

"I'm a late addition, sir. To Colonel Pierce's security team." Lucien raised his non-alcoholic glass. "I'm on duty." He looked from John to Jani, added two and two, and nailed four. Eyes flashing cold, he set down his drink and held out his hand to Jani. "Care to dance, ma'am?"

Jani pretended to ponder, until she saw the hand waver and uncertainty flicker in those chill eyes. Only then did she take Lucien's hand and let him lead her out on the floor. "Are you really a member of Niall's security?" she asked after they had picked up the step to the à deux that the orchestra played.

"He signed me up because I used to work for Ani. I think he was concerned she might try to pull something. Or maybe he was concerned I might try to pull something."

"Is dancing with me on the duty list? I didn't check."

"We're all supposed to keep an eye on you. What better way?" Lucien stepped back and gave her a lengthy head to toe examination. "You look beautiful."

"Thank you." Jani drank in that inestimable face. "So do you."

"Hmm." Lucien pulled her close. "You covered your eyes."

Jani tried to ignore the press of his body against hers, a feat she didn't quite manage. "Niall and I worked out a protocol. Official government functions where I'm acting in some sort of intermediary capacity for the idomeni, the films come off. Purely social stuff, like this, they stay on."

"How about if the person you're with simply prefers you without them?"

Jani felt the blush rise. She hoped Lucien wasn't close enough to feel it, too. She looked toward the table, where John watched them, drink in hand, and steered until she had turned her back to him.

Lucien hugged Jani closer. "How—are you?" For the first time, his voice sounded stilted, rehearsed, as though it was a question he had never asked before. Her beautiful, fractured prince.

This princess isn't so intact herself. Jani rested her cheek on his shoulder. The polywool felt pleasantly rough. "Fine." The orchestra played Eduard, and she savored the rise and fall of the strings. "Usual aches and pains."

"Umm." Lucien sounded like he knew the feeling. "I assume you heard about Tsecha."

"Yes. Considering all Cèel could have done, he got off easy. But he wanted it. I think he decided that becoming true Haárin was the best way for him to work toward his new order."

"Well, like everything he does, his new order means more work for everybody. They've signed me up for another class. Haárin Language Protocols—what a surprise." Lucien paused. "It's next week."

Jani grinned. "Is it?"

"Yeah." Lucien sighed. "I guess I'll have to get to know our friendly in-city BOQ."

"I guess you will."

"Heard you moved upstairs to a bigger flat."

"Yes."

"Hmm." Lucien tried another angle of approach. "Is dinner out of the question?"

Jani counted to ten before answering. "Dinner's fine."

"Then that will have to do, I guess." He pulled her closer. "For now." His fingers fluttered along the seam of her fitted top. "This opens up along the side."

They finished that dance, and the next, and the next. The monster prince and his changeling princess, in a world where survival was a happy ending and you took your magic where you found it. By the time they returned to the table for Lucien's lid, John had departed, the only signs of his presence three glasses depleted of their contents and a linen napkin crumpled into a tight ball.

After being introduced to Jamira and impressing her mightily, Lucien took his leave to return to the command center. Jani made rounds, talked with the people who had been anx-

ious to meet her, and kept a daughterly eye on her parents,
who appeared ready to waltz, eat, and talk until the last candle guttered to extinction.

She finally broke away, taking refuge in a secluded hallway that was far enough away from the ballroom to discourage casual visitation. She found a narrow windowseat,
wedged into it, and watched the activity on the terrace.

"How are you holding up?"

Jani turned to find Niall standing in a doorway. Since his
job kept him behind the scenes, he had opted for dress blue-
greys rather than the more formal whites. He looked as tired
as she felt. A half-smoked 'stick dangled from his lips. "I
would have to say, Colonel, that I have just about reached
my limit."

Niall took the 'stick from his mouth and studied it. "I
know just what you need." He pulled a handcom from his
pocket and barked a few terse orders. "Follow me, please,
ma'am," he said as he repocketed the device.

They exited through a side door. Pullman waited for them
with the skimmer of the day, a black two-door. They closed
themselves in, and Niall steered into the early morning
quiet.

"If you want to change . . . ?" He reached behind his seat
and pulled out a small duffel. "I've got a set of casuals.
You'll swim in them, but they might be more comfortable
than that get-up." He glanced at her sidelong and grinned in
bemusement. "Never saw so much damned metal in my
life."

"You should see all the stuff I didn't wear." Jani piled into
the backseat and unclasped earrings and bracelets, then
paused as she unpinned her sari. "You know, if an enterpris-
ing reporter gets holos of this, I'll entertain Chicago for at
least a month." That kept them both laughing until they left
the city behind.

They drove through Bluffs neighborhoods that Jani recognized, then down darker streets that she didn't, finally ending up on a dirt trail that led down to a secluded stretch of
beach.

"Belongs to a friend." Niall popped both gullwings and
walked out onto the sand, unclasping the neck of his tunic

along the way. As he activated an underground fuel vent, Jani gathered wood and leaves and heaped them around the outlet. After she finished, Niall activated a 'stick and tossed it on the pile. The fire sputtered, then caught when he increased the fuel flow. He and Jani lowered to the seat offered by a convenient log, and watched the flames.

"Haven't seen you much these past few days." Niall braced his tietops against the fire containment ring. "How are you?"

"Fine." Jani uncovered a stick that had been buried in the sand and poked at the fire.

Niall picked up a pinecone and tossed it from hand to hand. "When my love swears that she is made of truth, I do believe her, though I know she lies."

Jani racked her brain for the titles of all the books Niall had lent her that she'd never read. "More Keats?"

He mimed throwing the pinecone at her head. "Shakespeare. Sonnet 138. I keep meaning—"

"—to lend me the sonnets." Jani scooted nearer the fire and rubbed her cold hands. "There was one thing of his that you lent me that I read, and it stuck with me." She raised one finger like an instructor's pointer. "Exit, pursued by a bear."

"That's from *The Winter's Tale.*" Niall emitted a bear-like growl himself. "That's not what I had in mind."

"No, but it is remarkably descriptive of my life thus far." Jani stared into the flames, the heat pulling the moisture from her films. "It just might remain so."

Niall made as though to speak, but before he could, something in his tunic beeped. "Excuse me." He pulled out his handcom and listened, then muttered an "Out" and stashed it away again. "We're going to have company."

Jani let her head drop between her knees. "You want to hear me whine like Angevin, don't you?"

Niall smiled. "Oh, somehow I don't think you'll mind." He rose and walked toward the water.

The lights began as pinpoints far to the south. As they neared, Jani picked up the blue sidelights, as well. Lakeskimmer lights. She rose to join Niall. "You called him?"

Niall turned around and tossed the pinecone in the fire, where it sizzled and flared. "I thought you could use some cheering up."

The lakeskimmer drew close and slowed to a hover. Tsecha stood up in his seat while next to him, Dathim worked to hold the craft level. *"Nìa! It is pretty damned cold out here!"*

"It's warm by the fire!" Jani swatted her head of security when he burst out laughing. They stepped out to the water's edge to grab hold of the skimmer and guide it ashore. As Jani walked around to the pilot's side, she looked up at Dathim. He stared back, the arrogant cast of their first meeting absent. Then he nodded, once, a motion so slight as to be almost undetectable.

"I have not sat at a fire such as this since I schooled at Temple." Tsecha clambered over the side of the skimmer and strode along the sand. "We would sit and tell one another of our homes, and the cities from where we had come." He wore a shirt that matched the blue sidelights in color and brightness, dark green trousers, and covered it all with the same brown coat he had worn during his first city expedition with Dathim. He had wrapped his head, as well, with a length of green cloth. "We shall do that," he said as he dragged another log seat closer to the fire. "We shall talk of the cities from where we came, then we will talk of the cities to which we will go."

And so they did, until the rising sun backlit the lake horizon. Every so often, sparks shot up from the fire and spread across the sky, like new stars looking for a home.

**Transcript of conversation appended to Patient File S-1.
Participant key: JS-John Shroud; ED-
Eamon DeVries; VP-Valentin Parini
\<start conversation\>**

JS: Eamon, have you sent your comments on Jani's prostheses to her file? Staff meeting's in an hour—I want to evaluate your findings before we sit.

ED: You'll be evaluating *my* findings? Since when? You handle the genetics muck, I play with the gadgets and flashing lights, remember?

JS: Just send me the updates.

ED: \<pause\> Fine—see attached. As you can no doubt conclude from the stress and balance scans—adept as you are at your new-found specialty—she needs a new left arm and leg.

JS: \<pause\> We just switched out limbs a few months ago.

ED: \<laughter\> Yes, well, she's a growing gel, John. No matter what your experts do to try and slow her down, she brushes it off and continues on her merry hybrid way.

JS: We can discuss that at the meeting—I have a few ideas—

ED: Filled to the brim with ideas, aren't you, Johnny? Just like the first day we met. Ah, will I ever forget it? Me pushing through the crowds at the Rauta Shèràa shuttleport, on the lookout for that white head of yours and not finding it. Then just when I figured you'd stood me up, you emerged from the shadows. Somber as a judge pronouncing sentence, you were, with your hellbound pup at your heels.

VP: Thanks, Eamon.

ED: Ah, Valentin. I wondered when you'd speak up. But you

always did wait to gauge your master's mood before opening your mouth.

VP: Bit of a son of a bitch yourself, aren't you? You came soon enough when John called, just like you did twenty years ago. "For the thrill and the hell of it." Isn't that what you said in Rauta Shèràa? "For the joy of sticking it to Morden nìRau Cèel."

JS: I think we've all grown beyond that, Val.

VP: No, we haven't. We've been battling Cèel ever since he tried to convince the Laumrau to reject our applications to work at the Rauta Shèràa consulate.

JS: Cèel tried to convince the Laumrau to block every application. He didn't trust any human who wanted to come to Shèrá. He's from the warrior skein—distrust is his job.

VP: Can the charitable assessment. Cèel knew why you wanted to work there, just like he knew why Eamon and I came when you called us. Nema's rumblings about a new universal order had just escaped Temple confines and made it out into the Commonwealth. You heard the stories at Oxbridge, same as I did at Harvard, and Eamon at Lyon. A hybrid race—the idea grabbed us by the collective throat and didn't let go until we banded together and made our own hash of it!

JS: Val? <pause> Why the nerves? What's bothering you?

ED: His conscience is gripping him, like it did in the basement. I always told him to leave it beneath the nearest lamppost where it belonged, but he never listened to me.

VP: It—it's just that now that I can see Jani every day . . . I see what she has to go through and I wonder if we did the right thing.

JS: Val, if we hadn't, she wouldn't be here today.

VP: I know, but—

ED: It's too late for regrets, boyo. Ten years ago you'd have been able to put the genie back in the bottle, but now any attempt to change Kilian back to fully human would kill her. She is what she is. John's labor of misplaced love, tumbled from her pedestal straight into the scrum of Commonwealth-idomeni politics. If you're looking for something to be sorry for, be sorry for that!

We hope you've enjoyed this Eos book. As part of our mission to give readers the best science fiction and fantasy being written today, the following pages contain a glimpse into the fascinating worlds of a select group of Eos authors.

Join us as acclaimed editor David G. Hartwell brings you the best fantasy stories of the year and Juliet E. McKenna returns to the fascinating world of the Einarinn and the adventures of the thief Livak. As Dave Duncan sweeps you away to a land of swords, sorcery, intrigue, and the finest swordsmen ever. As Kristine Smith builds a suspenseful story of military secrets, interstellar politics, and alien intrigue and James Alan Gardner returns to the fascinating world of Melaquin—and the deadly adventures of Explorer Festina Ramos. And as Martha Wells tells an epic story of endings, beginnings, and a malevolent plot to keep the world from being reborn.

Whether you like science fiction or fantasy (or both!), Eos has something for you in Fall 2001.

Year's Best Fantasy

Edited by David G. Hartwell

Coming July 2001

In the tradition of the popular YEAR'S BEST SF series, acclaimed editor David G. Hartwell now gathers together the best fantasy stories of the last year, in the inaugural volume of the YEAR'S BEST FANTASY. Travel to exotic worlds—far-off and just around the corner—with this dazzling collection of fantastic fiction.

Never before published in book form, the best fantasy stories of the last year (and the first year of the new millennium!) appear here in one volume—tales of adventure and possibility from both established masters of fantasy and rising new stars.

In "Debt of Bones" fantasy titan Terry Goodkind regales us with a long-ago adventure of the Wizard Zedd and the price of honor, in a story set in the dark times before Richard Cypher discovered his destiny to wield the *Sword of Truth*.

New York Times bestselling author George R. R. Martin returns to the *Song of Fire and Ice* with "Path of the Dragon," as Daenerys Stormborn crosses the ocean on a dangerous mission to build an army of vengeance.

In "Greedy Choke Puppy," critically acclaimed, award-winning author Nalo Hopkinson tells a tale of life and death, and the night-raids of the soucouyant, while reader favorite Charles de Lint weaves a story about injustice and making a stand—for honor and beauty and life—in "Making a Noise in this World."

The YEAR'S BEST FANTASY also includes stories of wonder and imagination from Storm Constantine, Nicola Griffith, Sherwood Smith, Michael Swanwick, Gene Wolfe, and many more.

The Gambler's Fortune
The Third Tale of Einarinn

Juliet E. McKenna

Coming August 2001

'So what's the offer? No offence, Livak, but the last I heard you'd gone off with Halice to work for some wizards again. I can't say I fancy that. Charoleia told us she'd had a letter from Halice all the way from some new land clear across the ocean. The Archmage discovered it?' He gestured towards the stage, where the heroine was now weeping alone. 'People sleeping in a cave for thirty generations, heartless villains trying to steal their lands, wizards raising dragons to drive them off; Niello couldn't make a masquerade out of a story like that and expect people to swallow it!'

'I know it sounds incredible, but those people in the cave were the Tormalin colony that Nemith the Last lost track of just before the fall of the Old Empire,' I explained.

Sorgrad looked more interested, despite himself. 'We've all heard the stories about that lost colony, rivers running over golden gravel, diamonds loose in the grass. People have been trying to find it again ever since the Chaos.'

'I don't know about any of that, the gold and the gems, I mean,' I said hastily, 'but do you remember those islands out in the eastern ocean, the ones where I was taken when I was forced into thieving for that wizard?'

Sorgrad nodded warily and I strove to keep my voice level, ignoring memories of that ordeal. 'Don't forget how much coin I brought back from that trip, Sorgrad. Say what you like about wizards, they certainly pay well.' If you come back alive, I added silently to myself. 'It was these Ice Islanders—well, their forefathers—who stamped the original settlers into the mud. The ones that managed to escape hid themselves in a cave, wrapped themselves up in enchantments and the Archmage sent an expedition to find them last summer. That's what Halice and me got ourselves mixed up in. These people had magic, 'Grad, old magic, not the flash tricks of the Archmage and his like, but lost enchantments that put them to sleep and kept them safe while all these generations passed. Truthfully, I saw it with my own eyes, saw them roused.'

'I've heard no word of any such threat,' interrupted Sorgrad skeptically.

'That's because Planir and Messire have put their heads together and decided to keep it all quiet until they've got some plan in place.' Ryshad and I had argued ourselves breathless over that one, advocating instead the circulation of detailed descriptions of the Elietimm in their distinctive liveries, so that they'd stand out like the stones on a stag hound if they ever tried to make landfall again. I still thought our so-called leaders were wrong. 'Some time soon, the Emperor and his cronies will be facing organized soldiery backed by enchanters who can pull the wits out through someone's nose from half a league away,' I continued. 'My master knows he'll need magic to fight back.'

I held Sorgrad's gaze with my own. 'Messire D'Olbriot wants to understand this old magic, ideally before anyone else thinks to start looking, to know what he might be up against. It gets better. The Archmage wants to learn all about this old magic as well. Artifice, that's what they're calling it now, or aetheric magic, take your pick. The point is, the wizards of Hadrumal can't use this old magic, don't ask me why. That's got Planir worried, so he's doing everything he can to find out what he might be facing.'

'So your patron, if he has the information the Archmage is so keen on finding, he can trade it for some mages to start throwing fire and lightning at any Ice Islander who wants to come ashore without paying his harbor dues?' Sorgrad was still looking thoughtful but less hostile. 'That makes sense.'

'I knew you'd see it,' I grinned. Messire D'Olbriot hadn't, not until I put it to him, for all his years of shuffling the pieces around the games of Tormalin politics. The whole notion of getting involved with mages and wizardry was still about as welcome in Toremal as dancing with a pox-rotted whore. 'As I say, this is a job that could pay very well indeed. We might even be able to play both ends against the middle and double our winnings.'

Sky of Swords
A Tale of the King's Blades

Dave Duncan

Coming September 2001

"Malinda of Ranulf, you are summoned in the King's name to—"

"The Usurper's name!"

The Chancellor's dark eyes were filmy, as if he had spilled milk in them, and hair like white cobwebs fringed his red hat, but age had not softened him. "You are indicted of high treason, numerous murders, evil and illegal conjuration, fornication, misprision, conspiracy to—"

"Considering my youth, I must have been exceedingly busy! As rightful Queen of Chivial, I do not recognize the authority of this court to try me on these or any other charges."

His name had been Horatio Lambskin on the night he swore allegiance to her. Now, as Chancellor, he would be Lord Something-or-other. He posed always as a bloodless state servant, an altruistic tool serving only the common weal. He probably believed his own lie, so he would not view his change of allegiance as a crime, just a higher loyalty. At the moment his mission was to see her condemned to death, but if he failed and she ever won back the throne that was rightfully hers, he might well turn up for work the following morning in full expectation of carrying on as before.

"I will acknowledge nothing less than a jury of my peers," she said.

They had found a way around that argument, of course. "This is not a court, mistress. A bill of attainder has been laid before Parliament, condemning you to death for high treason, diverse murders, evil—"

"You sound like a parrot."

Nothing changed on the skull face. "If this bill is passed by Parliament and signed into law by His Majesty, then your head will be struck off. Parliament has therefore appointed a committee to consider the evidence against you. If you do not wish to testify, you have the right to remain silent."

Strategy . . . she must think strategy. Somewhere beyond these gruesome walls, out in the world of smiles and sunshine, her supporters would be plotting on her behalf, although of course they dare do little while she was a prisoner. The Usurper could not rest easy on his ill-gotten throne as long as the rightful Queen of Chivial lived. Assassination was what she had expected: poison or poniard or the silken noose. Every new dawn had been a surprise. She had not seriously considered the possibility of a public execution, and a public trial she had never even dreamed of before the warrant for this inquiry was thrust in her hand the previous day. Perhaps Lord Chancellor Whatever-his-name-was-now did not have Parliament quite so much under control as he would like. Had an outcry forced the Usurper to stage this farce?

Dare she consider the faint possibility that she might not be going to die of it? Alas, when hope flickered, the rage that had sustained her waned and gave way to fear, so that the skin on her arms puckered in gooseflesh and her fingers began to shake. She was on trial for her life and the deck was stacked against her.

The clerk had stopped.

One of the peers jumped in with a question. ". . . that you conspired to effect the murder of your father, His Late Majesty Ambrose IV—"

"No!" she snapped. "I deny that charge utterly."

"How would you describe your relations with your father? Warm? Loyal? Dutiful?"

"It was no secret," Malinda said deliberately. "As a child I was taught to hate him, fear him, and despise him. When I

was old enough to make up my own mind, I found no reason
to alter those opinions. He drove his first two wives insane
and murdered the third; his fourth was to be a girl a month
younger than I. I sincerely believe that he was a strong and
effective king of Chivial and the realm has suffered greatly
from his untimely death. In his private life he was a tyrant,
and I never loved him, but his death was not something I
planned or desired."

   She had never intended to kill him. That had been an over-
sight.

Ascending

James Alan Gardner

Coming November 2001

The red beam worked like a rope, reeling us toward the navy ship. I wondered if we would feel anything as we passed through the edge of the milky FTL field . . . but there was only the softest jerk forward, and a tiny bit of dizziness wherein my toes felt momentarily tingly.

Ahead of us, a great round door opened in the rear of the ship—almost big enough to have swallowed our ship whole. The instant we crossed the threshold, gravity returned; we slammed down hard onto a metal floor, bounced once, and juddered forward until we jolted to a stop against the far wall. *Hmmph*, I thought, *these navy humans are clumsy. Either that, or they are intentionally treating us coarsely because they are great arrogant bullies.*

While I worked to free myself, the navy ship closed its hatch behind us, sealing us in completely.

Lights on the navy ship's ceiling suddenly grew brighter, and the walls around us made ominous crinkling sounds. "Our hosts are pressurizing the transport bay," Uclod said. "Any second now, the place'll be swarming with Security mooks."

Apparently, a mook was a humorless person wearing olive body armor and brandishing a truncheon or stun-pistol with great officiousness. A troop of such persons clattered into the chamber with bustling self-importance, racing to take up positions around our little chunk of Starbiter and training their weapons upon us in a most aggressive manner.

Their leader (of a gender I could not identify, thanks to the armor and a voice more howl than human) shouted something that did not sound like words in any language I knew. One of the others jumped forward, pistol at the ready; the mook fired directly at our outer wall, and a splooge of noxious green splatted from the gun barrel. The substance must have been some chemical—the instant it struck our chamber's membrane, the tissue began hissing and spitting, bubbling up clouds of vile smoke. In less than ten seconds, a ragged hole had burned itself open, letting air from the human ship gust into our little chamber.

"Harout!" cried the mookish leader. "How, how, how!"

"What language is that person speaking?" I whispered to Uclod.

"Soldierese," he replied. "Start with English, then skip any consonants that sound too effeminate."

"Hout!" shouted the mook. "How!"

"Yeah, yeah," Uclod said. "We're coming."

He took a step toward the gash in the wall. I put my hand on his shoulder to stop him. "Wait—we must do this correctly."

I glanced around the room and saw what I wanted, lying against one wall: the black Explorer jacket I had brought from Melaquin. Snatching it up, I pushed my arms into it, discovering the fit was very fine indeed. The coat was not so heavy, and not at all tight; it also hung down to the middle of my thighs. I took another moment to straighten the garment and slap-fasten the strip down the front, just as I had seen Explorers do. Then I stepped out through the hole and historically made First Contact.

"Greetings," I said in a loud clear voice. "I am a sentient citizen of the League of Peoples. I beg your Hospitality."

For a long moment, nobody spoke. I could see the mooks' faces through their clear visors; several appeared disconcerted to be confronted by someone dressed as one of their own Explorers. "I come in peace," I said. "My name is Oar. An oar is an implement used to propel boats."

Someone gasped at the far end of the room. I turned and saw an unarmored person standing in the doorway.

"Oar? *Oar?*"

Festina Ramos hurled herself across the floor and wrapped her arms around me.

Wheel of the Infinite

Martha Wells

Coming December 2001

Maskelle paused at the dropped tailgate, looking into the dark. She could see the temple from here.

The massive domed spire was black against the lighter shade of the sky, the moon shape of the portal below it barely visible; male and female phallic symbols woven together. The detail of the terraced carvings was entirely lost in shadow. They had passed small sanctuaries along the way, but this was the first time in too many years that she had been so close to a true temple.

She moved away from the wagon, one of the oxen snuffling at her as she drifted past. The temple was calling to her, not the stone shell, but what it represented, and the power that likeness gave it.

She walked through the sodden grass until she came to the edge of the baray and stepped up onto the stone bank. The Koshan priests had the custody of the temples, but they were only static forms. It was the End of Year Rite that remade the universe in its own image, and that was only performed by the Voices of the Ancestors. The End of Decade rites were even more crucial.

This year would be the End of a Hundred Years rite.

Maskelle lifted her staff, holding it above her head. An echo whispered through her, a reflection from the Infinite through the structure of the temple. After all these years, it still knew her. "I helped another stranger tonight," she whispered. "I didn't kill anyone to do it. Not intentionally, at least. Is that enough for you?"

A slow wave of darkness climbed the temple wall, the lamps in the windows winking out one by one.

She lowered the staff and let out her breath. No, it wasn't enough. *And now they will all know you're back.* Oh, the delight in the power never died, that was the curse, and her true punishment, whatever the Adversary had decreed. She shook her head at her own folly and turned back to the camp.

She reached the wagon and climbed up the back steps, closing the panels that faced the campsite. She sat on the still damp wooden floor, looking out at the temple and the silver surface of the baray in the distance.

She was facing the right direction for an illusion of privacy, though voices from the other campsites, oddly distorted over the plain, came to her occasionally. The night breeze was chilly on her wet clothes, the drying mud itchy on her legs. And someone was watching her. She knew it by the way the oxen, caught in the firelight from behind the wagon, cocked their ears. She found his outline in the dark finally, about twenty feet away, sitting on his heels just out of reach of the light. She might have walked within ten feet of him on the way to the baray. Again, the shock of being so taken by surprise was like ice on her skin. She waited until it drained away, then quietly she said, "Come here."

The breeze moved the short grass. He stood up and came toward the wagon.

Her staff, as much a part of her as her hands or feet, lay on the wooden bench of the wagon. He stopped just out of arm's reach. Her arm's reach. She was within easy range of his sword.